FLAME OF SHADOW
DARK WORLD TRILOGY

AMARAH CALDERINI

This is a work of fiction. All of the characters, organizations, places, and events portrayed in this novel are either the products of the author's imagination or used fictitiously.

FLAME OF SHADOW
Copyright © 2022 by Amarah Calderini

All rights reserved.
No part of this book may be reproduced in any form or by any electronic or mechanical means, including information storage and retrieval systems, without written permission from the author, except for the use of brief quotations in a book review.

Cover Artwork and Design: Sarah Hansen of Okay Creations
Interior Formatting: Tiarra Blandin
Editorial: Tiarra Blandin of Allotrope Editorial

For my sister.
And for all the ocean-hearted girls who've ever been told they are too much.

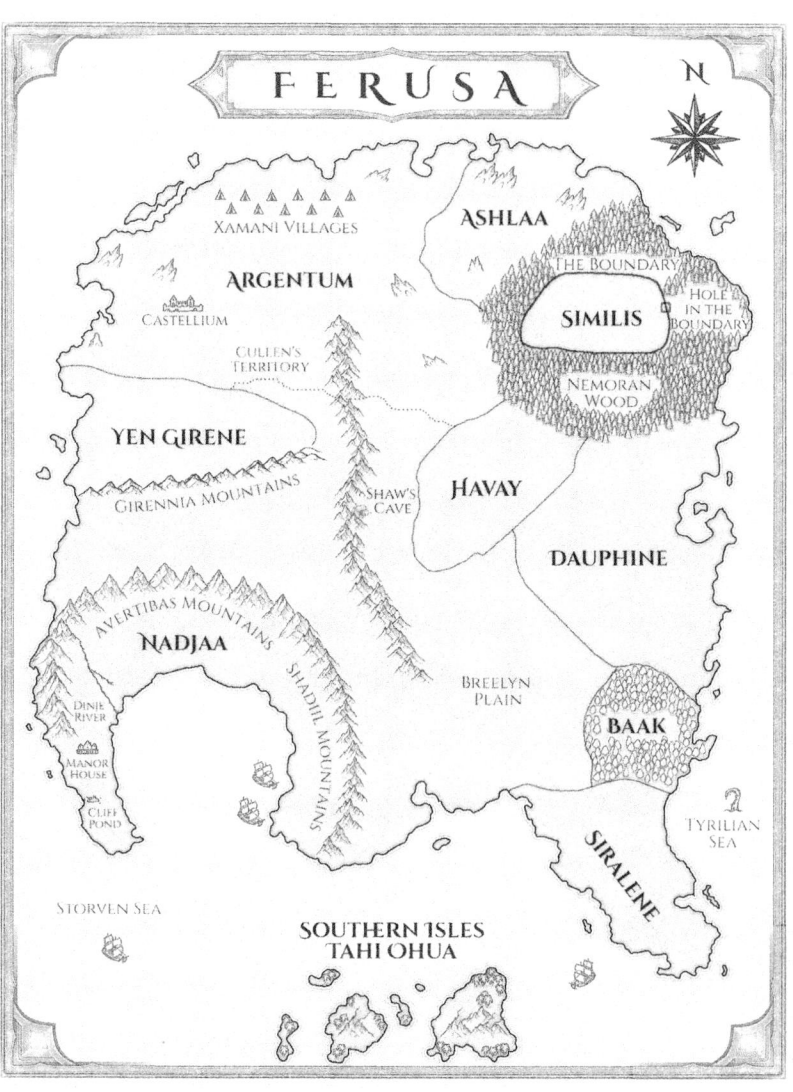

CHAPTER
ONE

Shaw

It is always cold here. Frigid and deep, the kind of cold that settles in your bones and never relents. Even in the late months of summer, my father's city of Argentum is blanketed by heavy, roiling clouds and a freezing mist. I think I remember a place where the sun caressed my skin, but it's hard to tell if the memory is true. It's hard to tell if any of them are true.

The Praeceptor tells me the amnesia is temporary, a side effect of my body adjusting to being soulless. In time, the memories will return as events and places, but they will never be as vivid as they once were. Emotion is what cements memory after all: what adheres it to your heart and lungs.

I have no heart now. I only have the cold.

Dim light spills from small, rectangular windows cut high in the stone walls, giving the corridor the semblance of a prison as I make my way through the slices of light. My father's fortress, aptly named the Castellium, was built to withstand a siege. It is brutal and efficient but could never be mistaken for comfortable. Everything is hard and sharp, an outward manifestation of the fortress' master.

I grimace when I feel a familiar tug inside the echoing emptiness of my chest. The Praeceptor grows impatient. Hastening my pace, I trace the familiar stone path from the dungeons to the throne room.

The doors, which reach two stories high and are carved from black metal, are already ajar when I arrive. Not bothering to acknowledge the two militia members stationed on either side, I stalk through the arched threshold. Cold billows through the expansive room as I make my way past the bustle of Argentian nobility and the chatter of emissaries from almost every warlord between here and the Shadiil mountain range. The warlords themselves are notably absent with good reason. This meeting is supposed to be peaceful, an arduous feat if fourteen power hungry monsters were to be trapped in the same cage.

An ornate throne sits at the head of the room, the only adornment in the otherwise barren hall. It, too, is black and solidly constructed, with large spires arranged around the crown. Though similar in shape, the throne is an inverse of the natural sun: where the sun gives light, the metal throne appears to absorb it.

My father, who usually enjoys lording over others from the seat of power, hasn't bothered with it today. Instead, he leans over a table with two of his *legatus,* their heads bowed together in discussion.

The Praeceptor doesn't even flinch as I approach at his back. He only turns to me with a shrewd gaze, his mouth set in a thin line of disapproval. It would take far more than silent feet to catch my father off guard. "You're late," he observes levelly.

"I came when you called," I reply.

Cullen's lips peel back from his teeth in distaste. He's never been one to stomach insolence, but mine will go unpunished for now. The time has come for him to demonstrate his weapon and he won't risk making the emissaries wait just to prove a point.

And if he did, it wouldn't matter. In taking my soul, he also stole my ability to care. The last time he visited me in the dungeon, I laughed and laughed until he was finally forced to step away before he killed me. He never gives in to my mania—I am useless if I'm dead.

"You would do well to remember whose leash you wear," my father growls, and the emptiness in my chest contracts until I'm forced to gasp for air. Cullen raises his chin, studying every miniscule movement of my face, from the slight dilation of my pupils to the tightening of my jaw.

He's directed my every movement for two months, and still, he doesn't completely trust his control. I face him with dead eyes. "You are more than generous in feeding me the bloodshed I desire. I have no want of anything except more of it."

He nods, sated for now. But never for long.

Turning to the room at large, he raises his hands. The din immediately falls silent. They fear the repercussions of the Praeceptor's Dark Militia, having witnessed firsthand the destruction even one member can reap. It was the militia who infiltrated the warlords' territories. Shadows that crawled through cracks their leaders hadn't even known existed, lingering on the edges of society until the Praeceptor gave them the signal.

And that's when all hell broke loose.

The attacks were sly and anonymous. A flood that destroyed a quarter of the city, a fire that ravaged influential neighborhoods. Attacks so well planned, it wasn't long before half the populations were convinced it was something otherworldly waging war against them. Nature spirits and old gods come back for vengeance against the Dark World.

The Darkness breeds terror of the unseeable and my father has always been more than willing to paint a picture of what lies beyond sight. News of the Ocean-wielder spread, along with hatred of everything she represents. Citizens of Baak, Ashlaa, and Kin Rylene, all rose up, demanding their warlords do something to fight against the terror of the supernatural. Whispers of Nadjaa's involvement, of the influence of their absurd Chancellor spread like wildfire. By the time my father stepped in, most of the warlords greeted him as a long-lost savior, willing to give him whatever he demanded.

The Praeceptor thrives on the brutality of war, but he is also pragmatic. His militia is greater in number than Ferusa has ever seen, and he never even needed it. He only needed to sow fear to reap control, terror oftentimes a greater motivator than violence.

Which I suspect is why he's finally let me out of my cage. The people fear the Dark Militia, but they are just men. Soon, they will know the horror of the monster in the shadows.

"Citizens of Argentum, ladies and gentlemen of Ferusa. Unnatural wickedness has returned to our land—evil that endangers our reigns." The Praeceptor watches each of the emissaries in turn, his pale eyes glinting in the torchlight. Some still possess their souls while others relinquished them long ago, but all shy away from his gaze.

"There are those too weak to stand against the immoral powers that seek to corrupt our land. And there are those who strive to gain power at the expense of our morality."

I've not been allowed into the Praeceptor's confidence since I've returned, kept as I am in the dungeons—but my guards are a chatty bunch when they believe I'm asleep. I've learned enough to know my father speaks of Akari Ilinka, warlord of Siralene and self-titled queen. Power-hungry and ruthless, the witch-queen has been shoring up her defenses against the Praeceptor, while simultaneously searching for a way to control the newfound magic crawling the continent.

Clothing rustles as the emissaries shift uncomfortably. None want to appear sympathetic to Ilinka's cause in the Praeceptor's presence.

"The completion of the Dead Prophecy looms ever closer. Already, there is an ocean-wielder hiding behind the Boundary of Similis. An abhorrent creature masking herself as human walking among us. She is beyond our control for now, but the time has come to act before any more spirits reveal themselves. To weed them out from where they hide in the shadows of *our* Darkness and destroy them all."

No one is foolish enough to mistake the Praeceptor's words as a request. I've heard whispers of plans to destroy any who show signs of magic but haven't discovered how he intends to find them. I stretch my neck and plant my feet more firmly into the stone floor, as the void inside me rises. Perhaps he will finally allow me out of my cage—allow me to feed on the fear and blood of battle.

My father's face is utterly impassible, and his strides are neat as he surveys the emissaries. It has always been a strength of his, to keep his emotions so fully in check. Even when his anger is palpable, he hides it beneath a façade of calm objectivity. It is what he wanted from me, once. Now, he demands my rage.

"I mercifully offered each of your warlords a place in my

vision for the land, asking little in return. They were all wise, and chose to accept, rather than face my wrath. And still, there are those who betray my generosity." The Praeceptor's voice is deathly calm as utter silence falls over the emissaries. Terror wafts from them in stinking clouds and I eye them with disgust. Cowards.

The Praeceptor stops his pacing in front of the Baakan emissary. A stout man, with thinning hair and large jowls that quiver when he stares up at my father. "Baak would never betray you, Praeceptor. Our citizens and our armies are dedicated to eradicating the prophecy."

Cullen studies the man, his mouth pressed into a thin line. The only outward sign of rage he'll show. "Is that so?" he asks, turning from the emissary in abrupt dismissal. He waves at the soldiers stationed by the door. They disappear into the hallway, black swords sheathed at their hip, high powered rifles tucked beneath their armpits.

The Praeceptor drums his fingers along the balustrade as if suddenly bored of the entire proceeding, the sound echoing off the dark stone walls. After a long moment, he says, "I gave my word your territories would be safe, so long as you assisted in the destruction of the Dead Prophecy. You have not turned over the would-be magic wielders as promised."

The emissaries opens and closes his mouth in quick succession, his speechlessness reminiscent of a largemouth bass. "S-s-sir, I—"

My father raises his hand, and the emissary immediately falls silent. Perhaps he's smarter than I gave him credit for. After a moment, the soldiers return, dragging two bound people with them. Both are dressed in the heavy fabrics favored in Baak, though these look as though they've been dragged through a thorn thicket. Tears roll down the woman's face, pooling above the gag tied roughly around her head. I watch with vague distaste as snot soaks into the fabric, her wails of fear vibrating uncomfortably in my ears.

In contrast, the boy next to her makes no noise. Young, barely on the verge of manhood, he stares at my father hatefully. His hands and feet are bound, and his face has been sliced almost beyond recognition and then left to fester, a mark of his defiance.

The emissary bellows in anguish. "My family had nothing to do with the warlord's decision! Please, show mercy, Lord Praeceptor."

Absurd laughter bubbles in my chest. I swallow it down as my father gazes down at the man's panic. "Your warlord met with the witch-queen."

Horrified gasps echo through the room, loud as a thunderclap. With no windows in the cavernous throne room, sound is just as trapped as the rest of us.

The emissary doesn't take his eyes from his wife and son as he shakes his head mutinously. "Never, my lord! The Baakan warlord is committed to overthrowing magic and keeping the Darkness. The shipment you demanded must have simply been delayed!"

"Akari Ilinka thinks to outsmart me. She believes she can bring the Dead Prophecy to fruition and bend the light to her control."

"She is insane, Praeceptor! We would never—"

"SILENCE!" My father's voice booms. My chest contracts once more, and on his command, I melt from the shadows.

The emissary pales, his watery gaze terrified as I stride lazily toward his family. His son's eyes are a clear blue, and rage flashes in them when I come to stand over him.

His strength of character might be admirable if I still had a soul, but now, I have no use for it. The void in me begins to swirl and my blood heats in anticipation. The agony of patience is almost too much to bear, for this is the only thing I live for—feeding the hunger of the abyss. Feeling a moment's reprieve as I breathe in fire and pain.

Warmth, however brief.

"A son is a father's greatest pride," the Praeceptor tells the emissary. I am not my father's pride; I am his reckoning. The words are not meant to be sentimental. Because a son is either a weakness or a weapon and it's clear by the emotion staining the emissary's rotund cheeks which his is. "I'm sure you've heard the rumors of my own's *gifts*."

I lick my lips as my body trembles. Newfound heat blisters in my veins. I breathe deeply through the pain as it sizzles each of my nerve endings. Everything has hurt since losing my soul, but *this* pain, I crave. It burns through the aching emptiness and brings the blurry edges of my new reality into stark clarity.

"A gift from the Darkness itself, my son is a reminder of what will happen if we do not stop the spirits *now*. He follows the will of the Praeceptor, but what if that peace-loving fool in Nadjaa finds ten of him to wield? What will your warlords do then? Give their freedoms over to the demands of a power-hungry Chancellor? Willingly be enslaved, as the Similians are?"

I shake with the need to let the pain go, to push it outside myself, but I remain frozen until my father's command. If I disobey, he may not gift me with another chance. He will leave me to drown in my own ash-ridden wasteland.

"My son's power is proof of the danger that lies in sitting by while the prophecy comes to pass. And since your warlord seems in need of *proof,* emissary, I shall give it to you in spades."

The Praeceptor flicks his wrist lazily, my unleashing.

There was once a place where sunlight caressed my face, a place where I felt warm. But now, I am a weapon and a weapon's only warmth comes from the blood that adorns its blade. My father's men drop the boy to the ground and step back, giving me a wide berth. As if I may not find the boy's pain to be enough and decide to devour theirs next.

The boy thrashes against his bonds as I reach out to him. Though his jaw is set, and his eyes are sharp as stone, his body trembles. The air is tinged with the sour scent of his fear. Closing my eyes, I breathe in deeply and let the scent settle in my chest.

When I brush his bare shoulder with my fingertips, he jolts in agony. When I set both my hands to his skin, his hateful determination is lost in a haze of pain, and he screams. The sound reverberates against my ear drums, and I swear I can feel the thrum of his pulse in time with my own.

Both stubborn. Both living on borrowed time.

The emissary sobs, his pleas twisting around the boy's screams in malevolent harmony. His mother wails, pulling at her hair and cursing the old gods. As if there is anything holy left in this Darkness.

I drink it all in—the misery, the pain, the fear—and exhale a sigh of relief. Because my abyss has risen, filled me to the brim, and for the first time in weeks, I am not hollow.

When the screaming ceases, I pull my hand away and stuff it in my pocket. I stare down at the boy's remains, feeling nothing. No tinge of regret, or guilt, or even pleasure. Just the emptiness climbing back up my throat. It never leaves me for long.

The boy's mother is no more than a pile of rags on the floor, having fainted between the guards. The emissary sags between the two militia members who hold him, snot bubbling beneath his nose, eyes red-rimmed and empty. Silent sobs rack his body, as if his son's death has robbed him of the ability to make noise. I watch him detachedly.

My father does, too. His face is emotionless, but for the glint in his eye. The one he usually keeps buried far beneath a mask of humanity.

The emissary stands shakily, shoving at a militia member with haphazard determination. "This is not justice!" he cries, his voice sounding like it's been dragged over miles of gravel.

Goosebumps rise on my skin as I laugh, the humorless ring ricocheting from the ceiling. The man is a fool to think there is anything like justice within the Castellium walls. The cold returns to the room with fervor, settling in my bones. Soon, I will be back in the dungeon, cold and hungry once more. As I deserve.

"This is the Praeceptor's law," I tell the man. "The only form of justice that matters."

Mirren

The stage lights are too bright. I pluck at my jumpsuit, attempting to peel the thick fabric from my clammy skin as sweat pools uncomfortably between my breasts. There are hardly any shadows here, nowhere to gain respite from the eyes of my Community as they gaze up at the stage. Everything is illuminated—from the sickly pallor of my skin to the slight tremor in my hand.

Balling said hand into a fist at my side, I paste a serene smile on my face. "Trust in your Covinus," I tell them.

I don't wait for their murmur of response, instead, ducking backstage where the lights are dimmer and my brother's hopeful face waits.

"You did a wonderful job," he says, handing me a cold bottle of water. I stare at it for a moment before tucking it into my backpack.

Easton frowns. Since my return, I hardly eat or drink and it worries him. But the loss of my power has left me with a pounding headache and the constant twist of nausea. On the rare occasion I feel well enough to eat, food turns to ash in my mouth. And water—the cool splash of it against the raw ache of my throat is a cruel reminder of everything stolen from my body.

Given. Not stolen.

Easton opens his mouth, and for a minute, I think he'll protest my refusal. But he only smiles. Arguing is against the Keys and since his miraculous recovery, Easton never goes against them, even in the privacy of our own quarterage. There is no more lenience for the volume of my voice, no more secret laughter.

The last time he allowed me to hug him was at the Boundary gates right after he woke.

I can't decide if I'm relieved he now adheres to the rules so well he will never risk losing his safety, or if I hate him for being blind to how trapped we are.

I can't decide how I feel about most things anymore. Whether it's the loss of my power, or the echoing ache of losing Shaw, my chest feels like it's been stuffed with a thick blanket. It's hard to breathe, or care, or do much of anything beyond exist.

Easton glances at his watch just as a golden head

appears around the corner. His mouth tightens as Harlan strides toward us, hair glowing under the lights as if lit from behind. His blue Covinus jumpsuit is starched and crisp and his smile is easy as his eyes move past my brother to find mine. "Good evening, Mirren. I trust your speech went well."

It's generous to call what I've been doing since I returned a 'speech'. I stand on the stage, reading robotically from a Covinus issued card and try not to pass out as I tell my Community the dangers of the Dark World.

"She was wonderful," Easton says proudly, all signs of strain cleared so well from his face, I almost believe I imagined it.

"I have no doubt," Harlan replies genially.

The sight of him sets my stomach churning once more. I was so relieved to find he'd somehow survived while I was in Ferusa, but it seems he spared himself by becoming a Covinus loyalist. He's been my personal jailer in the months since my return, showing up each morning to escort me to whatever speaking event has been arranged, and then waiting to usher me back to our quarterage each evening. I haven't figured out if this is a punishment for me or for him.

"I'll be ready in a moment," I tell Harlan with a wan smile. I don't wait for his reply as I shoulder my way into the nearest bathroom.

Determinedly avoiding my reflection, I splash cool water on my face. I don't need to see the mirror to know my cheeks are sunken and my skin waxen, as if in the absence of my *other's* nourishment, my body has begun to eat itself. The Covinus, at least, appreciates my new appearance. Along with regaling tales of the horrors of the Dark World, my wasting away helps sell his agenda that the land beyond the Boundary is nothing but an evil wasteland.

My return was just the thing he needed to quell rumors of unrest.

Sighing, I don't bother to dry my hands as I push the bathroom door open. Whispered voices halt me in my tracks, their fervor unheard in Similian hallways.

I peek around the corner to see Harlan crowding Easton into the nearest wall, their bodies close enough to touch. A flush has risen to his skin as he leans over my brother and pure instinct has me rushing forward to force myself between the two of them.

It takes a full moment for Harlan to tear his gaze away from Easton to meet my eyes. Looking slightly dazed, his chest rises and falls rapidly, and his usually neat hair sticks up like he's just raked his hands through it.

Easton, however, appears perfectly unruffled as he steps out from behind me. "Harlan was just saying how much he's looking forward to moving into your residence at the end of the week," he explains, and though I try, I don't detect anything other than polite deference in his voice. Nothing of whatever heat just sparked between them.

Harlan straightens, suddenly remembering himself. He clears his throat. "Ah, yes. I'm so pleased to begin our Community service together."

I work to keep from rolling my eyes. Whatever Harlan has done to keep himself alive isn't enough to keep him from being Bound to the Community traitor.

"Let's go," he says, and without a backward glance at my brother, he shoves through the door and out into the street.

Easton watches him go with a hard glint in his eye. After a moment, he says, "I'm so proud of you, Mirren. I know the Covinus has been so pleased with how effective you've been at soothing the Community."

That is not at all the impression I've gotten the few times the Covinus has summoned me. In fact, he seemed to imply that my brother's livelihood depends on how well I sell his story. Convince the Community that only horror lies beyond the Boundary. That Similis' safety is the only thing needed; that things like love, freedom and friendship only lead to heartbreak and violence.

Convincing them should be easy since that's exactly what happened. Since my heart was shredded and thrown into a black pit alongside the man who brought it to life. But after everything, I still cannot speak ill of Ferusa without my throat feeling like it will seal shut. Because for all its faults, half my heart exists there. And no matter how I try, I cannot seem to forget the feeling of being *awake*.

"Are you coming?"

Easton presses his lips into a thin line and shakes his head, and the previous tension of the hallway blooms once more. "I have a few things to finish up here. I'll see you at the quarterage."

When I emerge into the cool night air, Harlan starts walking without bothering to check if I'm following. Whatever passed between him and Easton was enough to make him forget he's supposed to keep an eye on my every movement.

The color on his cheeks has deepened to scarlet, a precise match to the bricks of the red square. I lower my brow and ask hesitantly, "Are—are you alright?"

Harlan lets out a rough sound that could be a scoff or a laugh. "Of course I am," he says, "why do you ask?"

I suck in a labored breath. "The fact that you appear to be the only participant in some sort of race to my quarterage," I reply as I struggle to keep pace. My lack of power has sapped the stamina I built in the Dark World. Some days, I can barely keep up a slow walk.

Harlan immediately slows, but his hands are squeezed tightly at his sides, like it takes a concerted effort. "I'm sorry." For once, he doesn't sound sorry at all.

Something heavy settles between us. I'm tempted to ask what's dimmed his usual sunshine. What sort of burden does he bear so heavily it's settled between his brows? I open my mouth, but Harlan stops short with a shake of his head.

"Please don't, Mirren," he says miserably. "I can't answer you. It will only get us both in trouble."

"No one will know—"

"Someone *always* knows."

He begins walking once more, and I stare after him, trying to determine what it is about his statement that's so bothersome. It isn't his words as I've known their truth forever. It's the *way* he said it—with bitterness.

In the months I've been back, Harlan has been nothing but a resolute Similian in my presence. He's made no mention of the power he witnessed on the Boundary, said nothing of the lies encased in the speeches the Covinus' has prepared for me. He's never shown any sign of discontent with his life in Similis. Which begs the question, what in the Darkness did my brother say to him?

"Harlan, if this is about being Bound, maybe I can talk to the Covinus. I'm sure he'd agree you deserve an upstanding Community member after how hard you've worked at reintegration."

Harlan runs his fingers over his Binding brand absently, the raised design still an angry red on the smooth skin of his forearm all these months later. "I have no wish to be

Bound to anyone but you, Mirren. In this, the Covinus knows best. For me, the end of the week cannot come soon enough." When he meets my eyes, his gaze is fierce.

I stare at him, my words disappearing down my throat. When Harlan sacrificed himself for me, I wasn't versed in the strength of emotion. How they drive a person and spur them to bravery. But my time in Ferusa was like lifting a thick fog and I now see Harlan's actions with new clarity.

We haven't spoken of that night and fear has kept me from examining it too closely.

I have nothing to give you. There's nothing left.

"Harlan, I—"

I never get the words out, because at that moment, the lights of Similis, which shine at all hours of the night, flicker.

Harlan reaches for me just before the square goes dark, a hand that speaks most by the Keys it breaks, but I can't catch it. Because in time with the darkness, something *surges* from the deepest parts of me. It crashes violently, my body an arid shore at the edge of a great sea. My lungs have been so dry and my bones so brittle, I can't withstand its surge. I collapse to the ground, my knees scraping against the brick.

I am lost in the all-consuming blanket of night.

Far off, someone screams.

Light floods the square once more and it is just as disorienting as the dark. I blink wildly, tears sticky on my cheeks, as Harlan helps me gently to my feet.

He pulls away his hand and shoves it in his pocket. "Are you okay?" Though his voice is calm, his eyes flutter around the square, unsettled.

When they land on me, curiosity burns alongside his concern. I force a smile and nod. "Just a scrape."

Relief washes over his face. "Let's get you home and cleaned up."

I don't tell him that my knees may be bleeding, but I feel better than I have in months. My head no longer aches and I'm suddenly ravenous.

Because whatever happened didn't just bring a wave of darkness—it brought my magic to life.

CHAPTER
TWO

Mirren

The streets vibrate with quiet panic as Harlan and I race toward my quarterage. A child cries somewhere in the distance, unaccustomed to the inky black of night. Community members in every Sector emerge from their residences, pale faces squinting up at the lights as if they will fail again at any moment. I understand their fear, even if I don't share it. The Darkness is only supposed to exist outside the Boundary. It isn't supposed to crawl through the cracks, breeding the unknown.

As we round the last corner, pain has settled back into my bones and my head throbs. My breaths become more ragged, but Harlan doesn't slow. If he understands why I collapsed, he's given me no indication. Only drags me along, as if getting inside the walls of the quarterage will be enough to protect us from whatever knocks at our Boundary.

Sweat beads on his brow as we reach my Sector. A child stands alone in the street and Harlan yanks me roughly past with no hesitation. My feet tangle up in each other and it's only his hand on my shoulder that keeps me upright. For the first time, it occurs to me I'm not who he means to protect.

Harlan saw my power at the Boundary. He knows better than anyone the magnitude of it.

We reach my quarterage, the plain door appearing the same as it always does beneath the lights. Each scratch illuminated for the world to see. There is no hiding here. I open my mouth, to explain or lie, I haven't decided. But Harlan shakes his head and gives me a warning look.

When I step inside, I see why.

Seated at the small, scrubbed dining table, is the Covinus.

His white-blonde hair is combed to perfection and his complexion appears oddly sallow beneath the harsh kitchen lights. His eyes run from my tangled braid to my tear-stained cheeks, then down to the bloodstained holes at the knees of my jumpsuit. While he has never been anything but outwardly polite, there is something beneath his skin that feels...inhuman. It is disquieting when a person shows no outward emotion at all, not even now, when his Community has been threatened.

"Good evening, Ms. Ellis," he says evenly, motioning for me to sit as if I've arrived at his table and not the other way around.

I look around for the Boundary men that usually accompany him, but the rest of the quarterage is still. Even Farrah, who only leaves the quarterage for Community meetings, has gone somewhere for the evening. The Covinus follows my confused gaze with a flick of his gray eyes.

"I wish this conversation to remain private," he says in answer to my silent question. He looks to Harlan, motioning for him to sit as well. "You may stay, Harlan. Of all Community members, you are most aware what happens when we don't put the greater good first."

What does that mean? I glance at Harlan uncertainly, but his face remains inscrutable. He watches the Covinus like the mild-mannered man is likely to leap at him at any moment, but to my relief, he sits. Harlan may be a loyalist, but since I've returned, I've tried to avoid being alone with the Covinus at all costs.

"Where were you at 7:30 this evening, Ms. Ellis?"

I stare at him dumbly before finding my tongue. "I was —we were leaving my speaking engagement."

The Covinus looks to Harlan who nods in confirmation. Annoyance surges that he doesn't believe me, but I swallow it down. I thwarted our Community rules and everything he holds dear only a few months earlier—of course, he doesn't believe me.

"You were in the red square, then? Did you happen to notice something out of the ordinary?"

I chew on my lip to buy myself a moment of reprieve before answering. Lights that have shone for thousands of years failed, eerily similar to Shaw blowing through a Boundary that has stood for a millennium. I had nothing to do with either, but the Covinus' question feels dangerous, like I'm being lured off a cliff. "The lights flickered, sir."

He watches me with those odd gray eyes, eyes I could have sworn were pure black when we first met. A trick of the light, I suppose, in my panic over my brother, but every time I look at the Covinus, I still expect to see them.

"It was not just the lights, Ms. Ellis."

My eyebrows shoot up.

"It was *everything* that flickered." His eyes glint. "Was there anything *else* odd at that moment you wish to inform me of?"

Fear squeezes my throat. *He knows.* It was just a flicker, a caress, and somehow, the Covinus *knows* my *other* awoke in those moments of darkness. But if I confirm my power has come back, he won't hesitate to Outcast me. To tear me away from Easton. I swallow roughly and straighten my shoulders, looking him directly in the eye. "No, sir. The sudden darkness was disorienting. I lost my balance and fell, but it's only a scrape."

I don't dare look at Harlan, knowing one word from him will give me away. Will he voice his suspicions and sell me out to cement his reentry into the Community? Turning me in would certainly get him out of being Bound to me.

But Harlan remains silent.

The Covinus studies me a moment longer before pushing himself to standing. His blue jumpsuit is starched and flawless in contrast with mine, scuffed with dirt and bloodstained along the knees. "It is more imperative than ever, Ms. Ellis, for you to use the platform I have gifted you. You will ensure there is no panic. You will reassure your Community members that Similis is the safest place to be. Remind them of the desolation that lies on the other side and the ruin it brings."

He walks to the front door, his steps measured like a cat circling a bird. *You are not caged,* I remind myself for the thousandth time, *you have wings. You chose this.*

"If you prove yourself incapable of quelling the unrest, there will be...*consequences*. Do you understand me?"

I don't trust myself to rein in the words I wish to hurl

like a dagger, so I settle for nodding. With a quick bow of his head, he disappears into the brightly lit street.

A strong exhale escapes me, and I collapse into the nearest armchair. Even holding myself straight for a few moments takes a physical toll and suddenly, I feel as though I could sleep for days even though sleep rarely comes. The night is too bright here, the rooms too clinical. And when I lie still for too long, I am haunted by glacial blue eyes turning black.

"Why did the Covinus come?" Harlan asks the room at large, startling me from my thoughts. His hands flutter nervously over his face like two overlarge birds. "He should have waited for my report like usual."

I shrug indifferently, too exhausted to puzzle out the meaning of any of it. "You'll have to ask him why he suddenly doesn't trust his spy."

Harlan doesn't even narrow his eyes at the accusation, and I find myself wishing for some of his anger. For *something,* other than the tedium of civility I've been subject to since my return. What I wouldn't give for the light of Cal's laughter or the heat of Max's anger. Anything other than tepid banality.

"It's not good he was here, Mirren. It means you aren't convincing him—that you aren't convincing the Community. And it's dangerous to be an outsider."

Something snaps inside me, reminiscent of my power but entirely my own. "What do you care?" I bark out bitterly. "If I get myself Outcast, you won't be stuck with babysitting duty anymore. And you won't be saddled with a half-dead traitor for a life partner."

Harlan's face softens and for an absurd moment, I consider hitting him; forcing him to show something other than kindness, when I most certainly don't deserve anything of the sort. "Mirren, I want you," he says in a voice so low heat climbs my cheeks. "Please listen to me."

He settles himself across from me, his face oddly earnest. "There are rumors of desertions. Of Community members who saw you come back from the Dark World alive and *powerful*. Your speeches haven't been enough to convince them there is nothing but darkness on the other side. There are whispers of the Covinus' lies. And this blackout...it's exactly the sort of thing that could start a revolt."

I stare at him. I didn't know anyone else had gone through the Boundary. The hole Shaw put through it has never been able to be repaired, only laid over with plain brick, easily broken through. Worry and guilt gnaw at my stomach as I remember what awaits the unprepared on the other side. I wish I'd been able to tell my Community members the truth, so if they went into Ferusa, they did it with their eyes open.

Harlan braces his hands on his knees, sinking further into the chair Easton collapsed in just months ago, the catalyst of everything that's happened since. "I know you aren't afraid of being Outcast, but there are...*other* things they will do to you if you aren't convincing enough."

"What do you mean?"

Harlan looks torn between being sick or crossing the space between us to shake me. Instead, he sighs and shakes his head, rubbing a hand roughly over his thigh. "It doesn't matter. Think of Easton and everything you've gone through to be with him. It will hurt him if you're Outcast. Just promise me you'll be more careful."

There is so much more layered beneath Harlan's words but worry for him and my brother keeps me from asking.

He was right earlier—someone always knows. "I'll try harder."

He nods, relief settling over him. I don't tell him how hopeless it all feels; that I'm using all the energy I have to be good enough to stay with Easton. That I'm a half-wraith, incapable of more than going through the motions of life. I can only live on the lines, possessing no energy for the color that should fill them. Shaw told me to heal Easton, but that wasn't his worst request—he also told me to *live*. And so, I try to honor his last wishes while simultaneously hating him for it. How dare he leave me, taking fragments of my heart with him, and then implore me to live as half a person?

Harlan stands, smoothing his Covinus uniform. "Please be careful, Mirren. And trust me, there are far worse things than being Outcast."

If only Harlan knew.

Shaw

I stare at the fissures in the stone wall of my father's dungeon. Droplets of water seep through them, *drip, drip, drip*, the result of a climate heavy with moisture and fog. I don't think of the iron manacles that spread my hands and feet wide or of the thick leather strap that digs into my skull. I don't think of the clinical efficiency of the blade that peels my skin from my bones. I certainly don't think of the interested fervor in my father's eyes as he watches my blood splatter over the stone floor.

Instead, I imagine the cracks spreading like black vines. Slowly growing, crawling, weakening the stone. Until the entire Castellium collapses down on top of us. My father's creation brought low. I wonder what it would feel like to be crushed by thousands of pounds of rock. I think it would be warm.

The Praeceptor let me out of my cage for the display upstairs, but his leash never goes far. He ordered me back here, my home for the past two months where he tests my limits and then punishes me for there being any limits at all. Reminds me who holds my tether. Squeezes until I remember only that I am his.

Sometimes I laugh. Sometimes I scream. But I don't ever cry.

The soulless have no tears.

Today, I don't do anything. I lie motionless on the table as the Praeceptor retires the instrument to a small cart without bothering to wipe my blood from its blade. Crimson, the same color as when I was human. My father nods to the man next to him, a low-ranking militia member. The soldier wheels the instruments from the room, leaving us alone.

We are always alone for what comes next. I used to fight against it, straining against my bonds until my shoulders popped out of place. I would attempt to claw my way across the table, my body's pathetic attempt to save itself, but it never made any difference. So now, I only wait.

The Praeceptor drapes a cloth over my face, and I am shrouded in darkness. There are no more walls to focus on, only the roughshod pound of my heart. The beat is erratic and painful, but I know better than to try and calm it. Once my father begins, there is no controlling the physical responses. No convincing my lungs that breath isn't worth the energy needed to sustain it.

When the first wave of water splashes over the cloth, my body seizes, and I want to weep at its weakness.

"I'm doing this for your own good." My father's breath is hot against my ear as he dumps a fresh pitcher over my face. My lungs flare as I try to keep from inhaling, struggling against the demand to breathe. The hollow ache inside me expands, but the only power in this room belongs to *him*.

I am empty, nothing. A vessel to be filled with only his desires.

He pours more and I writhe on the table as the cloth seals against my nose and mouth. But there is nowhere to go. Water burns in my nostrils and spills down my throat until I gag violently, choking on my own bile. And then my traitorous body gasps, desperate for air.

Though it's water that fills my throat, it feels like flame, as I wrench unnaturally on the cold table. My ears ring and pressure pops behind my eyes. Black edges my vision. He's gorged himself on retribution, and finally satiated, this is when he will kill me. The Darkness calls and my body fights against it, pulling against my restraints until I feel the bones of my wrist crumple.

Because there will be no peace in the Darkness. There is no peace anywhere.

There is only the Praeceptor and the cold and the blood.

Moments or hours later, my father removes the cloth from my face. The manacles drop away from my hands and feet with a sharp clank and without them to hold me in place, I collapse to the floor. The wounds on my legs reopen as I retch, my throat burning as water and bile pour from my mouth.

I suck in violent breaths, my battered lungs rattling in the silence of the stone dungeon. My naked body trembles and I hate it for its need to survive. For its willingness to get down on its knees and serve.

When I open my eyes, my father stands to my left, his expression sharp as he examines me. Every miniscule reaction, the Praeceptor devours it all, nourishment of his twisted desires. Normally, I'm adept at keeping it from him, but the water always breaks me. Lingering so close to death day after day has opened up a chasm of dichotomy inside me, with one side wanting to tumble into it and the other, terrified of even stepping toward the edge.

I want to die. And I'm too cowardly to do it.

"The time has come for you to leave Argentum," my father says.

My cheek scrapes across the stone as I struggle to face him, too exhausted for even an echo of suspicion. Years in the Darkness have not aged my father as they do others. Aside from slight graying at his temples, he appears virile and strong. Undefeatable.

"The Prophecy is coming to pass, and we will not be caught out when it does."

The prophecy. Something tugs at me, something from before, but I can't hold onto it. The fire in my head has receded, leaving behind a fuzzy cloud of ash. Thoughts stick there in fragments, but none come together enough for me to form any sort of response. Exactly as my father prefers me. On my knees and mute.

"You will take a battalion from Havay to Siralene. You will ferret out the potential nature-wielders so that when the Prophecy does come to pass, it will no longer matter. There will be none left to oppose us. And if any try, you will burn their cities to the ground."

Burn. Their screams of terror, the heat of the flame, the wash of their blood—it will all feel so *warm.* My father grants me a gift, and I want to grovel on my belly in gratitude. I have been in this dungeon for so long, wet and cold.

My joints scream as I scrabble to a sitting position, the tendons in my shoulder stretched and inflamed. I will heal, I always do. Maybe this time, I'll be thankful for it. "It would be my honor, sir." My voice is wretched, the sound of flayed skin.

"You will not go near the Boundary or Nadjaa for the time being. The seeds of unrest have not had enough time to take root there. And you will show those who would oppose us no mercy."

The word echoes strangely off the walls, distorted and distant. I've been shown no mercy, does the rest of Ferusa not deserve the same? Why should they be spared the pain and terror I've known? The Darkness has no *mercy* and neither do I. "I will melt the skin from their bones, Father. They will feel your wrath."

He purses his lips, the only sign of approval I'll receive, but I cling to it as though I'm starving and it's a morsel of food. Finally, I have been granted the opportunity to prove my worth. If the Praeceptor wants his justice, that is exactly what I'll give him. I will make myself so valuable to him, he will have no choice but to free me from this cage.

My father's eyes narrow and sharpen. "There will be consequences for failure."

"I won't fail," I tell him eagerly, as the hunger in my chest begins to burn anew. It hides so deep when we are trapped in this dungeon, but now, it roars its approval.

"And if the sparkle of water ever tempts you from your place beside me, Fire-Bringer, you'd do well to remember the lessons I've instilled in this dungeon."

I shift uncomfortably, my throat still raw, my lungs still flaming. Everything hurts and it is because of the water.

Deep cold and stolen breath. I would evaporate it all if I had the chance, so there is no more pain.

Cullen caresses a finger over my jaw, as a doting mother would to a child, but there is no warmth in his eyes. Only cool calculation as he says, "The water is no place for a boy who burns."

CHAPTER
THREE

Mirren

The wailing startles me awake.

Similis has never possessed the silence of the wilds of Ferusa. There is always the metal clank of working factories, the hum of mobile engines, the buzzing of the Boundary lights. But there are rarely sounds of people.

The uproar tears through the usual quiet with harrowing precision, somehow sounding more like a knife than a noise. I shoot up in bed, my heart thumping close to my throat. Even when Shaw broke through the Boundary last spring, the screams were short lived, only coming from the few closest to the explosion.

But now, bone deep keening reverberates through the Sector.

I shove my feet into my boots and tear into the living room. Easton is already there. His hair sticks up from the cowlick at the back of his head and he blinks wildly, as if trying to determine whether he's still asleep. I don't say anything as I rush past and throw open the front door, before sprinting into the street in my pajamas.

The normally quaint Sector has descended into chaos. All around, people have emerged from their quarterages, most in their pajamas, some half-stuffed into coats and boots. It isn't the quiet terror of the blackout last night, but a loud, breathing thing, that billows between them like an icy fog. Running into the middle of the street, people swirl around me as I try to determine the source of panic. Dread coils around my stomach as my gaze settles on a residence a few quarterages down.

There, pinned to the brick like a grotesque marionette, is a woman's body. Or what *used* to be a woman. Now, her mouth gapes in horror, her skin as ghastly pale as a fresh snow. When I note the large pool of blood congealed beneath her, the Achijj's face flashes before my eyes. Bile climbs my throat, and my breaths feel too demanding in my lungs.

I swallow my nausea down. This wasn't Cullen. It can't be.

"By the Covinus," Harlan mutters in horrified awe, running up beside me.

How he got here so fast from his own Sector, I have no idea. Maybe the Covinus has him sleeping outside our quarterage to watch me at all hours, but I don't bother to ask. Instead, I dash down the street, my untied boots slipping on loose asphalt as I round the corner toward the next Sector. Harlan is right on my heels as we follow the sound of more screams.

I fall motionless at the end of the next street, blood roaring in my ears. Pinned to another quarterage by steel stakes is another body.

My Community's fear is sour on my tongue. All around me, the silence of Similis is broken by wails of horror.

Screams of anguish. And the sound is not just here—it comes from *every* Sector.

"Mirren," Harlan says, his voice oddly hollow, "I recognize that man."

I whip my head toward him, but he doesn't wait for my response. He doesn't even look at me, his eyes glued to the decimated corpse. "That's one of the deserters."

I bite my lip, hoping the pain will stop my mounting panic. Is Cullen rounding up every Similian he can find and murdering them in cold blood? And if it really was him, how did he sneak in unnoticed when the hole in the Boundary is guarded day and night?

My stomach clenches. What if the blackout last night wasn't a coincidence? What if it was caused by another failure at the Boundary?

Similis has always been untouchable to the Praeceptor, but now, he has something he didn't before. *Someone.*

Shaw blew a hole through our safety net once before. And now, with the loss of his humanity, he's capable of so much more devastation. The Praeceptor has always wanted Nadjaa, a seat of power in the Dark World, but has never managed to take it. But what if he's found a way to do just that? Because if he gets his hands on Similian technology, Nadjaa won't stand a chance.

Was it Shaw who let the Praeceptor inside the Boundary? Ice forms in my throat. I've seen what Cullen can do to an entire city when he's set loose inside its walls.

The lights of the Boundary flicker once more. I gasp, feeling as if the ground itself rumbles beneath my feet. The outage is barely noticeable in the rising morning sun, as distracted as everyone is by their shock. But I *know* they've failed again, because my *other* flares to life, a violent wave rising within me, ready to take its revenge at being so starved.

As quickly as it comes, it's gone. I struggle to remain on my feet as my bones go dry once again and nausea clenches my stomach. Harlan steadies me with a hand to my elbow. Twice, he's broken the Keys by touching me. By *helping* me. His gaze meets mine, scared and warm and tender, and seeing emotion worn so openly flares a light in my chest I thought to be long extinguished. I want to tell him how handsome it looks on his face, shining and genuine as it is.

Instead, I say, "We need to find the Covinus. Now."

∽

We don't even make it to the red square before the Covinus guards find us. One of them, a woman with brassy blonde hair pulled into a tight knot so severe, it pulls up the corners of her eyebrows, steps in front of us. She tilts her head slightly, but her face gives nothing away as she says, "The Covinus summons."

I take a deep breath and nod. It can't mean anything good that he's summoned me so soon after the attacks. He knows I've had flares of my power, but he can't possibly think I have something to do with this. Can he?

Even if he does, it doesn't matter. I have to warn him about the Praeceptor. About the things Shaw can do. So, I step forward, despite my misgivings. Harlan makes to follow, but the woman holds up a firm hand. "You will file into the Community center along with the rest of the population and await instructions from your trusted Covinus. You have been relieved from duty for now."

Harlan glances at me uneasily and I try to give him a reassuring smile, but it feels heavy. His worry tickles my neck like tendrils of grass as the guards lead me away and into the Center, and for a moment, I fear he'll do something stupid. But he lets me go without a word.

As the woman leads me to the staging area, three other guards fall in at my back as if I'm liable to make a run for it any moment. The Covinus stands to the side of the stage, peering out as his citizens file into their seats. The screams have dwindled, replaced by the quiet I used to fervently crave. I would have given anything, then, for the whispers to be silenced, for the calm appearance of every other Community member. But right now, when blood coats our streets and violence has shredded our peace, the hush doesn't feel like trust—it feels like apathy.

"Ah, Ms. Ellis," the Covinus says perfunctorily, turning toward me with an expressionless face. "I'm glad you've arrived so quickly."

"Sir, I have to talk to you—"

"And I have need of you as well. It seems an opportunity has presented itself, and if we are to use it to its full potential, we must make haste."

"I—what?" I stare with my mouth agape, my words momentarily forgotten. *Opportunity?* Is he calling the horrific death of over fifty of our Community members an *opportunity?*

The Covinus is unruffled by my shock. Where my hands flutter like dislodged birds, his remain relaxed at his sides. "I told you your words have not been enough to persuade your fellow Similians of the dangers of the Dark World. Now, the realities of the gruesome curse have been dropped into their laps as a violent reminder. It is up to you to drive the point home, Ms. Ellis. To weave a tale of the soulless who stalk the Darkness."

My mouth goes dry. I've never told the Covinus the cost

of the queen's curse, only that Ferusians being unable to kill is a myth. But he must not be as ignorant of Ferusa as he's appeared.

"After today," he continues, "there shall be no more deserters. There shall be no more talk of freedom. There shall be no more *dissent.*" He speaks the last word so passionately he bares his teeth, and for a moment, all I can do is gape.

He never appears anything but serene. I thought his robotic nature was disquieting, that I'd be assuaged by his emotion. But something wriggles beneath it now that sets my teeth on edge.

"Sir, if I may...there are more important things than speaking to the Community right now."

The Covinus sets his eyes on me, and in the dim lighting, I swear they flash black. I blink, and they're the same color gray they've always been. "And what could possibly be more important?"

"I think the bodies have been left by the Praeceptor. I think he has a way into the Boundary. Was there another breach?"

The Covinus' mouth twists in what could be amusement. "It was not the Praeceptor. These citizens defected the safety of our Community and were met with the violence of the Boundary hunters that lurk outside our gates. The fault is their own."

I frown. The hunters are despicable human beings, but as far as I know, they don't mutilate the people they capture. You can't sell damaged goods, after all; it would cut into their profits.

I lick my lips and try again. "Sir, the Boundary was breached last time by—"

"ENOUGH!" the Covinus roars so loudly, I flinch in

surprise. I haven't heard a raised voice in months, and certainly not from someone as contained as he is. "The Boundary has *not* been breached, and if you breathe one word of this nonsense to anyone, you will find yourself outside of it. I grow tired of your resistance. If you are not a willing Community member, perhaps your purpose here has been served."

I swallow roughly. *Think of Easton.* I've gone through hell and back to make sure we stayed together. If I fail now, it will all be for nothing. Anrai's sacrifice will be for nothing.

Heal Easton and live.

I dip my head in deference. "Yes, sir. I will do my best to persuade our Community."

He motions to the stage, and I force my eyes down. My feet forward.

The Community all stares up at me, waiting to be told of the dangers of Ferusa and the safety that only lies in Similis.

But as I stare at them each in turn, the Covinus' words echo in my head.

The Boundary has not been breached.

He seemed so sure there was no breach. And if there was no damage to the Boundary, that means...

Whoever did this walked right through the front gate.

∽

Shaw

I sit apart from the militia, tucked into shadows cast by the large trees of the Nemoran wood. Soldiers carouse around the fire, lively with drink and the promise of battle by the end of the week. None of them glance in my direction, but I prefer it this way. When one happens to catch my gaze, the unpleasant stink of their fear fills my nostrils and makes the abyss ache with blood lust.

It's been hard enough to keep it sated on our journey. We've made fast travel, but there's been little excitement. The Praeceptor has the allegiance of most of the warlords this side of Similis and the few villages who previously resisted, folded quickly. My father has made quick work of spreading my reputation up and down Ferusa, stoking rumors of the man with dead eyes who rains horror upon those who would defy the Praeceptor. The past two nights, in places barely large enough to be deemed towns, they handed over their children and mothers and brothers with little to no resistance.

They knew they could recover from the loss of a loved one, but there would be no recovering from *me*.

Only a few more days until we reach Havay, and then, I'll be able to let go. To quell the ache and the cold and fill it with the screams of those who seek to align themselves with the witch-queen of the south and the peace-loving Chancellor of Nadjaa. My father's enemies and therefore, mine.

The Praeceptor spoke much of the Chancellor in my time in the dungeon. A man too weak to hold the territory he does and too idealistic for continued survival. The Chancellor miraculously survived my father's ministrations, thanks to the ocean-wielder, no doubt. Though she's hidden herself in Similis for now, her meddling has proven to have long term effects on Ferusa. If she ever steps foot over the Boundary again, she will learn she is no longer the only one with power to change the tides of the land.

I once knew the Chancellor and the ocean-wielder, though I've still no recollection of either of them. I felt untethered at first, with no concrete memories to tie me to the world, but I've been rebuilt in the bowels of the Castellium as something else. Monsters have no need of memories.

There are those in this camp, specifically Ivo, who would disagree. He is one of the few *legatus* in the Dark Militia who still retains their soul, though he's obviously comfortable enough with destruction to have risen quickly in the ranks. In spite of his own violent tendencies, the man doesn't trust me.

I meet Ivo's eyes across the fire, his battle-hardened face tight as he watches me. I let a cruel smile crawl across my face, and he turns away with a look of disgust, taking a long swig from his tankard.

He's wise to keep his guard up. I've no allegiance to him or anyone else in this gods-forsaken camp and would just as soon spill their blood as anyone else's if it accomplished my goal. Only the Praeceptor's leash spares them. I feel his hold even from this distance, coiled around my lungs like a snake waiting to strike. I still don't know whether my father sent Ivo to lead the militia, or to keep an eye on me.

A disturbance from the south end of camp tears me from my thoughts. The *legatus* tenses, before pushing himself upward with the lithe movements of a much younger man to head toward the noise.

I follow him, weaving through the soldiers on silent feet. Perhaps I'll be able to feed the abyss tonight after all. Pain threads through me as it rises like a wave of destruction, spearing for each of the soldiers I pass.

"What's happening?" Ivo growls at the nearest sentry, his eyes on the intruders beyond. A travel-worn family cowers in the trees, surrounded by armed militia members. The husband, malnourished and weary, stretches himself over his wife and two children as if his ragged body will do anything to stop bullets. This far from any city, they can only have come from one of the villages we just visited.

The sentry's eyes slide from Ivo to me, his throat bobbing. "We're handling it, Legatus."

"Is it not standard procedure to call upon *me* for any who wander near this camp?" I cheerily ask no one in particular. The militia had obviously been seconds away from shooting them all, but I am charged with deciding whether a person has the capacity for nature-wielding and shooting someone first is a breach of protocol. None of those who have the potential for power are to die, though I'm sure for most, death would be preferable. Instead, they are to be rounded up and sent back to Argentum. For what purposes, I have no idea.

I also don't care. Maybe filling the Castellium dungeons will keep the Praeceptor's attention from me.

The sentry closest to us gapes up at Ivo before his gaze flicks fearfully to me. "Sir, we were just about to call for the Heir, when the man claimed to have information. We thought, perhaps, to hear him out before he faced..." His voice trails off and his throat bobs again as he swallows down his disgust.

It could be true, but it isn't the reason for his hesitation. He would rather see the children shot in the head than subjected to my more...barbaric method. The soul-ridden are so predictably weak.

Ivo grits his teeth, his eyes on the children. What he sees there that gives him pause, I can't imagine. Floppy brown hair, knobby knees and elbows. An off-putting amount of snot and tears caked to round cheeks.

"Sir!" the father cries, his pleading eyes finding Ivo's.

"We have no quarrel with the Praeceptor or his reign. We are just weary merchants, traveling to the next village."

With a pithy glare at the *legatus,* I saunter forward. "If you have no fight with our prestigious warlord, then you'll have no qualms submitting to the small examination he's requested of all Ferusians."

His lower lip wobbles as fearful eyes volley between Ivo and me. The *legatus* stiffens at my side and the traveler's face lights up hopefully when he sees Ivo's hand go to the pommel of his sword, as if perhaps the *legatus* may stand between his family and me. But when Ivo makes no further move, the man's lips turn down in resignation. "It won't—it won't hurt my children, will it?"

I almost laugh. His voice is heavy with enough dread, it's clear he's heard the rumors. So maybe, he isn't an innocent merchant after all, but was instead trying to spare his family from me.

Instead of answering, I close my eyes and put my hand to his cheek.

Screams fill the forest. They bounce off the thick trunks and lash back, filling my ears with a harmony of pain. Man or woman or child, it doesn't matter to the abyss. It breathes and lives, satiated by only moments of agony. The coin that hangs around my neck shudders against my chest, the power inside it winding around my own before plunging deep into the man's soul like a dagger into a heart. Our power scrapes and searches, claws and tears, and the rest of the world falls away. It is only me and the man's soul, and for a moment, I allow myself to consume it.

To remember the brush of emotions. The feeling of fullness.

It seems only a brief second passes before I receive my answer, but when I open my eyes, several militia members have passed out. Another retches behind me, the contents of his dinner spilling to the forest floor.

Only Ivo stands straight, watching me with narrowed eyes. Making note of exactly what kind of monster I am in case he ever has to face me. He senses how much I enjoy the scraping, the agony, and knows: nothing that thrives on such horror can be human.

I grin at him as I set my hands to the wife.

When I am finished with her, and then the children after, they lay in heap at my feet. Alive, but certainly emptier.

When the father finally comes to, I answer his unspoken question. "Your family is not capable of hosting a nature spirit. You are free to go."

Tears spill from his eyes as he hugs his wife to him. He sags in relief that his family won't be taken to Argentum, that they've survived the Praeceptor's demands. Relief still in place, as I bring my dagger across their throats, happiness etched forevermore, even as their blood splashes my boots.

CHAPTER
FOUR

Mirren

I shuffle past Easton into the living room, exhaustion weighing heavily on my shoulders. My stomach is sour though I haven't eaten anything all day. The Covinus had me speaking to crowds until late into the night and it's sapped what little strength I possessed, besieged as I was by their terror, their mistrust, their anger. I did my best to soothe their worries, but I don't know that it was enough. I've felt a lot of things from my Community through the years, but this was the first time a pervasive restlessness moved through them, spreading invisibly from person to person.

The lights flickered twice more during the stretch of the day, and by the second time, I was able to keep to my feet. I was ready for the resurgence of my *other,* ready for its smothering sense of agitation and hunger. I fed it as fast I could, channeling my desperation and heartbreak into it, before it flickered out again a moment later.

Perhaps your purpose here has been served.

The Covinus' threat lingered over every word I spoke, over every lie I told.

My brother's effortless smile eases something in my chest as I shoulder my way into a dining room chair and collapse across from him. For a moment, I consider throwing my arms around him. It would be so nice to glean comfort from the feel of his hand in mine, like I did when we were children. But I know better now. So, I just smile back, the gesture wan.

"I've been waiting to speak with you all day. Are you alright?"

I stare at him for a moment, deciding how best to answer his question. Does he want the true answer? That I feel mired in Darkness and have since the moment I set foot over the Boundary all those months ago? That I am riddled with worry, not only for him, but for our Community?

Or is he looking for a Similian platitude that brings him such comfort? Even hollowed out and cut down, I am still too much for Similis—too much for my brother. No matter how I contort, there is never enough room for all of me here.

"I'm sure seeing such violence brought you right back to the trauma of the Dark World. I asked the Covinus if you could simply rest for the day, but he insisted it was best for the Community if you spoke with them and I know he's right."

Easton has no idea of the trauma I endured in Ferusa. I tried to speak with him upon returning—I wanted *someone* to know the terror and beauty of it all. I wanted to tell him of the tenderness of friendship with Cal and Max; of the exhilaration of being fully yourself around someone like Anrai; of the way it felt to let our father break my heart once more. But Easton wouldn't allow it—the Covinus deemed it treasonous to speak of the outside world and Easton insisted what happened in the past didn't matter: we were together and safe in Similis.

"Trust in the Covinus," I mutter bitterly.

His gaze softens. "Trust isn't always easy, Mirren. But trusting when it's difficult is what makes faith so powerful."

My lips twist in a frown as I study him. "What if someone you trust has lied to you?"

An impenetrable wall falls over Easton's face, more surely than if it were actually made of brick. His eyes narrow warily. "What do you mean?"

"Easton, I—" I cut myself off with a curse and his eyes widen. If I tell him my suspicions about the deserters, Easton will be breaking a Key just by listening to my treason. But it feels like an ever-expanding swamp in my chest, and if I don't tell *someone,* I fear I'll be lost within it. When I finally open my mouth, Easton stiffens like he expects to be hit. "I don't think the Covinus is telling the truth about those deserters."

For an absurd moment, I think I see something like relief in the line of his mouth, and it occurs to me that perhaps I'm not the only one in Similis who keeps secrets. Whatever relief he holds, it's quickly replaced by alarm. His eyes flutter wildly around the quarterage, as if the Covinus and his guard will burst in at any moment.

"It just doesn't make sense that someone from Ferusa got past the Boundary. The hole is guarded around the clock. Someone would have seen *something.*"

"Mirren, what are you saying? It sounds like you're—like you think the Covinus had something to do with the murder of his own people." Easton's eyebrows climb halfway up his forehead as he shakes his head in disbelief.

"I don't think we're as safe here as you think. He said if I didn't manage to convince the Community it was the Dark Worlders, there'd be consequences. And he's hiding something—"

"Enough." My brother's voice is calm, but firmer than I've ever heard it. I don't like the way he now looks at me: the way he would a Community-traitor. "I've given you certain liberties as I know you've gone through a lot, but I will not have you speaking ill of our leader. He allowed you to heal me and welcomed you back with open arms, in spite of betraying the Keys. And you thank him by accusing him of murder?" He pushes an exasperated sigh through his teeth. "The Covinus keeps us safe from the twisted monsters that live in the Darkness and I will hear no different."

I bristle, remembering the way I lobbed the same word at Anrai. What would Easton call me if he knew the truth? That I murdered Shivhai and fractured my soul? And worse, that I don't even regret it? "People, Easton. They are *people* in Ferusa, the same as you and I."

"They are *not!*" he hisses back.

For a moment, I consider screaming at him. Shaking him until he hears reason. But instead, I stand up so suddenly, the chair legs screech against the floor. The sound echoes in the silence of the room. Easton stares up at me in alarm, and though I try to push it away, I'm forcibly reminded of our father. In the set of my brother's jaw, in the weakness shining in his eyes—in the way he can so staunchly ignore anything that threatens the way he sees the world.

I glare down at him and my heart wrenches, because I no longer see anything of the little boy who clung to me when we only had each other. "It was one of those *twisted monsters* that gave up every piece of himself so you could live. Your precious Covinus didn't care whether you lived or died because you mean *nothing* here. So remember with every breath you take, it is only by Ferusian grace you even breathe at all."

For the first time, I choose to leave my brother alone.

~

My eyes burn as I stare at the bare white ceiling. Light pours in through slats in the blinds, giving my room the appearance of a shadowed prison cell. The icy numbness that has plagued me since Anrai was taken is now replaced by the heat of anger. How, after everything, can Easton still believe in the truth of the Covinus? Where is his anger at being deemed useless, discarded like yesterday's trash?

I toss and turn, the sheets scratching against my skin. How did I ever sleep before, with the Boundary lights glaring obnoxiously? How did I never notice the thrum of electricity buzzing against my eardrums?

When I finally succumb to the pull of exhaustion, it is only to be jostled awake once more. Panic squeezes my throat as my eyes struggle to adjust to the darkness. It takes me another moment to realize the Boundary lights haven't gone out, but rather, a hood has been pulled over my head. I thrash out as shadows move around me, grabbing my arms and pulling me from the bed. Pure instinct drives me as I jab, thumb squarely planted on the outside of my fists. An angry *harrumph* exhales from the nearest person as I make contact and I don't pause before I stomp down, my bare feet connecting with the booted arch of someone else's.

Another set of hands pulls my arms behind my back, and I kick out, my movements turning from efficient to erratic. Being this weak feels too familiar. Like a dank cave, hundreds of miles from here, when all I could do was scream.

I don't scream now, only thrash wildly, my bare toes connecting with fleshy stomachs and rock-hard kneecaps. My face is wrenched between two overlarge hands, pinching my jaw open as a gag is shoved into my mouth.

Someone yanks off the hood and dread pinches my stomach as I set my eyes on the Covinus loyalists.

Two large men hold me, their blue jumpsuits startling in the gray of the room. Three more act as a human blockade in front of my bedroom door. The woman who summoned me earlier now stares back at me calmly, her blonde hair still tied in a neat knot at the base of her skull. "It will be better for your brother if you don't struggle," she says quietly.

I snarl against the gag.

She doesn't even flinch at my insanity. Only motions for the others to haul me forward. I force a deep breath through my nose, letting it leak back out through my teeth. I've lived the last months in a haze of pain and emptiness, but now, anger hones my mind into sharp lines. There is no more appeasing the Covinus now—there is only escaping him.

I can't fight off six guards in the middle of Similis with no power. Even if I get lucky, and the lights flare again, I have no guarantee it will last. I have to be smart if both my brother and I are going to make it out of this unharmed.

The men yank me forward and I stumble through the doorway as I try to keep to my feet. My cheeks burn as they drag my along, their combined strength no match for my weakened body.

Easton bursts from his bedroom, his night clothes

twisting behind him as he chases after us. "What's going on?" he cries, his wide eyes finding mine. "What did you do?!" he shouts. When no one answers, he runs to block the door. "What did she do?!"

The blonde woman stops short, fitting him with a perfunctory look. "Your Covinus wishes to speak with her. You trust your Covinus, do you not?"

To his credit, Easton looks torn. He raises his hand, and for a heartbreakingly hopeful moment, I think he might fight for me. But instead, his look of panicked resignation is the last thing I see as I'm shoved unceremoniously into the back of a Covinus mobile.

I tear the gag out of my mouth and brace myself against one of the bench seats, my fingertips biting into the cold metal sides as the van surges forward. The only windows are two small slits at the top of the back doors, and I clamber toward them, balancing precariously with one foot on the bench and the other wedged against the corner. The streets are as brightly lit as noontime, the only thing denoting the lateness of the evening being the lack of any movement. We move swiftly through them, and my stomach flips as I realize they haven't turned on the sirens or lights. It doesn't bode well for me that they want this to be a secret.

The van tilts as we maneuver through Sectors and I almost fly off the seat. Clawing at the window, I manage to keep myself upright, but when the metropolis finally comes into view, I almost tumble backward once more. Understanding mingled with a sense of dread settles in my chest, extinguishing the miniscule hope there's still some way to assuage the Covinus.

The red square is no longer visible beneath the crowd of people covering it. Thousands of Community members gathered so close their shoulders touch. The crowd undulates, a giant organism that makes the heart of Similis appear like it's actually alive. The sound of their anger reverberates around the van, shouts and chants of discontent flowing together in a song of chaos.

"What is this?" I breathe aloud, but no one is there to answer.

The van doesn't slow as the crowd swarms. Fists pound against the sides, the sound like thunder. My throat clenches, fear for my Community members fluttering in my chest. Their bodies are so breakable compared to the steel of the mobile; their will so breakable against the might of the Covinus. He can't possibly punish them all, can he?

Beneath my anxiety, something like pride wends through me. Whatever happens to me when I face the Covinus, whether I be Outcast or worse, I'm not leaving my Community completely in the dark. They've at least begun to question the wisdom of trusting in the Covinus over themselves.

The tires bounce over the last of the red bricks and then go smoothly silent as we turn into an underground garage. The brakes squeal and the van jerks to a stop. Doors slam and I scramble away from the window, cursing loudly as my toes catch the edge of the seat, sending me sprawling forward. I'm still huffily blowing errant tangles of hair out of my eyes and pawing my way to standing when the loyalists open the door to usher me out.

One of them picks me up by the armpits and sets me on the ground like a child. Swiping sticky strands of hair off my face, I glare up at him indignantly. He doesn't meet my eyes, only prods me forward. I'm herded into an elevator and the six of them file in silently around me, blocking any chance of exit as the doors slide closed. My stomach lurches as we're shuttled upward. When we jerk to an unsettling stop, I swallow roughly, dread clogging my throat. We're at the topmost floor.

As far as I know, no one has access to this floor, not even the guard. No one but the Covinus.

The doors creak open, but no one moves. They all just watch me expectantly. When I don't step forward, the blonde woman finally brings her gaze to mine, her lips pursed. "Think of your brother," she tells me again.

I bare my teeth in a sneer, but her words have their intended effect. I step off the elevator.

The doors close behind me, the metallic grind like a knife through the silence. My feet sink into thick carpet as I take in the room, blinking as wildly. It's as though I've been transported somewhere far from the austerity of the Covinus building. The room is beautifully open, framed entirely by floor to ceiling glass windows. The Boundary lights sparkle through the glass walls, bathing everything in a soft glow that reminds me more of the lantern light of Ferusa than the electricity of Similis. Sofas made of luxurious fabric are placed throughout, their cushions as plush as clouds. Paintings in rich colors are displayed beneath the subtle glow of electric lamps, their subjects depicted in whimsical blues and fanciful purples.

For a moment, all I can do is gape around the room, frozen in awe. There is nothing beautiful in Similis, nothing meant for simple enjoyment or excessive beauty. And by the Covinus, I didn't realize how starved I've been for it. I allow the splendor to wash over me, sinking beneath my skin, before taking in the shelves lining the interior walls that encase the elevator shaft.

Books.

The shelves stretch at least fifteen feet high, filled with

novels of all shapes and sizes. I gawk up at them, shock warring with disbelief. The Covinus has denied us every pleasure of life, convinced us they're selfish—all the while, enjoying them for himself.

"Good evening, Ms. Ellis."

The Covinus' voice sounds from the far side of the room and my stomach leaps into my throat as I whip toward it. Hands clasped behind his back, he stands next to a large desk, gazing down at the riot in the red square. His face is bathed in shadows and he's entirely still as he watches the unrest he so feared unfold beneath him.

I stand frozen, staring at the outline of his slight frame and the glare of the lights in his white-blonde hair. Out of nervous habit, I reach to caress my *other,* but of course, all I touch is emptiness. Barren and dry. It will only be me here in this cavernous office that, in spite of its splendor, suddenly feels as desolate as Yen Girene.

The Covinus says nothing further, apparently in no hurry to inform me why he ordered me dragged from my bed in the middle of the night. Surely, he can't think I organized the Community to rise against him when all I've done is tell his lies. Shifting impatiently from foot to foot, I prompt, "you wished to speak with me?"

He makes a noncommittal noise in the back of his throat, before sighing heavily. "Protests are a funny thing," he says, though his tone indicates he doesn't find them the least bit humorous. "They've plagued civilizations for as long as time, and yet, what do they ever really accomplish other than destruction?"

Uncertain whether or not he intends for me to respond, I finally say, "they make voices heard. Voices the powerful may not have listened to otherwise."

Even though I can only see his back, I sense the man's

sneer. "Do you know why the First Queen cursed the Dark World, Ms. Ellis?" He turns away from the window. The Boundary lights leech the color from him, and he looks spectral against the glass. "Too many *voices*. Uniformed mouths, spewing opinions as if they were facts causing confusion and dissension. She sought to silence their wickedness."

I frown. I'd once believed the Covinus version of history without question, but having seen the beauty and the horror of Ferusa for myself, I know things aren't so linear. But I swallow down my disagreement, because something about the leader standing before me has shifted. He is no longer the amiable man who welcomed me home, or even the stern one who admonished me in the Community Center. There is a desperate edge to him now, razor-sharp, and haven't I seen what desperation can drive a person to?

A warning tingles up my spine. I am not speaking with the benign leader of a peaceful society—in his place stands a dictator on the verge of losing his power. No different than Cullen or Denver.

"I'm sure you disagree. You've shown flagrant disregard for the wellbeing of your Community since before your parents were even Outcast. There have always been rumors dissension is passed through the bloodline, but I've never put much stock in mythical nonsense." He meets my eyes and I force myself to hold still beneath his piercing gaze. "Until you. Selfish to the very core, exactly like your parents."

There's no denying it's true of my father now, but once, a giving heart beat in his body. A heart that dreamed and loved so fiercely, he was willing to give up everything for it. Until the man in front of me punished him with it, shattered it too irrevocably to ever be repaired. The familiar sting of anger rises in my throat. "You know nothing of my parents."

Why didn't I ask Denver more about what happened all those years ago? Why didn't I at least try to listen?

The Covinus smiles as if sensing my ignorance, the skeletal effect making him all the more frightening. "Outcast for *love,* was it? I suppose you imagine that as some revolutionary act, all passion and rebellion? Let me tell you something about their supposed love. Your father was Outcast, but your mother was not. Do you know why?"

I remain willfully silent. As much as I hate the Covinus, a part of me remains desperate for any piece of my mother.

"Your mother wasn't willing to be Outcast. She threw herself at my feet, groveling and claiming to care nothing for the man. Said she only loved her Covinus and would do *anything* for me in order to stay in Similis." The Covinus begins to pace behind his desk as I work to keep my face neutral.

It can't be true. The only thing that kept Denver's refusal to help Easton bearable is that once, he was not as he is now. Once, he was noble and selfless and kind.

The Covinus' eyes are fervid, focused on a memory far from this room. When they settle back on me, they are fathomless. "Do you know what I did with her love for me?"

I squeeze my eyes shut against the words, but it doesn't save me from them.

"I *killed* her for it. You are alone in this world because love is not revolutionary. It's selfish. A destructive force to be fought against, never celebrated. Look how low it brought you, Ms. Ellis. Willing to walk past cages of children without blinking. To ignore the plea of dying men. Willing to play as a god and take another's life as if it's less worthy than your own."

Emptiness is a wave of defeat in my chest threatening to breach my resolve, but I refuse to fear it. I can swim, after all.

And love may have taken everything from me, but it has given me as much in return. It's given me Easton, alive and safe. *For Easton,* I repeat to myself, *it's all for Easton.*

"I can calm the protests," I assure the Covinus, uncertain if I'll be able to affect them at all. Is there any stopping the ripple of a pond once a stone has been thrown?

To honor Anrai's sacrifice, to stay with my brother—I have to try.

"In a healthy Community, every member serves a purpose. No member more or less important than another, just like in the human body. But when an organ becomes diseased, do we allow it to poison the rest?"

I steel my spine, dread crawling through my chest.

"We cut it out. Even the deserters served a purpose. Warning others what would happen if they, too, leave the safety of my arms. But you, Ms. Ellis..." his words taper off as he slowly lowers himself into the chair. Opening a drawer of the desk, he pulls out a revolver. Cocking the hammer, he feigns a look of regret. "I'm afraid you no longer serve a purpose."

My throat burns as I stare down the barrel. I've come too far to let this small man shoot me in his office, alone and unheard. He as good as admitted he was behind the murders of the deserters, and if he mutilated fifty of his own citizens, what's to stop him from disposing of my brother once I'm gone?

More instinct than thought, I dive to the left, the crack of the shot ricocheting sharply off the glass and back to my ears. Another shot rings out as I crawl toward the bookshelves on my belly, the plush carpet littered with feathers from a nearby couch. Throwing my arms over my head, I duck behind the sofa as books explode over me in puffs of parchment. My ears ring sharply, my stomach in my throat as I flatten myself to the floor.

My breaths come in short wheezes and panic presses against my chest as I try to think. The elevator can't be the only way out of here. If I can just find another door, I might have a chance to lose myself in the protest crowd.

And then what?

Powerless, weaponless, and weak. How in the Darkness' am I ever going to get my brother and I through the Boundary safely?

One fight at a time, Lemming. Anrai's voice. Survive first; worry about the rest later.

I pull myself across the floor on my elbows as another shot cracks through the silence. It's only a matter of time before the elevator doors open and the guards come to restrain me. Fear begins to squeeze—my throat, my stomach, my limbs. I'm trapped. Just as I've been since I stepped back into Similis.

This is not a cage. Think.

The Covinus' chair scrapes against the floor, as if he's finally deemed killing me important enough to stand for. His footsteps are measured as he prowls closer. I snatch a book from the shelf and hurtle it at him. My aim is good enough that he's forced off course, ducking with a snarl. Arming myself once more, I spot the only other door in the room and a relieved breath hisses out of me. Small, squat, and situated on the opposite side as the elevator. It's stairs —it *has* to be stairs.

I throw another book and then another. They're only distractions, and sorry ones at that, but at least I'm not waiting here to die. Because gods, isn't that exactly what

I've been doing the last few months? Waiting for the Darkness to envelop me so I could just fall into it and spare myself the toll of trying to live in a world where guilt and heartbreak tear me to shreds?

No more. *You are not caged.*

It may be my fault Anrai is gone, but he would *never* approve of giving in the way I have. He didn't allow even an inch of the possibility of failure, and he chose *me* as his match. It's time I remember why I was worthy of it.

"You are only delaying the inevitable," the Covinus taunts, "a few books are nothing to the power of the Covinus."

I hurl another one at his head. It collides with his nose with a sickening *crack*. My nails claw the plush carpet as I scramble to my feet. Atrophied muscles screaming, I race to the door, praying to whatever Dark World gods used to exist it's unlocked. Terrified to slow down for even a moment, I crash into the metal, the impact clacking my teeth together.

The door swings open revealing a concrete set of stairs, and a terrified sob escapes me as I hurtle down them, the Covinus' angry roar echoing behind me. Painful breaths saw out of my lungs, but I don't slow as I descend, down, down, down. The bones of my legs feel as though they'll collapse at any moment, and I curse myself for allowing my body to waste away.

I should have fought harder. How did I forget the wildness inside me, the dark recesses that have always powered me forward? That were mine long before my *other*?

Finally, I reach the bottom of the winding corridor, bursting through the last door. Wheezing, I bend forward, hands on my knees as something like relief courses through me.

The elevator next to the stairwell dings cheerily and my relief dissipates as the loyalists stream out. I try to run, but they swarm me. Hands grip my arms, yanking them behind my back. I shriek, kicking and thrashing, but there are so many of them.

Looking past the crowd of bodies, I see the Covinus standing in the elevator. Blood pours from his nostrils, his emotionless face gleaming crimson as he watches his guard subdue me. A machine, even under attack, is still a machine.

My shins crack against the concrete as I'm forced to my knees before him.

I'm going to die here alone, having never told Easton I love him; above a Community of people I've hated and loved and lied to, who deserve to know the truth of their world; a world away from the friends that hold my heart, the city that cradles my mind and the man—the man who owns my soul.

I squeeze my eyes shut, a desperate sob clogging my throat. Will Anrai's soul meet mine in the Darkness? Or will it turn away from me, disgusted by my weak heart?

"You parents thought to defy my power," the Covinus says, stepping toward me, his voice barely above a whisper. "And look what happened to them. You will die, and then I will end your brother. It will be as if the Ellis family never existed."

Oh gods.

The Covinus raises the gun until all I can see is the smooth metal of the barrel. I trembled the first time a gun was pointed at me, but now I raise my eyes away from the weapon, to stare down its wielder.

I have the heart of ocean, even if I can no longer touch it. And I will not die on my knees.

My heart pounds against my rib cage and my muscles cry out in agony as I push against the guards' hold. The Covinus watches inscrutably as I shake off their hands. Coming to a stand, I face my journey to the endless Darkness with my eyes wide open.

CHAPTER
FIVE

Calloway

The pounding on my bedroom door is nothing to the pounding inside my skull. Max and I had somehow decided drinking three bottles of cherry wine between the two of us would be the height of the evening prior, but when I sit up and have to clamp my mouth shut to keep from retching, I can't for the life of me remember why.

The knocking continues and I chuck my pillow at the door. "Go away," I bark irritably, before collapsing back onto the bed and burying my face in the plush mattress.

Even with my eyes squeezed firmly shut, I know it's Max by the no nonsense way the door slams open against my bedroom wall. Rhonwen would never be so rude.

Or loud.

She strides purposefully to the window, and before I can so much as object, whips open the curtains. Light pours into the room, the buttery slices of the Nadjaan sun like sharp daggers to the eyeballs.

"You've poisoned me," I mutter pitifully, my voice

muffled by the mattress. "Must you come in here to finish the job?"

Max laughs, the sound warming my chest. Oh, yes. *That* was why drinking had seemed like such a good plan, because it's always a surefire path to hearing more of my friend's delight—something that's been rare as of late. I'd dance on my head if it earned me the smallest fraction of a giggle, even if such movement would be ill advised at present, because Max, in all her fiery spirit, is one of the only people on earth I truly love.

The coverlet is ripped from me unceremoniously and I curse loudly.

Perhaps I don't love her. Perhaps I hate her.

I lunge forward, wrestling the blanket from her hand and she lets out a squeal as we both fall back in a tangle of scrabbling limbs. I may be stronger physically, but Max has always been more determined, so after a moment, we come to a stalemate and both lay back onto the bed, still gripping our portion of the covers.

I turn to her, my head swimming with the motion. She's dressed as immaculately as ever in a tunic of rich emerald green, her hair coifed and hanging down her back in perfect coils. Her face is devoid of makeup, but freshly washed, and missing all the signs of death I currently feel. I whine at the unfairness, pursing my lips grumpily. "How are you so chipper?"

She grins, her teeth gleaming. "If you can't keep up with me, I may need to find myself a new partner in crime."

I shove my portion of the blanket at her with a grunt. "As if you could find anyone with such great taste."

She smiles in assent. Then says, "Denver wants us in his office in twenty minutes."

Groaning, I slump off the bed, more resembling a

puddle of goo than a person, but I manage to keep my feet beneath me as I come to my full height. The room sways slightly and nausea rises once more, but the mention of Denver has a sobering effect. "Why?" I grunt, searching in vain for a pair of pants.

The man who took me in as a teenager, who was always affectionate with his words and intentional with his actions, has been more like a ghost than a person since we returned from Yen Girene. At first, I'd tried to share in his grief—surely, being tortured for months on end needed to be spoken of—and then tried to include him in mine. He'd loved Anni like a son, and yet, has made no mention of him at all.

Then again, he never mentioned Mirren or her brother, either.

Maybe to Denver, heartbreak is better kept behind an impenetrable wall. Contained, it can't hurt him.

That, I'd understand well.

On the rare occasion he's called us to his office, it's always been as a guard of sorts in lieu of Shaw's absence, a job I despise. I'm trained well enough, I suppose, but life is too short to be standing around, wielding a sword in the middle of civilized conversation like some sort of fool. There are too many wines to drink, jigs to dance, and mouths to kiss, to stand around like a menacing statue.

I shove my leg into a pair of trousers, one hand balanced on my wardrobe to keep myself from toppling over. Once I finally manage to work the other leg in, Max jumps up and shoves my bow and sword into my arms, before pulling me into the hallway.

"Hey!" I shout, making to shove my way past her back into the room. "What about my hair?!"

Meeting or no, I have no intention of walking around all

willy-nilly with hair that looks as if I've been playing with lightning bolts. Though a few inches shorter than me, Max is as impossible to move as a brick wall and when I take note of the haunted look in her eyes, I relent, and allow myself to be manhandled down the hall with a beleaguered sigh.

As much as I despise these meetings, Max lives for them.

For a snippet of news that never comes. The other side of the continent has been disturbingly quiet since Anni's departure. I haven't decided whether it's an encouraging sign or an ominous one, but Max has taken it as her personal mission to discover his whereabouts. What she plans to do when she does, I can only guess.

Shuddering, I push thoughts of Anni from my mind. I pointedly don't think about how his father is punishing him for his betrayal as a child—I certainly don't think of the things Shaw himself is willingly doing as a capable assassin with no soul or morality to adhere to.

Instead, I loop my arm through Max's. We all have our ways of dealing with losing Anni; I can't fault her for hers. "The details of the night are a little foggy. Remind me, did you invite that handsome fisherman to your bed?"

"He was a coppersmith, and no. I was too busy keeping you from toppling into the Storven," she replies with a wry grin in my direction.

"Too bad, the swim may have sobered me up a bit." We spin around the corner and down the stairs to the first floor. "He was an excellent dancer. Which probably means he could move his way around a body—" My words end in a spurt of laughter as Max shoves me into the nearest wall.

She laughs too and something eases in my chest. We've been so off balance without Anni, a boat teetering back and forth with nothing to anchor it, but this—being ribald and loud and fun—feels familiar. Hopeful, that there's at least a small chance we can find our way back to some semblance of normal.

When we round the final corner to Denver's office, our laughter dies.

The Chancellor blinks up at us from his seat at the desk, his eyes appearing twice their normal size behind a pair of round spectacles. "Ah, Calloway, Maxwell, thank you for coming so quickly." His hands flutter over paperwork, as he shuffles and reshuffles various stacks. Hands that appear miraculously unscarred in contrast with the rest of his body. "This shouldn't take long, but the reporting general is from Jayan's district, so it would be best if we appeared in alliance."

His eyebrows climb higher as he notes the state of my hair, but he makes no comment and motions us forward. Max moves behind him silently, while I scuff my feet and kick obstinately at the ornate rug. Great. Another meeting standing behind Denver, listening to that slimeball of a councilmen's grating voice and feeling like I'm solely in charge holding up a wall.

My head throbs and I swallow down the dryness in my throat, my stomach roiling. Perhaps it would have been prudent to eat something before coming here.

I suppose if I puke, I'll just have to make the best of it and aim for Jayan's shoes.

The aforementioned slimeball enters the room, his watery blue eyes shrewdly moving between Max and me. The general strides in behind him, looking windswept and handsome in the white uniform of the guard, his helmet tucked beneath a muscular arm. The man scans the room with the natural assuredness of a well-seasoned soldier, but his confidence wavers when he sets his gaze on me.

Unable to help myself, I give him a roguish wink. The general had the pleasure of my company for more than a week last winter when in between guard rounds. His cheeks redden in remembrance of our exploits, and he swallows visibly, his masculine throat bobbing as he determinedly avoids my gaze. I can almost feel the roll of Max's eyes beside me, further adding to the thread of delight winding through me.

Jayan clears his throat pointedly. "Tell the Chancellor what you've learned, Rocher."

The name rings no memories. Had I even bothered to learn it before sending him back to whatever country outpost he occupied?

The general shifts awkwardly, before steeling his spine and turning to Denver. "The Dark Militia is on the move. A select legion that appears to be led by his heir."

Anni is leading the Dark Militia? Max exhales a small breath, barely audible. Denver doesn't move at all, his face betraying none of the heartbreak suddenly swirling through me. Is that something he learned as a Similian, once upon a time, or is the lack of emotion at devastating news something he practices as Chancellor? Either way, it forcibly reminds me why I so despise these meetings, aside from the obvious.

Denver has always treated us like family in this manor, laughing around the dinner table, teaching us in the study. I have never felt a burden to him, never felt like I needed to *earn* my place here. But in this office, standing behind him like his own personal assassins, distaste threads through me. Here, he does not treat us like his children. He treats us like his followers.

"What's Cullen's goal with this faction?" Denver muses thoughtfully.

"We aren't sure, Chancellor. But there have been rumors circulating that he's been rounding up parts of the population and shipping them back to Argentum."

Denver makes a humming noise in the back of his throat. "To what end?" he murmurs, more to himself than the general.

"Slaves?" Rocher offers. Max stiffens next to me and my heart tugs with the need to take her hand, even though she won't approve of being made to look weak in present company. "Maybe he's in need of more soldiers? Whatever the reason, apparently those who refuse or try to escape are being burned alive. Our spies report an entire village in the north is now nothing but ash."

Gods.

The room is suddenly stifling, the air gone stale. Anni has always been determined, his heart as much of a driving factor in his ruthless choices as his unyielding nature. It was his soul that kept him tethered, pulled him from the edge of darkness. I've been bracing myself for months now, knowing this was a possibility—that without a soul, Anni would be bloodthirsty enough to work for his father. But nothing prepared me for hearing it confirmed, or the way it would feel like my lungs have been hit with a sledgehammer.

I steal a glance at Max. Rage radiates from her eyes as if she's forcibly projecting it. I bump her shoulder with mine, undeterred by the power of her anger, because it's simply how Max processes things. Emotions are more manageable when you keep the most vulnerable of them buried behind a wall of something else. I'd know.

Her shoulders move with a deep breath, and I know I've calmed her slightly.

"Have you heard enough now, Denver?" Jayan says hastily, his eyes glowing like a mountain cat about to pounce. "Every day we hide away in our valley, the Praeceptor grows stronger. Isn't it time to wage war, to conquer his lands to be sure they will never rise up against us?"

"There will be no war." Denver's determined gaze lands squarely on Jayan and I feel the cool reassurance of relief. *This* is why Denver leads Nadjaa, why the city is as magnificent as it is. He will never be bullied; never be torn from the path he believes is right. "Nadjaa does not conquer. We will do as we have been. Keep our defenses prepared and our ears open."

"And what of Similis?" Jayan demands. I whip my head toward him, narrowing my eyes. Anni tasked me with one thing before sacrificing himself and the weight of my promise hasn't lessened since losing him. Keeping Mirren safe. "There have been reports of the lights flickering. If there is a time to break through the Boundary and take their technology as ours, it's now!"

"Flickering lights mean nothing," Denver replies coolly. "It certainly doesn't mean we should sacrifice our citizens on a whim."

Jayan twists his lips in a distasteful sneer, but I hardly see it.

Instead, I remember Anni last spring, crouched in the Darkness next to the towering wall. We'd spent almost every penny we had on those explosives, and even then, we hadn't been hopeful, because in a thousand years, no one had ever even made a dent.

But things like odds had never mattered to Anni. It was one of the first things that drew me to him. After everything that happened to my family, by the time Denver found me, I'd given up on trying to direct my life in any sort of manner. If I wasn't exactly content to ride the wave, I was too tired by that point to swim against it. But Anni—he'd been fighting against the current his entire life.

There was no obstacle too steep to overcome, no moral line that would ever stop him from protecting what he saw as his. As someone who'd failed miserably at keeping loved ones safe, I found Anni's resolute defiance mesmerizing. It's why I followed him last spring, why I believed wholeheartedly that my brother would be the one to break into Similis even though no one ever had.

Max had held my hand and together, we watched Anni light the spark and fracture the world as we knew it. And when he turned back to us, pale eyes alight with the reflection of flame, he didn't look victorious. He looked self-possessed and poised, as if failure had never even occurred to him.

And now, that same determination has no soul to tether it to earth, no soft heart to remind Anni of his humanity. The man who never fails is marching across Ferusa, burning villages as he goes. With each passing day, he grows closer to Similis. To Mirren.

Denver doesn't seem to find the news of the Boundary lights flickering unsettling, but he didn't witness how easily that wall collapsed beneath Anni's determination, as if it were made of water rather than unnatural stone. And Denver didn't swear a pact with his soul-brother. He doesn't feel the resounding levity of it with every beat of his heart, with every breath of his lungs.

Because if Mirren isn't safe, I've failed to give Anni the only thing he's ever asked me for.

Shaw

I stay awake for days on end as the militia marches further south. The journey to Havay takes longer than usual, a result of the deep superstitions the Argentians hold about the Nemoran wood. Raised too close to the Xamani, stories of the trees' magic, of the unnatural creatures born and bred within the shadows of their leaves, the soldiers are wary of the forest's power.

If I heard any of the stories as a child, I don't remember them now. But I respect the soldier's fear as we camp on the edge of the ancient trees, because I, too, imagine I feel something heavy wind around my throat and settle in the emptiness of my chest. Something that whispers to me, ancient words, soft and lilting.

Raw and ageless, it searches.

My eyelids grow heavy, but catching myself, I snap them back open. I don't want to sleep. The night brings dreams of my time in the dungeon, and of the time before, when I was lost in the chasm. But the leaves rustle above me, their rolling hush whispering to my body's pursuit of survival, of its need to eat and breathe and sleep.

And before long, I am tumbling into the Darkness.

Creatures tear my skin into ribbons, their claws digging beneath my ribs and pulling until they crack. They are relentless, shredding me from the outside in. I scream into the void until my throat goes raw.

Desperate, I scramble to find the pieces of myself. Their edges are razor-sharp, and my fingertips bleed as I try to grip them together, to reassemble them into the shape of myself. But the blood is slippery, and no matter how hard I try, I can never keep the pieces together. They escape me, drifting into the endless black.

Lost. Always lost.

And I cannot follow, for somewhere in those velvet depths, lies a sea. And oh, how it *rages*. Before, when I was trapped in the void, I tried to fight my way toward it thinking those savage waves held relief. But now I know, water only holds destruction.

Abandoning the lost pieces of myself to the sea, I run. But it feeds on the fragments left behind and its appetite only grows stronger. It stalks me with its fury. Plunges down my throat and steals the breath from my lungs. Its emerald waves reach for me, pulling me under and refusing to let go. The waves demand things I cannot give, things I cannot even understand. I plead and I cry, but its power won't cease until I am consumed.

I wake with a violent start, breaths sawing out of me in whistling huffs. My hands are clammy as I run them roughly over my thighs. Sweat drips into my eyes, blurring my vision as I try to remember where I am, why I'm here.

The air is quiet but for the occasional rustle of a bed roll or the soft snuff of a snore.

I am Fire-Bringer, Soul-Eater. Heir of the Praeceptor and edge of his blade.

I do not need to hold onto lost pieces of myself, because there *is* no self. There is only the emptiness, the hunger, the abyss.

Why, then, does something stir within its depths? I have pushed it down, starved it—neglected and abused it—but now, it moves in the darkest corners of this body. It crashes like a wave, but curves like a river. It smells like warm rain.

I shiver. I don't like rain or waves or rivers. Water is the enemy of someone who burns; its depths only hold suffocation and death. It must be the presence of these godsdamn trees, their unnatural presence burrowing into my head.

I grip my chest and let out a snarl. Paw at my sternum, as if I can dig the feeling of that sea out with my bare hands—as if I can snuff out the way the waves call to me now, even in waking. Though I scratch my skin raw, the feeling remains rooted.

Several militia members rouse awake at my roar of defeat, their wide eyes shining in the darkness as they remember I am not human. Not one of them. A monster rides in their presence and it is only a matter of time before they find themselves the focus his fury.

My eyes move to the blood still splattered across the leather of my boots. Blood of that family. A wife, a child, a husband. A smile crawls across my face as I remember the ripe taste of their fear on my tongue. In a few days' time, I'll be able to gorge myself on an entire city of it. Until then, I will not give myself over to the tricks of dreams.

Fire-Bringer. Soul-Eater.

Empty.

~

Mirren

The bullet never comes.

Because at that moment, the Boundary lights go out, dousing the garage in disorienting darkness. The ground rumbles beneath us and the building begins to sway, as if it's made of fabric rather than concrete. The lights surge again, the explosive flash blinding me. The elevator dings as the electronic systems reset, and realizing what's happening, the Covinus lunges forward with a roar just as the doors begin to slide closed.

But when the lights fail again, the darkness holds.

My *other* sings to life. And it isn't the weak trickle I've clung to during the other blackouts. It's a storm surge against an ocean cliff, crashing against my lungs, filling every crevice of my broken heart and body. I gasp as its fury, *my* fury, swirls inside me, a violent cyclone of wills. I struggle to keep myself afloat—from plunging into its depths—and losing myself entirely.

I stared at the crevasse of my power once before, in the dungeons of Yen Girene. It felt endless then, like I could jump in and never find my way back to the surface. I teeter atop it now, breathing in deeply to steady myself. To stabilize the pull of the void. Now is not the time to lose myself to the unknown—not when I may possess the ability to not only take down this entire building, but perhaps, all of Similis.

The Covinus pounds against the elevator door, his fury at having been thwarted now muted behind the thick metal. There are no lights here, not even the glow of the moon. The Covinus guard flail around me, tripping over each other as they feel their way toward the sounds of their leader's panic. The Boundary lights have been their crutch for so long, they don't know how to move in the natural state of the world.

They don't know their eyes will adjust and the night that once seemed so blinding will welcome them, its folds of inky black as much a blanket of protection as it is a shadow for mischief. They don't yet understand that Darkness is what you make it.

I don't wait for them to adapt, instead turning and sprinting through the garage, working to keep my foot falls silent. My body feels strong as I race toward the muffled sounds of protestors. There are still wounds—the loss of Anrai and the hole I gave up when I killed Shivhai—but for the first time in months, I don't feel completely shattered.

There are no lanterns in Similis, no candlelight—nothing to pepper the endless void—so I don't know I've reached the protestors until something forceful slams me into a concrete wall. Terrified screams sound as a wave of bodies pushes against me, their hysteria feeling like a solid force. The pressure on my chest increases, and for a panicked moment, I'm sure I'll be crushed beneath the mob.

But the wave ebbs and footsteps around me stumble as the crowd surges in the opposite direction. Fresh air barrels into my lungs and I move blindly again, relying more on memory than sight. Above the sounds of fear, voices rise in the dim moonlight—anger at the Covinus, demands for the truth—and pride expands in my chest. Maybe our voices were never truly lost or stolen. Maybe we've forgotten how to use them.

I tear free from the undulating crowd and hurtle through the streets. Away from the towering buildings of the red square, the moon's dim light illuminating the bustle of the sectors. No one has abided the curfew tonight: there are people everywhere, whispering frantically, their wide eyes drawn to the sound of the protestors. The blackouts have never lasted this long before, and I might be making a fatal mistake by not tearing through the Boundary while my power is awake.

But I can't leave Easton.

Somehow, we have to make it out of here together. I can't have come this far just to lose him now.

He's on the roof when I reach our quarterage, staring in

the direction of the red square as if he can somehow see straight to it. He faces me calmly, even as I burst unceremoniously through the door, the old wood creaking as it slams into the outer wall. I paw at the curls plastered to my forehead, my eyes stinging as sweat drips into them, but Easton appears entirely unruffled by the evening.

"Easton," I pant, throwing a hand on my hip and bending over in an attempt to calm my breathing, "we have to go."

My brother gives me an indulgent smile. "Mirren, you will just need to work harder. Whatever you've done to upset the Covinus, we can fix it. Together."

Our Community is poised to explode and somehow, he is still the epitome of the Keys. Unfortunately, I have no time for Similian nonsense.

"NOW!" I roar over him. "We have to go *now*!"

Easton's eyes pop and he takes a step backward. "Mirri, we aren't going to leave our Community," he says, as aghast as if I've suggested murdering someone. "Trust in the Covinus. He will restore peace and you will regain his faith."

I swallow down the bitter rage climbing my throat and force a measured breath through my teeth. Easton's entire life has been a lie. I can spare a moment of patience for him to adjust, even if I feel the weight of the Covinus' anger ensnaring my throat more with every passing moment. "Easton, he plans to restore peace by killing me. *He's* the one who murdered those deserters—"

He pinches his brow between his fingers and shakes his head. "That isn't true—"

"—*he's* the one who killed Mom!"

My words come out as a jumbled shout and I instantly regret them. Face flushed, Easton backs away from me like I've launched a weapon rather than words. He shakes his head wildly, his eyes shining with fear. "That isn't true," he insists again.

"IT IS!"

At that moment, the door to the roof bursts open so loudly, both Easton and I jump in surprise. Pure instinct has me calling to the humidity in the air and raising it as a wall of protection in front of us. Gaping at my show of power, Easton curls further into himself. Emotion clogs my throat as I witness his fear.

Because it's no longer fear of the unknown or leaving Similis that clouds his face.

It's fear of *me*.

I'm expecting the entire Covinus guard to pour through the door, but it is only Harlan, golden hair looking distinctly windswept and cheeks ruddy with exertion. He looks massive in the shadowed doorway, all tensed muscles and uncharacteristic fervor as he takes in the scene before him. Water threads between my fingers and up my arms, before swirling in a shimmering vortex between us. Harlan is motionless, watching my power with an unreadable expression, even as my brother backs away in terror from the magic that once healed him.

I note the Covinus-issued rifle tucked tightly at Harlan's side and my throat clenches. I don't want to hurt him—he's only done what he needed to survive—but I won't let him take me back to the Covinus.

After what feels like ages of tense silence, Harlan's eyes find mine. "We need to get you out of here."

"I—*what?*"

Easton stares at Harlan, his fear momentarily forgotten in the midst of his shock. "Yeah, *what?*"

Harlan ignores my brother completely. Instead, he sets

the rifle against the doorjamb and charges toward me. "They're going to kill you, Mirren."

"I gathered that," I reply distantly, feeling like the world has shifted once more, and I'm the last to notice. Is Harlan truly helping me again? After he spent the last few months acting as my prison warden?

"Your only chance is to get through the Boundary before the lights come back on. The men guarding the hole have been called to quell the protest. We have to move *now*."

There isn't time to ask how, exactly, Harlan knows all this, but I don't miss his use of the word *we*. I'd expected many things from the golden boy, but for some reason, helping me hadn't been one of them. He risked his life for me once and it almost ruined him. And now, when he's finally climbed his way back into the Covinus' good graces, he has no reason to risk his status once more. If anything, he should cement his position by dragging me back to the red square.

Something like guilt tugs at my stomach as I remember the way he looked at me when he pleaded for me to be careful. I shouldn't let him do this, not when I don't understand the true reason why—not when I have nothing to give him because Anrai will always hold my heart. But I find myself nodding anyway. "I'm leaving as soon as Easton does."

"Harlan, you agreed to follow the Keys!" my brother cries, his voice strangled, and his face stricken.

Harlan finally turns to Easton, the shadow of whatever passed between them earlier now as thick as a physical wall. Harlan's throat bobs and I stare at him, wondering what the emotion he is trying to swallow down would look like if he allowed it free. "Are you coming?" he quietly asks my brother.

Easton blinks furiously. He clears his throat. And finally, sounding betrayed and defeated at once, he answers, "No."

The sound of sirens rent the air, tearing through the distant hum of the protestors, but the sound of my heart breaking is the only thing echoing in my ears. "Easton, please—"

His lips press together so fiercely, they've lost their color. "No. No more of this, Mirri. I don't know what Harlan's told you, but this can be sorted. We will wait for the Covinus to get here, and you'll see! It's all been a misunderstanding."

Hot tears brim. I wipe at them furiously, my brother's face blurring through a watery haze. The soft curve of his jaw and the cowlick to the left of his temple: a face I've loved with every piece of myself for as long as I can remember. "They'll kill me if I stay here. Come with me." It doesn't come out strong as I intend it; instead, it rings as a plea.

"They won't—they would never do that!"

Harlan steps between us. "I wish I'd seen how weakhearted you are." His mouth twists in disgust and he stares at my brother like he's never seen him before. Tension pulls taut in the air. My brother's eyes volley between Harlan and I, his anguish plain. And for a brief moment, I believe Easton will choose me.

Choose me as I've always chosen him.

But when he doesn't move, his face white with terror and his cheeks still dry, I understand. Even before Harlan says, "Mirren, we have to go. Even if he won't."

My tears spill unchecked now as I let go of my power and the wall of water crashes at our feet, soaking the hem of my jumpsuit. "I can't—I can't leave him here!"

Because if I do, everything I've gone through will have been pointless. The pieces of myself and others sacrificed so

Easton would live. If I leave him alone and unprotected, all of it will be rendered useless.

Easton steps toward me, his arm outstretched. His eyes flick in the direction of the protest, the wail of the sirens, before they fall back on me. "Mirri, just wait a few more moments. For me. Please."

I find myself nodding, because of course, *of course,* I'll give him a moment. He's my baby brother, a piece of my heart, and I'll always give him whatever he needs.

But then Harlan takes hold of my hand. His palm is warm against mine, the touch so human, so *alive,* that more tears slide down my cheeks, because *gods,* how long has it been since I've been touched? When I don't pull away, he wraps his arms around my shoulders and gently pulls me toward the door. "If you die now, no one will ever know the truth. You've more to do in this world," he whispers near my ear.

If I die, the truth dies with me. And Similis will be left even more vulnerable to the Praeceptor.

"Mirren, please. Stay," Easton pleads, following us as we move slowly toward the door. He drops his outstretched hand, his fingers curling into a fist. Even now, desperate and terrified, he won't break the Keys to touch me.

"You are *killing* her right now, Easton! If you don't let her go, her death will be on your hands. Do you trust the Covinus enough to bear the weight of your sister's life on your shoulders?"

Easton mouth drops in horror as I let Harlan usher me into the open doorway of the quarterage. Because Harlan's right. I have seen the power of voice, and now, I cannot lay down and die in silence, even if my brother asks it of me.

I meet his eyes and there are so many things I wish to

say. *I wish you weren't so weak. I wish you to be free of the stain of darkness I bring. I miss you. I hate you.*

"I love you," I tell him. The only honesty I can grant in this moment, the one thought that rings truer than the rest.

I turn away before I know whether he will accept or condemn me for it.

∽

Numb shock threads down my limbs as Harlan and I emerge into the street. I managed to shove a few rations into a backpack, but otherwise, we carry nothing. Once again, I'm planning to cross the Boundary with little more than the clothes on my back.

And once again, I'll be leaving Easton behind.

The smell of smoke tinges the air, the sounds of the protestors now entirely consumed by the screech of sirens. Engines rumble closer and Harlan drags me to the far wall, pressing my body into it before we can be seen. The Boundary lights surge, and I grapple against him, momentarily blind as my *other* leaves me, before we're once again plunged into darkness. I only manage to keep to my feet because I'm pinned between Harlan and the wall. "We're never going to make it to the hole," I tell him, wiping my tearstained cheeks impatiently in an attempt to soothe my rising panic.

I take a ragged breath, trying to erase Easton's terrified face from my mind.

Trying not to hate him for it.

Whatever emotion overtook Harlan on the rooftop has ebbed, giving way to his usual tranquility. If he is as terrified as I am, it hardly shows. He studies me calmly and I realize with some discomfort how close we are. Too close for Similis. His golden eyes appear oddly wolflike, almost glowing in the alleyway shadows. "Just how powerful is your magic?"

I whip my gaze to his. It's the first he's mentioned the spectacle he witnessed as a Boundary guard, the first time he's alluded to the power simmering in my blood every time the lights go out. Ignoring my silence, he presses, "Can you break through the Boundary with it?"

My eyebrows jump up in alarm. Break through something indestructible? After months of starving my *other* to the point of near death?

"I—I'm not sure," I admit honestly. I broke through my father's chains, but I almost lost myself doing it. And those were only made of iron—the Boundary is made of something entirely unknowable, not seen before or since its creation.

But it *isn't* indestructible, is it? Shaw, whether it was with his ruthless heart or determined focus, he conquered it. Can I, too? Am I willing to risk my life, and Harlan's, on a such a slight chance?

I throw my hands over my head as the sound of wood exploding reverberates through the alley—the door to my quarterage. Harlan presses himself against me, a wall of warmth and muscle, and something tugs at my heart as I realize it's to shield me. Whatever Harlan's reasons for helping me, it's too late to turn back. If I don't figure out a way through the Boundary, we'll both die.

"It's our best shot," I say determinedly.

He nods. His throat bobs and his shoulders rise shakily as his eyes rake across my face, searching for something. Then he takes my hand and together, we run into the dark.

The lights flicker on twice more as we sprint past quarterages. Harlan catches me both times, dragging me along next to him as I struggle to remain conscious. Each time I lose my power, agony rips through me, my bones threatening to shatter into dust. Whatever the connection between the lights and my *other,* if they're restored completely, we stand no chance.

There are only two sectors between mine and the agricultural fields, but by the time we reach the edge of the second, my breaths come in ragged wheezes and my muscles scream with exertion. I haven't been on more than a brisk walk in months and I'm suddenly nostalgic for the hard set of my body Ferusa carved last spring.

Too soft. Too weak. It's why everyone around you is gone.

You don't look like you've fought for anything a day in your life.

Gunshots crack somewhere far off and Harlan tenses beside me. His jaw goes rigid as his eyes move toward the direction of the sound—the red square. He's never spoken of those harrowing moments during my escape last spring, but I know he's remembering now. The agony of that bullet ripping through him.

I curl my fingers into fists as I imagine the Covinus doing the same to all those innocent people in the square, simply for disagreeing with him. My *other* is with me now —it'd be easy to storm the square and drown the Covinus and his guard where they stand.

Sensing my intentions, Harlan squeezes my hand. "We'll come back and set things right. But first, we have to survive."

I meet his eyes, so steadfastly earnest, that I actually believe him. Gripping his fingers tighter in mine, we traverse the small descent into the fields.

The world is hushed inside the cornstalks and as we move further into them, the cacophony of the red square fades, leaving only the dry rustle of the leaves. Harlan has to turn sideways to keep his broad shoulders from brushing against the stalks and alerting the Covinus to our location, but he doesn't let go of my hand and I don't ask him to.

It feels so good to not be alone, to have someone's skin against mine. But in spite of the comfort of Harlan's presence, guilt winds through me, leaving me more breathless than I already am. "Harlan," I whisper. "You've done enough. You could go back. Tell them I threatened you with magic. That you didn't want to help me. That you tried to stop me."

"Easton will tell them the truth, even if I wanted to turn back," he replies bitterly. Bile rises in my throat at the thought of my brother, so beholden to the Covinus, he'd send someone to their death. Harlan turns to me. "But I don't want to, Mirren."

The lights pulse once more, and my legs turn to jelly beneath me. I pitch forward, but Harlan catches me and pulls me upright, until our chests are pressed together and the rhythm of my breathing slows to match his. His big hands are splayed across the small of my back and something intense flares in his eyes as he says, "There's nothing for me here. We stay together."

Unable to tear my gaze away from his, I swallow roughly, but it's useless. Guilt cannot be cleared away by a swallow.

Neither can gratitude.

The lights wink out, the fresh layer of darkness now more welcoming than disorienting. My *other* floods through me and I find my feet, distancing myself from the heat of Harlan. Shoving my hands awkwardly into my pockets and clearing my throat, I avoid his gaze. We wait for our eyes to adjust and then continue on slowly through the cornstalks.

I know we're nearing the Boundary even before the stalks begin to thin, because something odd permeates the air. It's weighted and thick, and somehow feels like discord—like oppression and violence.

I shake my head. Walls don't create feelings.

Even so, as we emerge from the cornstalks to see the Boundary glinting in the moonlight, a wave of nausea rises in my throat and a cold sweat breaks out over my skin. Wrong. It feels *wrong*.

"Are you alright?" Harlan asks, brows furrowed in concern.

I nod weakly, not trusting myself to speak. Forcing a deep breath into my lungs, I step toward the wall, ignoring how every part of me rebels against it. Like my own body fights against me, tries to drag me back from whatever makes up this wall. Stepping through the gates on my return was terrible, but I thought it was the result of my power being drained—not that the Boundary itself caused the feeling.

When I set my hands to it, my sense of wrongness only deepens. It's foreign and clammy, both alive and horribly dead all at once.

Closing my eyes and breathing heavily, I'm about to reach for my *other* when the ground rumbles beneath my feet. Glancing wildly behind us, we watch as the corn fields begin to roll like the swells of an eerie ocean; far beyond, buildings that have never been anything but stationary, sway like distorted trees. Harlan throws an arm around my head as we're both thrown to the ground. The earth groans and stretches, angry, *awake*.

Glass shatters in the distance, bricks crash. Waves reverberate in my chest, sound or pressure, I can't be sure, until all that surrounds me is an obscure crescendo of power. I can't breathe, can't think, can feel nothing but the swell in me, around me.

My ears ring when the world finally stills, the silence as menacing as the cacophony. I climb to my feet, swaying unsteadily as if the earth still rolls beneath me. Helping Harlan up beside me, we stare out at the dark imprint of Similis as screams ring out anew.

Dirt scuffs his cheek and corn stalks poke out from his hair, matching its golden tone almost exactly. "What in Covinus' name was that?" he breathes.

I shake my head and turn back to the Boundary. Whatever it was, hopefully it distracted the Covinus long enough for me to figure a way into Ferusa. I should have asked Anrai more questions about how he broke through. Maybe then, I'd have *some* idea what I'm doing. All I know is how woefully unprepared I am. Shaw, at least, had explosives. I only have my hands.

Prepared this time for the awfulness of the stone, I press my palms to its cool surface once more. My *other* rears up instantly, furious and agitated. It yanks at me, its waves frenzied as it tries to move us away, but I resist, keeping my hands firmly planted. The Boundary shudders beneath my touch, rising to protect itself. It is the desiccation of death laced with the sentience of life.

And then, it begins to feed.

The Boundary pulls at my *other*, aggressive and greedy. I jump back with a gasp, my chest heaving.

"What's wrong?" Harlan asks.

I lick my lips, trying to shake off the sense of thievery. Of violation. "I—I think the Boundary is trying to...I don't know—*absorb* my power, somehow?"

Harlan eyes me warily. "Like it's alive?"

"Not alive, exactly. But not dead either." I'm making no

sense, but I don't clarify as another thought settles over me. "I think the Boundary is the reason my power doesn't work inside Similis. Like...like it's its *own* power." And if it's this strong during a blackout, I don't want to be anywhere near it at its full strength. How did Anrai stand it? Does it only feel terrible if you have power?

With a firm grip on my *other*, I touch the stone once more. I call to the water of the field, settled deep in the roots of the cornstalks. I swirl it over my skin, watching the way the droplets magnify everything they touch and encircle them in sparkling moonlight. Then, I push them into the wall.

The Boundary pulls, but I hold tight, burrowing further into its horrible depths. Water swirls around me, tangling in my hair and sluicing down my chest. The same chasm I gazed into when I freed my father gapes open beneath me, and I tilt further toward its edge. A part of it, and yet, separate. What would it feel like to fall to into it? To merge ourselves until we are only each other?

"It's working!" Harlan exclaims, but I don't dare open my eyes.

I feed my heartbreak into the widening hole: my devastation at my brother's refusal to choose me. I push my loneliness, the desperation that's weighed me down until I could barely stand. The Boundary accepts it all greedily, siphoning everything around us, an insatiable black hole. But the well of power in me grows. Perhaps just one more step. One step and I can leave the ache behind—

"Mirren, you've done it!" Harlan threads his fingers through mine and the warmth of his skin jolts me back into myself.

What did I almost do? Had I really been about to lose myself to my power? And what would have happened if I did? Would I cease to be Mirren entirely, no longer possessing a human heart, somehow only waves and currents?

I open my eyes to see Harlan's right. Staring back at me is a hole just wide enough for Harlan to squeeze through. Even from a few steps back, it feels like a festering wound. Unnatural and sticky. Steeling my nerve, I slide through it.

On the other side, I scrabble to my feet, closing my eyes once more. The sweet air of the Nemoran barrels into my lungs and my *other* settles inside me as if I've sung it a lullaby. We're still so close to the Similian factories, the freshness of the Dark World air has to be only in my mind, but for the first time in months, I feel like I can breathe deeply.

It takes a fair bit of wiggling for him to push his wide shoulders through, but after a moment, Harlan makes it through the Boundary as well. He climbs to his feet, looking distinctly out of place as he brushes dust off his jumpsuit. We're going to need to find clothes as soon as possible.

And weapons. It isn't wise to be unarmed here.

Though I am never unarmed on this side of the Boundary, am I? I have my *other,* endless and foreign, forever intertwined. Aggie said we are the commenia flower and the bayani tree, one nothing without the other. Why is it, then, for a few moments, I couldn't remember myself at all?

And worse, I hadn't wanted to.

CHAPTER
SIX

Mirren

Awake.

I feel *awake* for the first time in so long, as if clearing the Boundary also cleared the fog pressed against my mind. The ache of loss is sharper—how could it not be, when I walk through the woods Anrai was born to—but I'm no longer mired in it, as if having a goal has renewed my sense of purpose, my sense of self.

The Nemoran expands around us as we disappear into the trees, and though I know what resides in the shadows, I feel heartened, nonetheless. There is room in this forest for all of me—there will be no more shaving off parts deemed unworthy, no more contorting myself into being less than I am.

"Where are we going?" Harlan asks, as he plods alongside me. His footfalls are heavy, and I have to keep myself from wincing with each one. By the Covinus, was I this loud when Anrai found me? No wonder he'd been so exasperated.

"To get some weapons and clothes." I think longingly of the Covinus-issued rifle Harlan left leaning against the quarterage door. If I'd been thinking clearly, I would have grabbed it on the way out, but I was too lost in the pain of leaving Easton.

"Weapons?" Harlan asks, his eyes widening in alarm.

"You know how to shoot, don't you? They must have trained you when you joined the Boundary men." I don't mean to sound accusing, but something in my tone stops Harlan in his tracks.

"I *had* to join the Boundary men. I never wanted to shoot anyone, Dark Worlder or otherwise."

"Ferusian," I reply hotly, narrowing my eyes. "They call themselves Ferusians. And if you didn't want to shoot anyone, what exactly did you think the gun they gave you was for?"

"I didn't," Harlan answers so honestly, I almost back up in surprise. "I wasn't thinking a moment beyond my survival."

Gods. Have I truly been harboring bitterness at Harlan for doing what he must to survive? After everything I've seen—after everything I've *done*—how could I possibly condemn him for doing the same? Darkness knows, the world is not dissected with lines of black and white.

Softening, I tell him, "You don't have to answer to me for what you had to do. You don't have to answer to anyone."

He drops his head, his jaw working. "I have to answer to myself."

I have no argument, so we walk on in silence.

After an hour or so, shadows begin to dance over the thick tree trunks. Harlan hasn't appeared to notice the direction we're headed, content to follow my lead without question, which I'm thankful for, because he isn't going to like what comes next.

I press a finger to my lips and motion for him to stay put. With a start, he finally notices the flicker of firelight through the trees and his eyes grow wide at what that means. I almost smile at the hunters' predictability, camped as they are outside the Similan gates. Waiting for unsuspecting Outcasts to stumble upon them.

Harlan eyes widen even more as I saunter directly into their camp, allowing the first grin in months to spread across my face.

The Boundary hunters gape at me, not quite believing their luck. I may be more scarred than the last time I was here, but I'd still make them quite a bit of coin. Similians are rare, after all. I let the nearest one reach for his revolver, and then, while I'm still smiling, the water from his canteen bursts into his face.

At the same time, every canteen in the camp explodes. The hunters rear back with howls, scratching at their mouths and throats as I stride toward the fire where they've laid their cookware to dry. Weighing a frying pan in my hand, I happily give it a few test spins, before throttling the closest man. He slumps into a heap at my feet.

I go around the fire, perfunctorily swinging the iron pan, until the howling goes silent, and all the men are still.

When Harlan steps out from behind the tree, his mouth hangs wide open, as if his jaw has come unhinged. He creeps toward me gingerly, eyeing the unconscious bodies with a look of mingling distaste and awe. "I thought you said we were finding clothes?"

Sizing up each of the bodies, I point to a man similar in

size to Harlan. "Those look like they'll fit. Be quick about it, there may be others close by."

Harlan's eyes widen as he interprets my meaning, and his open mouth turns down in horrified frown. "You want me to—to *steal* from them?!"

"Did you think we were stopping by a seamstress in the middle of the forest?" It's a strain to keep my eyes from rolling at his sanctimonious tone, and it's only by focusing on stripping the smallest of the hunters that I manage it. The hunter is still much larger than me, but any Ferusian clothes will be better than my jumpsuit. "If it makes you feel any better, these men make a living by *selling* Similian Outcasts like cattle," I tell Harlan over my shoulder.

Harlan regards the men doubtfully as I move to the next slumped body and relieve him of his daggers. Rudimentary in design, but sharp enough. The man's bandolier is far too large, so I put one of the weapons into my boot and shove the rest into my knapsack.

The golden boy hasn't moved. "Just because someone else is reprehensible, doesn't give me leave to be as well."

I swallow down the dam in my throat as I remember the girl I was when I first stumbled into Ferusa. Naïve and idealistic, kept alive only by Anrai's protection.

There is no one else now. Our survival depends on me.

In a perfect world, Harlan is right. What have I done, dragging him into a world where around every corner, something waits to maim or kill you; to break your spirit so thoroughly you can't remember ever *wanting* to be kind? Why didn't I consider what it would cost him before I allowed him to follow me through the Boundary?

Because danger lies inside the Boundary, too. It is different, but Harlan and I both know, it can be just as destructive.

I inhale sharply. "If you don't want to steal from him, I understand. But the jumpsuit you're wearing is a dead giveaway to where you come from, and Similian is a dangerous thing to be in Ferusa."

Harlan considers me for a moment, warmth pooling in his eyes. I look away before I can determine its cost, shoving a few more weapons into the knapsack. Gods, I should never have been selfish enough to bring him with me. The binding mark on my arm suddenly feels like a fresh burn. At the very least, I should have been honest with him about my feelings for Anrai.

Harlan kneels next to the unconscious man. "I am very sorry, sir," he mumbles before hesitantly pulling off the man's boots.

After we've thoroughly raided the hunters' supplies and changed into their clothes, burning our jumpsuits in their fire, we set off into the wood. Harlan keeps pace with me, as we navigate slowly through the dark, over roots and underbrush. Soon, the sirens of Similis fade completely and if the Boundary lights have come back on, they'd be impossible to see so deep in the trees.

A howl sounds in the distance followed by the distinct *yap yap yap* of the Ditya wolf, but instead of dread, I only feel relief ballooning in my chest. The Dark World expands before us, and I am no longer caged. *You've got wings, little bird.*

"Alright, Mirren," Harlan begins. "What's our plan? We can't let the Covinus get away with murdering his own Community." Unbidden, his hand trails to the stock of the rifle he took off the hunter, the gun so similar to those carried by the Boundary men.

I feel like a bird who's only just settled on its perch before a gust of wind blows it askew. "My father," –the word sticks in my throat— "is the Chancellor of Nadjaa. I think he's our best chance at protecting Similis."

Harlan absorbs my proclamation much more calmly than I did. "Your father...he's still alive after being Outcast?" His eyes shine intensely. "Are there others out there? Other Outcasts that will help us overthrow the Covinus?"

"My father won't help us overthrow the Covinus," I answer immediately, bitterness tasting like acid in my mouth. Once, my father may have tried to set things right in Similis, but he's washed his hands of it now. He cares only for the safety and freedom of Nadjaa. "He won't do anything unless it serves his goals. But I think we can convince him that Similis is in danger of falling to the Praeceptor." At Harlan's look of confusion, I explain, "He's another warlord, my father's enemy. He's been taking over Ferusa a territory at a time and if he finds out Similis is weak, it's only a matter of time before he invades."

"You think this warlord would concern himself with Similis?"

I consider everything Anrai told me of Cullen, even before I realized he spoke of his own father. Of his desire for power and control. Similis, with its electricity and factories, represents all of that. I've gone over that day in the cave, how the Praeceptor was so willing to let me go, even though it risked the Dead Prophecy coming to pass.

It was because he *knew* he had a way past the Boundary. Shaw. And with the Covinus losing control of his people and the lights flickering, it's only a matter of time before the Praeceptor comes calling.

"We have to tell my father the lights in Similis are failing. He'll help if he thinks the Praeceptor is going to invade. Especially with the Praeceptor having a way in."

Harlan's head snaps toward me. "What do you mean?"

I pick at my fingers, guilt ensnaring my throat. There's so much I haven't told him. I take a breath. "The hole last spring. I...I know the man who did it. And the Praeceptor has him now."

My throat bobs and my foot taps, almost of its own accord. Harlan tilts his head thoughtfully. If the news a bloodthirsty warlord has access to his family upsets him, it hardly shows. There is no panic, only curiosity as he asks, "How did he get through? Does he have power like you?"

I bite at my lower lip. "No. I don't truly know how he got through. But we're going to have to find out."

Harlan nods. "So, we go to Nadjaa."

My heart aches just hearing the moon city's name spoken in Harlan's stiff Similian accent. How I've longed for the smell of the sea and the thrum of life beating in Nadjaa. The open, endless sky speckled with stars. "To Nadjaa," I agree. "We're going to need to find some horses. It's a long journey on foot." If I can somehow manage to find the way there. Through the Nemoran and the Praeceptor's territory.

One problem at a time. We pilfered enough coin from the hunters, we should be able to purchase at least one. "The closest city to Similis I know of is Havay. We'll head there first."

∼

Shaw

"What news?" I bark at Ivo.

I heard him coming a mile away, lumbering through the trees like a man whose life has never depended on remaining invisible. At 6'5 and roughly the size of a Nemoran tree, it probably hasn't. He doesn't understand the whisper of shadows or the call of the Darkness: only brute strength that's as useless as a dull sword.

What my father sees in him, I can't begin to guess.

"The Praeceptor has sent his orders," Ivo replies. I turn to him with a wry smile, eyeing the way his hand grips the pommel of his sword. As if he could draw it fast enough to save himself from my rage.

"He has information that Akari Ilinka may visit the city and if she does, he wants her alive. We are to stay our hand for a few days and observe."

I frown. "Alive?" What reason would the witch-queen have to be so far north, in the heart of the Praeceptor's territory? And why would my father spare her life when the quickest way to gain Siraleni compliance would be to murder their leader?

"She has something the Praeceptor desires. Something important."

I know better than to ask what it is. My father would never trust all the information to anyone, let alone this soul-ridden militia *legatus*. "And did my father specify how long we are supposed to sit here like rats in their hole *observing?*"

"Until he can verify the information. Until then, we wait."

Without another word, the *legatus* turns and heads back toward where our soldiers are camped, hidden on the other side of the ravine, between the crumbling ruins of a civilization long ago overtaken by the Nemoran. The soldiers grow restless and paranoid camped so close to the wood. Just last night, a foot soldier slit open the bellies of three of his sleeping bunkmates before he could be apprehended. He swore until the moment he was shot in the head that the trees had made him do it.

The night before that the outskirts of camp were set upon by a yamardu. The beast drained two men and deafened four others before it could be run out of camp.

And still, my father wishes us to wait?

I turn toward Havay, the stalwart city nestled against the border of the wood before sprawling across the Breelyn Plain. Unlike the Xamani who revere the Nemoran's power, Havians are determined to pretend it doesn't exist, accustomed as they are to its oddities. Twisted creatures routinely crawl from beneath the canopy to ravage the city and no one bats an eye. The creature is exterminated, and everyone goes about their lives as if nothing about the wood is at all odd.

It's probably this stubborn practicality that has kept the Havians from being swayed by the militia's infiltrations. Rumors of the supernatural would never spook someone who faces Ditya wolves multiple times a week.

Havay is where I'll get my fight. No one here will hand over their children because of rumors of a prophecy. My nerves feel as though they've been singed, one by one, as I imagine the screams and blood I'll finally be able to gorge myself on. The chasm inside me hungers, the ravenous need growing more agonizing with each passing day. I can hardly move, hardly think beyond it. I've become practically immobile, barely able to hold a sword, for all the concentration it takes to keep it from spearing out and feeding on every soldier that passes.

Waiting is only another test of my will: one I won't fail. I'll give the Praeceptor no reason to doubt my willingness to dole out his justice. No reason to take me away from what I so truly desire.

I'll wait, but I do not have to sit in my pain. My throat

aches and the hollow inside me scratches. If I cannot yet turn my fury outward, I will turn it inward instead.

With a bloodcurdling scream, I rip into the abyss and send it hurtling into my lungs, my blood, my skin. It balloons inside my chest until I thrash on the ground, until I burn from the inside out—until I am nothing but Darkness once more.

Chapter Seven

Mirren

Wind whips off the Breelyn Plain, yanking my hair from its plait. As Harlan and I wind our way through the dirt streets of Havay, I swat at it, cursing under my breath when it flutters out of my reach.

Both the houses and the people of the city are weather-worn and robust, both looking to have endured their fair share of storms. To protect from the winds, every building is squat and hugs the rolling ground, the only thing reaching higher than one story being a small, wooden water tower. No one meets our eyes as we wander in search of a stable—some going so far as to slam their doors before we can approach. Perhaps having survived so long in the shadow of the Nemoran wood breeds such suspicion of strangers, but it unnerves me all the same.

Harlan takes in everything quietly; the rough-hewn squalor so stark in contrast with the sterile façade of Similis. But there is something familiar about it all the same, because as in Similis, nothing here is built for beauty, only survival.

A rotund woman in a wool spun brown dress meets my eyes for only a moment, before dropping the basket full of laundry she had propped on her hip and ushering her children inside their small house. Harlan and I agreed it would be safer not to call attention to ourselves by using my power, but I caress my *other* anyway. The feel of it settles my worry slightly and I grip the dagger in the pocket of my trousers.

Of course, the Havians would be suspicious of newcomers, when the Praeceptor has taken over everything else on this side of Nadjaa.

When we come to a tavern, I motion Harlan inside. "They'll know where the stables are, and we can get something to eat before we move on."

He nods and follows me into the ramshackle building. The door squeaks on its hinges, the wood so warped it doesn't close properly behind us, only bounces uselessly on the frame.

"Closed for curfew," the barkeep barks from behind the counter. A stout woman with silver hair tucked into a neat bun, she scrubs at the buckled wood for a few more seconds before looking up at us with shrewd eyes.

Glancing around, I realize we are indeed the only customers. The emptiness is odd, when the sun has hardly set, but maybe it's a Havian custom I'm unaware of.

"We're sorry," Harlan immediately apologizes.

The woman narrows her eyes at the deference in his voice. She drops the soiled rag into a bucket with a plop, before throwing her hands on her hips and stepping out from behind the counter. In spite of her girth and the steep slant of the floor toward the door, she moves on steady feet.

"Could you point us in the direction of the stables?" I

ask quickly, not wanting to give her time to determine why Harlan speaks the way he does.

She pulls on the strings of her apron, securing the already tight knot as she turns to me. "I could, but you'll find them empty."

"Empty?"

She huffs a sigh as she ambles closer, shoving in errant barstools as she goes. "Warlord made a deal with that witch-queen. Paid him a sum worthy of Yen Girene's treasury for almost every resource we had."

"Why?"

The woman's gaze turns hard. "Where'd you say you's from again?"

"We didn't."

The distinct metal click of a revolver sounds from behind me. I whirl, drawing my daggers, to find two armed men blocking the tavern door.

Harlan gazes stonily at the guns, but he doesn't move toward his own.

"What's the meaning of this?" I demand. "We mean no harm. We came to trade for horses, but since there are none to be found, we'll be on our way."

The woman nods to the men, clearly the one who alerted them. "Another time, I'd ask you's no questions, sell ya a horse and have ya on your way. But this isn't no ordinary time, what with the Praeceptor's men camped over the ravine and unnaturals like *you* on the lose."

Dread squeezes my stomach as my *other* twitches in my veins. "The Praeceptor's men are here?"

The woman watches me with interest, her shrewd gaze drinking in the way all color leeched from my face at the mention of Cullen's name and not the proclamation that she knows who I am. "People like you have all of Ferusa up in arms, pledging themselves to the Praeceptor so he'll protect them from magic. Havians have always protected ourselves, but he's still demanding we pledge our allegiance and submit our citizens to his so-called 'testing'. Including our children." Her accusing stare feels like a brand, as if I'm the one who's led the Praeceptor here.

"I—I've been in Similis with no power. I've threatened no one, including the Praeceptor."

"Well, the man is under the impression there are more of you out there. So, we've rounded up the children to be guarded around the clock in the middle of town and enforced a curfew. Any and all strangers are to be held until we determine their allegiance. That certainly includes the girl who has brought this down upon all of us."

The men move toward us, but I raise my dagger with a snarl. My mind whirls. More nature spirits? Is it possible the Dead Prophecy named more than just me? Something like hope blossoms inside me, only to be smothered by my next thought. "Is the Praeceptor with the militia? Has he made these demands himself?"

"He's sent the Heir in his stead. But even that inhumane monster won't scare us into giving over our children. Havians haven't survived this long by giving into threats of Darkness."

My mouth goes dry. *Shaw.* Shaw is here.

And if he's here, that means whatever the Havians have done to protect themselves won't be enough. Shaw doesn't lose. If he's set his mind to accomplishing his father's goals, he'll rip the city—and himself—apart before he fails.

Despair surges through me at the thought of him serving his father, the man who has already stolen so much from him.

And it's your fault. He did it to save you.

I lower my dagger and the men surge forward, pulling Harlan and I into the street. Thrashing against him, I stomp on the arch of one's foot just as Harlan elbows another in the nose. "Listen to us!" I cry out. "I'm not here to harm you! You need to listen to me about the Heir! The children —whatever you've done with them isn't enough!"

The woman stands in the doorway, the lights of the tavern casting her into a dark shadow. "Don't you worry about the children. We protect our own here, always have. We've got no need of *your* kind here," she spits at me distastefully. "Go quietly now. Show them there's no need to fear you and you might be let go after this mess is sorted."

Grimacing, I look to Harlan. He nods his head imperceptibly and shifts his stance. He may be Similian, but he's also proven himself a survivor. Even when surviving was against the Keys.

We ready ourselves for a fight that never comes as screams sound from the city entrance. For a moment, Harlan, the guards, even the barkeep, are all frozen in place listening to the sounds of chaos erupt. Sounds of pain and fear.

And something else. Something that *roars*.

"Oh gods, he's here—" White hot panic grips me as the men abandon us, sprinting toward the entrance to the city. Whatever danger they think I pose, it is nothing to the danger of the Heir of the Praeceptor.

Shaw was never able to fully tell me all of his father's tactics, but I know enough of the man to understand there is no moral line he won't cross to achieve his goals. Including sacrificing children.

I yank my daggers from my pockets and Harlan fumbles with his pack, finally freeing the gun. The barkeep reappears, a sword in one hand, a small revolver in the other. Her gray hair sparkles in the lantern light and for a moment we just stare at each other. "What's your name?" I ask breathlessly.

"Lettie."

"Lettie, you don't have to trust me. I'm sure the rumors you've heard about my power are terrifying. But right now, we need to go protect those children. Whoever is guarding them won't be enough to stop the Heir. Where are they?"

Lettie's stare is hard as if she can weigh my character by peering straight into me. After a moment, her stance relaxes, and she readjusts her grip on the pommel of her sword. "They're in the basement of the council house. Let's go."

We take off in the opposite direction of the city entrance. Harlan cocks the shotgun. "Who is this Heir?"

My heart. My enemy. "Someone dangerous," I finally reply, the only honest answer I can settle on. "He's the man who broke through the Boundary."

When we round the corner, my heart drops into my stomach like weighted lead. The town square spreads before us, lined on each side by squat, wooden shops. On the far side sits the council house. The only building made at least partially of stone; it looks far sturdier than any other structure in Havay. Heavy steel doors have been barricaded and at least thirty men stand guard around its façade.

If they were facing a different enemy, it may be enough.

But Shaw has no soul. No morals. No limits.

My breath freezes in my chest as I stare at the man I've spent months longing for. He looks exactly the same from this distance, all sharp ridges and angles; handsome in that savagely careless way only he seems to manage.

He stands perfectly still in the center of the square. There's no sign of the Dark Militia, no sign of anyone as he cavalierly saunters down the middle of the street. He is too far away for me to see his face properly, but I plaster myself to the side of a building anyway, as my heart pounds in my throat and my lungs struggle for air.

I'd have given anything to see him, just one more time, but nothing could have prepared me for the acute *hurt* of it.

Shaw tilts his head as he moves closer and breathes in deeply, as if he can smell my scent on the wind. For a terrifying moment, I think he'll take one more step and see me where I cower.

But instead, he turns toward the council house.

Fear grips me, for the children and the men guarding them, but I soothe my nerves and calm my heart. As skilled as he is, Shaw is only one man. And I have the power of the ocean on my side, stronger than his guns or steel.

But Shaw doesn't reach for any of the black knives strapped across his chest. Instead, he cocks his head and lets out laugh, its humorless ring piercing the square.

And then, he erupts into pure flame.

CHAPTER
EIGHT

Mirren

I clutch my hands across my mouth in horror as fire trails harmlessly over Shaw's skin. His laugh fades as he watches the flame, until it coats him like an odd sort of armor. *What has Cullen done to him?*

Shaw coaxes it into his hands, stoking the flames until they are too bright to look at. The guards around the council house throw up their hands, their weapons clattering to the ground as they attempt to save their eyes from the shocking flare. I want to run toward them, to yell for them to keep hold of their weapons, but something keeps me in place. Shaw remains still, grinning maniacally, as the ball of flame grows bigger and brighter.

And then, he begins hurtling them into buildings.

One by one, each storefront lining the street erupts in a torrent of fire. And now, I understand whatever is happening at the city gates is a distraction. Shaw needs no militia.

"Come out, come out, wherever you are," he calls gleefully, watching with delight as people begin to pour from the buildings. Smoked from their hiding places, they choke on fumes and cower from the heat of his creation.

This is why Cullen was so willing to let me go, why he was so eager to possess Shaw. It wasn't just to settle his petty need for revenge—he must have known that buried somewhere deep was the potential for this destruction. Had Anrai known too?

The men guarding the door abandon their posts and run toward Shaw. They shoot arrows and discharge guns, but nothing touches him through that armor of flame.

I turn to Harlan and Lettie. "Lettie, is there another entrance to the council house?"

She nods, her face pale as she takes in the otherworldly power destroying her home. All her fears of nature spirits confirmed in the sweep of Shaw's hands. Careless, overpowered. No wonder average Ferusians are terrified of people like him. Like *me*.

"Good, you and Harlan sneak to the back and get those children out of there. I'll distract the Heir."

Harlan shakes his head stubbornly, gripping the sleeves of my jacket. "I'm not leaving you to...to *that!*"

Lettie nods. "That monster was spawned in the Darkness itself, girl. He'll eat you alive."

I breathe in deeply, settling my feet more firmly on the ground. Before I let myself be made small in Similis once again, I vowed to cower before no one. My *other* rises to the surface, spearing out for any bit of moisture Shaw's fire hasn't evaporated. I eye the small water tower, held aloft by spindled logs. Harlan follows my gaze, understanding my intention, even before I say, "I'm probably the *only* one who can distract him."

Even if the idea of facing him, of seeing those black eyes in place of crystal blue, will tear me apart. Imagining him without a soul was one thing, but seeing it—watching a face that once brought me such comfort twisted to malice—it will be unbearable.

Harlan looks as if he wants to argue, but finally, he nods. Lettie just shrugs, indicating her clear opinion that I'm insane, but she isn't going to waste her energy on changing my mind.

"Get them out," I say again.

Then, bracing myself, I turn toward the square.

Flames lick up the buildings and tresses crumble beneath the heat. The roof of a dress shop collapses, sending sparks shooting in all directions. People run screaming, frantically patting out smoldering clothes. Others gather behind an overturned wagon, shooting arrows at Shaw. An acrid smell permeates the air and bile rises in my throat as I realize it is charred skin and hair.

Shaw takes no notice of the few arrows that manage their way through the fire to whiz by his head. He's created a maelstrom of chaos around him, flames whipping in all directions like a burning storm. As I grow closer, I realize his eyes are not the black of the soulless—nor are they the pale blue of a glacier. Now, they burn from the inside out: the color of the hottest flame.

He has always been filled with quiet rage, but this—*this*...it's what I imagine his anger would look like if someone fed it for millennia. Fed it every twisted, dark, horrible thing in the world until it combusted, its dark power hot enough to melt the very sky.

I draw steadily closer, each step feeling like I'm moving toward the sun. As if sensing my presence, Shaw turns suddenly, and it takes everything in me not to flinch from his gaze. There is nothing remotely human in his face, only cold indifference and wild, primal anger. It heats the air between us to an unendurable level, and I know only my *other* keeps my skin from blistering, my blood from boiling.

Shaw tilts his head as I come slowly toward him, but there is no recognition in his face. Only mild curiosity.

He wonders why I do not burn. Why I'm the one thing his fire doesn't destroy, even as I keep my power inside of me.

"Have you come to play, girl?" he asks, wrapping tendrils of flame around his arms like deadly whips. "Everyone else cowers in their fear, leaving you to face the dreaded beast alone?" Sparks burst from his arms, even as the flames snake around his throat. "I'm afraid the stories never end well for the damsel in distress."

Damsel be damned. "Shaw!" I yell for no other reason than desperation. Because in spite of him burning down an entire square—in spite of the cold way he regards me—I still feel him. He lives along the lines of my heart and in the depths of my *other*. Crumpled and beaten as it is, I've kept a small hope alive that some part of him remains in the shell of his body. Something of the man I knew.

His lips cut into a terrible grin, and something inside me shreds its claws through my lungs. If there is any part of him left, it doesn't remember who I am. Who *we* were. I once found adventure in the curve of his mouth, but there is no softness now. Only cruelty. Grin still firmly affixed, he carelessly flicks his wrist, and ten of the men guarding the council house go up in flames.

Their cries of agony rent the night, their glowing forms scrambling to find some relief from the pain. My *other* surges, my rage becoming its own, at what's become of Shaw. But I force past my hurt, feeding it to my power and breathing deeply against the crash of its waves. We are strong enough for this. "Shaw, stop this! You will kill everyone in the city!"

"They were warned." It's his voice, but it isn't. The tenor is the same, but it's edged with none of self-deprecation Shaw had even at his most arrogant.

"There are children here!" I try once more, wondering if my pleas only echo in the empty chamber where his soul used to reside. The soul he gave up for me. "There are innocents!"

His face twists and the flames surge around him, the conflagration so bright, I'm forced to shield my eyes. "No one is *innocent,* Lemming," he snarls, half-mad.

My mouth parts. My heart speeds.

Lemming.

He called me Lemming.

Shaw

Fire swirls.

I feed it, stoking the flames carefully. Lovingly.

Because their warmth fills the cold nothingness that's echoed inside me for months.

The more people scream, the more ash that fills the air, the more powerful it grows. No more ache of starvation, trapped beneath the ground. Wild rage is so much better than being empty. *Anything* is better than being empty.

I throw fire at the men who once guarded the council house and then with a flick of my hands, watch as the wagon explodes, taking the archers with it. Screams ring out around me and I savor them all. The Havians were warned. They were told what happens to those who would defy the Praeceptor. They foolishly thought because they've survived the beasts of the Nemoran, they would also survive *me*.

But I am a monster of a different sort. One bred in the Darkness and forged at my father's blade.

Their sounds of anguish echo in the hollow of my chest. My fire bathes in them, flaming higher and higher inside me until my vision turns red. I've turned the hideousness of my power inward for so long, burning myself from the inside out, never able to feed it what it craves.

So now, I gorge myself on it. The relief of others' pain. The absence of my own.

The girl moves toward me still. Braver than all the men in this town, all of which tried to run from me and now burn for their cowardice. But that bravery will be her downfall, useless in the face of the Darkness.

My flames reach for her hungrily, but they do not devour her.

They tug at her curls and play across her lips. Gently. Her eyes churn like the waves of a great sea and when I meet her gaze head on, the chasm inside me rears back.

That sea. The one from my dreams that seeks to consume me.

Witch. Enchantress.

The abyss writhes within me, slithering and cold, and still the girl does not retreat. Surely, a siren sent to test the depths of my loyalty. But I will not fail. I won't be trapped again in the dungeons while my power eats me from the inside out.

I thrust my flames toward her, a wall of boiling heat, but she doesn't waver.

Lemming.

A resounding clang powers through me, vibrating my jaw and tearing through my skull with such force, I double over, clutching my head. Pain—so much pain. Pain like before I came to the Castellium, when the Darkness tore every bit of me apart and then forced me back together. Pieces missing and parts shoved where they don't fit. Pain like the dungeons where I gasp for air and the air never comes. Only the water, icy and consuming.

The girls comes closer and my power spears for her. She will burn, I know she will burn. I can end this, and my father will be proud and there will be no more pain.

But my flames only dance harmlessly over her skin. They circle around her throat, a noose of fire, and still she doesn't run. She calls me by a name long-dead, one I no longer claim. I am only Fire-Bringer, Soul-Eater. Heir of the Praeceptor and Darkness incarnate.

I roar in agony and my inferno swirls higher around us, drowning out the Havians' screams. The steel doors of the council house begin to droop, even metal no match for the blistering heat. I watch the glow of the steel, try to focus on destroying the doors and remember why I'm here.

The nerves in my head sizzle. I claw at my face, determined to unroot the agony, but it persists.

You are made to destroy.

I am. I am.

I dig my palms into my eyes and then blink furiously, roaring my fury. Behind the girl, children are being shepherded out the back of the council house, the sight of them tinged red with the flow of power. Even as the entire square crumbles around them, there are still those who seek to defy the Praeceptor. The girl and whatever hold she has on me won't stop me. I will bring him his vengeance.

Her gaze follows mine, and her face pales in realization. "Shaw, no!" she cries, lunging toward me. She will give herself over to my flames to keep me from the children, but it's too late. I unleash the fury within me, the swirling chasm of ash and emptiness. The girl will never be able to reach me through the cyclone of flames.

But instead of retreating, she throws her hands up and closes her eyes. I stare at her through a wall of fire, at the way her petite face furrows in concentration. And then, with dread, I realize my mistake.

Water crashes against the tank of the water tower as if it seeks vengeance for my flame. In burning the square, I've weakened the stilts holding it up, and the entire thing wobbles as the water collides against the barreled sides. I raise my arms with a shout of anger, but it's too late. The large tank splits open with an unnatural groan and the water surges toward us in a tidal wave. A man yanks the remaining children to higher ground as the wave consumes the council house, the square and everything else in its path.

I shake my head, backing away from the surge. Panic closes my throat. The water, *oh gods,* the water.

My flames are extinguished, and I'm swept off my feet. Carried away in the tide of all my nightmares.

But somewhere inside my turbulent fear, one word sounds in time with the frantic beating of my heart.

Lemming.

CHAPTER NINE

Mirren

My dreams are filled with raging infernos. Everything is consumed by billowing flames, even the oxygen—until there is nothing left but ash and destruction. And pain. So much pain.

I wake with a gasp, clutching my throat. My heart pounds frenetically against my ribs as the night comes back to me in sharp flashes.

Anrai. Oh gods, Anrai.

I squeeze my eyes shut once more, but it makes no difference when his face is imprinted on my mind. The inhuman beauty of his wrath. The empty wasteland of his eyes. The way he *burned.*

What did Cullen do to him to awake such destruction? What kind of pain has he endured since he was taken from me?

Your fault. It's your fault.

"Mirren," a familiar voice calls, shaking me from my thoughts, "you've been asleep for days."

"Cal?" I don't dare open my eyes, even as the ache inside me relents momentarily. I must still be dreaming, lost in the obscure depths of my power that still long for what could have been if only I'd stayed in Ferusa. Because that isn't what happened, and my friends are not in Havay. I left them, just as I left Anrai. How long have I been asleep to be imagining Cal's voice beside me?

I steel myself with a sharp inhale, but when I peek my eyes open, it isn't the ramshackle strength of Havay that greets me. Instead, everything is polished and tidy, made of deep colored woods and creamy fabrics. Bright sunshine filters in through a window, a cerulean sea twinkling in the distance.

My breath catches in my throat.

Home. I am home.

And indeed, it is Cal's lanky form that unfurls like a lazy cat from the armchair next to the window. His mouth pulls into a smile. "Is it too soon to tell you that you look like absolute hell?"

With something between a sob and a laugh, I launch from the bed, colliding with him in a half-hug, half-tackle. Without hesitation, his arms come around me as I press my face into his chest. "Seriously though...you look as though you were dragged through the actual Darkness by your face. And then given a haircut by a yamardu."

Tears run unabashedly down my cheeks as Calloway tucks me in close, resting his lips atop my head like I'm a child to be soothed. The loneliness and terror and hardship of the past few months bubble to the surface; and though the visibility hurts in what it reveals, it also eases the burden somehow. "Shh...you're safe now. We've brought you home."

We.

I pull back and wipe furiously at my eyes, looking wildly around the room. In the corner, stands Max. She holds her arms stiffly across her chest, her cutting gaze and regal face looking as though they've been carved by an ice goddess. Vengeful and beautiful, my friend. Somehow, I've even missed the way her anger feels.

Unable to help it, I cry harder. Despite the divide between us, they *came* for me. Through the Praeceptor's lands, even though I told them I didn't need them. Even though I left them to get through the loss of Anrai on their own. "H-how?" My lower lip trembles as I attempt to gather myself. "How did I get here? How did you find me?"

"The tidal wave in the town square made you kind of hard to miss," Cal points out, ruffling my hair.

He glances at Max, who rolls her eyes irritably and says with a huff, "*someone* vowed to Anrai he would protect you and apparently, that doesn't expire upon the removal of one's soul." She throws a hand on her hip, accusing gaze turned to Cal. "And I wasn't about to let that *someone* venture into Cullen's territory alone."

I lower myself slowly back onto the bed, my head spinning. Cal smiles sadly. "I promised Anni I'd look out for you. We heard rumors of blackouts at the Boundary and that meant anyone who wanted to stop the prophecy had a chance of getting to you. So, we journeyed north. We were just outside of Havay when we saw the fires. By the time we found you in the square, you were—" Cal shakes his head and pushes a breath through his teeth, "—you were almost in…a sort of trance? Your eyes were open, but it was like…it was like you weren't here. You've been that way for almost five days."

Max's throat bobs and she softens slightly as she asks, "What happened?"

I curl my bare toes against the wooden floor and try to recall the moments before I passed out, but they are a blur of desperation and fear. One moment, I was trying to save the children—to save Shaw from himself—and the next, I'd been lost. Drowning in a sea of my own making. How had I fallen so far into those unexplored depths without meaning to? And how did I find my way back?

A muffled sound comes from beside Max, and I leap up with an alarmed cry when the disheveled lump next to her feet shifts. "Max, is that—by the Covinus, is that *Harlan?!*"

Max blinks slowly. "Is that what you call the lemming?"

Indeed, Harlan is bound at her feet, a wide-eyed ball of muscle and golden skin. He makes another desperate noise around the bright pink gag stuffed haphazardly into his mouth. I lunge toward him, glaring pointedly at Max. "What in the Darkness have you done to him?"

"Do you know him, then?" she replies with a heedless tilt of her head.

I tear the gag from Harlan's mouth. He spits a few times, recoating his tongue with saliva as I quickly untie his hands and ankles. "I *told* you I know her!" he retorts hotly, glowering up at Max.

Max shrugs. "One can never be too careful," she says blithely to no one in particular. Then, to me, adds, "He got upset when we tried to take you. Shouting nonsense and drawing all sorts of attention. This was the best way to gain his compliance without alerting the entire Dark Militia we were there."

"She means the *easiest* way," Cal quips helpfully.

Max shrugs again. "I *could* have just stabbed him."

"Oh yes, you should really be applauded for your self-restraint," Cal replies with an eyeroll.

I unravel the last of the knots binding Harlan and help him to his feet. A bruise mars his left temple, and his face is smudged with soot, but otherwise, he appears mostly unharmed. "You saved the children," he tells me. "They're all okay."

Smiling softly, I meet his gaze, seeing myself reflected in the calm of those golden pools. "Are you okay?"

He rubs a hand slowly over his hair, furrowing his brow in consternation. "That depends...have we, in fact, been kidnapped?"

I laugh. "We have not."

He shoots Max a suspicious glare. "Are you certain? *That* one has an awful lot of weapons."

"And there's plenty more where those came from," Max says with a wicked grin.

Harlan turns a shade so red his cheeks could color a robin's belly at Max's implication.

"Before he combusts from our indecency, perhaps you should introduce us properly," Calloway implores from his perch on my bed. "It was a bit hard to catch his name, what, with the gag and all."

I glare at him over my shoulder, but he's right. If Harlan is going to be with me in Ferusa, he has to accept Max and Cal as they are—penchant for kidnapping first and asking questions later included. Being back in the manor, listening to their lighthearted bickering, has smoothed something jagged inside me and I won't give them up so easily this time. "Harlan, these are my friends. Calloway and Max."

Harlan's brows shoot up at the term of familiarity, before he remembers himself and schools his face into its usual Similian contentment. "It's a pleasure to make your acquaintance."

Max groans loudly, throwing up her hands. "Darkness save me, there's two of them! Is it *truly* a pleasure to meet me after I walloped you with my sword and then tied you to a horse?" She eyes Harlan distastefully, before flicking her eyes to me. "Do you know he didn't once threaten to murder me, even when he thought I was going to hurt you?" She throws her hands on her hips. "Not a very good friend, if you ask me."

Ignoring Max, Calloway slinks across the room like a cat. He bows in front of Harlan with relish: the former looking positively wicked and the latter, distinctly uncomfortable. "It is indeed a *pleasure,* Harlan," Cal purrs with a cheeky smile. "I have a feeling we'll all be the closest of friends."

The tips of Harlan's ears go red, and he clears his throat awkwardly.

"That's enough you two," I say with an air of long-suffering patience. Cal retreats with a devilish wink. Max sets me with an unrepentant stare. Chewing my lip, I settle myself next to Cal on the plush mattress. "When you were in Havay, did you—did you see Shaw?"

Cal immediately sobers. "You mean, did we see Anni become a human torch and try to burn children alive?" He shifts, licking his lips and nodding his head. "Yes. Yes, we did."

A lump rises in my throat, shame mingling fiercely in the pit of my stomach. How could I allow myself to feel the relief of being home, even momentarily, while Shaw is trapped in a soulless hell? How could let myself enjoy the comfort of our friends when he's alone? I hazard a glance at

Max, my guilt and agony mirrored in her expression. "Did you know?"

They know what I mean. *Did you know Anrai holds the power of flame?*

Calloway shakes his head slowly. Max's face hardens, her eyes glinting like the edge of a blade. After a moment, she says, "No. If he knew, he never told us. I've—I've never seen anything like that."

Neither have I. In my short experience with magic, Shaw's was like nothing I've ever imagined. A maelstrom of fury, a physical explosion of rage. "It was like...like he didn't even know who I was. Like he didn't remember who *he* was."

Harlan's eyes volley between the three of us, questions apparent on his face. But he remains silent, as Max lowers herself into the armchair. Spreading her legs, she props her elbows on her knees and lifts her gaze to mine. "Shaw has been rounding people up and shipping them back to Argentum for weeks. Anyone who refuses is burned alive and now we know, it isn't the sort of fire that can just be put out unless Shaw wills it. We've basically handed Cullen an unbeatable weapon. You're the only one who can stand against something that powerful."

She says it as a challenge, searching my face warily, as if expecting me to duck and run at any moment. I can't say I blame her. I've given her no reason to believe I'll stick around when things get hard.

But the truth is, I don't know if I *can* stand against Shaw. It wasn't just the water tower that split open in that square—it was something inside me as well. Something I fear I can't take back. "Everything happened so fast in the square. I couldn't let Shaw kill all those children and when I summoned that wave, I scared myself. I was desperate and careless and...and I didn't *think*—I just dove in. And it was like...like I got lost inside my power." I stare down at my hands, remembering how for a moment, I couldn't feel my body at all. Only my *other*. "It felt...I dunno, like I couldn't find my way back to my own humanity. I think that's why I was unconscious. I was too far gone to remember the way home."

I swallow audibly, then voice the fear that's plagued me since I first laid eyes on Shaw in the square. "What if...what if the only way to match Shaw's power is to lose my own soul?"

Cal and Max are silent, mulling over my words. Harlan rubs his wrists thoughtfully. "That wave was pretty powerful. Do you think he even survived it?"

I nod miserably. If I'd killed Shaw, I would feel it in the cracks of my soul. But there is only a hollowness in the places my power has touched him, and I don't know whether or not to be thankful for it.

Calloway swallows roughly and rises to his full height, steeling his spine as if preparing himself. "We have to kill him," he says resolutely.

I whip my head toward him. "I will *not!*" Shaking my head vehemently, I shove myself to standing. Cal's lanky frame towers over me, but he doesn't look threatening—only sad. "There has to be another way."

"There is no other way, Mirren. He cannot be allowed to burn villages full of people on the Praeceptor's whims. And we can't risk you delving so deeply into your power before you're ready. You were unconscious so long, we started to think you wouldn't wake up. What if the next time you face him, you never find your way back to us? It's too risky."

Max watches Cal with an inscrutable face. I wait for her vehement objection, but when it doesn't come, I realize this is something they've already discussed. Perhaps while I was still in Similis, ignorant of everything that's been happening.

"The Praeceptor has already turned half of Ferusa against us. If we don't take Anni out of the equation, it's only a matter of time before he comes for Siralene. And Nadjaa after that," Cal continues. "And with the Boundary lights flickering," he hesitates, but his gaze is unwavering, as though he knows what he's about to say will hurt. "Mirren, your brother isn't safe in Similis. Anni *will* get in, unless we take him out first."

I hate that he speaks so levelly, like a general discussing war strategy in a cushioned room far from battle, rather than his best friend. "We are *not* killing Shaw," I tell Cal tersely. "I am not Ferusian and I'd never be able to sacrifice someone I care about, just to win some war."

Cal's eyes harden. "Anni was my soul-brother. I will forever have a hole in my heart where he resided, but he is *gone*. And we cannot allow the monster wearing his face to ravage the land he so loved."

I press my eyes closed tightly. "*Don't*—don't call him that." *Monster*. What he always saw himself as; what he could never see beyond.

"Anni would do it," Cal pleads gently, and my anger deflates. He is still trying to do right by his friend, to honor him in the only way he knows how. Protecting Nadjaa. Protecting me. "Anni would put his own feelings aside and make the hard choices. The choices that don't feel good but are the right thing to do. If the situation was reversed, Shaw would do it."

"I'm not Shaw," I reply, my voice sounding strangled.

Max lets out a sob: one I feel in the deepest parts of my chest. I am not Shaw—none of us are. He was our strength, the unyielding flame in our hearts, and without him, we're left floundering.

Harlan watches me with soft eyes, and I want to shy away from his kindness. Because though Cal is right, there lies a selfish part of me that will never let Anrai go, even to protect an entire continent. After all this time, I still can't embody the best of the Keys and choose the greater good over my own wants. My heart was dark and hungry long before I crossed the Boundary or fractured my soul. Will I ever learn to be better? To stop wanting so fiercely?

"You cannot kill Anrai," Denver says from the open doorway, startling us all so greatly that Max's hand flies to her sword.

My father's scars shine in the sunlight, and he leans heavily on a cane as he limps inside the room. Something tugs at my heart as I take in the thick wave of his regrown chestnut hair and the set of his mouth, familiar, despite the unnatural pull of the healed burns.

"Denver, I know you care for him—" Cal begins, but Denver shakes his head with impatience.

"That is not why."

Whatever warmth seeing my father healed has rendered, quickly drains from me. Of course, it isn't why. Denver cares for no one but his power and his city. Not Easton or me, and certainly not for his adopted son who sacrificed himself so that Denver could be free. I turn away in disgust as my power rises in an agitated cyclone. Inhaling sharply, I force it back down.

I am still human, I remind my *other*. And despite Denver's many faults, he is still my father.

His gaze meets mine, his green eyes sparkling behind wire rimmed glasses. "Hello, Mirri."

I stare at him mutely, not trusting myself to speak. If I

open my mouth, certainly, every spiteful thing I've thought about him in the past months will come spilling out. Poisonous, black thoughts.

"You cannot kill Anrai because the prophecy demands his existence," Denver explains gravely.

My breath catches. Max narrows her eyes. "I thought you only knew the first line," she says slowly.

"Before—" Denver's normally smooth tenor wobbles fractionally, and I try to ignore the tug of empathy at his obvious trauma. I was too ruined to ask the extent of what happened to him during the length of his abduction, but knowing Cullen, it was unspeakable. "Before I was captured, I managed to translate not one, but *two* lines of the Dead Prophecy. The second line speaks of a fire-bearer. Mirri, you aren't the only one needed to bring back balance. We also need Shaw."

"Well, that is unfortunate, seeing as he's quite busy terrorizing the countryside," Cal bites out acerbically.

I study my father. "You knew this before you were captured," I repeat, the repercussions slowly dawning. "Does this mean Cullen knows as well?"

A tremor racks Denver's body as he nods. "He knew before he took Shaw."

~

Shaw

"What happened?" My father's words reverberate off the Castellium walls, an angry scrape of stone against stone. He doesn't even need to yell to make the soldiers nearest him flinch.

What happened?

I still can't answer that for myself.

When I woke, water in my lungs and a roaring pain in my skull, I could barely remember my own name. I had to be dragged from the town square by Ivo and tied atop a horse like an invalid. Now, five days later, strength has finally returned to my muscles. But the echo of whatever that witch did to me still sizzles in the emptiness of my abyss.

It wasn't just that she forced an endless swirl of ice water into my lungs—it's the unending pain she caused without even touching me. As if she took the rawest parts of me and molded them to her liking. And the worst part is, I can't be sure everything went back to the way it was before. I still feel the agonizing touch of her, though she's nowhere near Argentum.

How? *How?*

The truth is, I don't know. An answer I cannot give the Praeceptor if I wish to keep my head attached to my body.

I clear my throat, still raw from drowning. "According to our intelligence, the girl was supposed to be in Similis. I was unprepared to meet her in Havay. The fault is entirely my own and will not happen again."

My father narrows his eyes. I feel Ivo stiffen beside me as the Praeceptor stalks toward us, his booted footsteps echoing menacingly. The throne room is empty today aside from us and the two soldiers stationed as sentries, but the lack of audience only furthers my dread. My father is at his worst when we are alone, as there is no reason to for him to pretend to be human. No audience to play a part for.

We did not gain compliance from Havay and there was no sign of Akari Ilinka when we arrived. By all accounts, the mission was a complete disaster, and Ivo and I led it; it will not be the soldiers who pay my father's price.

I feel the familiar constriction in my chest as the Praeceptor tests his control and I sway on my feet. He squeezes until there is no more air in my lungs, until I am drowning with no water. "You are never unprepared," he growls, coming close enough I can see his eyes. Everyone believes them to be the same color as mine, but they aren't. Cullen's are flecked with pinpricks of yellow, as if the rot inside him seeps through his irises.

He squeezes until I clutch at my chest with both hands. My cheeks heat with rage at my show of weakness, at how my body responds in spite of my resolve: always so desperate to survive, never realizing survival is a curse.

My father looks down on me, his lips peeled back from his teeth. "I trained you. I've fought you. You are *never* unprepared. I told you to burn Havay to the ground. What weakness holds you back?" At once, pain explodes in my chest, like I'm being clawed from the inside out. My eyes pop and the veins in my neck go taut, my mouth opening in a silent scream. "Tell me, son. Tell me, and I will *dig it out.*" My lungs are being shredded and all I can do is gape up at the man who gave me life, as I crash to my knees. "Shall we peel open your ribs and see what fragility festers beneath them?"

Finally, my father relents and fresh air barrels into my lungs. I wheeze, collapsing to all fours. My arms shake beneath me, but there is no room here for weakness, so I force myself back up. Something unfamiliar glints in the Praeceptor's eyes as he gazes at me, but I don't take the time to place it as I struggle to my feet. The quicker I get out of here the quicker I figure out what in the Darkness happened: why my power faltered in the girl's presence. And why my very blood sparked when she drew close.

The Praeceptor sets his cold gaze on Ivo. The *legatus* possesses more strength than I gave him credit for, because he meets those pale eyes without flinching. "And did you find Akari Ilinka while my son was otherwise engaged?"

Ivo sets his jaw, his feet spread apart, and his hands clamped stiffly behind his back. "No, sir. There was no sign of the witch-queen."

"I practically handed her to you on a platter. I fed you her exact location and all you needed to do was bring her and the man to me alive."

Ivo wisely says nothing. *Is the man Ilinka travels with the reason my father wants her alive? If so, he must be someone important. If I can get to him before Ivo, perhaps I can keep myself out of the dungeon. Maybe even buy a fraction of freedom.*

"You have been a good *legatus* to me all these years, Ivo. One who's always known the cost of failure. I trust I will have no argument when I collect payment for this one."

Ivo closes his eyes briefly, no more than a fraction of a second, but it's enough for me to know whatever my father plans to take from him, he doesn't give willingly. Everyone always does whatever it takes to scrape their way up the ranks in the Castellium, hungry for power and prestige. But my father is like the sun—too close to his splendor and you will only be scorched. And by the time you realize it, it's always too late.

"Now that the ocean-wielder moves freely, the prophecy is back in play. We need to move faster to exterminate those with the potential for magic." Cullen sets his eyes on me. "And you son, will remember just how great a threat water is to you. You are her only equal. The only one capable of finding that witch and bringing her to me. Do you understand?"

Her only equal. A thrill of power rises to the surface of my skin as I remember the way my flames caressed her body, drawn to their own deaths by her magnetism. Willing to be smothered beneath her power, if only they could take their last breath on her lips.

Lemming.

She means to outwit me, but water is not all powerful. It evaporates. So, I will need to burn hotter.

I meet my father's gaze. "I will be ready for her this time. When I find her, she will burn like the rest of them."

CHAPTER TEN

Mirren

My anger is so potent as I gaze at my father, I fear it will boil the power inside me, turning it into something rancid and festering. I force myself to take count of his injuries, the angry red burns that cover his face and throat, the puckered skin of stab wounds at his arms, the ravaged remains of his right ear. Though he's regained some of his muscle mass, he is an echo of the father who tucked me in and told me stories—the man who painted my dreams in such vibrant colors. He was destroyed by Cullen as much as the rest of us and I take a deep breath, trying to remember he doesn't deserve to be maligned for his choices under duress.

But my empathy is tangled up in my feelings of betrayal. Shaw, Easton and I have always been worthy sacrifices to him, bricks in his vision for the world remade. Where I have always held on too tightly, my father has always been the first to let go in service of the greater good. Which is more selfish? Or are they both borne of the same dark things, one only better in the end result?

"So, you not only gave Cullen your daughter, but sold

him your son as well?" I spit out. Denver flinches like I've hit him, and it's only the sick satisfaction of hurting him that finally cools the burning in my throat.

"I didn't know the prophecy spoke of you," Denver says quietly. I wish he would yell back: that he would show his outrage at what the world has done to us. But even hundreds of miles outside the Boundary, his Similian shows through.

His words suddenly sink into my chest like iron daggers. "But you knew...you *knew* it spoke of Shaw!"

Denver's eyes widen. "It was only a suspicion and Cullen was already hellbent on getting Shaw back. Shaw's power hadn't come to fruition, and it seemed like the safest option to satisfy Cullen's greed—"

My *other* surges to my skin and the wash pitcher on the wardrobe bursts into pieces, soaking the wood floor.

"Mirren, you know it isn't as simple as that," Cal reminds me gently. "No one thinks clearly under torture."

But I can no longer see past my rage—past the look on Shaw's face as he gave up his soul for a man he thought loved him. "It *is* as simple as that! You said it yourself, Cal, Shaw would have made the hard choices. If the situation was reversed, Shaw would have *died* before giving Denver to the Praeceptor. And now, he is worse than dead, for *him!*" My power swirls, agitated and restless, as I turn to my father. "You sold him out to the person who hurt him most in this world!"

Calloway falls silent, tears glistening in his eyes. Max simply gapes at Denver, shock and horror mingled on her face. Harlan watches Denver with an unreadable expression, as if he's just come to a conclusion about something and isn't pleased with it.

Denver straightens, his cane digging into the floor as he

shifts his weight. "We have been making decisions without all the information, to our detriment. It's more important than ever that we translate the rest of the prophecy. Cullen's raids have not been random. There's evidence he's singling out parts of the population and taking them to Argentum to be exterminated."

Max's nostrils flare. "He's killing them? Why?"

"I believe he's found a way to determine if someone has the potential for magic. If the prophecy doesn't come to pass soon, there may be no one left for the nature spirits. Balance will never return to the continent." He studies me, and for a moment, I feel like I'm five years old under his gaze. "I take it by your presence here, the rumors of blackouts at the Boundary are true?"

"Yes, and instead of doing anything about it, the Covinus is trying to create scapegoats and hold onto his power."

Max twists her mouth in distaste. "They're all the same, aren't they?" I don't miss the way her eyes travel to Denver. "All warlords, just with different names."

Denver doesn't seem to hear her. "The Boundary failed long enough for you to escape, Mirri. It may be only a matter of time before it fails completely and Cullen comes for the Similians. The Xamani Kashan who first helped me with the prophecy has arrived in Nadjaa. I believe he can help us translate it and stop Cullen before it's too late."

I cut my eyes toward him. "Asa's here?" The brave man Shaw and I rescued from the Praeceptor's camp.

Denver nods. "I have a suspicion about the next few lines of the prophecy, but I need his help to confirm it. Unfortunately, he's refused to meet with me." His gaze settles heavily on me, and I realize my father didn't come to my room to check on my wellbeing, or to keep us from plotting Shaw's murder. He needs something from me.

"Why?" Max asks.

Denver glances to her. "He is untrusting of warlords. And though I am not one, he won't consider my invitation."

I purse my lips and mutter, "He has a good sense about people."

Denver ignores the jab. "Cullen has taken over Xamani land in the north and I've granted Asa asylum here at great risk to Nadjaa." He doesn't say what he's gained from allowing Asa's people a haven. "He's asked after you, Mirri. Perhaps you could speak with him and impress upon him the importance of learning the last lines of the prophecy."

Part of me feels like being a stubborn child—to cross my arms and dig in my heels just to spite my father. But when Harlan eyes me meaningfully, I swallow down my pride. Denver may be a terrible father, but if Cullen really is killing potential magic wielders, things on the continent are worse than I thought. "If I help you, you have to promise to help Similis as well...to not only care about Nadjaa. Cullen could use Shaw at any moment to break through the Boundary and if he takes over...it isn't just the Similians who will be hurt."

Denver tilts his head in a way that reminds me so much of Easton, for a moment, I feel bereft. "I founded this city on the idea of help."

I shake my head. "You founded it on freedom first, and those two things don't always align. Promise you'll help the Similians, even if it means working with the Covinus."

My father's face darkens, and I wonder again how much of the Covinus' story is true. Did my mother truly abandon Denver to stay in Similis? Is that why my father now refuses to let his heart dictate his actions?

"I promise to do whatever I can to keep Similis out of the Praeceptor's grasp. That much technology in his hands will be a danger to all of Ferusa."

It's the best I'm going to get: the promise to help only because it furthers his own goals. Harlan and I will only be able to bring change to Similis if there's a city left to go back to. So for now, Denver and I's goals align. I wiggle my toes against the floor, the worn wood so different from the cold concrete of my quarterage. If Denver is so quick to forget the feel of the place he comes from, I will just have to work to keep it in his mind.

∼

The Xamani camp is nestled outside the city, framed by the looming magnificence of the Averitbas mountains. Temporary shelters have been constructed of thick hides, each one intricately painted in bright cherry reds and cobalt blues. Meat smokes slowly over small fires, enveloping the entire camp in the mouthwatering scent of foreign spices.

My stomach gives a large rumble as Cal and I make our way through the worn dirt paths between tents. We find Asa near the center of camp. His face, once hollowed out by starvation, is now full and handsome. His bronze skin has regained its luminous pallor, stretched across a prominent nose and high cheek bones. His long hair hangs in a thick braid down his back, the shining black strands interwoven with dyed straps of leather.

Children surround him, their mouths agape, their small bodies still with rapt attention. One sits in his lap, chubby hands clinging to the Kashan's neck, watching with wide eyes as Asa tells a story. Even while sitting, the Kashan moves with a fluid sort of grace: his voice, his hands, his eyes—they all weave the tale so intricately, I don't even realize I've been staring, frozen, until his warm brown eyes meet mine.

Surprise flickers there for only a moment, before being replaced with genuine delight. "Mirren!" He says my name with the same veracity as one of his stories, and I can't help but smile. "Come, come!"

To the children, he whispers dramatically, "This is the heroine of one of our tales! The brave one who faced the dragon in his lair to free the stories from their cold prison. *She* is the reason our words breathe open air to this day."

I shift uncomfortably as their awed gazes all shift to me. "It wasn't quite that spectacular," I mumble.

Asa grins, disentangling the little boy from his neck and setting him to the ground gently. He tilts his head and winks conspiratorially. "The best heroes are always humble, wouldn't you say?" The little boy nods so fervently, I gather he'd agree to anything if it garnered him the attention of his beloved Kashan. Asa laughs and shoos the children. "Alright, run along now. The stories have exhausted your Kashan for now."

The children disperse in a blossom of chaos, little feet running in all directions, screeches and giggles echoing behind them.

Asa motions for us to sit. I settle next to Cal on a brightly woven rug, his knees knocking mine as he curls his long legs beneath him. "I had so hoped to see you, brave one. It seems much has happened to both of us since we last met." His eyes drift curiously to Cal. "That is a beautiful bow you have," he says, nodding to the weapon strung over Cal's back.

I jump, startled at forgetting my manners. "Asa, this is my friend Calloway. He came to rescue me in Havay."

Cal shoves my shoulder good-naturedly. "Nice to meet you, Kashan. But as I'm sure you know, Mirren was in no need of rescuing." He releases his bow sling and offers it to Asa for inspection. "It was a gift from my father. Traded for a bushel of wheat and a few wool blankets years ago outside of Siralene."

Asa runs his fingers lightly over the bow's curve, as if he can absorb the stories carved there by simple touch. "A nurturer of the land. A fine calling," he says with a nod of approval. "One I've never had the patience for, I'm afraid." He hands the bow back to Cal. "There is a distinguished weapons master on the north side of camp who will have arrows worthy of your bow. My gift for your honored friendship of Mirren."

Cal looks at me in question and I flash him an encouraging smile. Though he's still beholden to his vow, I didn't ask him to accompany me as a guard. Only a friend.

"Thank you, Asa," he says with a deferential nod, before taking his leave to find the weapons master.

When he disappears behind the furthest tent, Asa says, "I was sorry to hear about our friend." He smiles sadly, watching as I attempt to swallow down my sudden grief. When will the mere mention of Anrai no longer feel like a knife to the gut? Hearing my unspoken question, Asa continues, "our soul never feels the same when a piece of it is gone."

I glance to him in surprise, but he shakes his head. "I don't mean one taken by the curse. I mean one given freely to another...in love."

Love. Anrai and I never said the word to each other, but I'd be lying if I said I haven't thought it most every day since I lost him. What else would have the power to keep a wound from ever healing? To shred me apart the moment I wake to his memories every morning? His loss is still as raw as the day after Yen Girene.

I clear my throat. "Asa, I need your help."

The Kashan gives a knowing sigh. "I feared your father had sent you."

"He has," I admit, "but that's not why I'm here. He wants your help with the next line of the prophecy, but...so do I. The Praeceptor is rounding up potential magic wielders and murdering them."

Asa furrows his dark brow, staring at the fire thoughtfully. "How is he targeting them? The nature spirits were always fickle in nature—it would be the height of hubris to assume you can predict who they would choose if given the opportunity."

I wring my hands. "I don't know. But it isn't just that... the Praeceptor controls almost every territory in the north. And the Boundary is failing. It's only a matter of time before he comes for Similis. The Covinus has done nothing to prepare for an invasion—he won't even admit there's a risk. And I don't want what happened in Yen Girene to happen to the Similians."

Asa tilts his head. "There are some who would say they deserve their fate. They've sat safely behind their Boundary for millennia, never reaching out a hand to their brothers suffering in the Darkness around them," he says neutrally.

"Do you think that?"

"No," he replies without hesitation, "but it is not my opinion that matters. The Xamani are warriors, but we do not seek war. We have been driven from the land to which we're bonded, forced to wander under the heat of another sun, because we are no match for the might of the Dark Militia. I am sorry, *zaabi*, but it is not my help you'll need. To save Similis, you will need the Chancellor's."

"What if I don't?"

Asa raises a doubtful brow. "I have heard of your power, brave one, but I do not think even that is enough to overcome the Praeceptor's shadow of evil."

The idea swirling in my head like mist since my father first spoke of Shaw's involvement in the prophecy now begins to solidify, taking form like cliffs out of a heavy fog. "Alone, it's not. But what if I wasn't alone?"

"You seek to bring back magic." It isn't a question.

I nod fervently. "Not for my father. Or any other warlord. But for balance. If the nature spirits were reborn and blessed the land once more, the Darkness wouldn't have such an easy path against the light."

"Sometimes light is only so bright to blind you from the truth. Have you considered what will happen if you resurrect magic and birth an army of men like your Shaw?"

I bite my lip. Asa is right—giving magic free rein could make everything worse than it is. After a beat, I finally say, "I have to believe in the good of people, Asa. I know there are those capable of horrifying things..." My eyes travel to the scars dissecting his hands, put there by Cullen himself. "But I have to believe that in their hearts, most people are still good if they're given the chance to be."

Asa beams as if I've passed an unspoken test. "It's settled then. Where do we begin?"

"Well," I suck in a breath. This part is guesswork, led only by a feeling in my stomach. Silly, really, but it's all I have. "If I am water and Shaw is fire, I think...I think somewhere out there is air and earth. All the elements have awakened."

Asa nods slowly. "This has occurred to me as well. You believe you all need to be together to bring the prophecy to life?"

I nod. I've no proof, nothing other than the way the thought *feels*—as if something ragged has been smoothed. Something broken, mended.

"Do you think you can translate the exact words? Without Denver?" I ask hopefully.

"You don't wish to inform your father?"

Not yet. Denver may think he means well, but Nadjaa will always be his priority and I don't trust that he'll choose the good of Ferusa over his own city. "I don't think any leader should have access to that kind of control. It should be neutral, for the good of Ferusa. Not to win a war."

Asa looks as if he wants to say something but shakes his head when he thinks better of it. "It may be possible without Denver. Xamani stories are not written down. They are passed from generation to generation, as ever-changing and fluid as a river. The language of the old gods is long forgotten, evolved into something different. But I remember every story. The work will be recalling the correct one."

He speaks of stories as living things, as if the words themselves live and breathe. Reminiscent of the way Anrai spoke of his books. For a brief moment, I long to sit at Asa's fire and just listen. But the world moves too fast around me. "I might have someone who can help sort through the right stories."

For the first time since I sat down, Asa looks distinctly disgruntled. "If you speak of the witch at the edge of the forest, I have already had the unpleasant experience of making her acquaintance."

A loud laugh escapes me. Aggie really knows how to make a lasting impression.

Asa raises his chin indignantly. "She seemed to imply

that I am cursed to a violent death by cobblestone. There are cobblestones in every city in Ferusa!"

I stifle another laugh, remembering her vague warning to Cal. It's been hard to tell whether Aggie's warnings are serious, or if she just finds it amusing to keep men on their toes by threatening violent deaths. "She's eccentric, but she isn't a fraud. She's familiar with prophecies...like some fragment of old magic still lives in her. She could help."

Asa grimaces, as if he's swallowed something repugnant. "For you, brave one, and the debt I owe you, I will seek out the old witch." After a slight pause, he adds, "and perhaps avoid cobblestones for the time being."

"Gods, has she done it to you too, Kashan?" Cal says, rounding a corner with a new quiver full of arrows slung over his shoulder. "I swear, the old loon has given me a permanent twitch," he says darkly, eyeing the distant skyline of Nadjaa, as if one of the bricks will launch itself this way at any moment.

Asa laughs, just as a ball of dark hair darts out from behind Calloway. "Mirren, this girl says she knows you—" He trails off as Sura collides into me, wrapping her spindly arms around me in a fierce hug. "—and apparently she does." Cal sighs.

Sura pulls back, swatting at the cloud of dark hair around her and beaming at me. "You're here! We were so worried when the grumpy man never came for us that something had happened to you both!"

I hug her back, appreciating the full set of her face and the renewed strength of her limbs. She no longer looks Darkness-edged and starving; she looks happy. "I'm okay. And you! You look so well."

Sura beams, motioning behind Cal to where Luwei stands, shyly observing. His hands are stuffed into the pockets of his buckskin trousers, and he blushes fiercely when Sura declares, "Luwei tried to convince the Chancellor to go after you, but he wouldn't listen, even after we told him you saved our Kashan. But Luwei refused to take no for an answer—"

"Enough, Sura," Luwei interrupts desperately. "We're glad you're safe."

I smile. "I'm so glad you're both safe. I was just enlisting the help of your Kashan. Sura, you mentioned Asa was bringing you up as a Kashan. Perhaps you could act as a buffer between Asa and Aggie?"

"Your assistance would prove most helpful, Sura," Asa nods and Sura blushes under his attention.

"Yeah, Aggie doesn't seem inclined to predict women's deaths," Cal quips, elbowing Luwei lightly. "Might hang back if I were you. She's liable to tell you you'll be strangled by tent cloth."

Luwei has the good sense to look perturbed. Asa says, "And you, Mirren...what do you intend to do?"

"I'm going to find earth and air before Cullen does," I tell him, pushing myself to my feet. The sun has already begun to sink behind the mountains, and Cal and I still have a long way back to the manor.

Asa nods, his smiling mouth turning grave. "They may not want to be found. Look at how the world hunts you and your kind. If they do indeed have power, they've most likely taken heart and hidden themselves."

I give the Kashan a small smile. I don't possess the Praeceptor's secret weapon for finding potential wielders, but I think I have something just as effective. "I know someone who can help finding the unfindable."

CHAPTER
ELEVEN

Shaw

The air in Dauphine is heavy, as if all the moisture has been pulled from the ground and hung up like twinkle lights. But the sun shines. I close my eyes, appreciating the way it heats my skin, even as the rest of me remains cold and hollow.

I peer down from my perch atop the clay roof, the market below bustling with midday activity. Sellers hock their wares, each trying to out proclaim their neighbor, resulting in a cacophony of muddled shouts. A crowd gathers at the far end of the street, goggling the stage where a slaver parades his latest merchandise. A young boy, by the looks of it, trembling and malnourished. The slaver cracks a whip and the boy yelps, squeezing his eyes shut.

I turn away, eyeing the other end of the street. The woman ambles through merchants, pausing every once and awhile to finger an odd trinket or admire a necklace. A large basket is slung over one of her forearms, packed with her purchases, and she adds one more to the top of the pile with a smile. She wasn't hard to track down after I burned her tavern in Havay. She did what most Havians without the money to rebuild did—move onto the closest territory that isn't controlled by the Praeceptor.

Dauphine will only enjoy a few more days of freedom. The militia travels behind me, but I can no longer afford to keep to their slow pace. The longer the ocean-wielder roams free, the more damage she'll cause to the Praeceptor's reign. Now that I've emerged from the fog of the dungeons and can think beyond the unendurable hunger, my drive has become clearer. The girl stands in the way of everything I seek to accomplish. I must bring her to my father. Now.

I leap nimbly to the next roof, tracking the woman as she makes her way through the remainder of the market. Her Havian neighbors were more than willing to give her up when threatened with my brand of justice and I imagine it'll be much the same with her. Normal people aren't trained to hold up under interrogation, and as far as I know, she owes the ocean-wielder no loyalty. They'd only met moments before my attack.

The woman rounds a corner and heads down a mostly deserted street, back toward the hovel she inhabits. I scale the nearest wall and drop silently in front of her. She startles, throwing her hand to her chest and stumbling backward, but she doesn't scream.

I smile, pleased. Perhaps this will be more exciting than I thought. "Hello," I purr.

My smile does not put her at ease. Smiles are only comforting when something lives behind them. If there is only ash and destruction, they are unsettling at best—threatening at worst. She eyes my daggers and takes another step back, which only makes me smile wider. Maybe she'll run and I can give chase. Maybe I've found a worthy opponent; someone who won't break at the first wave of pain.

"What do you want?" she barks. Her words are steady, but the way she clutches her basket to her chest like it will protect her, denotes her uncertainty.

"Just to ask a few questions," I reply conversationally. Grinding my jaw and stretching my neck, I will my power to settle inside my chest. Sometimes, it feels like it lives apart from me, ravenous in its need to feed. Keeping it leashed and starving, even momentarily, is exhausting.

I take a step toward her, crowding her further against the building. Her eyes dart toward the ends of the street, but she will find no help there.

"I heard you made the acquaintance of a girl in Havay."

She shakes her head fervently. "I grew up with the beasts of the Nemoran and I know better than to ask travelers questions. I don't know no girl beyond seeing her in my tavern."

My smile grows painful. "Now, now, Lettie. I am a dangerous person to lie to. I only want to know where the girl went after the attack." I pull a dagger from the black bandolier crossed over my chest, standard issue for the Dark Militia but with a few enhanced modifications to fit my personal needs.

Lettie's chin wobbles, but she jams her lips together, mastering her fear. Interesting. I'd only needed to draw a knife to pry answers from the others, but I was right in assuming this one was made of stronger stock. I cock my head curiously and run the blade along her cheek lightly. She presses her eyes closed with a whimper. "I'm sure you've heard of me, Lettie. Which means you know there are consequences for not giving me what I want."

Her eyes fly open as I dig the dagger into her flesh. As

much as I'd love to play with her longer, I'm on borrowed time. The face is the fastest way to get information—no one wants to be marred for life. But the tavern maid only snarls at me as blood begins to leak from the small incision. "I know exactly who you are," she growls, "The Praeceptor's monster. That girl saved those children, and I won't give her up to the likes of you."

A wave of nausea rises in my throat, and suddenly, I can no longer see the alley in front of me. I am far away from Dauphine, in a familiar mountain cave, the girl's body pinned beneath mine as my blood peppers her face.

Not now, not now.

This has happened with terrifying frequency since the ocean-wielder touched me and I wonder again what exactly she did. My father says it's only my memory coming back in disjointed fragments, but there is no relief in the remembering. It is heavy and warped by the girl's touch.

I'm certain, now, that I knew her intimately. Her scent is visceral, and her taste lingers in my mouth hours after I've spiraled back into the present. I've determined it was *fear* I witnessed in the Castellium from my father, as if somehow my attachment to the girl could overpower his control. He thinks I spared her life on purpose.

I'll prove him wrong and earn his trust by meting out his justice. By bringing the ocean-wielder to him weak and on her knees.

I lash out at Lettie, opening up her other cheek with one deft slice. She whimpers and drops the basket to clutch her wounds, her fingers growing slippery as blood pours from the laceration. The ocean-wielders face remains at the edges of my vision, the curve of her lips and the defiance in her eyes, so I shake my head to rid myself of it and allow my power to rise. It needs no prompting, a reminder of the feeble hold I had to begin with, and surges past my skin. Hungry for Lettie and her pain. Always hungry.

I stare down at the barmaid, the demented pit of emptiness burning so furiously in my eyes that she gasps in horror. The girl has garnered some sort of loyalty from this woman, but no matter—my fire burns through anything. It was made in the pits of Darkness, only to destroy.

"Tell me where the girl is, or I will burn you alive where you stand."

Lettie sets her jaw, and a thrill runs through me. Have I finally met someone who is strong enough to withstand my power's need? Someone it can gorge on and finally be full, rather than the paltry sips on which it's been subsisting?

She cries out as I run it along her skin and watch with detached interest as blisters rise in its wake. "And then I will find your daughter, Lettie. Do you think she'll be lucky enough to be saved from me twice?"

Lettie sags and I know I have her. Disappointment threads through me. Ridiculous to think I'd find someone equal of the monster inside me in this pathetic barmaid. I have only one equal, one strong enough to withstand its demands—powerful enough to give me the fight I so crave, the one that will finally relieve the aching hunger and biting emptiness.

"She left Havay after the attack," Lettie sobs.

It's what I wanted, but there is no calling my fire back now. It spears further toward her, intent on devouring every bit of pain it can wring from her. It melts the skin of her arm until she screams. "There were two people! A redhaired man with a bow and a curly-haired woman with twin swords."

Abruptly, my power flares before receding back into me,

though I haven't called it. And then I am gone from this alley once more.

I'm in a gym as a copper-haired boy grins at me. Then I'm in the dining room of the Castellium as a scrawny girl meets my gaze with angry defiance.

By the time I'm hurtled back into the present, Lettie is gone. But no matter.

I know who's helping the ocean-wielder.

~

Mirren

I've been crouched so long in the alleyway my feet are numb. Yanking my cloak tighter around my neck, I curse inwardly as an icy breeze skitters over my exposed skin. Darkness fell hours ago, and though the loud ruckus of the taverns lining the main street are still going strong, I'm beginning to wonder whether Max was right and I'm wasting my time.

Baak is a large territory, set between the thick evergreens of the eastern-most coast. There is nothing of the squalid air of Havay, nor is there the sense of war with nature that Yen Girene carried. Here, everything is built in service of the pines, which provide not only natural protection for their city, but also their livelihood. The residences and shops wind through the trees, some built into their actual branches, with stairs curling around the trunks. Even in this alley, in a clearly disreputable section of the city, dark green pine boughs curve overhead, creating the illusion of a natural ceiling.

It might be beautiful if it weren't crawling with Dark Militia. In one of Denver's meetings, Cal and Max heard rumors Baak was holding out against the Praeceptor in favor of the warlord of Siralene, but it appears the intel was wrong. Crimson-clad soldiers stalk the forested streets—they hang out of taverns with local women strung around their necks and lounge in front of stores, bawdy and loud, looking entirely at home beneath the trees.

Cal and Harlan had both wanted to accompany me into the city, but three of us would be far more conspicuous than one. Besides, I hadn't been exactly sure how to explain what it is I'm trying to do.

I have no actual idea *where* I'm supposed to be looking —only a tugging sense of a place my *other* has traveled. At first, it was barely noticeable, and Max had declared me insane for setting off in search of a feeling. But the closer we got to this territory, the heavier the feeling grew, until neither Max nor myself could ignore it. Familiar and alien at once, I know now what I search for is in Baak.

Somewhere.

There was another reason I'd insisted everyone else stay behind. On the off chance I *do* manage to find what I'm looking for—well, it may very well end with my death. Because I know without a doubt, what I search for does not wish to be found.

I shift, wincing as the blood rushes painfully back to my toes. While I'm gingerly rubbing the arch in my foot, the darkness at the end of the alley stirs. So subtle, it could be written off as a trick of the moonlight, but when my *other* undulates against my chest, I know it's what I've been waiting for.

I pull a dagger, ignoring the stiffness in my muscles as I silently follow the movement.

Before I can so much as blink, my dagger is yanked from my hand.

The cool blade of a sword presses to my throat and a

whisper sounds in my ear. "Hasn't anyone ever told you it is unwise to stalk assassins in dark alleyways?" Avedis asks genially, removing his sword from my throat with a flourish and stepping from me with a polite nod. Having been almost murdered by him last year, adrenaline should be racing through me at how close his blade just was to my jugular, but I can't help but smile at his prim tone.

"Assassin. Singular." I correct pointedly.

He hums in neither agreement nor dispute, examining his blade with disinterest. "If you're here to finish me off, I would have greatly preferred a quick knife to the throat while I slept. Or perhaps a healthy dose of poison in my ale. I can't say that drowning much suited me."

I grin sheepishly. "That's not why I'm here. I need your help."

Avedis tilts his head curiously, his dark eyes glinting in the moonlight. He wears sturdy boots and is clad in dark leather, his hands encased by a matching pair of gloves. His thick hair has been shaved close to his scalp once more and though I detect no weapons aside from his sword, it occurs to me I may have interrupted one of his jobs. "Lost the taste for offing men yourself, then, eh?" he muses.

I blanche. "How did you—" I stop myself with a roll of my eyes. "You know what, it doesn't matter. I don't want you to kill anyone. I want you to help me *find* someone."

"If this has anything to do you with your wayward assassin's new penchant for burning down cities, I respectfully decline."

I swallow roughly. I should have known Avedis would have knowledge of both Shivhai and Shaw: it's his penchant for always knowing things he shouldn't that's drawn me back to him in the first place, despite both Max and Cal claiming the idea was insane. I raise my chin. "I didn't think you were afraid of Shaw."

He purses his lips ruefully. "Afraid? Hardly. Possess a healthy attachment to my skin and limbs? Indeed."

"This isn't about Shaw. Is there somewhere we can talk?"

Avedis watches me skeptically for a moment before tipping over in a dramatic bow. "After you, m'lady."

⁓

The main street winds its way around several large trees, their branches spread out against the night sky. The assassin leads me straight past militia soldiers, most deep in their drink. Women call out from windows set high in the branches, selling entertainment, their voices lost in the din of music that pours from the various establishments.

Finally, we come to a tavern so decrepit, the sign hanging above the door is no longer legible. "Isn't there somewhere...quieter we can go?" I ask with an uncertain glance at the nearest soldier. The man wobbles and then glares at the ground beneath him as if it's had the nerve to move without his permission.

Avedis only smiles, pushing the door open. It sticks stubbornly as he shoves his shoulder into it, before finally relenting with a loud squeal. "Best place to hide is in plain sight. The militia would hardly believe the ocean-wielder would be foolish enough to walk right through them."

He ushers me in impatiently and the door closes behind us with another ungodly squeak. "Besides, if I'm going to drown tonight, I would prefer it to be in my cups rather than at your hand."

Bowing as deeply as he would to a highborn lady,

Avedis flashes the barmaid a charming smile. Her full cheeks flush a pretty pink and with something halfway between a giggle and a breathy sigh, she motions us to a table and promises to return with food and drink. Avedis settles himself into a chair in the corner, the small table looking like it was built for a child rather than his hulking form.

He folds his hands in front of him as I collapse into the remaining chair. "Now, what is it you wish to speak to me about, Oh Lady of the Watery Grave? The last I was aware, you were safely ensconced behind the Boundary, enjoying your electricity and studying the Keys. Or whatever other odious eccentricities it is you Similians entertain yourselves with."

"It's Mirren," I retort irritably. "And how do you know where I've been? Have you been keeping tabs on me?"

"Is it only you who's allowed to do that, then?" He replies airily.

The barmaid returns with two large mugs and two steaming bowls of stew. "Why thank you, miss," Avedis says with a wicked smile, causing a fresh blush to bloom on her cheeks as she hurries back toward the kitchen.

"What?" He asks in response to the skeptical look on my face. "I may deal in death, but that's no reason to forget my manners." In demonstration, he takes a delicate sip of the stew and swallows it demurely. "Really, it's a shame I wasn't born on your side of the Boundary."

My stomach growls loudly as the scent of the stew wafts toward me, overpowering the stench of stale beer which coats the rest of the tavern. Avedis only smiles knowingly as I pull the bowl toward me and eat with decidedly less manners than the murderer across from me. Through a mouthful, I ask, "What else have you heard about Shaw?"

Avedis throws his hands behind his head and leans back in his chair. The thick muscles of his arms bulge as he watches me in that peculiarly curious way of his. "Some things are best left unknown. Remember who he was and don't spare a thought for who he is now, because they are not the same man."

If only it were that easy. If only I could clear his face from my thoughts and the weight of his sacrifice from my conscience. How I wish I could sleep through the night without reaching for his warmth. Without imagining the curve of his lips and the feel of his body beside mine.

I level a stare and after a moment, Avedis throws a hand up in relent. "If you insist on torturing yourself with knowledge, who am I to stand in your way? I've heard Shaw is a most-willing heir to the Praeceptor and has become his father's personal hand of justice. Anyone who resists the warlord is met with the flames of his son. He has no conscience, no empathy, and thrives on the pain of others: man, woman *or* child. Most say meeting the Darkness is preferable to meeting those pale eyes."

By the Covinus. I should be thankful Anrai is truly gone, because the weight of his sins would crush him. The ember of hope I've nurtured since hearing him say the word *Lemming* is smothered—even if I could somehow find a way to return his soul, would he even allow it? He can't even remember who he used to be.

Who *we* used to be.

My eyes fall on Avedis, and I suddenly remember who he is: a man intimately familiar with the sacrifices paid in tithe to the first queen's curse. "Do you think he can remember? Who he used to be?"

Avedis gazes at me with pity. "There is a time after losing one's soul when memories are gone, but in my experience, they do return eventually." At the glint of hope in my eyes, he shakes his head. "Memories are connected to your soul, but they are also imprinted on your body. On your skin and in your lungs. Because of this, he will be able to remember events, but not the emotions connected to them. And without the emotions behind them, memories are essentially rendered useless."

The assassin speaks so mournfully, I stare at him in horror. How did it not occur to me before now? "Avedis, do you—do you have a soul?"

His dark eyes flicker and his gaze turns cold. "Why have you come, Mirren?" he demands, his voice like ice.

"I told you. I need your help finding someone."

He drains the contents of his mug in three large gulps before bothering to respond. "And why have you come to *me?* From what I recall, those friends of yours are more than capable of hunting someone. Especially the one who favors hot pink gags and twin falchions. And if not them, why not your father?"

"You know things. Things you shouldn't. And I didn't know where else to start to find someone who is unfindable." I pause, weighing my words. It's folly to trust a man who once tried to kill me; a man whose morals are available to purchase for the right price. Trusting the wrong person in Ferusa is a death sentence, but my power has traveled through Avedis—and he didn't feel like someone incapable of being good. "The next line of the Dead Prophecy says it isn't just me who will bring back magic."

Avedis' gaze is inscrutable. He crosses his arms over his chest, his jaw suddenly made of marble. "Shaw?" he growls.

I nod. "Not just Shaw. We are water and fire, but there will be two more. Earth and air. It will take all the natural elements returning to break the queen's curse and restore magic. I need to find the other two before Cullen does. He is hunting down potential wielders so that none will be left to oppose him."

Avedis doesn't move, his eyes suddenly ruthless enough to remind me who it is I sit across from. "And what will *you* do with them when you find them? Turn them over to *your* father so he can keep his seat of power?"

I stiffen. "Of course not. We're going to bring back the nature spirits. Restore balance and overthrow the warlords. *All* of them. Ferusa won't have to live in darkness anymore."

His nostrils flare. "I have no interest in Ferusian power struggles or dead spirits coming back to play magic tricks," he bites out roughly. "And even if I did, how do you propose we get your evil, soulless boyfriend to cooperate?"

"We'll figure that part out when we come to it."

Avedis narrows his eyes, the thick scar that dissects his face stretching and contracting with each movement. "Why would you trust me with this information? I am nothing more than a paid blade. One that would have cut you down with no hesitation. I paid my life debt to you, and we are once more on equal footing. If someone were to offer the right sum, there would be nothing to hold me back from completing the job this very moment. So again, I ask *why?*"

Because there is something in Avedis reminiscent of Shaw. They are not the same, but both fought tooth and nail to survive in a world hellbent on destroying them. My faith in Avedis isn't based in logic: it's rooted somewhere deeper. Somewhere less tangible. "Because I trust you."

He doesn't scoff as Shaw would, definitive proof of their true differences. Instead, he raises his eyebrows in surprise. "That seems...foolhardy," he says hesitantly, looking slightly abashed.

"Shaw would think so, too," I admit. "But I'm not him.

There's something good in you, Avedis, soul or not. You helped me when you had no reason to and you won't do anything to hurt me now, including betraying my trust."

Avedis stares at me like I have three heads, looking both torn and flattered, but I press on anyway. "You're the only one I trust enough to help us find air and earth. You know things no one else does. I know you can find them."

The assassin clears his throat and shifts in his chair, appearing uncharacteristically flustered. "Your search won't be as difficult as you imagine," he says in a soft voice. "I already know the location of the wind-whisperer."

My eyes widen. "You do?"

He doesn't smile when he says, "It is I."

CHAPTER
TWELVE

Mirren

Dawn stains the sky in watery shades of pink by the time Avedis and I wind our way through Baak. Avedis strolls past the Dark Militia as if he has nothing to hide, and though I attempt to do the same, my movements are jerky and unnatural. One overlong glance and I'm positive they'll know who I am and shoot me on sight, but none of them take any notice, hardly even turning our way as we walk past them and disappear into the surrounding forest.

The woods are thicker here, the crash of the north Tyrilian Sea against the steep rock cliffs muffling any sound. I eye Avedis thoughtfully. "When you came to...to..."

"Kill you?" he supplies helpfully, without breaking stride.

I roll my eyes upward. "Yes, *that*. You said something... you said you were disappointed I was ordinary."

He hums in assent. "There were whispers around you. Too many for someone of no note or skill and it piqued my curiosity. I spent a long time alone... but I never gave up the distant hope of finding others like me."

"Did you ever find anyone else?"

Avedis watches me for a moment. "You are the first."

When we arrive at our makeshift camp on the edge of the sea cliff, Max immediately draws her sword, the distinct ring of the blade echoing off the tree trunks. Avedis assesses her with a haughty air, as if he's amused by her show of strength rather than threatened.

He's never actually seen Max in action.

She swipes her tongue over her lips, more than willing to give him a demonstration.

"Sword down, Max. Avedis is a friend."

Her weapon remains high in the air. "Generally, my friends don't try to assassinate one another."

Avedis cocks his head, surveying Max with renewed interest. "Well, as I have no friends, you'll have to forgive me for not being aware of the protocol. But duly noted."

My heart twists at his words, but there is no mercy on Max's face.

Cal stands next to her, running his eyes over the multitude of places I now know weapons are hidden on Avedis. Back, chest, legs and arms. "Are you still murdering people for money?" he asks bluntly.

If his frankness surprises Avedis, he doesn't show it. "When the situation calls for it," he replies airily. He scans our camp, not with restless vigilance, but rather, tepid curiosity. After a beat, his blithe gaze settles back on Cal. "Are you still a stooge for your warlord who calls himself a Chancellor?"

Cal's lips twist in annoyance, but he doesn't take the bait. Instead, he turns to me with a harried shake of his head. "I still think we'll have more luck finding earth and air on our own."

I hesitate, shooting a sidelong look at Avedis. His secret

is not mine to tell, but it will certainly help my friends to understand why he's needed; now, more than ever. He bows his head in assent. "Actually, we have the location of the air wielder," I admit.

Cal's brows leap up in surprise, while Max's lower in suspicion. "Already?" How?" she asks doubtfully, lowering her sword just an inch.

Avedis puts his hands on his hips, rolling his gaze lazily to me. "It's no wonder you need my help, if the company you keep is so dimwitted."

"It's him," I snap, jerking my thumb toward the assassin with a glare. "He's the wind-whisperer."

"Who is?" Harlan asks curiously from where he's come sauntering in through the trees. "Oh Mirren, you've returned!" He makes to come toward me when Max slaps him in the stomach with the flat of her sword. He elicits an unceremonious grunt and shoots her an injured look. "Hey!"

"Are you crazy? You're *unarmed!*" Her nostrils flare. "You can't just saunter up to assassins, especially *this* one!" She gives me a long-suffering look, as if she still can't believe she now has *two* naïve Similians to deal with.

A gust of wind blasts through the tree, blowing my hair into my eyes and knocking Max's sword decisively from her hand. She lunges for it with a cry of outrage, but Avedis is already ambling past her toward the fire. "Now that that's settled, shall we discuss our strategy for finding the earth shaker?" he asks conversationally, situating himself on Cal's bedroll and helping himself to one of Rhonwen's mini cakes Cal had been saving.

"I do love raspberry jam," the assassin says to the cake with relish, before taking a dainty taste.

I bite my lip to keep from laughing and follow Avedis'

lead, sitting next to him. Harlan immediately follows suit as does Cal, albeit, after a bit of grumbling. Max remains standing with her arms crossed over her chest, looking positively murderous.

"How long have you had your power?" Harlan asks and I find myself grateful for his presence. He may not be worldly, or particularly skilled with a weapon, but his easy mannerism is capable of smoothing almost as many problems.

"As long as I can remember." Avedis licks errant jam from his fingertips. Cal watches mournfully as the remainder of his dessert disappears. "It is how I caught the attention of my previous master. And also, how I escaped."

Harlan's gaze travels to the thick scar that dissects the assassin's left eye. "Was it your master who gave you that?"

The air grows thick with tension. Cal averts his eyes as I shift uncomfortably. I've wondered about Avedis' scar since the night we met, but it seemed indelicate to ask. But Harlan is so guileless in his inquiry, the assassin doesn't appear to take offense. "The witch-queen was merciless. The wind whispers its secrets to me. I was punished for learning one of hers and being foolish enough to attempt to barter for my freedom with it."

I stare at him. The warlord of Siralene was his old master: the woman who ruined his childhood and mutilated his face is the same one who now seeks to defy the Praeceptor.

"I grew up in the slums of Siralene. My mother and I were barely above the slaves, always starving. When I was caught stealing, my power rose up and defended me from certain death, slaying the guards who intended to hang me. Murders committed by a child are an unusual occurrence to be sure, and these in particular caught the warlord's eye for their...*finesse.*"

"She drafted me into her service when I was ten. Older than most child soldiers, but always more powerful. I did what I had to do to survive, but I never let my power slip in front of her. I knew if I did, she'd keep me forever. Akari Ilinka is drawn to power, you see. She collects those more powerful than herself and drains them like a succubus. It is how she's held onto her territory for so long, even against the Praeceptor."

"So, I waited...waited until the time was right and she trusted me enough to loosen my leash. And then I escaped. My air covered the trail and allowed me to disappear into Ferusa. She hunts me still. The wind whispers hints of my location in her ear, always pulling her in the wrong direction. It's how I've avoided capture for so long."

Max's jaw tightens. "If you don't work for her anymore, why do you still murder for hire?"

Avedis meets her gaze, the dark brown of his eyes unrelenting. "We all do what we must to survive the Darkness, do we not, *Maxwell?*"

Something like fear flickers on Max's face, and as the two stare at each other, I get the distinct impression Avedis has discovered something important about her. Something she hasn't told even us. He remains silent, however, content to keep her secret and after a moment, Max straightens her shoulders and gives him a nod. A temporary truce.

"You killed for Ilinka?" Cal asks, his voice deadly quiet. He's gone still beside me, and his face is suddenly ruthless as he gazes at the assassin, his usual good-natured ambiance giving way to violence.

"Cal?" Max asks, worry tingeing her voice.

He doesn't look at her as he stands and strings his bow, leveling an arrow at Avedis' heart. "Answer the question."

The assassin stiffens as he senses the change in atmosphere, but he doesn't reach for a weapon. He meets Calloway's gaze gravely. "Did she take someone from you?"

Cal's jaw goes rigid as he pulls back on the bowstring. Avedis' gaze snags on Cal's hair, and as if he's just noticed it, he pushes a small exhale through his teeth. "Are you asking if I was her weapon that burned your kin?"

Calloway swallows roughly. For a moment, we're all frozen as he teeters on an unseen ledge: poised to either thread an arrow straight through Avedis' heart or fall to his knees and sob with anguish. Unable to speak through it, he gives a rough nod.

Avedis watches him, and for once, there is none of his endless curiosity: only miserable understanding. "It was not me, Calloway. But I was there when she ordered your family's destruction."

My eyes flare. "Oh gods, Cal, I'm so sorry—" I begin, but he shakes his head fiercely and drops his bow with a curse.

"I'm a hypocrite," he says softly, kneeling to the ground and dropping his head into his hands. "I told Anni he needed to forgive himself for what he was forced to do—that he wasn't responsible for the horrors his father made him commit. But here I am, faced with it and...and I don't think I could do the same." His voice is thick, and his eyes shine as he gazes at the assassin. "If it had been you, Avedis, I—" he shakes his head again. "I don't know what I was just willing to do."

Avedis bows his head. "If it was I, Calloway, I would have knelt before you and accepted whatever punishment you deemed fit. But if it soothes your soul at all, please know, I remember all their names and faces. Every last one.

And whoever was assigned to your family assuredly does, too. They are not forgotten."

Cal presses his eyes closed, his throat working. After a moment, he says, "Thank you for agreeing to help us, Avedis."

Avedis inclines his head. For someone who claims not to understand friendship, he is certainly adept at navigating the emotion of it.

"So...where do we begin looking for the earth-wielder?" Harlan asks, the weight of the moment dissipating with the sincerity of Avedis' words. He turns from Cal, giving him a moment to gather himself. "Can you read people's minds?"

Avedis laughs. "It's a tad more nuanced than that, but the easiest answer is no."

"Have you heard anything...unusual?" I ask.

Avedis grins wickedly. "Of course, O Siren of the Deep. The world is filled with rumors of wonderfully strange things. I never concern myself with the banality of the well-behaved."

I breathe deeply to keep from rolling my eyes as he gives me a silky look. "What about something odd having to do with the land?" I clarify. When my *other* healed Shaw, I hadn't even known I was the one who controlled it. What if the earth-wielder has made something happen without realizing they did?

Harlan looks thoughtful. "What about rumblings in the land? Crevasses appearing where they normally wouldn't?"

I look to him as we both remember the way the ground rolled the night of our escape. "You think they're somewhere near Similis?"

He shrugs. "It would explain what in Covinus' name that earth-shake was."

Avedis hums and closes his eyes, appearing deep in

thought. He goes completely still aside from the drumming of his fingers against his thigh. When more than half an hour passes and he still hasn't moved, Max lets out an irritated scoff and after muttering something about 'nonsense', announces she's going to find more firewood. Harlan offers to join, and in her immense agitation, she forgets to argue.

I scuff my toes in the dirt and Cal leans back on his elbows, face turned toward the last few rays of sun. He is almost completely asleep when Avedis finally speaks. "There have been earth shakes."

It's only then I remember Avedis' words to Shaw when they first spoke at the manor. *The wind told me.* I'd thought he was simply provoking us and knew the things he did because of his work as an assassin. But the wind *actually* speaks to him, sentient and listening. I stare at him, imagining the things the air has heard, the words swept up in its ever present current.

Avedis pushes himself to standing, stretching his legs and adjusting a few of his more delicately placed weapons. "There was an earthquake in Ashlaa, just north of Similis and the Nemoran. It was at the exact time of the planned execution of a thief almost two months ago. No one has seen the thief since, and it's been written off by the warlord as an oddity of nature. A coincidence that the earthquake saved him."

My eyes are wide as they meet his, our thoughts mirrored. "What if he saved himself?"

~

Shaw

"Any word on the girl?" Ivo's words are gruff, and he

follows them with a long gulp of mead. He motions to the barmaid for another, before finally meeting my gaze. In the weeks since I last saw him the circles beneath his shrewd eyes have darkened considerably but otherwise, he appears unharmed. I wonder again what my father's done to him, what pound of flesh he's rendered in payment of Ivo's failures. Obviously not a trip to the dungeons.

I don't ask though. It doesn't matter one way or the other, and I'd be a fool to think the Praeceptor punishes Ivo the way he punishes me. There are certain things he reserves only for the Heir.

Instead, I paste an obnoxiously arrogant smile on my face and lean back in my chair as though I don't have a care in the world. I set my eyes on the *legatus* and relish the way he stiffens, subtle as it is. "I have a few leads. What of the witch-queen?"

Ivo sneers and takes another slurp of his drink. We both know Akari Ilinka is safely back in her territory, and he stands no chance of capturing her now. Though he still leads the Dark Militia—still supervises the shipments of all those I deem potential magic wielders back to Argentum—his failure is a gaping wound that stands no chance of being remedied.

I tilt my head as he determinedly avoids my gaze. "Ah. So you haven't let it go, have you? What do you know?"

He stares at me flatly, considering. The barmaid saunters over, setting a fresh tankard in front of him, the honeyed liquid sloshing over the rim and splashing onto the table. Acid climbs my throat as her eyes rove over me, hungry and interested. I swallow it down, glaring at her with as much of my power as I dare. This is a nameless town on the border of Baak and Dauphine: she may not yet have heard of me. But as she takes in the depthless pits of my eyes, her hands fly to her mouth in horror.

With a yelp, she hurries away.

Ivo cocks his head.

"What?" I snarl, grabbing his mug and gulping it down, as if it's somehow capable of soothing the burning in my throat.

"I've known many soulless in my time leading your father's armies," he says slowly. "None would scare a woman off before using her."

My eyes flick to his as he examines me. "Unlike the militia, I have no interest in entertaining simpering weakness."

He shrugs and slides the mug back to his side of the table. "Even weakness can warm a cold bed for an hour or two."

I twist my mouth in distaste. The suggestion echoes inside the empty cavern of my chest, wriggling and slimy. There is nothing warm about it, nothing soothing. Even my fire lays dormant, instead of rearing up and demanding we drink the barmaid's pain.

And so it's been since I met the ocean-wielder in Havay. Each day, I am accosted by memories until the line between past and present blurs so fully, they become indeterminable. Memories of her spitting mad, climbing from beneath the carcass of a Ditya; of her body twisting to unheard music, cloaked in a gown of sea-green; of her beneath me, skin flush with pleasure and moonlight.

There are no particular feelings attached to any of them, other than mild curiosity. What would her bare skin look like now, laced in flame? What would that mouth look like parted in pain, as she feels my power's frenetic hunger?

"So you've made no progress on finding the ocean-wielder," Ivo presses, startling me from my thoughts.

I glare at his intrusion. "What do you care?" Ivo may work for my father, but that doesn't mean I'll share my intel with him. Soul-ridden he may be, but he is still a *legatus*, which means he'll stab me in the back the first chance he gets if it means more power. There's no way I'll allow him to be the one to bring the girl to my father.

His eyes flick around the room, dingy and sparsely populated as it is. They take note of the door and the pair of men next to us, so deep in their drink, one has sprawled face down in his soup. "The Praeceptor cannot yet invade Siralene. Their armies are too great and their defenses too well fortified. They are not susceptible to rumors of the supernatural, as they all believe their queen *is* supernatural and therefore, will protect them all. Your father will not declare war until he has the other territories, and the prophecy, well controlled and can be sure the Chancellor of Nadjaa will offer no assistance."

I roll my eyes to the ceiling and sigh loudly. "Are we just here to list your failures, Ivo? Because I can assure you, there is not enough time in the world."

The *legatus* ignores my jab. "I believe there is a way we can both find what we seek."

The man next to us grunts in his sleepy stupor and glasses clank at the near empty counter as the maid dries each of them in turn. I lean back in my chair, assessing the captain. After a beat, I say, "Is that so? Perhaps you are more enterprising than I've given you credit for, Ivo."

"The witch-queen collects those more powerful than herself. She always has. It's how she's held her seat for so long, despite many attempts on her life. She was in Ashlaa to find one of those people."

Ashlaa is a small territory on the northern side of Similis. Its warlord was one of the first to pledge allegiance to the Praeceptor as its army is so small, it would never stand a chance against the might of the Dark Militia. It's odd, then, for Ilinka to venture into Praeceptor controlled territory unless she had an exceptionally good reason.

"What is your point?"

"Who do you think she will try to collect next?"

I cross my arms over my chest, the handles of my daggers pressing into my skin. Even though I've hardly a reason to use knives anymore, I rarely take them off, their weight something of a comfort. "So, you think if we follow Ilinka, we'll find the ocean-wielder?"

Ivo nods. Irritation flares that this didn't occur to me first, but I've spent so much time obsessing over the girl's movements, I haven't spared a thought for the witch-queen. But Ivo, it seems, is not willing to lay down and accept his failure. For the first time, I understand why he's ranked so high.

"The girl is supposed to be traveling with two of the Nadjaan Chancellor's stooges, but my most recent information puts her in Baak."

Ivo looks thoughtful. "It would make the witch-queen's job easier if she is not protected in Nadjaa. And therefore, ours. What was she doing in Baak?"

I roll my shoulders, irritation climbing my spine. "She didn't rent a room and only stayed for what appeared to be a sad excuse for a dinner. She was seen in the company of an unknown man dressed in black, but that is all anyone seems to be able to tell me. One has said his hair was white, another was positive it was black. The other didn't seem sure the fellow had even *possessed* any hair."

Ivo frowns. "Are you sure your information is good?"

I wave him off grumpily. This far away, my father's hold on me is near extinct, but I still feel the distant pull of his commands. *Bring the girl to me.* He fears my connection to her will override my loyalty, but he forgets one important thing: the only loyalty I possess is to myself. And I have no intention of hiding from the Praeceptor my entire life.

I will give him everything he asks of me until his trust is unshakeable. I will deliver the girl to him on a silver platter, proving my worth once and for all. And when he finally welcomes me back into his arms, then—then, I will devour him.

And until that moment arrives, I have the fight of the ocean-wielder to look forward to. "My information is always good," I reply airily. "I believe there's a reason these people cannot describe her companion."

"And what would that be?"

As far as I know, the only thing that causes one to lose their memories is losing their soul. But every person at the tavern that night couldn't be soulless. It has to be something else, though what, I have no idea. "Things stir in the Darkness. Surely you know that."

The *legatus* shudders and his shrewd gaze whips around the tavern, as if the Darkness itself hears my words and will strike up in retaliation. He makes a motion over his chest, a superstitious movement familiar to the Xamani tribes of the north. Perhaps it wasn't just the militia who feared the pull of the Nemoran wood: it was their captain as well. I tilt my head. "Do you fear the Darkness, Ivo?"

Hesitation flashes in his eyes. "There are things in this world that don't wish to be spoken of. Things your father wakes in service of power. You'd do well to have some respect for them, boy."

I laugh humorlessly. "I was torn apart and remade in the Darkness, Ivo. *I* am what's been awoken."

Ivo's gaze sharpens as he remembers what sits across

from him. It's become easier to feign humanity over the past few weeks, to pretend that rot doesn't fester beneath my skin, if only for a few moments at a time. But the emptiness inside me has not changed; the hollow that demands to be fed pain; the bloodlust that shades my vision in crimson. Each village I burn, each person I ravage in search of magic, has only proven to me that the ache cannot be satisfied by mediocrity.

You are her only equal.

There is only one person who has never cowed to me. One person strong enough to sate the jagged need of my appetite. The idea has driven me more surely than my father's rage, even more so than my want for revenge against him, though I've yet to speak it aloud.

"Let's go to Siralene and watch Ilinka. If she leads us to the ocean-wielder, we'll both be able to save our necks."

CHAPTER
THIRTEEN

Mirren

We spend the next few days following Avedis down a path only visible to him. We pass through the remainder of the Baakan trees and trail along the rocky cliffs of the far coast. The air is heavy with moisture and sea salt, and the sun grows hotter as we move further south. Every so often, Avedis sits down in the middle of the path, long legs beneath him, and goes completely still. Sometimes it's only for a matter of seconds, and other times, he remains frozen that way for the better part of an hour before he picks the next direction.

Once, after a particularly long session, his face turns white, and he gasps suddenly as if the air has been choked from his lungs.

"What is it?" Cal asks warily.

Dahiitii nickers, and I sway on top of her as she paws at the thick clay dirt. Avedis avoids Cal's gaze, hoisting himself gracefully back atop his own steed. He never listens to the wind from his horse, perhaps afraid he'll be too lost in the whispers and topple out of the saddle. "It has nothing to do with our mission," he hedges. Not an answer.

Fear grips me because I know immediately, he's heard something about Shaw—something that will only further ravage my heart. But still, I find myself asking, "What did he do?"

Avedis sighs and shakes his head, knowing my curiosity won't allow me to let it go. "There has been another village annihilated. A small one, outside Dauphine." He drops his gaze and shakes out his reins. "There were no survivors this time. No one sent to Argentum."

Oh gods.

Calloway swears violently. For a moment, I think he'll turn his horse around and track down Anrai, prophecy be damned. But he only squeezes his eyes shut and rubs his temples, perhaps talking himself out of it.

Max says nothing but raises her gaze to mine. Behind the hard anger, a deep sorrow flickers. It isn't until we've begun riding again that she pulls her horse beside mine and says, "I understand, now... why you left."

I look to her in surprise. It isn't an apology, but she's never owed me one—it's an acknowledgement of her understanding of my heart; that I never would have gone back to Similis if there'd been any piece of Shaw left. "It tore me apart to leave, Max. It felt like admitting he was truly gone."

She looks to the trail ahead, the foliage far lusher than it was in the north. It sprawls across the trail in dense swaths, and dangles from tree limbs in verdant curtains. The entire forest buzzes with life, the chirp of insects and the warble of birds rising and falling in a never-ending melody. "He *is*," Max says firmly. "I couldn't admit it before, but now—now, I know. Anrai is dead. Because if there were even a piece of his true soul left, he would find a way to cut the head off the monster. You know him, Mirren. You know he'd rather be dead than be used as a weapon for his father."

She's right, but the wave of grief that overcomes me is so powerful, it's as if Anrai is giving himself up all over again. I saw his eyes turn black, saw the way he tried to burn children alive with no remorse; I've known my Anrai is gone. But still, I've kept a small, unacknowledged part of me hidden in the back of my mind that somewhere out there, a piece of his soul remains. A piece I inexplicably feel at times, as if it follows me on the breeze, teasing my hair and winding around my heart.

A piece kept alive by Max's assured belief Anrai can still be saved. Because as strong as Max is, she guards her heart well, and she would never allow herself to believe in something that would only hurt her in the end. Her belief bolstered mine that somewhere, our Anrai still exists. I blink back tears. If Max has chosen to accept he's gone, I should, too.

I watch as Cal and Harlan speak softly to one another. Cal motions to something in the distance and Harlan nods with interest. A shy smile spreads across Harlan's face, even as he bounces uncomfortably on the horse. Cal laughs, and something eases minutely in my chest. I breathe in the smell of damp earth and allow my *other* to gently lap up against my heart. *This* is why Anrai is gone. Small moments, big moments—moments of love and pain and life. He wanted those he cared about most to live.

As much as it hurts, as much as I both hate him and love him for it, I can't bring myself to regret the decision. It was his—and he made it with the heart that loved us so well.

"He isn't gone," I tell Max resolutely. "Because we all

carry a piece of him. He cannot remember his heart, but we can. As long as we do, he'll never be truly gone."

Tears shine in Max's eyes and her mouth twists with emotion. But she only nods and clicks her tongue, speeding up her horse to join Cal and Harlan.

∼

When we stop for the night, Avedis sinks to the ground once more, his long lashes brushing his cheekbones as he closes his eyes. He looks so peaceful, he could be sleeping, if not for the upright angle of his spine.

"I suppose that means he isn't going to help with dinner," Cal says with a roll of his eyes. "How convenient."

He settles in to skin a rabbit he caught earlier in the day, and Max begins to build a fire. Their movements are well practiced and efficient, but off balance without Anrai's presence, like walking a well-trod path with only one leg.

Harlan sits next to me as I remove Anrai's bandolier and begin tending each blade. Calloway set them on my bed upon my return to Nadjaa, claiming he preferred his bow, but I recognize the kindness of it: giving me something of Anrai's to touch. Their handles glint in the setting sun, the ornate carvings appearing somehow more alive in the light.

"Those are nice," Harlan says, watching with interest as I begin to sharpen the first blade. He sets the Boundary hunter's gun down beside him, the sleek lines of the weapon uncomfortably discordant against the rustic view of the trees. We haven't talked much on the journey here, but all my worry for Harlan fitting into Ferusa was misplaced. His countenance is as pleasant here as it was in Similis. He jokes with Cal and has convinced Avedis to teach him how to use a sword during quiet nights on the road. He's even managed to win Max over, content to allow her to admonish his naivete and then act as his personal bodyguard.

I stiffen, my throat suddenly feeling like sand. "They are—they *were*—Shaw's."

"The man with the fire?" Harlan asks, but his voice holds no judgement. "It seems you know him well."

"Knew," I correct in a strangled voice. "Not anymore."

It feels wrong, to sit here with Harlan and speak of Anrai, though I'm not sure why. I've made Harlan no promises other than to help Similis and he's made no declarations to me. But the Binding mark is permanently branded on our arms, and I've been too cowardly to ask if he expects everything that comes along with that. I don't think I can bear to know if those expectations are why he followed me through the Boundary—why he continues to see the good in me that I'm not even sure exists any longer.

His golden hair has grown longer in our short time in Ferusa, his skin subtly darkened by the sun. The fresh air and wild living somehow suit him, having only grown more handsome. He gazes at me so warmly, I have to look away before I fall before him and confess all the ways I don't deserve that look.

You are the light, and I am the dark. I will ruin you.

Hadn't that been my first thought when we were Bound? I hadn't even known all the ways it would come true. He's uprooted his entire existence and gotten himself Outcast, all for a girl whose heart has been utterly shattered by someone else. A girl only filled with bitterness and regret, who lives every moment fearing she will tumble too far into it.

Before I can say any of this, Avedis' eyes flick open. He's to his feet with his sword drawn before I can blink, staring into the depths of the trees. Cal strings his bow, wide eyed and wary, and Max unsheathes her twin falchions, looking almost excited for whatever comes next.

Harlan and I scramble to our feet as a strong wind begins to blow through the trees. It isn't like any wind I've ever witnessed, its power bending thousand-year-old trees at their trunks. The gale roars as branches rip free and shoot into the shadows. I feel breathless against the pressure of it, watching as Avedis stands perfectly still, directing the maelstrom of sudden chaos.

After another moment, the wind dies down, the calm silence disconcerting in contrast with the noise of the storm. Avedis nods toward the forest. "They're in there," he says to Cal and Max.

Cal disappears into the trees with his bow still drawn, while Max glares warily at Avedis. After a moment, Cal returns, this time moving much more slowly, and dragging an unconscious body with him.

"There are two more," Avedis tells Max, sounding almost bored. "But we only need one."

The man is dark skinned, dressed in regalia that looks as if it used to be a pristine shade of white, but has now been scuffed and dirtied by his unconscious trip through the forest. Cal drops him in front of us, panting slightly. His eyes rove over the soldier and something in his face hardens.

"Who are they?" Max asks.

Avedis doesn't bother to reply, stepping over the soldier. His face holds none of the affable charm I've grown accustomed to. Now, as he stares down, he is emotionless and sharp—the man who once tried to kill me. After a beat, he says, "I know who has the earth-shaker." There is no victory in his voice. Instead, he sounds oddly hollow.

Avedis slaps the soldier perfunctorily across the face. The man's head lolls, but he groans softly as he comes to. The assassin's lips peel back from his teeth, but it is not a smile that graces his face. It's more like the snarl of a Ditya wolf. He stares at the soldier, his dark eyes glittering. "You tell your witch-queen you've found the ocean-wielder as she asked." He brings his fist down hard against the man's face, and I swallow roughly as the sound of shattering bone cracks through the silence.

Avedis straightens, his eyes still bright, as he says, "you tell Akari Ilinka she will rue the day she gave the order to hunt the ocean-wielder. Because now, she is coming."

CHAPTER
FOURTEEN

Mirren

Siralene is a tropical paradise at the southernmost tip of the continent. It protrudes further into the Storven Sea than Nadjaa, a mecca of pristine white buildings and bright verdant roofs. Plants of all shapes and sizes spill from hanging boxes lining the street, their plump leaves and vibrant flowers painting the city in splashes of color. The city's beauty is equal to Nadjaa's with one distinct difference—Siralene's dazzling skyline is the fruit of slave labor.

Slaves work everywhere in the thick heat: some rebuild roads, their malnourished bodies bowing beneath huge loads of rock; some tend to the plants that line the streets and walkways, while others carry water and scrub the wash with red-chapped hands. Though the slaves are of differing heritages, pilfered as they were from every corner of Ferusa, it is easy to distinguish them from the Siraleni citizens as thick black bands have been tattooed around their necks. Even the children's.

"Are they all spoils of war?" I ask Max, watching as the citizens of Siralene carry about their lives, clad in draping silks of pale blues, sky pinks and shimmering golds, oblivious to the people who serve them and clean up after them. As if they are no more than pieces of machinery.

"Some of them," Max replies, falling into step beside me. The dark gray of her loose-fitting clothes is perfect for traveling and training, but here, the color stands out like a sore thumb. "Cal told me some of them are Siraleni themselves. If you're homeless, or troubled, or any other sort of slight on their territory, the guards steal you away to a workhouse."

My *other* surges inside me, fed both by anger at the injustice and the close proximity to the sea. So near, its call ensnares me. Max, feeling me tense, says softly, "There will be a time, Mirren. But it isn't now."

A woman pushes a slave boy down the stairs, her voice echoing shrilly between buildings as she berates him. My power thrashes. "I won't placate myself by saying there will be a better time to free someone, Max. How is there ever a better time than now?"

On the other side of me, Harlan agrees, looking torn between disgust and outright devastation. He grips the rifle wedged under his shoulder, the first time I've ever seen him willingly reach for the weapon.

"When we grant these slaves the power you have and they are able to take their own vengeance," Max replies without looking at either of us. Instead, she begins climbing the stairs to the ivory palace with a pleasant smile pasted on her face. It looks so out of character, for a moment, I almost forget my anger and remember why we're here. To play a part to distract a bloodthirsty queen from our true goal. "We cannot take on Ilinka's entire army by ourselves and the slaves will be punished if we try. But if we succeed in freeing magic and restoring balance, the people *can*. We work for them, Mirren. For them and every other downtrodden person in Ferusa. Don't lose sight of that."

I breathe in her words, letting them settle over my power, but it's become more difficult to soothe. Maybe it's because the only things I have to feed it lately are anger and sorrow and loss; or it's because I gave too much of myself when I faced Shaw, falling so far over the edge, it's no longer possible to restore a healthy balance.

Fear has kept me from examining the answer too closely. I still awaken in the night, straddled between humanity and the depths of my *other,* the feeling of falling imprinted on my lungs. I fell without thought when I faced Shaw; what will happen if I do it again? If I go too far, will I become like him? A shell of who I used to be, everything tying me to life forgotten somewhere on the surface?

"She's right," Harlan says ruefully, his grip relaxing on the rifle. "We'll play our part to help Avedis and Cal and then we'll get out of here as soon as we can."

Akari Ilinka's home can only be described as an opulent palace. Made of shining white stone and elaborate arches, it stretches for what seems like miles of coastline. The entrance is open and airy, filled with creamy light and gauzy curtains that billow lightly in the ocean breeze. Everything gleams in the sunlight, but I know better than most: sometimes light only exists to blind you from the twisted shades of reality.

Guards line every entrance of the palace, but just like the ones at the city's boundary, they pay us no mind. They stand eerily still, hands curled around long spears and eyes scanning the horizon. Avedis knew we were being followed, shortly after determining it was Akari Ilinka that possesses the earth-wielder. He said the queen was laying low, determining the best way to add me to her collection of powerful subjects. Aside from the one guard we freed to relay our message, the rest of them remain tied up in the forest outside the city.

Now, the queen knows I will not be taken by force. I come only of my own accord.

A woman with dark skin and closely shorn hair steps from behind the guards, her figure diminutive in comparison with the bulk of the guards'. She gestures us forward with a warm smile, as if we haven't accosted her soldiers and she's merely been expecting us for tea. Dressed in Siraleni garb, strategically knotted silks drape her petite body and flow down past her sandaled feet. "Hello, Ocean-wielder," she says, her voice like warm butter. "I am Shina, the queen's personal attendant. Her Majesty was so pleased to learn you've come to Siralene to form an alliance."

I swallow, forcing myself not to look at Max. We knew the warlord wanted me on her side, whether by force or alliance, it didn't appear to matter, but I still wasn't expecting to be ushered straight into the palace. Ilinka must be very confident in her soldiers if she thinks to control me so easily.

Pasting a smile on my face, I bow my head to the woman and step forward. Witch-queen or not, with the sea this close, I'm a formidable foe and we need to buy time for Avedis and Cal to discover where she keeps the earth-wielder.

Shina leads us past the guards and down a few sprawling hallways, white pillars sparkling against the cerulean sky. We pass a slave woman scrubbing the white floors, while others bustle between rooms, polishing marble busts and gold fixtures. They look more well fed than those we passed in the streets, but none of them lift their eyes to meet my gaze.

After a few moments, Shina bows us through an ornate archway leading to a large balcony.

"Here goes nothing," Max mutters.

It's not the throne room I expect from a woman who fancies herself a queen, but instead, a lush terrace that fans out against the eastern horizon. Thick vines cover the walls in deep green, contrasted by the curtains of exotic blooms that thread between them. A small stream winds across the marble floor, bubbling cheerfully over sparkling gold pebbles, until it finally spills out over the exposed edge. A low table made of scrubbed sea wood is set for an elaborate dinner, gilded plates and silverware polished until they gleam in the sun.

And seated at the head is the most regal-looking woman I've ever seen.

She is dressed in the same fashion as Shina, gossamer and golden ties woven seductively around her body, but unlike the attendant, everything about this woman screams extravagance. Fat jewels sparkle between the ties, the largest one, a gem of clear emerald, set in a circlet atop her head. Her umber skin has been dusted with gold, her full lips painted a deadly shade of red. Her hair is a silky curtain that spills over her shoulder, more gemstones sparkling between its inky black strands, and she pushes it back with a delicately painted hand as her upturned eyes take in our disheveled appearance.

Indeed, Akari Ilinka looks every bit the queen and not at all the witch. I suddenly wish we'd brought any sort of clothing with us that isn't the overlarge cloak and dusty leggings I've been traveling in for Covinus-knows how long.

"Your Majesty, Akari Ilinka, Queen of Siralene and the Southern Realm," Shina announces.

I can almost hear the roll of Max's eyes as we sink into a reluctant bow.

The queen watches us for a long moment, seeming to enjoy the sight of me beneath her. Finally, she waves us up lazily. "Shina, have the slaves prepare a meal for our esteemed guests," she says, eyeing her blood-red nails as if they're more interesting than we are. "Something lavish," she adds as an afterthought.

The thought of a slave being forced to prepare my food sends a hot wave of nausea through me. "That won't be necessary, Your Majesty."

The witch-queen's face twists in quick displeasure, her graciousness suddenly knife-edged. "Is there something wrong with the food I offer you, Ocean-wielder?"

I press my lips together, considering my words. I've never mastered the clever tongue or smooth manners needed to navigate politics, my mouth having always been more of a hindrance than a help. Someone like Avedis would know exactly how to weave the precise amounts of courtesy and savagery needed, but he didn't volunteer to show his face and I never could have asked him to. He's better left to the shadows with Cal, searching the wind for any sign of the earth-wielder and protecting us from afar.

"The ocean-wielder is Similian," Harlan explains genially, and my shoulders relax slightly. Harlan, who's always embodied the best of the Keys, is adept at soothing words and polite banter. "It is considered bad form to eat food prepared by another's hand."

The queen's red mouth turns down in disgust, but something like respect shines in her eyes as she runs them up the length of Harlan. "And who are you?"

"Harlan Astor, Your Majesty."

"He's the ocean-wielder's advisor," Max interrupts, the blunt force of her tone drawing the queen's greedy gaze away from Harlan. "As am I."

Akari narrows her eyes shrewdly. "You look familiar girl."

"I'd imagine so as your soldiers have been following us for a week." Max smiles sweetly.

The witch-queen is undeterred. "Are you from the Isles?"

"No." Max raises her chin defiantly.

Akari tilts her head, her gaze growing sharp as if she can pierce through Max's skin and see into her secrets beneath. "What is your name?"

"Maxwell."

"That...is not a name of island descent," the queen concedes slowly, but she doesn't seem appeased. If anything, her interest in Max only appears to grow, her eyes shining with the same sort of greed she'd focused on Harlan. A collector, Avedis had said. Apparently, it is not only power she desires.

"I am not from the islands. I am Nadjaan," Max replies with a bored look.

I school my face into neutrality at Max's bold-faced lie. She hardly speaks of where she is from, but Anrai mentioned once she was born in the southern isles. I wonder again at what secrets Max's past holds.

Akari Ilinka makes a noncommittal noise, and as if losing interest in the entire conversation, abruptly barks at Shina, "Go. Now."

The attendant hurries off, leaving the three of us alone. There are no guards I can see, and I wonder again what the queen is playing at, allowing me to walk so freely into the heart of her home. Does she not see me as a threat? Or is it her belief she is more powerful?

She crosses her legs languidly, revealing jeweled slippers and a long swath of shining skin. "Normally, I'd wait until after dinner to discuss alliances like a civilized person, but as you all appear unversed in manners, shall we be frank?" She motions for us to sit across from her with an air of irritation.

We sink low into the emerald-green cushions, an affect I'm sure is intentional as we now have to stare up at the warlord like children. "Are you here on behalf of yourselves, or on behalf of your foolish Chancellor?"

"We're here because you had your soldiers hunt us like animals," Max bites out.

The witch-queen's mouth curves into a cutting smile. "I would be remiss if I didn't keep tabs on someone as dangerous," her eyes rove over me and I swat my braid over my shoulder uncomfortably, "or as powerful as you are."

"An alliance with Nadjaa would be helpful to your fight against the Praeceptor," Harlan offers, attempting to redirect the conversation.

Akari tilts her head, looking bored once more. "Your Chancellor would see the whole world shrivel to dust if it meant Nadjaa still thrives. He won't move from his safe little bay until he is forced, and even then, it would only be to *talk*. Men like him do not shape the world," her eyes glow as they meet mine. "Women like us do."

I try not to shift again under her scrutiny, even as her words lay unpleasantly on my chest. No matter the power I possess, I will never seek to wield it against others as she does.

Unless you lose your humanity. Then, who knows what you'd be capable of.

Pushing the words away, I focus on the witch-queen. "We speak only for ourselves. We have no desire to watch the Praeceptor burn Ferusa and wished to extend our friendship."

"Friendship," Akari muses, wiggling her hips in her chair. "You have a lot to learn about the world if you think *friendship* will keep the Praeceptor at bay. Men will not be defeated by good hearts and happy thoughts. Do you know why they call me a witch-queen, Ocean-wielder?"

I shake my head.

"Because men *fear* powerful women. They think us soft-hearted and weak and if one of us manages to claw our way to the top, they cannot understand how. And so, they decry it supernatural to soothe their cowardly souls. Men will take everything for themselves and nothing, especially something as idealistic as friendship, will keep them from it. If you wish to get anywhere in this world, you will understand this now: power is the only language they speak, and power is what you will give me if you wish to defeat Cullen."

I grit my teeth. "I will kill for no one. Including you, Your Majesty."

"No one?" she asks with a shrewd smile that sends my heart plummeting into my stomach. "From what I've heard, that isn't quite true."

At her words, I hear the sound of Shivhai's last gasp and the fracture in my soul suddenly aches ferociously. The queen watches me with a malicious glint, and I force myself to meet her gaze. She wishes to unsettle me with her knowledge, but as someone who keeps company with a wind-speaker, it will be more difficult than that. "I've heard you collect weapons, Queen. I won't be one of them."

Akari heaves a long-suffering sigh. "Then why have you

come into the heart of my city, if not to kill for me? Do you know that I do not accept defeat? Have you not heard the stories of the time before the Blood Alliance when the Praeceptor came for my land? I slayed every one of his soldiers and drank their blood on the battlefield. I gutted his wife and strung her up for Ferusa to see. I have always known what I want and how to take it. You may have power, Ocean-wielder, but make no mistake—you are *not* powerful. One is not gifted power; one must *take* it. And I will take yours, whether you wish me to or not."

Max stands, sliding a dagger from beneath her cloak. She'd given up her twin falchions in favor of appearing less threatening when entering the palace, but I should have known she'd never leave herself vulnerable. "Is that a threat, *Queen?*"

Ilinka only laughs, the contrast of her venomous red lips against sparkling white teeth reminding me eerily of blood. "It is a promise, Maxwell of Nadjaa. Is it not better to be mine, to share in power and be safe in the womb of Siralene? Safe from men who would burn the world?"

I've seen the scars left from belonging to the witch-queen. There will be no sharing of anything. She will use me as she used Avedis, and even if she does defeat Cullen, Ferusa will be no better off. Warlords and their desires only ravage the land; sacrificing whoever they deem lesser to reach their goals. The only way to rise from the Darkness is to *ruin* people like Akari Ilinka: people that deem themselves worthy of deciding who lives and who dies. And the only way to do that is to complete the Prophecy.

My *other* laps at the shores of my anger, reminding me again why I'm here.

She keeps him well hidden, Sea Speaker, Avedis' voice whispers in my ear, carried on the slight breeze blowing in off the Storven. I start, looking around wildly for any sign of the assassin, but no one else appears to have heard. *You must stall longer. We will have to continue our search through the night.*

Akari gazes at me hungrily, awaiting my response. Max still looks murderous. Only Harlan appears at ease as he watches me quietly

I look to the witch-queen. "I have no wish for the Praeceptor's rule. May we take the night to consider your offer?"

The queen looks pleased at my sudden change of heart. At her quick nod, more than thirty guards appear from behind the thick curtains of foliage. I was right to think we weren't alone. Had she planned on ambushing me? "Escort the girl and her advisors to the east wing. Make sure they enjoy all the luxuries Siralene has to offer."

We stand, Harlan looking distinctly relieved as Max sheaths her daggers rather unwillingly. Akari doesn't take her dark eyes from mine. "Only the weak put others before themselves. You would do well to forget your Similian upbringing and spare yourself the pain of trying to save people who won't even be grateful. Take the safety I offer you."

∼

Despite being little more than prisoners, the queen houses us in luxurious quarters, a distinct reminder of what we're to gain by serving her. The apartments are as airy as the rest of the palace, the large room opening to another small balcony draped in opulent foliage. A large bed swathed in light silks looks particularly inviting, but I'll never be able to sleep with the film of travel dust that coats my skin.

The bathtub is more of a pool, bubbling and sunk

deeply into the floor. I step into it reluctantly, guilt weighing on my heart. There is no running water here as there is in Nadjaa and I wonder how many slaves were forced to carry buckets up the tower stairs in order for me to be clean. Though sloughing the grime from my skin is necessary, I refuse to enjoy it. Washing quickly, I jump from the water as if somehow, the speed of the bath can make any of this right.

Are you safe, lady? Avedis' voice swirls through the room, just as I slip a gauzy nightgown over my head. His soft breeze rustles the leaves outside, the sound soft and tinkling. I blush at having almost been caught naked, distinctly thankful Avedis can only hear what the wind does, rather than see.

"I'm fine," I tell the empty room, feeling rather foolish. "I don't know how long we'll be able to keep her suspended like this. She seems inclined to take me forcefully if I don't agree to serve her."

I swear, the breeze itself laughs ruefully. *She is not one to be denied,* Avedis replies in a voice so bitter, I wonder what else she took from him. Judging by the way she appeared ready to devour Harlan, I can guess. *Calloway and I continue our search and hope to know more by morning. If you need help, just whisper on the wind. I won't be far away.*

I nod, heading toward the bed. The weight of the day feels so heavy, I find myself saying, "Avedis?"

After a moment's pause, the wind sweeps through the room once more. *Yes?*

"Thank you for coming here to help us. It was too much to ask of anyone, to return to the place of their trauma. Most would have refused."

I can almost feel his blush. Finally, he replies, *it is you who has helped me, Mirren. I have not felt the warmth of another's trust since I was a boy. And I thank you for yours.*

With one last gust, the room falls still once more. I climb into the bed, nestling into the soft blankets, but sleep won't come. I stare at the canopy, wondering what my brother is doing half a continent away. Does he miss me? Does he regret not coming?

Does he know the entire world is falling apart around Similis and that I may not be strong enough to save it?

After what feels like ages of worry gnawing at my throat, the flower vines rustle outside the archway once more. I roll my eyes with a smile. "I said I'll be fine," I call out in a sing song voice. Hopping out of bed, I step onto the balcony, the chill of the white stone biting my bare feet. The night smells of sweet blooms and ocean and air. My *other* settles contently as I gaze at the shores of the Storven. This close to the sea, Avedis is silly to worry about leaving me unprotected. For an assassin, he can also be something of an overgrown mother hen.

"Will you, though?"

Every bit of my *other* freezes in my veins as the voice trails back to me. A sound both haunting and familiar; one I've longed to hear a million times and also, never wish to hear again.

It is not Avedis who steps from the shadows of the eves.

Grinning wickedly, pale eyes glinting in the moonlight, Anrai Shaw steps toward me. "Hello, Lemming."

CHAPTER
FIFTEEN

Mirren

His face is breathlessly cruel and just as handsome as it is in every one of my dreams. He smiles as he steps from the shadows, and I hate that after everything, it still devastates me. Until this moment, I believed my heart shattered. But now, as the fragments crumble to a dust finer than sand, I understand there is still so much more hurt to feel.

"Mirren," Shaw drawls, slinking toward me.

I flinch at the sound of my name on his lips, lilting in his accent, but somehow, still razor-sharp. "What?" He cocks his head curiously. "Don't like being called by your name these days? Prefer something more melodramatic?" He brings a long finger to his lower lip, pretending to ponder. His memory appears to have returned, but it has not brought his empathy with it. "Wave-tamer? Ocean-wielder? Or my personal favorite, as of late, Prophecy Bringer?"

"I'd prefer not to be called anything by you," I manage icily, as my hands tremble at my sides.

His grin turns decadent. "Surely you don't mean that,"

he tsks, sauntering closer. "A relationship such as ours deserves the intimacy of doing away with titles, don't you think?"

My heart runs roughshod in my chest and my *other* rises in an agitated wave. It crashes against me, wanting to both consume Shaw and destroy him at once. "You're no longer who you once were. We have no relationship," I tell him, steeling my voice.

He snarls, taking three large steps forward, crowding me against the palace wall. Leaves and flower petals tangle in my hair as I try to stretch as far from him as I can. He smells the same, the scent of open air and woodsmoke and spice, and I struggle not to inhale. How unfair, that his scent remains delicious as ever, while the rest of him is a toiling pit of depravity.

"No relationship?" he growls. He shoves his nose into the juncture of my throat and inhales sharply, all without touching me. "I know the scent of you," he whispers, his hot breath tickling my skin, "I know the sweet taste of you on my tongue and the timbre of your moans when you find your pleasure."

I slam my eyes shut and go still. Remind my traitorous body he is soulless. Murderous. Utterly evil. But heat ravages through me anyway, insistent and wanting.

"Shall I remind you just how deserving I am of your name?" Shaw murmurs against my ear, his voice so low, I have to clench my thighs together. His hands are planted on either side of my head, but in spite of his words, he keeps his body apart from mine. "Or perhaps I could remind you how much you loved to scream mine?"

I open my eyes. Force myself to meet his gaze. Shaw used to burn so hot when he looked at me, an all-consuming inferno that sparked in my soul. Now, there is only ash and destruction. The chilled emptiness of a forest after a wildfire has torn through, gray and dead. At once, my body goes cold. "Why are you here?"

"For you," he replies as if this is obvious.

"To kill me, you mean?"

Shaw chuckles lightly, waving an indolent hand. "I have orders to bring you to the Praeceptor. What he does with you is not my concern."

I study the casual sweep of his brow, the relaxed set of his chiseled jaw—indeed, he looks highly unbothered by the thought of me being tortured at his father's hand. His movements are languid, lazy even; there is none of the taut readiness that was once a defining feature of his. Heat of a different sort rises within me, a maelstrom of anger and hurt that has my mouth moving before I can consider my words. "And do you always do what you're told?"

His face hardens, all laziness gone in an instant. "I am the Heir of the Praeceptor. His wants are mine. And if he wants to bleed you dry in his dungeons and find how deeply that power of yours is rooted, then I desire it as well."

I scoff in disgust. His nostrils flare in response. Of all we've lost, it seems the way under each other's skin still remains, the path to the wildest parts of ourselves as familiar as ever. "I guess it was your soul that made you strong." Disentangling my braid irritably from the flower vines, I take two large steps toward him. His feet measure mine as he backs up, always keeping the same amount of distance between us. "Without it, you're a coward—an addict, willing to degrade yourself for your father just to get your fix of pain."

Shaw's gaze is no longer a desolate wasteland. The pale blue seems to surge, an explosion of heated malice. His mouth twists in rage and I feel a glimmer of satisfaction. He is capable of feeling *something* even if it's only anger. "You know nothing of *pain*, Lemming. Nothing of hunger. Perhaps my father will allow me into the dark of your cell to teach you all the ways of Darkness in which you're ignorant."

I swallow roughly. Once, the promise of a dark place alone with him was enough to turn me molten, but now, it sinks in my stomach like heavy lead. Max is right—Anrai is truly gone. Protecting those he cared about defined the shape of him, resided in the very lining of his skin, and if there were any bit of him left inside the shell of Shaw's body, he would ravage the world with it to keep me safe.

I have been grief-stricken and angry and bitter, but for the first time since Cullen took Anrai's soul, I find myself hopeless. Whatever it is that whispers in my ear as I dream, whatever it is that caresses me in the light of the moon—it has all been desperate imagination. Nothing of Anrai survives.

"Get out," I growl as shades of red overtake my vision. How dare he stand here and torture me with the face of my dead. How arrogant of him to assume I won't strike him down where he stands; that I won't end Anrai's suffering once and for all. I should have done it when I saw him in Havay, should have put an end to all the destruction.

Only the vague memory of the prophecy keeps my power balled tightly inside me as I rush at him, pounding my fists against his chest. "Get out!" I scream, finally undone.

The moment my hands touch him, he roars in agony. I back up in horror as he doubles over in pain, pulling at his hair and clawing at his face the same way he did in Havay. The action is more animal than human, desperate and brutal. I stare down at my hands in shock. What have I done to him?

His breathing comes in pained gasps, his shoulders heaving as he raises his eyes to mine. I flinch for the second time tonight: because the hatred and hunger that stare back at me is inhuman.

"You will regret this, witch. Every soul I send to the Darkness after this will be on your hands until you give yourself to me. Every child's scream of pain as I melt their skin from their bones will echo in the chamber of your soul." He backs away from me, his lips curled back from his teeth, his eyes sparkling.

He looks like he did in Havay—utterly mad.

"I will find a way to touch you and when I do—when I do, I will take every memory of pleasure you have and turn them to pain. You will feed *my* hunger, until you feel it in every shadowed place of you...and by the end, you will beg for the Darkness as a reprieve." Before I can respond, he leaps from the balcony into the shadows below.

I stand frozen, staring at the spot he stood for a long time after. Anrai is gone, but I still need Shaw for the prophecy.

And he's just handed me the way to get to him.

⁓

Shaw

I'd waited days to see her. In the end, Ivo and I hadn't even needed to trail Akari's guard as I'd known where the ocean-wielder was long before we arrived in Siralene. Familiar agony had ravaged through me as if she stood next to me with an axe and cleaved my skull in half. I'd fallen from my horse and awoken hours later to the *legatus* staring at me warily, like I was insane and liable to have another fit at any moment.

But I felt no worry. After weeks of searching, she was close enough to be breathing the same ocean air. And to the Heir, pain is no obstacle. I was birthed in its depths; have grown strong on its bloody nectar. I know it as a child would know a mother.

So rather than fighting it, this time, I welcomed it.

I moved slowly, at first, drawing closer to the girl with each passing day. I would breathe through the agony, my lungs burning as I let it wash over me. I kept it close to my heart, feeding it to the flame, until everything burned. And when everything burned—when there was nothing but suffering and I couldn't remember ever living without it—I learned to move through it like it was the only way I'd ever moved.

But that was before she touched me.

If I thought I knew pain before, it was nothing to the feel of her hands on my chest. What I'd experienced in the bowels of the Castellium was a soft trickle to the weight of Mirren's touch, the crash as great as the Storven Sea. I couldn't breathe, couldn't think beyond the pure heaviness.

And still, somehow, I'd had to use every ounce of strength I had left to keep my body from sacrificing itself at her feet. It fought wildly, straining to touch her again as if it subsisted on the pain she served. For a body so willing to debase itself to survive, it was unnervingly quick to surrender.

Hours later, cold sweat still coats my skin and my heart pounds uncomfortably in my chest. Ivo has long since retired to his room, a meek slave girl trailing behind him, and still, I lie awake. If the *legatus* has any concerns about his ability to capture the witch-queen, he hasn't shared them with me. For as much as we're supposed to be working together, he's been cagey and secretive. He was gone for hours this morning and I still haven't determined where he'd been.

But I haven't concerned myself much with it. If he fails in his goal, it will only make my victory appear so much sweeter when I drag the ocean-wielder in front of my father, bound and weak.

If I can just figure out how to do that now that I've found her. My power cannot defeat Mirren, for hers matches mine in every sense of the word. And I cannot physically overpower her without the ability to touch her. Irritation rolls through me. I won't be able to take the girl by force.

You're going to be severely disappointed if you go around thinking everyone has the same heart you do.

The words echo back to me from another time, rising up from the depths of a memory that is someone else's. A wicked smile crawls across my face. I've hated the pull of these memories—the way they wind around me like a plague, infecting me with weakness. But what if they're exactly what I need to force the girl's hand?

Because just as she knows me—the way to goad my power, my anger, to the surface of my skin—*I know her.*

I close my eyes and lean back into the bed, enjoying the scratchy blankets against my bare skin. It's better than a cold metal table, at the very least. Better than rough stone.

I've never willingly waded into the murky depths of Anrai Shaw's memories and for a moment, I fear it won't work. There is nothing there but emptiness. I frown. Perhaps they are a separate entity from myself now that I'm soulless, controlled not by my will, but by their own wants.

It would certainly seem that way with their penchant for attacking me at the most inopportune times.

But as I relax into the mattress, they come: first as a whisper and then a wave. I fight my way through them, drowning at sea—the copper haired man washes over me first and I suck in a sharp breath, bracing myself against whatever it will be. But it is innocuous this time. Only the man, Cal, smiling at me while fixing a button on my shirt. I push the memory aside, twisting uncomfortably atop the thread-bare quilt. I don't like the man's smile, the way the familiar curve of it seems to call to me.

Max comes to me next, her indignant anger echoing in a kitchen. There is anger in most her memories, but it isn't the sort I understand—it doesn't rage and destroy, like mine. It protects, a hard shell of armor around a softness I find repulsive. I push through, the current of memory content to pull me along. Through the depths of a history I no longer feel and weaknesses I no longer possess.

Finally, I fall into the memory of Mirren. Balling the sheets in my fists, I remind myself to remain present, but it proves futile. I swim as hard as I can, my lungs expanding and my muscles straining, but my limbs are useless against the current of her. I'm pulled in a thousand directions, memories of the corner of her smile and the bob of her foot just as powerful as those of her stabbing a *legatus* in the neck and drowning an assassin on land.

I force my panic down and let myself be carried by the tide of her. Slowing my breathing, I allow Mirren's emotions to roll over me. I have none of my own, so they overtake my empty chest like the crash of a wave on a dry shore, just as quickly gone.

And in all of them, I feel her heart.

I thought it made of steel and resolve, airtight and

hardened by the strength of her fight. But it isn't. It's soft, like a sponge that soaks up other's pain. She feeds those who have earned no food and forgives those who have wronged her. I watch the moment she forgives *me* in the darkness outside a mountain cave—the man who kidnapped and hurt her.

She may be powerful, but the ocean-wielder is not impenetrable. I cannot touch her skin, but with some leverage, I'll be able to force her heart. My father fears my old memories are a weakness, but now, I see them for what they are: a weapon.

I sit up straight, grabbing for my shirt and throwing it over my head. I don't find Ivo. His failures are no concern to me, not when I now stand a chance of bringing my father the girl. Buckling my bandolier over my chest, I imagine the Praeceptor's face when I give him what he most wants.

Control of the Prophecy. It will be enough to prove my worth. To get close to him.

I shove my feet in my boots and head down the hall, not bothering to close the door. I won't be returning to the decrepit inn. The tavern below is empty, and I slip out the front door into the lantern lit streets. Daylight is still a few hours off, but I've always been more comfortable in the shadows.

And by the time dawn breaks, I'll have pulled Mirren into them with me.

Chapter
Sixteen

Calloway

After all these years, the smell still turns my stomach.

A scent unique only to Siralene: the tang of the sand-crusted shores that surround the city mingled with the earthiness of the sunbaked pavers snaking between houses. It smells of my sister Lila's mischievous smile, her flaming red hair lit by the long summer sun as she cajoled me into jumping from the tide pool cliffs. She was always braver than me—braver than anyone, really—and more than adept at weaponizing her seniority to goad my little sister Vee and I into an assortment of ill-fated adventures.

Vee, whose true name was Valeria but she insisted it was far too feminine, was of a far more serious nature. A permanent line creased the skin between her brows as she surveyed Lila's newest scheme, an indelible exhale of consternation on her lips. But she would always come, out of sibling responsibility or because she secretly enjoyed our romps, I'll never know. And on the rare occasion we made her laugh, it was magic. I turned into the silliest version of myself around Vee, willing to do whatever it took to earn that laugh.

The scent of Siralene is *them*. Mama and Papa. Lila and Vee. Home.

Bile fills my mouth again as I step out of the tavern and inhale sharply. By all accounts, it's the most pleasant-smelling city on the continent—the witch-queen and her guard force the slaves to clean at all hours of the day, and anything unsightly, including people, is immediately swept away—but for me, the fragrant air is always tinged with smoke. Burning skin and scorched hair.

I survey the familiar gleaming streets before continuing on to the next establishment. A frigid breeze sweeps up the bottom of my cloak, tickling the bare skin of my back with maddening accuracy. I swat at it like it's an errant bug. "Stop that," I mutter mutinously, garnering a few alarmed yelps from a nearby group of chattering wives.

I shoot them an apologetic look as the air shudders in silent laughter. I scowl, in no mood for the assassin's brand of humor. "Has anyone ever told you you're a nosey bastard?"

The wind blows the hood from my head in response, taking my hair from a coiffed masterpiece to something more closely resembling a bird's nest. I flip off the empty street, earning a wave of speculative whispers that follow me around the next corner. They probably think I'm mad, a dangerous thing to be in Siralene. One whiff of weakness and Ilinka's guards will come sweep you off to the nearest workhouse.

The risk is worth it, if only to stick it to Avedis.

"No one is going to tell me a thing with this hair," I grunt unhappily.

I was under the impression you weren't having much luck,

styled hair notwithstanding, Avedis replies, his voice more wind than words. It trails after me to my infernal irritation.

I flip him off once more for good measure, before continuing on. The sun set hours ago and fire dances cheerfully inside the iron lanterns lining the street. The assassin isn't wrong, but I'd rather listen to a yamardu sing than admit it to him. "The last three places are all frequented by the witch-queen's personal guard and drunk as they were, they knew nothing about an earth-wielder. Have you had any luck near the palace?"

The wind sweeps between my feet, causing the earth to feel rather unsteady and me to trip over my own ankles. I glare furiously at the empty air, wishing desperately there was something here of his solid enough to hit.

The palace is large, but I have swept almost every corner of it and found nothing. Not a whisper in the entire city of anyone with powers. They only speak of the power of their queen.

I scoff loudly, thankful no one is around to hear. "Ilinka's only power is stolen."

I take Avedis' silence as one of agreement. It's an odd truce I keep with the assassin. He was of the very guard I've spent my life hating, murderous and money seeking, but he is also one of the only people who truly understands the depravity of Akari Ilinka.

And he knows their names. Their farm has been given to another noble family in the queen's favor, their identities scratched from Siraleni record. Since their deaths, my family only exists in my memory, and it is something of a relief to share the burden with someone.

"You lived in the palace, Avedis. Where does she keep her prisoners?"

Everyone in the palace, in the guard and in Siralene, is

Akari's prisoner, Calloway. Even the nobles do not have the choices they imagine.

I grit my teeth. He's right. And the longer it takes to find the earth-wielder, the longer Mirren, Max, and Harlan are in her web. Anxiety clenches my stomach, along with shame. I should have accompanied them to the palace. Mirren said it was because I know the streets of Siralene that I'd be more helpful searching the city for any signs, but I know better. It was pity.

She didn't want to force me to face my family's killer, the same way she didn't want to force Avedis.

And for better or worse, for good reasons or bad, we both allowed it. Now, there is only getting through it.

It's beginning to feel like an impossible task. Avedis is more than effective at finding people, but only if someone speaks of them first. Even a whisper between friends. But Akari Ilinka has somehow managed to seal up every leak, even those of lovers. And if no one speaks, Siralene is too large a territory to physically search every corner.

I shiver, smoothing my hair and pulling my cloak close once more. "There's one more establishment known for being frequented by Ilinka's guards. I'll go see what I can find out. You've got an eye on our friends?"

They are safe as they can be, so close to the queen.

I don't miss the bitterness in his tone, but for now, I leave it alone. Someday, the conversation will be had, and I will have to decide once and for all which side I reside on. If the Darkness has taught me anything, it's that life is too short to hold a grudge. It's been easy to preach peace and forgiveness from the other side of the continent, to insist hatred only hurts those who harbor it. It's a different thing entirely to be faced with the truth of it—with the reality of allowing the person who stole your entire life to walk freely.

When I duck inside the tavern, I swallow tightly before pasting an easy grin on my face. A guard, his white regalia gleaming in the dim light, looks up in interest, his eyes roving down my body and then back up to my face. I wink, ordering a drink before stretching into the chair across from him.

"Hello there, handsome," I drawl, watching with delight as the tips of his ears turn pink.

He shifts under my gaze and drops his eyes demurely, before lifting them to meet mine through pale blonde lashes. They are a deep mahogany, a common enough color, but here, in the heart of my home city, it causes me to lose my breath. They are the exact color of Vee's.

"What's your name?" the guardsmen asks, but I barely hear him.

The air has grown stifling, and I yank at the collar of my tunic. Why is it so hot? Music blares from a musician onstage and for the first time in my life, it feels too loud. Smoke fills the bar and I shake my head to clear it away. It isn't really here. They've been gone for years.

But no matter how hard I rub at my eyes, the smoke remains.

Someone screams. The guardsmen blinks at me, befuddled, and without another word to him, I hurtle into the street.

Smoke. And not the smoke from my memories—true smoke.

I race down the street, toward the residential areas of the city where the screams sound the loudest. "Avedis, what's happening?" I bellow, not bothering to appear the least bit sane as I barrel past the same group of women.

I don't know. Something's shifted in the air, he replies, his wind a rush in my ears.

When I reach the first house, I skid to a stop, my stomach leaping up into my throat as I take in the scene inside the nearest window.

"Avedis," I say slowly, detached horror settling over me like a thick fog, "Shaw is here."

CHAPTER
SEVENTEEN

Mirren

The carved sea-wood door sounds like a gunshot as I burst into the hallway. It slams into the wall causing the two Siraleni guards stationed outside to startle. "Where is your queen?" I demand breathlessly, hopping up and down as I haphazardly shove my feet into boots.

My hair is a wild tangle of ringlets and I'm still clad in the gauzy nightgown, my emerald cloak thrown haphazardly over my shoulders, but there's no time to change. When Shaw left my room, he said the death of every child would now be on me. I thought he'd meant in his ongoing quest for the Praeceptor, but when Avedis' wind pummeled into my room, dread sunk low in my stomach.

Shaw doesn't accept defeat. Even if he can't touch me, I should have known he wasn't going to let me go so easily.

The nearest guard, a sturdy middle-aged man with a no-nonsense demeanor that denotes it will take much more than a half-clad woman to shock him, merely raises an eyebrow at my outburst. He elbows the guard next to him, a much younger boy who's been eyeing my nightgown with barely concealed interest. The younger guard immediately straightens, clearing his throat as his face flames red.

"We are not of the queen's personal guard, but it would be safe to assume she's sleeping, Ocean-wielder," the first guard replies stiffly.

"Mirren," I correct absently. If I'm called ocean-wielder ever again, it will be too soon. "And if you wish your queen to survive the night, you will tell me where she is right now."

The guard's face grows hard and his hand travels to the pommel of his sword. "Speak carefully, girl. Our queen does not respond well to threats."

I huff in frustration. "I'm not the one threatening her! The city is under attack and Akari Ilinka must know immediately."

I've already wasted precious time. I should have sprung into action immediately, knowing Shaw wouldn't simply leave, but instead, I stared into the darkness after him, attempting to draw the shattered pieces of myself into some semblance of human.

"And just how do you know that from the safety of your room?" the younger man asks with narrowed eyes.

The doors nearest mine shoot open, the loud bangs reverberating in the airy hall. Harlan steps out, freshly bathed, but much more appropriately dressed than I am. His jaw tightens as he takes in my appearance, a blush appearing high on his cheekbones as his gaze snags on my bare legs. Max steps out from the door next to his looking as if she never even sat down. She's still dressed in her traveling clothes, boots tightly laced and weapons still faithfully hidden. "What's going on?" she asks immediately.

I grind my teeth and meet her gaze, refusing to let any

weakness seep through the fissures Shaw's appearance has opened. "Shaw."

Harlan's eyes widen, but before he can ask any questions, Max has pulled two daggers from Covinus-knows where. The older guard shouts and draws his sword, but my friend is too quick. She yanks the younger guard toward her, pressing one blade to his throat and the other to the small of his spine. "You heard the woman," she growls in his ear. "Take us to your queen."

"You will regret this, Ocean-wielder," the older guard says with a beleaguered sigh, as if corralling vigilante women is not at all what he'd planned for the evening. "When the queen sees you've threatened her guard, she will hold no mercy."

Max appears wholly unaffected by his threat as she shoves the poor guard forward with a sardonic grin. "Lucky for Siralene, it is *Mirren's* mercy that matters now. If she had any sense, she'd leave your false queen to burn and be thankful there was one less warlord to worry about."

The guard's eyes grow wide, fear shining there for the first time. "The Heir? He is in Siralene?"

"That *is* what she's been trying to tell you," Harlan points out genially, from where he's been trailing behind us.

"But how? Our armies are stationed all around Siralene. There's no way he could have gotten through unnoticed."

"You clearly don't know Shaw," Max mutters.

The older guard nods reluctantly. "We will take you to the queen."

She only shoves the second guard forward, as if she expected no other outcome. Our footsteps echo in the hallways, empty save for a few slaves that tend to the lantern flames. I grab the nearest woman's arm. She startles, tensing immediately as if I mean to strike her. When she turns her face to mine, I see the right side has been mutilated much the same way as Avedis. Except whoever punished her, made sure it was done well enough to take her entire eye. "Take everyone you can find and go hide. Somewhere made of stone—the cellars, the dungeons, anywhere there's nothing to burn."

The woman's eyes dart to the guards, her fear of appraisal apparent enough. My *other* rises to my skin, so strong here on the edge of the sea. I feed it my worry and my heartbreak: my rage. "There will be no punishment for protecting yourselves. I'll make sure of it," I practically snarl the last words and the girl runs off. I can only hope away from wherever Shaw is.

"Mirren," Harlan whispers, falling into step beside me. His strides are so much longer than mine, but he keeps pace as if it's natural. "This is your way to the earth-wielder."

I glance at him uncertainly. "How?"

"Leverage your power. You're the only one who can match Shaw. If Akari wants to keep her people safe, she's going to have to give you what you want."

"Harlan—Shaw has *children* in rings of fire. I have to help no matter what Ilinka does." When I talked to Avedis, Cal had only made it to a few houses, but every sleeping child was surrounded by circles of flame. I don't know how many Shaw managed to snare, or how close he needs to be to keep his power burning, but I do know that even losing one child will be too much.

Max doesn't seem to share my hesitation, instead, eyeing Harlan with grudging respect. "That's not very Similian of you, Goldie. Which is probably why I like it."

Harlan blushes, and my power swirls, suddenly determined to protect him. How Shaw will relish breaking someone like Harlan: destroying his innocence and filling the cracks with misery.

"Mirren won't actually let the city burn," Harlan declares. "The witch-queen just needs to *think* she will."

Shame, slimy and potent, coats my throat at his faith in my goodness. He knows nothing of the true me: the selfish nature with which I cling to things I deem *mine*. How I've lied and tricked and killed for them. Harlan doesn't know the way I chafe against the rules of order, how I railed against them long before I ever fractured my soul. He doesn't know the temptation of losing my humanity entirely, of jumping into the depths of my *other* simply to protect myself from any more hurt. If he knew the true shades of my heart, he never would have followed me into the Darkness.

The smell of smoke shakes me from my thoughts, the acrid odor of burnt hair clinging to the stagnant air of the hallway. Max stiffens beside me and without speaking, we both break into a sprint. When we round the final corner, I can only be thankful Calloway isn't with us to witness what is surely a mirror to his family's horrible death.

Akari's entire guard is scattered across the marble floors, bodies steaming and skin melting, their faces no longer recognizable as human. Harlan gasps, burying his nose in his shirt, his throat bobbing as it works to keep down dinner. Max stares at the devastation, her gaze as sharp as the point of a sword. "He's here," is all she says, her voice distant.

Tears leak from my eyes, my *other* made physical, as together, we grieve at the sight before us. We pour ourselves over their bodies: the guards are already gone, but we spare them anymore mutilation. I call the water from the streams that run off the palace balconies and let it sink into my veins. I call on the Storven and it rises to my song. It circles around my head like a halo, pulling at my hair and dancing across my skin. Now is not the time to worry about falling too far—I will fall forever if it spares those children from *this*.

Harlan at my back and Max at my side, we burst into the witch-queen's chambers.

Shaw sits at a richly appointed table looking distinctly bored, his feet propped up on the ornately carved sea-wood as if he lounges in his own quarters and not the bedroom of a warlord queen. He doesn't appear to notice Shina silently sobbing behind him, clutching her cheek, a bright red burn apparent between her fingers. Instead, the entire focus of Shaw's arrogant smirk is on Akari Ilinka.

She stands frozen before him, surrounded by a ring of flame: a prison of Shaw's making. Her long hair has been singed, now falling just below her shoulders in scorched tatters and there is a bright red welt on the skin of her arm.

But her eyes show no weakness as they stare back at the Heir, and now, I understand why she is called queen—why her people think she is supernatural. Her jaw is set with defiance, her eyes bright with calculation. Her shoulders remain upright as the flames lick at her bare feet, and her chin is raised. She will give nothing, not even a small tremor, to whoever threatens her kingdom.

"It's about time you arrived, Lemming," Shaw says, rising from his seat with a wickedly lazy grin. "I should have remembered what a slow runner you are. I've been waiting for ages." His pale eyes flick from my face to Max's, where they narrow dangerously. There is no warmth there for his first friend in the world—for the woman who once saved his life. He raises an amused brow at the daggers in her hand. "Come to die by my flame, Maxwell, and you don't even bother to bring your best weapons," he sighs, as if extremely put off. "Still, fire is a fitting end to a woman who feels everything so very *brightly.*"

Max's face twists in rage and before I can stop her, she launches herself at Shaw. My heart freezes, terrified he will simply burn her midair, but he doesn't touch his power. Instead, he lets out a wild peal of laughter and meets her blade with his own, the black edge of the weapon glinting in the firelight.

Max slashes and jabs with incredible speed, slicing through Shaw's sleeve and then dancing backward. But Shaw is just as fast. He parries before moving on the counterattack, bobbing and weaving with the elegant grace I've always envied.

With Shaw distracted, Harlan and I run toward Akari. There is no gratitude on her face as she gazes at me from inside her burning prison. Only determination. "Are you going to free me, Ocean-wielder?" she asks wryly. We both know I have nothing to gain by freeing her, except, perhaps, to ensure my own enslavement. In the witch-queen's world, selflessness is an unimaginable quality.

"That depends on you, Queen. Give me the earth-wielder and I will spare both you and your people from the Heir."

A mixture of disgust and respect mingle on her beautiful face. "It seems I have misread you, girl. You never sought an alliance or protection. You only seek to reinforce your own power, same as any warlord. You wish to control the Dead Prophecy."

I raise my chin. "You're the one who told me I need to take in order to be truly powerful. I'm just following your advice."

"The Dark World is changing, and I sought the earth-wielder to protect my people from the Praeceptor and the Dead Prophecy. You would leave the innocents of my city unprotected?"

I breathe in heavily, weighing her words and the adept way she weaves them. After only speaking to me for an hour, she knows my weaknesses. Anrai once saw the tender places as strengths, but now, he's gone because of them. Because I couldn't sacrifice others to protect him.

To survive, I must harden. "You seek to negotiate, Queen, but there is no leverage to be had. Your palace may be made of stone, but your children are not, and the Heir keeps them in rings of fire. If you do not give me what I want, they will burn, and your people will turn on you for not protecting them." My *other* swirls in response to my words, filling the holes in my resolve until it is impenetrable. "Give me the earth-wielder and I will make sure the Heir harms no one else."

I follow Akari's gaze to Shaw. He's backed Max to the wall. Blood pours from a wound on her side and Shina trembles behind her as Max attempts to shield her with her own body. Her weapons lie out of reach and still, she refuses to relent to her oldest friend. Potent anger twists her face as Shaw moves languidly toward her. His breathing is even, not even slightly winded. He was never actually fighting her—he was only toying.

For the first time, something like fear flickers across the witch-queen's face. I recognize it not as fear for herself—not for her kingdom or her power—but fear for her heart. Shina means something to the queen. My *other* surges, spearing toward Shaw, but I force it still for a moment longer. Finally, Akari says quietly, "save her. Save my kingdom and the earth-wielder is yours."

She motions to a bookshelf next to her bed and I realize

why Avedis wasn't able to find the earth-wielder. She has kept them close, closer than Avedis would dare to venture, even with his wind. Harlan understands before I do, racing to toward the shelf and shoving it aside to reveal a small, carved chamber, barely large enough for a grown person. Inside, a middle-aged man dressed in only trousers, cowers on the cold stone floor.

I break the hold on my power. The water surges forward from my hands, dousing the prison that holds the queen in an icy wave. I shove her unceremoniously toward Harlan, who's draped the earth-wielder's skinny arm across his shoulder. Together, they limp slowly toward the door. "Go!" I yell, sending another wave toward Shaw, Max and Shina.

Max watches with wide eyes as it cascades toward them, a swirling typhoon. At the last moment, she dives out of the way with Shina in her arms.

The wave crashes against the stone wall, but it doesn't reach Shaw. Before a drop touches him, he lifts his hands and a barrage of flame shoots up between us, turning the water instantly to steam. Shadows dance across the sharp planes of his face and his eyes glint with hunger-lined madness as he stalks toward me. The wall of flame rises and curls, before cresting above me like a serpent poised to strike.

He doesn't spare a look for the witch-queen or the earth-wielder as they escape, his eyes only for me. Stoking the fire, embers burst to life at his feet and rise to join the cascade of flame.

Mirren, the circles around the children are shrinking. He's going to kill them, Avedis shouts, but I barely hear him. The room grows stifling, the pristine white stone beneath my feet beginning to feel tacky. How has he learned to wield his power like this? How far is his reach?

He has no soul to lose. He never has to fear falling or giving himself over completely, because there's nothing left that's human. How can I possibly match him?

As if reading my thoughts, he cocks his head and says, "Don't hold yourself back as you do for those weak sycophants." Flame dances in his hair and the pale of his eyes has grown molten. His voice is low, dangerous, and it brushes against my spine like the caress of fingertips. "Only *I* can withstand all of your power. Give me *all* of you, Mirren."

Gods.

I give into my anguish, my rage, my want—the darkest parts of myself that Anrai never once shied away from—and the strength of the Storven rises up in answer. My body is renewed at once, whole and strong, as I teeter atop the edge of the abyss. My *other* lashes out toward Shaw's flames, and together, they circle like a maelstrom: electric and terrifying. The fire surges at his urging, spearing toward me, only to be devoured by my sparkling whirlwind.

If I fall right now, I could take everything from Shaw. I could save those children with barely a thought. I could get lost in the endless waves and never again feel as though I'm too weak to save what I love. The storm surges between us, the floor beginning to crumble beneath the onslaught, and for a moment, I am tempted—tempted to give myself over to the inhumanity, to never feel another shatter of my heart, another tear in my soul. By the Covinus, wouldn't it feel good to do as Shaw asks and never stifle myself again? To let myself free of the self-inflicted prison?

Reading my face, his pale eyes light with fervor and he sends another thick tendril of flame shooting for me. He knows my temptation, he knows my longings—even with no soul, his memories know the path of mine. "The more the children scream, the more my power is fed. They feed into their own deaths without even knowing it," Shaw laughs, the cruel sound cutting through the furor of our storm. "You cannot save them by giving yourself in halves."

He's right. I won't be able to save them all if I don't give myself over to the depths.

Save them, Mirren. Save them and live.

Anrai's last words to me echo in the storm clouds of my soul and I want to scream at the unfairness, to rage that while he has the relief of inhumanity, I am forced to toil in its depths, fighting for his last wishes. Because my fight isn't over. And if I give myself up to the abyss, it never will be.

The Prophecy will never come to pass and millions of Ferusians will be cursed to the Darkness for eternity.

Heart pounding, sweat plastering my curls to my forehead, I abruptly drop my arms. Shaw's eyes flare, first in surprise, then in anger. My giving up doesn't feed the ache in his chest, the constant need for *more*.

"Let them all free. And I am yours."

His fire recedes, absorbing into his body as if he's made of living flame. "You would give up?" he asks in a hollow voice.

"The Praeceptor wants me taken to him alive, does he not? Leave the Siralenis alone and I will come without a fight."

A violent wind rushes through the open balcony, whipping the gossamer curtains. "Stay where you are," I murmur under my breath to Avedis. In response, the breeze becomes frenetic, a hurricane whipping through the queen's quarters. "Trust me."

The wind calms and I know Avedis has accepted my decision. Insane as it may be.

Shaw's eyes flash and for a moment, he seems to struggle, warring with something inside himself. He grimaces, his breaths coming in ragged pants. Finally, he stalks toward me, his strides charged and wild. "Weakness grows inside you like a vine," he hisses, stopping a hairsbreadth away from me. He won't touch me, the only assurance of safety I have. At least until we reach Argentum. "You are no equal of mine."

He raises his hands over his head and claps them together. With the sound, something lightens in the air, and I know he's released the Siraleni children. "It is done, then."

CHAPTER
EIGHTEEN

Shaw

By the third day of traveling back to Argentum, I think I hate the girl.

There is nothing of the spirited woman that haunts my memories, who always fought me tooth and nail. There is no arguing, no spitting; no screaming or cursing her fate. There is only silence and the weight of her gaze.

Though I've grown accustomed to the heaviness of her presence, now mostly able to move through the pressure in my skull and chest, whenever those piercing emerald eyes find me unprepared, it feels like the weight of the Castellium has crashed down upon me. But no matter how much I bait her, deride and prod, she refuses to rise to me. In all the time we've spent together on the road, she hasn't allowed me a single glimpse of her power.

Her way of punishing me, perhaps, though she only has herself to blame. I was so close to setting her free, to watching that wild, untamed power inside her come to life, when she stole it from me and locked it away. I hate her for that—for bowing to my father's will as everyone eventually bows. She was supposed to be stronger than him, my equal. It was a miscalculation on my part. I'd foolishly thought threatening the children would force her to fight harder, not sacrifice herself.

Because of her weakness, we're both headed back to the Praeceptor to plead our lives before him. Why is it that though she's given me exactly what I need to gain my father's trust, I feel like she's stolen everything from me?

I can only hope her presence is enough to earn the Praeceptor's forgiveness for leaving the witch-queen behind. I'd waited too long in Siralene and by the time Mirren surrendered, I'd barely managed to escape the might of Ilinka's military. I could have burned them all, perhaps, but I'd used most of my energy on the children and it hadn't been worth the chance my power would fail.

Ivo had been furious when he found us in the forests of Baak. I'd awoken to his sword pointed at my throat and I still can't be sure what kept him from gutting me. Ilinka is still in Siralene, the man she harbored now only gods know where, but I have what my father wanted from me. His approval overrode all deals I made with the *legatus*—it even overrode my desire for the girl to send us both into the Darkness. Because if I gain the Praeceptor's approval, there's a chance I can get close enough to unravel his hold on me.

In spite of the way Mirren unsettles me, I keep her close when we meet the Dark Militia near Havay. I tie her horse to mine when we travel and squirrel her away in my tent when we stop, as I would a precious gem. I burn anyone who happens too close, who looks too long. Though I hate her, she is *mine* and I won't let anyone take her from me until I deliver her to my father's hands.

She sits on a pallet of furs in the far corner of the tent,

full lips pouted, and cheeks flushed red in the heat of the fire. She eats when food is presented to her and bathes when given the opportunity, but she rarely speaks to me. A few times, I've caught her murmuring softly to herself, but it's always in the hushed depths of night and I can never determine her words.

Mostly, the girl sleeps.

I watch her greedily. How can she let her guard down in the presence of her sworn enemy, soulless and monstrous as I am? And yet she does, for hours and hours, as if she hasn't slept in a century. As if I won't take her and use her in every demented way my twisted mind has dreamed up in the long hours traveling behind her. The ache of the abyss has not subsided in her presence. It has only grown, hungry and demanding no one's pain but hers.

Her long lashes dance across her cheek, fluttering in the throes of a dream and I wonder briefly what her dreams look like. Mine are only of blood and fire and drowning in the sea, but an ocean-wielder cannot drown.

As if drawn to her bedside, I find myself watching the rhythm of her breaths and then reaching out to touch her, like a moth to a flame. What would it be like to run my hand along that luminescent skin and feel her power for myself?

A shock, hot and electric, runs up my arm at the contact and I snarl at the sleeping woman. *Why* can I not touch her?

I thread my power over my fingers. The flames dance from me to the soft curve of her cheek. I watch, mesmerized, as they don't burn—only warm—and she sighs contently, nestling further into the bed roll without waking.

I pull the flames back abruptly, lips peeling back from my teeth. Does she think me so weak as to not be a threat?

How ridiculous to sleep as if she's safe, as if the world doesn't burn at my hand. This is the woman who threatens the Praeceptor's reign? I scoff. She hasn't even enough sense to protect herself in her enemy's camp, let alone to bring down the might of the Dark Militia.

The sound of rustling near the tent entrance draws me from my thoughts. Another one of my father's soldiers, come to gawk at the ocean-wielder. "Go away," I bark out irritably, in no mood to don a mask of humanity.

"You do not wish to send me away, Heir," comes the muffled reply.

I stalk to the entrance, whipping the flap open with a snarl. But it is not one of my father's drooling men: it is not a man at all. Instead, a lithe woman only a few inches shorter than I, leans against the support pole. Her honey blonde hair shines in the firelight, brushing her bare shoulders as she sets sparkling dark eyes on me.

For a moment, all I can do is stare, my confusion palpable. The only women I've seen in this camp are members of the militia and they are generally clad in...well, in more. And if the woman doesn't belong to the militia, there is no way she means to be in my tent.

"Who are you?"

Her crimson-painted lips curl into a mischievous grin and she strides purposefully past me, the brush of her skin against mine eliciting a cold shiver. "Company," she replies, her voice low and sultry.

I don't close the tent flap and the cool night air blows through, causing the fire burning in the center to sputter. Mirren doesn't stir, now nestled so far into the pile of furs, only the top of her wild curls is visible. "I'm not fit for company," I tell the woman, my eyes still fixed on the ocean-wielder. "Not now, not ever."

The woman's gaze brushes over Mirren, but she makes no comment. Instead, she stretches out on my bedroll, positioning her ample chest so that it spills from her dress. Despite her apparent beauty, annoyance settles on the fringes of my nerves. Perhaps Ivo or some other *legatus* has sent her as a spy. Or she is here on her own twisted conquest, determined to be the one to have bedded the beast and lived to tell the tale. Either way, I don't have time for whatever sickness she seeks to amuse herself with. Especially not with Mirren lying in the corner, waiting for the moment my guard is down to make her escape.

I'm not foolish enough to believe the ocean-wielder's will is so easily quelled as to have given up completely. And we are far enough into the wilderness, away from any large cities, there is a distinct lack of innocents to threaten to force her compliance once more. It's a wonder she hasn't already tried.

Probably some remnants of her Similian morals and remaining true to her word. Absolute nonsense. But I remain ready and waiting, if only for another chance to press her to her limits. To crack her open and feed on what lives inside.

"I'm a gift from your father," the blonde woman explains, her long legs a spill of milky skin.

I scoff and throw the tent flap closed. *Cullen.* "And just what am I to do with this *gift?*" the word rolls off my tongue distastefully. The Praeceptor gives no gifts, especially not to heirs who have failed to bring him what he wants numerous times. My capture of Mirren is nothing to be rewarded; it's expected. Whatever this is, it is not meant to be pleasant.

The woman runs an inviting hand along the length of her thigh, dipping between her legs momentarily before sliding her hand up her stomach and up over the slope of her breast. "Whatever it is you wish, Heir."

I stalk over to her, not bothering to assume a face of humanity. If my father sent her, she's well aware what I am. Wrapping my fingers around the woman's delicate throat, I squeeze until her blue eyes tear. "*That* is a dangerous thing to say," I reply in a low voice, before finally relaxing my grip.

Even with my fingers about to crush her windpipe and the madness in my eyes, her smile doesn't waver. She is more terrified of my father than she is of me: if her seduction doesn't succeed, Cullen will take the failure as hers alone. "Your father simply wishes to ease your stress, Heir. And I am a very willing participant."

Bullshit. My father has no interest in providing comfort to anyone, let alone me. And the only willing participants housed in the godsforsaken Castellium are those as twisted as Cullen.

Removing my hand from her throat, I stand above her, examining her as if she isn't a half-naked woman, but a battle strategy. "Tell me," I draw a finger to my lips. "Did my father say why I am in such desperate need of comfort?"

For the first time, uncertainty flits across her face, quickly covered by a seductive tilt of her chin. "If a man's needs are not met in a time of war, he may lose his reasoning." She comes to her knees before me, and I allow her to run a finger from my sternum to my belly. "He may do things that are...*unwise*...in order to fulfill his desires."

"Ah." The woman begins to work the buttons of my shirt, but I hardly notice as the Praeceptor's intentions suddenly become crystal clear. Despite his control over me, he still doesn't trust my soullessness; he believes there is some shred of humanity in me that clings to the ocean-wielder. A smile crawls across my face.

Since I was a child, the Praeceptor has never had any detectable weakness. Even in his last battle campaign, when the witch-queen gutted his wife and strung her up outside of Siralene, it didn't have the intended effect. Ilinka thought it would devastate him, that he would be broken, but all it did was focus his rage. My father never loved his wife, as he's never loved anything. Emotion is death on the battlefield and so he's never shown even an inkling of it.

But now, I've been granted a rare gift. A chink in his impenetrable armor. Because my father's insecurity in the depth of his control means it is fallible. And now that I'm no longer mired in the fog of amnesia and the pain of his dungeons, my mind is finally clear enough to find the path forward. He made a crucial mistake in taking my soul, because just as I have no loyalty to the ocean-wielder, I possess none for him either. And if I maneuver carefully enough, I'll be free of him.

The Praeceptor's worries are for naught, even if the ocean-wielder's beauty is undeniable with those wide eyes and that mass of dark curls. And gods, my memories of her curves sprawled before me like an inviting feast is enough to make my mouth water. I don't have a soul, but I *do* inhabit a body, complete with all its primal urges. But that's all it is. Base instincts, like eating or relieving oneself. Even if I were to take the woman to my bed, it will never be more, because I have no more.

What I do have is cold emptiness and an insatiable hunger that's proven impossible to fill. If I can manage to free myself of my father's control before he kills the girl, perhaps I'll take her with me and do exactly what I promised on that balcony: feed from her pain and teach her all the ways of the Darkness until she's as empty as I am.

I swallow the frigid ache crawling along my tongue. I've

never let physical needs overpower me, but this is different. This is something that spears out of me beyond my control or ability to satisfy it.

With a predatory tilt of my head, I focus on the woman in front of me. She doesn't have Mirren's charms, but she is routinely beautiful—and her touch doesn't make my skull feel like it's been split open. In spite of his machinations, maybe in this, Cullen isn't wrong. Giving into her would soothe his suspicions, and perhaps giving into my body's desires will fill some of the ache. Maybe I'll feel more human.

Taking the woman's face in my hands, I press my lips to hers. She responds enthusiastically, sliding her tongue into my mouth and weaving her body around mine. She is warm, alive, but with the first brush of her lips, the swirling hollow doesn't recede. Instead, it balloons inside my chest, climbing my throat and reverberating against my lungs.

I shove her off me even as she strives to move closer, and wipe furiously at my mouth. She blinks up at me, her red lips parted in confusion, the paltry bit of fabric that constitutes her dress bunched at her waist. There is none of the warmth supposed to come with a woman's touch. As I glare at her bare chest, my body feels cold and unresponsive. Dead. And somehow, it is more unbearable than feeling that way by myself.

"Get out," I bark. Her crimson lipstick is smeared across the back of my hand like blood and I'm sure it's streaked across my face as well. Tears gather in her eyes as she gazes up at me, all traces of the worldly woman she just was, suddenly gone. Now, she looks young and impressionable. And vaguely familiar.

Ivo. *Godsdammit.* She's Ivo's daughter. *This* must be how my father chose to punish the *legatus,* feeding the innocence of his only daughter to the monstrous fire-bearer. What will he do now that Ivo's once again failed to bring him the witch-queen? Give the girl to the entire militia? For a moment, I consider laughing at the creativity of his punishments, of the new depths he continues to reach.

My power begins to sizzle in my veins, burning its way up my throat like raw acid. It's the only thing that ever lights the empty cavern in my chest, the only thing that's warm, and now it swirls with desperation to be let out. But Ivo's daughter doesn't move.

I whip open the tent flap. "Did you hear me? Get out of this fucking tent and don't come back."

The scent of her fear becomes potent, a wave of acrid stink that sends my power spiking toward her. It wants to feed, but the girl is not mine to burn. My father will send me back to the dungeons to drown if I kill the girl before his punishment is finished. "But sir—"

Flame scorches my lungs and the pressure in my chest builds. It needs a release, to be fed, before I combust. Acute pain sizzles through my head like an iron brand and it's all I can do not to tear at my own skin.

"The Praeceptor will punish me if I do not succeed in entertaining you. He will take my father from me. I cannot leave!"

I force my eyes open, focusing on the terror that wafts from her. I inhale sharply, devouring it, and my flames spring to the surface of my skin. Gritting my teeth, I stalk toward her. Never breaking my gaze, I bring my open hand hard across her cheek. Her head snaps sideways, a surprised whimper escaping her. The woman turns back toward me slowly, her eyes magnified by a sheen of tears. She clutches her cheek where an angry red imprint of my hand is now permanently burned. "Will that do?" I ask with an unnatural tilt of my head.

She bites her lip and nods, before tearing from the tent with a sob. I stare at the way the tent flap blows in the night breeze, struggling to keep my flames from spearing after her. The pain in my head has grown almost unbearable, but there is nothing to be done for it now. It's only a matter of time before Ivo comes for me: the girl is now marked forever, and the entirety of Argentum will believe I've had my way with her. The disrespect won't go unanswered for long.

Good. I'll burn the *legatus* in front of them all, melting his body bit by bit until he begs for death. Then, maybe, I'll be able to sleep.

Something rustles behind me, and I whip around, finding a pair of emerald eyes staring back at me.

Eyes like the sea—that roil with power fueled by a whirlwind of emotion: betrayal, disgust, lust, anger.

Mirren is the reason it feels like a Ditya wolf is clawing through my brain, but I find I can't move, not even to look away. We stand frozen, staring at each other. For an absurd moment, I wonder if she'll cry, having seen her former lover take another, but I feel no shame at the thought. Only mild curiosity.

But her cheeks remain dry. Renewed agony rips through my skull as she steels herself, lifting her chin and straightening her spine, a warrior readying herself for battle. And when her tongue darts out, swiping across those full lips, I realize my body isn't as dead as my soul.

Because as she examines me, her hands on her hips and her eyes churning like a summer storm, it sings to life: vibrant and heated and *alive*. Beneath the layers of pain, something stirs in my chest.

Like it's been awakened.

~

Calloway

The dock is teeming with activity when I step from the small skiff and onto the damp wooden boards of the Nadjaan marketplace. Reaching out a hand, I help Harlan from the boat, suppressing an amused smile as his bulky form teeters like a child learning to walk. Apparently, keeping to your feet on a swaying skiff is an acquired skill, one the Similian apparently lacks.

He smiles up at me, perfectly straight teeth gleaming white in the morning sun. I shrug irreverently, ignoring the slight pull in my stomach, and tie up the skiff. The sea air is warm today, but the breeze is cool in a way it never is in Siralene. Another reason to be grateful I'm home, even if that home feels fragmented at the moment.

With Shaw off being the scourge of humanity and Mirren his captive, the manor has felt larger than ever and far too quiet. Even Max's usual rambunctiousness and the task of nurturing the earth-wielder, Gislan, back to health hasn't seemed to help. I've always hated stillness. Quiet spaces. I'd take a room so loud I can barely hear myself think over an empty one any day.

Harlan wipes his brow as we step from the docks to the white-paved streets. Glancing down at the crumpled sheet of paper in his hands, he frowns as he attempts to decipher the messy scrawl of my handwriting. With a roll of my eyes, I swipe the list from him.

He freezes as our hands brush and for a moment, I ache. His fingers are long and unmarred by callouses or scars; so smooth, I'm sure they'd feel like pure bliss.

I yank my hand away abruptly. Something like hurt blooms in his eyes, bright and tender, but I turn away from that, too, before I fall headfirst into it. Why am I always drawn to wounded things? The creatures that are too delicate and vulnerable to survive my bed, let alone my love. Touch means something to Harlan in a way it never will to me. And besides, he is Mirren's. I don't entirely understand how, and I suspect he doesn't either, but somehow, they belong to each other.

It's best we don't touch.

His tongue darts out, moistening his lush bottom lip, and in spite of my newfound resolve, I follow the motion greedily.

Fuck.

I clear my throat loudly and flatten out the sheet of paper, a list of supplies Rhonwen needs for Gislan. The earth-wielder was half-starved and showing signs of heat stroke when we arrived back to the manor, and Rhonwen has made it her personal mission to see him fully recovered. After a week of her ministrations, Gislan is healthier than he's probably ever been. But when the housekeeper insisted she needed a few more things to see to him, I'd jumped at the chance to get out of the manor.

Personal errand boy or not, it's better than the emptiness of those rooms. Or having to play sentry behind Denver in another incessant meeting, listening to all the ways the world is going to the Darkness.

Crumpling up the list, I shove it haphazardly into my pocket. There will be plenty of time later for shopping. "I need a drink," I announce perfunctorily, before turning to saunter up the street. Harlan's delicacy aside, he's proven to be good company. He listens with rapt attention and when

I make a joke, he always looks sweetly embarrassed by his laughter, like it's taken him by surprise.

I can think of nothing better than amusing myself with his first taste of liquor.

The Similian furrows his pale brow, shoulders slumping as he hurries after me. "It's 9 o'clock in the morning," he replies dubiously. As if this will mean something to me.

I chuckle, as we turn down the street toward Seesa's, one of my favorite establishments. Painted an obnoxious shade of orange that looks somehow looks more offensive in the daylight, from the outside Seesa's looks derelict at best and abandoned at worst. But the time of day never matters, for music pulses from its walls at all hours. "Which means there's still plenty of daylight left to make up for our late start," I reply, opening the door and ushering in a very doubtful-looking Harlan.

His eyes, a golden yellow, even in the dim lantern light of the tavern, dart in every direction, growing more consternated by the minute. A band plays on a stage in the corner, the sound of their bass drum vibrating in my chest. People mill about in small groups, laughing and shouting. Some dance, woven together in a slick tangle of limbs that have Harlan's cheeks flaming crimson.

Breathing in deeply, I allow the noise to wash over me, the incessant chatter of my thoughts blissfully quiet for the first time in a week. I order two drinks from Seesa herself, before leading Harlan to a table in the corner and practically setting him into the chair like a child. Shoving the drink toward him, I grin. "After you, my sweet Similian."

Harlan eyes the drink as if its liable to jump up and strike him. He shakes his head, crossing his arms and shifting stiffly in the wobbly chair. "I don't think so," he says as his gaze drifts back to two men swaying back and forth, bodies pressed together.

"Suit yourself," I tell him. Undeterred, I toast the air and take three large swigs of my own drink. The alcohol burns pleasantly at the back of my throat, warming me from the inside out.

Harlan watches the dancers for a few long moments in silence, before he rubs roughly at his forehead and slides his eyes to mine. "Don't you think we should be getting Rhonwen her things?"

I shrug, my glass scraping the table as I set it down. "Rhonwen is just fussing. Gislan is Ashlaan," I say as if this explains everything, but then remember who I'm talking to. "Ashlaa is a small, poor territory in the north. Its warlord is selfish and greedy, and its people never have enough food. Gislan has probably eaten more this week than he has in his entire life."

Harlan doesn't look convinced. I sigh, conceding, "One drink and then we'll get the supplies."

The song changes, the fast tempo giving way to something slower: one that slides through the room and caresses the air. Harlan's gaze trails wistfully back to the dance floor, almost unbidden, and for a moment, I wonder if perhaps I've misread him, and he isn't scandalized by Seesa's. Maybe he wants to dance.

Then he says, "Do you think Mirren's okay? Do you think the Heir—Shaw—has hurt her?"

Harlan hasn't mentioned much of his feelings about Mirren giving herself over to Shaw and I haven't decided if it's an effect of his Similian upbringing, or just his own personal tendency to hold things close. He hardly ever appears anything other than pleasantly content, and I've spent more time than I care to admit, imagining what it would take to break through that smooth exterior.

I take another pull of the drink and lick my lips. Harlan's eyes follow the movement, his bowtie lips turned down in concern and suddenly, I feel his worry weighing between us. "More than likely, it's Shaw who needs the saving. Have you ever been on the receiving end of one of Mirren's waves? I'm sure she'll have him groveling for mercy in no time."

Clinking my glass with his stationary one, I down the rest of its contents and grin mischievously. "Now what do you say we go cause a ruckus to take your mind off things? Maybe...hold hands, read a book, or Covinus-forbid—" I clutch my mouth in feigned horror. "—*laugh?*"

Harlan presses his lips firmly together, his laugh so close, I can almost hear it. I wiggle my eyebrows suggestively. "Or maybe we can just stroll down the street and start an argument with everyone we pass. I'm sure that'd excite your Similian sensibilities, but I'm open to suggestions."

At this, Harlan does laugh. It sounds melodic, and somewhat surprised, as if it escaped against his will. Satisfaction threads through me, but it's quickly snuffed as he schools the humor on his face into a somber look. "You don't have to do that," he says softly.

"Do what?"

"Make me laugh."

"I *like* making people laugh."

He nods, his gaze wandering once again, snagging on a couple in the corner wrapped so tightly around each other it appears they've forgotten they're in public. Finishing my drink, I pull his toward me, newfound warmth buzzing in my stomach. After a moment, he says, "but you don't *have* to."

I freeze as his soft eyes fall on me. Somehow, they are the same color as the warmth in my belly. *What a ridiculous thought.*

"I heard you say Shaw was your brother before—and..." I stare at him as his cheeks flame, and he drops his gaze in embarrassment. "And I just meant you don't have to make me feel better when you're also worried. You don't have to pretend yours doesn't exist."

His embarrassed flush travels all the way down his neck, disappearing into the collar of his shirt. I stare at the hollow just below his throat, feeling seen in a way I haven't in an exceedingly long time, and unsure whether or not I like it.

I spoke the truth. I *love* making people laugh. It grants me a feeling of power no sword fight ever could, being the one to make someone forget their pain, even momentarily. It has since I was an eight-year-old boy, tripping purposely over my own feet just to hear Vee's cackling giggle.

But Harlan is also right. I use other people's happiness as a way to pretend my own worries, my own heartaches, don't exist.

Harlan shakes his head. "Forget it, it was stupid—"

"It wasn't stupid," I tell him earnestly, because as conflicted as I feel, that I know. "And you're right. I am worried about Shaw, but right now, I'm more worried about failing him. I—I made him a promise to protect Mirren. Letting her hand herself over to a soulless firebearer is not particularly the best way to do that."

Harlan nods, rubbing his hands on his thighs.

"But Avedis is with her. We'd know if anything had happened. And we have to trust Mirren. She was strong long before her magic and if she thinks this is the best way to capture him, we have to let her try. Besides," I say, stretching in the chair with a casualty I'm not quite sure I feel, "Anni would never have fallen in love with her if she wasn't capable of outmatching him." I drain the remainder of Harlan's drink, before looking over the rim of the glass to find he's gone oddly still.

Clearing my throat awkwardly, I set the glass down with a loud clink. A muscle feathers in his jaw and I don't know whether I've been loyal to Anni by speaking to Harlan of the past, or disloyal to Mirren. Maybe it's neither. Maybe I said it in service of the small, selfish part of myself that spends too much time thinking about the shape of Harlan's lips and how his broad shoulders and narrow waist form a perfectly tantalizing 'V'.

"He is—was—in love with her," Harlan repeats slowly and not as a question, so I don't answer. But then, "Is she in love with him?"

I'm spared having to respond by the door to the tavern opening with a screech and a spill of bright morning light pouring into the smoky room. Max spots us immediately, beelining toward our table. She'd been a stick in the mud, refusing to accompany us in favor of joining another of Denver's excessive meetings, but now, I can't think of when I've been more grateful for her timing.

Harlan glances up as she approaches our table, her long braids swinging behind her. He averts his eyes as she stops directly in front of him, the slip of midriff left bare by her shirt directly in his line of vision. He blushes again and I press my lips together to keep from laughing. Complications aside, watching Similians navigate Ferusa never gets old.

"Where have you been?" Max demands hotly, throwing

her hands on her hips. "I've checked every store Rhonwen said she sent you to!"

"We were absolutely parched, Maxi, and stopped for a quick pick me up." I drum my fingers on the table and grin at her. "And boy, am I happy to see you. Apparently, it's too *early* for this one to have any fun."

But Max doesn't smile, nor does she sit. Instead, she plants her feet as if readying herself for something, and ice replaces the warm buzz of alcohol in my stomach. "Cal, it's the Praeceptor. He's left Argentum."

Harlan's face pales in horror, and for once, I don't attempt to assuage it. "Where is he headed?" I ask, my voice sounding distant. Because I already know.

Max's face could be carved from steel for how sharp it is as she says, "to meet the Dark Militia. He's on his way to Mirren."

~

Mirren

Your time runs short, Siren.

Shaw has finally left me alone, gone to handle something on the outskirts of camp, leaving Avedis' voice free to rustle through the tent. I dip my hands into a bowl of warm water, scrubbing away the filth of travel as best I can with no soap.

Argentum lies only a few days north. We must move soon.

My chest tightens as I run my fingers through my hair and weave it into a simple plait that hangs to the small of my back. When I allowed Shaw to take me, it had mostly been to get him out of Siralene without hurting anyone else. But I'd also seen it as an opportunity. Whatever he is now, we still need him. With Gislan now ensconced comfortably at the manor, Shaw's fire is the last remaining element for the prophecy.

I had no real plan but was confident in the strength of my *other*. It would be easy enough to overpower him while he slept, fearful as he is of my touch.

Except that he hasn't slept. At all. I've woken hundreds of times, at all hours of the night, and each time, he's been staring at the fire, pale eyes reflecting the flame. How he's still functioning, I have no idea.

The opportune moment fell into my hands last night, while he'd been entangled with the blonde woman, but I'd wasted it. Instead of thinking strategically, it was all I could do to keep my *other* from wrestling its way outside me. I could only stand and watch as her greedy hands roamed over the small sliver of new skin above his hip, touching *our* history as if it belonged to her.

Thankfully, I hadn't drowned her where she stood, for when I heard why she was in Shaw's tent, my heart had broken for the girl. Another of the Praeceptor's pawns, thrown around and torn apart for his amusement.

And now, my time is dwindling. I have to get Shaw away from the militia before we reach Argentum. I vividly remember the way it felt when the Praeceptor stole my power, how weak and frail I'd been. I still don't know the nature of Cullen's magic or how he stole my *other* from inside my body, but I won't stand a chance if I get myself dragged in front of him.

Avedis' breeze winds around me, laced with the sweet scent of blooms. I wonder where he is and how he's kept himself so well hidden. After assuring the earth-wielder was safe at the manor with Max, Cal and Harlan, he's been trailing after me, his voice an ever-present comfort in the bowels of this horrible camp. It's him I've turned to when the sounds of misery and violence permeating the tent walls become too much, the Dark Militia a restless entity that wails in the night. It's Avedis I've confided in about my worries of falling too far into my *other,* of having to match Shaw's inhumanity if I have any hope of stopping him.

The assassin is a patient listener, and in the short time I've known him, I've come to rely on his sound council.

"Tonight," I tell him softly, peering at the tent flap to be sure Shaw hasn't yet returned. He never leaves me out of sight for long: either because he doesn't trust me, or he doesn't trust the militia. It's left me little time for plotting and a great deal of time to study his movements. "After dark, I'll distract him, and you can take him then. But after we escape, you have to stay far away from him, Avedis. Shaw can't see you."

The breeze shudders with the assassin's displeasure. *Our dear friend Maxwell may very well skin me alive if I leave you unaccompanied with a bloodthirsty flame-thrower.*

I roll my eyes with a smile. "I'll be unaccompanied with *Shaw*," I point out for no reason I can determine. By all accounts, Shaw is what Avedis says he is. Violent, selfish and completely unrepentant. I haven't been allowed out of his tent, but I've heard the screams when Shaw isn't here—I've smelled the acrid odor of burning skin, felt the pressure of his inferno billowing through the air, malevolent and ravening. The Praeceptor's order to bring me to Argentum alive is the only reason I've been spared. Because however Shaw felt about his father before he lost his soul, he now plays the willing heir, seemingly more than content to perpetuate Cullen's reign of horror.

In spite of all this, I sleep more soundly than I have since that day in Yen Girene. Maybe it's my body responding to his presence, as if it feels the remnants of safety Shaw has always provided. Or maybe, I've finally pushed myself to the point of exhaustion that I now just pass out on pure instinct. Whatever it is, I feel stronger than I have in a long while.

"I don't know what he remembers about you, Avedis, but I doubt it's anything good. I don't want to risk him killing you."

If the wind can grumble with displeasure, I swear, it does. *Who's the mother hen now? I'd like to see him try. Fire cannot live without air.*

I laugh softly just as the tent flap opens. My face sobers, humor fading into the morning air. Shaw ducks through the opening, laden with plates of food. His dark hair is damp, curling upward at his temples and he's clad in leather gear that is, for once, thankfully absent of any blood. When he straightens to his full height, I feel his presence like a strike to the chest. It heats the entire tent, and for the thousandth time, I wonder how I never guessed at Shaw's power before. He's always burned so hot, always felt like he drained the oxygen from every room. I thought it was the connection we shared, an effect of my feelings for him, but I never saw it for what it truly was—*him.*

"Breakfast," he mutters, dropping the plate in my lap without touching me. He doesn't wait to see if I'll eat, instead, going to sit in the only chair in the tent. Situated before a small writing desk and positioned as far away from me as the cramped quarters will allow. Turning his back, he begins to eat.

Sighing, I push around a bit of the food with my fork before taking a bite. The militia food is rarely good, but it's always hot and I force myself to eat it every day without argument. As malnourished as I was in Similis, I can't afford to refuse a meal if I'm ever to regain my full strength.

He doesn't speak of love because it hurts him—he's trying to hurt me.

And in spite of my resolve, the wound in my soul gapes as if he's physically stabbed me. I never allowed myself to *think* the word when we were together, let alone speak of it aloud. It was too powerful, too consuming. An emotion outlawed by the Keys because it's brought down entire civilizations, spurned continent-wide wars. I was terrified of the power it would give the world over me: the chance to steal it away and leave me with nothing.

By the time I realized everything it granted me was worth the risk, it had been too late.

I stare at the broken husk of the other half of my heart, suddenly sick with the unfairness of it all. But my heartbreak isn't his to feed on; it is mine alone.

So, I will feed him something else. "Is that why you're so willing to hand me over to your father?" My feet are bare on the fur-lined floor, only serving to further demonstrate how much taller he is, but it doesn't matter. It never has when it comes to him, all my feelings always rising up like a tidal wave to fuel our battles. "Because you think you've been spurned?"

Shaw's eyes light with fervor. He thinks he's finally won. That I'll lose my temper and give him a glimpse of the part of my *other* that is as inhuman as him, that rages as he does.

I twist my lips in disgust, and his nostrils flare as his eyes snap to my mouth. "If so, how weak to hand the revenge that should be yours over to your father. Are you truly going to let him be the one to teach me the ways of the Darkness, when I'm the one who cost you your soul? Are you really going to let *him* be the one to grow stronger on my suffering?"

I take a step toward him, and he measures it. Always so careful not to touch me, fearful of what it might do. Nausea clenches my throat as I remember the way he screamed and trembled on the balcony in Siralene. Is my touch truly torture for him now? How has something once so sacred been twisted into something unbearable?

"You think yourself all-powerful. And yet you give everything to your father. If he commanded you to lick his boots, you'd grovel at his feet." I crowd him further, his face unreadable as he uses up the last bit of space before falling back into the chair. "You think I haven't felt your hunger for me? I see how you crave my power...how you fight against the urge to devour me. And still, you would hand it over to someone who hasn't even bothered to leave his city."

"I am the Praeceptor's Heir. His wishes are mine." Even now, when I'm so close I can see his power writhing in the depths of his eyes, his face appears utterly unaffected as he watches me. The warlord's Heir through and through.

I step between his legs and without taking my eyes from his, reach out to run my fingertips down the length of his arm. He tenses beneath my touch and snaps his eyes closed. Something between a growl and a whimper sounds from his throat, as if my skin against his is both agony and pleasure. I pull away. "Is it the Praeceptor's command you not touch me? Has your fear of him kept your hands tied?"

Shaw's eyes flick open, the pupils flaring so wide only a thin, pale circle remains. "I'm perfectly capable of touching you," he replies with a wicked tilt of his head. I tense when he circles his long fingers around my throat. It was foolish to taunt him, to expect anything other than pain.

But maybe it's pain I'm after; punishment for all the ways I've failed.

But Shaw doesn't squeeze. He examines his hand

around my throat for a long beat, so still, he could be made of stone. Then his fingers begin to move, trailing lazily down between my breasts, and my skin heats beneath his touch. "I can touch you whenever I want," he says, his voice so low my toes curl. We both watch as his hand traces the undercurve of my breasts, before wandering slowly over my stomach. "I could touch you until you remember nothing but the pleasure I give you. Until you sob before me, begging for more."

He cocks his head and inhales sharply, as if he can sense the want pooling between my legs. But still, his face doesn't move. "I just have no interest in it," he finishes with a humorless grin, removing his hand abruptly.

Anger and embarrassment heat my skin once more and my *other* rises in agitation. I hate his stoicism, hate that mask of stone. He wasn't always so controlled. There was a time he trembled beside me, a time he could hardly stand to keep his hands from my skin.

Anrai is gone, the weight of his want for me something I'll never feel again. But Shaw still possesses a human body with needs and wants. Even if it's a twisted echo of what it was before, will it sate my longing for him enough I'll be able to breathe around it once more? Will it dull the edge of my guilt and my need enough for me to focus on living once again?

Angst and desire mingle, as my *other* rises up and demands I take from Shaw what Anrai took from me. Crawling across his lap, I slam my lips against his.

CHAPTER
NINETEEN

Mirren

There is nothing soft about it, a rush of relief and rage and desire so potent, my body turns to liquid. And I hate myself for it—that in spite of everything, I still turn to flame beneath his touch.

And would gladly burn forever.

But it isn't my desire I'm after. It only takes a moment for Shaw to relax around me, whatever pain or hesitation he felt melting away between the heat of our bodies. As if suddenly coming alive beneath me, he closes his eyes and tangles one hand in my hair possessively, the other gripping my hip. He pulls me further on top of him, my legs at either side of his waist. Growling into my mouth, he bites at my bottom lip before soothing it with a deft flick of his tongue.

His soul may be gone, but his body remembers. My power is imprinted on his skin, the memory of my touch still enough to drive him wild, and he kisses me like he's terrified to lose it.

I pull away from his lips and grind my hips down on his

lap. He's already hard beneath me and he groans as I run my hands down his chest, before slowly unbuckling his bandolier and peeling his shirt above his head. I toss them both haphazardly to the floor and Shaw freezes, eyes still closed. Waiting. "There was a time you would bow only before me," I say breathily, tracing the knotted scar above his heart with the tips of my fingers. "A time when *I* was your only master to worship."

His eyes fly open and he snarls, animalistic and terrifying, but he makes no move to stop me. Only watches as I trail my hand down the length of his chest and then beneath the waistband of his pants. Fire flares in his eyes, hot and bright, as I wrap my fingers around the silken length of him.

His soul is dead, but his body lives, and it responds to me as if I command it.

In this moment, he is no longer the Praeceptor's, but *mine*.

You will never be his, Anrai, because you are mine. *Do you hear me? Mine.*

Emotion clogs my throat as I palm him. His eyes roll back, and he moans, thrusting himself further into my hand. I'll hate myself for this later, for knowing this will never be more than what it is and doing it anyway, but for now, I revel in it. Shaw's power begins to burn at the surface of his skin, but I feel no fear. It is not the devouring torrent of rage he uses to hurt, but beautiful embers that warm me from the inside out.

Stroking him gently at first, I don't take my gaze from his as he stretches his legs out and leans back to watch me. That same dark obsession flares, but now, mingled with his flame, it looks entirely different.

It looks like he's considering eating me alive.

A thrill runs through my chest, and I speed up my pace. He curses under his breath, throwing his head back. His body contracts and trembles with my every movement, his bare chest heaving with barely contained restraint. When he shudders and gasps beneath me, I drink in every minute detail. I never got to witness Shaw in the throes of his own pleasure, undone and out of control, and I find myself greedy and wonton for every bit of it. I commit it to memory with tears in my eyes, so that later, when my heart is shattered and my body aches for him, I can take them out and relive this small stolen moment.

But it isn't enough. It will never be enough.

He learns forward, hands gripping me to him, dark hair spilling over his forehead as he leans against my chest. "Mirren," he whispers, his voice a hot caress against my collarbone that makes me feel as if I'm going to come apart. His lips trail over my skin, sucking and licking every part he can reach, murmuring my name over and over, as I grip him more firmly. His body shudders and euphoria threads through me that my knowledge of him remains.

When his mouth finds mine once more, needy and hot, I come undone. Electricity shoots beneath my skin, pooling in an unbearable ache at my center. He runs his hands along the dips of my waist and up to my breasts, and though I know I imagine the reverence in his touch, the desperation, I throw my head back and allow myself to give into it.

For a moment, we are not water and fire, darkness and light. We are just Mirren and Shaw.

"I'm going to—" his voice is strangled, and he tries to brush away my hand. But as lost in pleasure as he is, the movement is halfhearted, and I speed up my strokes. I won't allow him to deny me this: this last time to remember the way he looks when he wants me.

With a roar, he explodes into my hand.

His head collapses against the swell of my chest and we sit in silence as the rapid pump of his heart slows. A few moments later, he raises his gaze to mine, pale blue and lovely as the first time I saw him outside the Boundary.

His mouth parts, but suddenly, I know I can't bear to hear his cruel words slice through whatever settled over this room when we touched. My heart can't withstand the ache of him ruining my memories with whatever monstrous thing he thinks to tell me. I disentangle myself from his arms and take a few large strides toward the other side of tent, swallowing down the tears threatening to spill over and never stop. I breathe in sharply, feeling entirely too full. Of hope, of heartbreak, of desperation. Every beautiful and terrible thing mingles furiously in my chest, and for a moment, I think I'll be sick.

When I gather myself enough to turn back toward Shaw, his demeanor has shifted entirely.

His body is rigid, his smile cuttingly cruel. And his eyes —they're a wasteland once more, nothing but cold ash. Had I really imagined them as anything different? How delusional am I, to pretend to see what I wanted in a ruthless killer?

In spite of my resolve, hot tears spring to my eyes. I chose this: chose it even when I knew it would fix nothing —that it would only serve to break me further.

Shaw opens his mouth, but before he can spew whatever horrible comment he seeks to destroy me with, his eyes go wide. His nostrils flare as a terrible gasping noise sounds from his mouth. The tendons in his throat go taut and he claws at them like he's being strangled by invisible hands.

Heart racing, I start toward him in a panic. "Shaw?"

But before I reach him, his head lolls and he slumps over in the chair. Out cold.

Still staring at his unconscious form, my stomach leaps into my throat as a polite drawl sounds from the shadows. "As usual, it seems my timing is impeccable."

CHAPTER
TWENTY

Mirren

My cheeks flame as Avedis steps from the shadows with a sparkling grin.

"How long have you been over there?" I hiss furiously.

The assassin shrugs. "Long enough for this to be awkward," he replies frankly, moving soundlessly into the center of the tent. "You *are* the one who told me to catch him while he was distracted, are you not?" He runs his gaze over me appraisingly, taking in my disheveled clothes and the mussed state of my braid. "I must admit, you are unexpectedly adept at diversions for a Similian."

"Oh, shut up," I mutter mutinously. I peer at Shaw, his legs sprawled before him like an overlarge ragdoll. "You haven't killed him, have you?"

Avedis doesn't bother to answer, instead looking around the tent with a low whistle. "I'd imagined being captured by the Heir of the Praeceptor to be less...comfortable."

I wave him off. "I told you to wait until dark. How are

we going to get him out of camp in broad daylight without alerting the rest of the militia?"

"During the nights, the Heir has guards posted around this tent, but during the day, they steer clear as he apparently burns anyone alive who looks at you overlong." He says all this with the air of one discussing the mundane. He toes Shaw's bed pallet with distaste, before moving to rifle through the small desk drawer. "And your fire-bearer has made camp on the edge of a cliff."

I raise a brow. "You can't mean—we aren't going to throw him off of it?"

Avedis laughs. "Would you agree to it if that were my plan? It risks damaging certain *parts* you may deem quite useful."

I blush furiously. "You're horrible. You know that, right?"

Avedis grins brightly, smooth charm oozing as if I've given him high praise. "I *am* a world-class assassin." His face sobers, concentration lining his brows. "And no, as much as I despise the arsonist, I am not going to throw him off the cliff." Avedis pulls his sword and opens up the back of the canvas tent in one deft slice, creating a slit large enough to walk through. "But I am going to carry him off it."

Shaw has had me blindfolded whenever we traveled, no doubt in case I ever escaped I'd have no idea where I am. Through the slit, I see the cliff Avedis spoke of. We're no longer near the Nemoran wood, which means we must be north of Similis. Here, the sky is painted in tortured shades of gray and purple, appearing violent and morose. The landscape is jagged, with spires of thick rock jutting from the ground and canyons cutting through the earth like wounds in flesh.

We are camped on the side of one of the deepest, the cliff behind our tent a near vertical wall of rock most likely chosen for its defensibility. No one would survive the climb up or down.

Avedis purses his lips and thrusts his hands in front of him. After a moment, Shaw's prone body rises from the chair, held by invisible strings. His hair falls across his forehead in thick waves, and his lips, kiss-worn and pink, are slightly parted. For a moment, he doesn't look like the man who has destroyed entire towns—he looks like a boy, sleeping and innocent.

I swallow roughly as I peer down the sheer drop. "Avedis...you've done this before, haven't you?"

The assassin remains as whimsically untroubled as ever. "Have I levitated a soulless terrorist down thousands of feet while his forlorn lover looked on? Can't say that I have."

If I hit him, it will only break his concentration and he could drop Shaw, so I settle for a hateful glower.

He grins sidelong. "Relax, dear Siren. The air is forgiving when I ask it to be. He'll be safe as long as you will it so."

I nod nervously as Shaw floats through the tear in the canvas. His head lolls and his arms dangle listlessly at his sides, as if he's unconscious in the arms of an unseen giant. My stomach leaps as he disappears over the cliff edge.

Taking a settling breath, I shove my feet into boots and begin to dig through Shaw's belongings. I've no clothes beyond the nightgown I wore that night in Siralene, my cloak having been burned beyond saving, so I wrap the spare militia-issued one I've been using while traveling around my arms. Then I yank open the writing desk drawer and find the leather bandolier Shaw confiscated from me. The daggers are beautiful as ever, their carvings seeming to move along the handles in the dim morning light. I'd feared Shaw had disposed of them, as distasteful as he finds sentiment for his past life.

I buckle the bandolier over my chest and am just about to turn back toward Avedis when the soft wink of metal catches my eye. Shuffling aside a few random reports, my breath catches in my throat.

My coin.

The one that began my entire journey—that led me to Shaw.

It gleams as if it's been recently polished and the tattered pillowcase scrap I used as a necklace when I first crossed the Boundary has been replaced with a fine gold chain. I pick it up gingerly, my mind racing. I thought I'd lost the coin in the scuffle of Yen Girene. What, then, is it doing hundreds of miles away in this drawer?

"Heir, your services are required by the guards." A muffled voice sounds from outside the tent, freezing me in my tracks.

Avedis' hands are still raised, his face furrowed in concentration. His eyes dart from me to the outside interloper and I understand he will be no help. Not unless he drops Shaw.

"We've found a few holdouts from Havay. They need to be tested."

Tested?

Anger bubbles in my chest as my *other* flitters in agitation. *Magic.* They need to be tested for their potential for magic. Punished for something they don't even yet possess.

"Heir?" the man says again, albeit somewhat hesitantly. From what I've gathered, Shaw's own militia steers clear of him, terrified of his violent tempers. I can't say I blame them. "Permission to enter?"

I curse under my breath and draw a dagger. "Don't you dare drop him," I threaten Avedis.

"Understood." His dark eyes flick to the dagger. "Perhaps your power would be more prudent?"

As the soldier ducks into the tent, I realize Avedis may have a point. The soldier is roughly the size of a small boulder, his neck nearly twice as thick as my thighs. His red regalia is decorated similarly to Shivhai's, so he must be high ranking and well trained. His hesitation at garnering the Heir's furor fades quickly as he takes in the tent and Shaw's conspicuous absence.

The man draws his sword, lunging for me just as I let the dagger fly. It spins, end over end, before lodging in his thigh. He bellows in rage, arcing his sword toward my throat. The water from the wash basin rises to my call, wrapping around the man's mouth. His shout dies immediately, replaced by coughs and sputters. The soldier tries to move through it, but my water winds tighter and tighter, covering his mouth and nose until he's forced to stop. He grapples at his face, but upon finding my power isn't a curtain to be pulled away, he succumbs and collapses to the ground.

Two more militia members duck into the tent, drawn by the sound of the first man's cries. I can only hope they alerted no one else. A woman rushes toward me, leveling her revolver at my chest. The shot sounds, metallic and sharp against the silence of the tent, but it hardly takes a thought to turn my water to ice and raise it like a shield before me. The bullet ricochets, bouncing off the ice and embedding itself in the writing desk.

"He's almost there," Avedis whispers, his voice strained for the first time. "Hold strong, Ocean-heart."

I wind the condensation of the morning around my

fingers as the two soldiers charge. Delving into the deep of my *other*, the tent suddenly feels as cold as the darkest parts of the sea and just as fathomless. I linger on the edge of the crevasse once again, toeing the line between my human soul and the unimaginable. The droplets begin to swirl, a tempest that takes pieces of me until I am no longer Mirren.

I am the sea, and I am ageless. I am all-powerful; both the creator of life and the thief of it.

I blind the soldiers, stealing their breath. Their power is mine to consume. I don't relent until they feel all my *other*, until they know our rage.

Somewhere small and far away, I feel a hand on my shoulder.

I don't want to acknowledge it, for touch is human and I am not. But the gentle tapping is insistent, and after a moment, I climb to the surface. Toward Avedis and the tent. Back toward my soul.

Blinking wildly, the assassin's shaved skull comes into view.

He dips his head in respect, as if he understands where I've been—and its cost. "The fire-bringer is safe. It is time you join him."

I breathe deeply, taking note of the way my nightgown scratches against my skin and the scent of smoke lingering in the old cloak. Simple things. Human things.

"Avedis," I begin, but he shakes his head.

"Worry is for another time. For now, do what you must to survive."

And isn't that the curse of the Darkness. Do what you have to for survival. Give up pieces of yourself until you have nothing left to give, because at least you still breathe. How had I ever judged those living in Ferusa for their choices?

Emotion clogging my throat, I throw Shaw's new black bandolier haphazardly over my shoulder. It is stiff and uncomfortable, but I can't afford to leave behind extra weapons. I nod to Avedis. "What about you? That was too much noise not to attract others."

"Do not worry about me. I've been breezing through war camps my entire life. Now, if I may suggest not looking down?" He quips playfully.

Before I can respond, a soft wind lifts me off my feet and I am tumbling out of the tent. To the Darkness with not looking down—as Avedis launches me over the cliff edge, I squeeze my eyes shut, determined not to look *at all*. My stomach drops as I sail into the air, an unmoored balloon alight on a breeze. If I weren't so terrified, I might wonder what the world looks like from this view, but the force of the wind keeps every thought from my head except for the distinct wish for it to end.

The sounds of movement from the militia grow louder as I float toward the bottom of the canyon and my chest tightens in fear for Avedis. There's no way the soldiers will be able to scale the cliff face in time to stop Shaw and I, but they're perfectly able to cut down the assassin. I forcefully remind myself how adept he is at remaining invisible. And even if he wasn't, I have no way of getting back to him now.

I push the worry from my mind as my feet finally find solid ground. Shouts sound from thousands of feet above, so steeling my nerves, I hurry toward where Shaw lays sprawled on the ground. Dahiitii stands next to him, nudging his unconscious form impatiently with her nose, unable to understand why he isn't showering her with his usual affection. His breaths are deep and rhythmic, and I find myself grateful he breathes at all. Avedis could have easily snuffed the life out of him and saved the people of Ferusa from the Heir, prophecy be damned.

Giving Dahiitii a quick nuzzle, I rummage through the saddle bags and determinedly ignore the peace that's crept over Shaw's stern features. He looks too much like Anrai in sleep—wild and beautiful. I can't make the mistake of believing him to be the same man I lost. One wrong step on the journey back to Nadjaa and he'll kill me without hesitation.

By the Covinus, what was I thinking in the moments before Avedis interrupted? I'd let my guard so low; Shaw could have taken my life at any moment, and I would have been too caught up in the revelry of him to do anything about it. Heat climbs my cheeks and I shake my head. There will be no more pretending Shaw is anything but soulless. No more giving in to the weakness of my heart.

I wrap a length of leather around Shaw's torso. If only Avedis' forethought had included setting Shaw's unconscious body on top of the horse rather than beside her. I turn, winding the rest of the leather around Dahiitii's saddle. With the right amount of leverage, I should be able to pull him up.

Planting my feet, I heave a deep breath. But when I turn for one last look at Shaw's sleeping form, there is only empty dirt.

∼

Shaw

When I wake, I breathe only ash. It swirls in my mouth and puffs clouds in my lungs. When I cough, flames scald my throat.

I peer up at the sheer rock face towering above me, the

violent gray sky of Argentum feeling so far away. Images of the moments before I was rendered unconscious flash in my mind and fill me with pain and luscious want. Sinful curves, delicate skin; the feeling of having crawled from a lightless pit and into a room drenched in sunshine. The way her mouth on mine had quenched the hollow inside me while simultaneously setting it aflame.

How I would have gladly allowed it to burn the rest of me.

The ocean-wielder's back is turned as she fiddles with a mare's saddle. I cut myself free with the small knife I always keep tucked in my boot and climb soundlessly to my feet. Her curls have pulled free from her braid and tumble down her back, blowing in the soft breeze along with the second-hand cloak. The sight of its tattered hem enrages me and as I creep around the side of her, I consider ripping it off.

I underestimated her ruthlessness. I hadn't honestly believed her a heartless seductress; I had only been taunting her to break through that unflappable *goodness*. To destroy it with some of my own Darkness, because what could be more satisfying than spoiling something pure?

But perhaps it is that very goodness that drives her. That lends her the strength to do whatever needs to be done to stop my evil.

Did she really seduce me in order to kidnap me? How had she even gotten me down this Darkness-forsaken cliff?

When she turns, her eyes widen for only a moment. I snarl at her, baring both my teeth and the depths of the toiling soullessness in my eyes. A look to remind her who exactly she seeks to trick and what the cost will be.

But Mirren doesn't flinch; she *laughs*. A mellisonant sound that rings in the emptiness of my chest. A thrill shoots through my center, and for a moment, all I can do is stare at her. Because how had I forgotten—even for a second—that she has always been my equal. Soul or not, she will never cower before me as the others do because she is perfectly matched, her strength and determination a mirror to my own.

A tender soul makes her no less a warrior: it only makes her a more dangerous one. Blinded by my rage and the echo of old memories, I thought her weak for giving up.

My father was right in believing our history compromised me. And now, he will assume the worst.

He'll think I've escaped *willingly* with the girl, that I've betrayed him a second time. And if she succeeds, I'll never be free of him. With the hold he has on me, there's nowhere to hide. He will find me wherever I am and strip everything from me until nothing remains but raw pain. He will shove me back into the dungeon where I am only emptiness, starved and freezing.

I've worked too hard to have my chance of freedom stolen now.

With a snarl, I lunge at Mirren, and we go tumbling to the ground in a tangle of limbs. She lets out a yelp of surprise but doesn't reach for her power. She scrabbles beneath me, her body lush and warm, but she is no match for my sheer size. My father will be upset when I bring her to him dead, but his disappointment is still better than him thinking I've colluded with her. He will understand I had no choice but to risk the prophecy and end her life—no choice but to put a stop to the madness before she ruins me.

As I pin her legs between mine, she pounds at my chest, the sharp pain of her small fists only serving to ground me further in my determination. I wrap my fingers around her throat and squeeze, feeling the delicate flutter of her pulse beneath my fingertips. My flame, which normally spirals out from me in search of nourishment, stays tightly balled in my chest.

The water is no place for a boy who burns.

She will only bring me destruction. I tighten my grip.

Her eyes widen, and for the first time, fear sparkles in the sea of endless green. After everything I've done, the children I've burned and the lives I've destroyed, she still foolishly believed there is something inside me other than infinite darkness. I squeeze harder because she was wrong. *I am empty, a vacuous void.*

My skull pounds, the heavy agony of touching her skin settling over me. My breaths come as rapidly as her desperate wheezes, and my fingers tremble around her throat as I try to work past the tortuous flare in my brain. But I don't release as her tendons go taut. I've lived through so much pain, surely, I can finish this.

Mirren coughs and sputters, tears springing to her eyes. She claws desperately at my hands, her nails drawing blood as she tries to save herself—and still, she doesn't reach for her power. Still, she seeks to save me.

Disgust threads through me. Her heart may drive her, but now, it will be her undoing.

Her body goes pliant beneath mine. "Anrai," she gasps, barely a word.

End this. End her.

But suddenly, I am frozen, drowning in the turmoiled sea of her gaze.

That sea. The sea that haunts my dreams, that never relents, even in waking.

Something shifts within the heaviness of her touch, the same as it had when she touched me in the tent. It is no longer just the searing of my nerves and the crushing of my skull. No longer just empty pain. Something spreads from my chest to the tips of my fingers, a maelstrom of *feeling*, aching and full and terrible.

What is she doing to me?

A rustle sounds from the end of the canyon, and I whip around to see a horse and rider heading straight toward us. Even from this distance, I know him—know him by the hard line of his shoulders, his stiff stance on the horse. By the way all the light of the day is drawn into him, as if the black of his sword is somehow capable of swallowing the sun.

My father.

Dust clouds the air as three more riders join him, the steady beat of horse hooves growing ever closer. Ivo, his bulking frame towering atop his steed, pulls back a bowstring on my father's command.

The Praeceptor is here for Mirren, to drag her back to his dungeons, bound on her knees. To pry her open and break her so thoroughly, the threat of the Dead Prophecy will be eliminated.

This can be over. With her end, I can prove to my father she has no hold over me.

Ivo pulls back the bowstring.

Fingers still around her throat, I meet Mirren's eyes. *Let it end. Let it end.*

My power surges to my skin, starting from my dead heart and shooting outward. There is no thought that drives me forward, no other word than *mine* echoing in my head. I yank Mirren to her feet just as Ivo sends the arrow careening toward us. It sings through the air, stabbing into the dry dirt where she'd been just a moment before.

Smoke fills the canyon as I shoot a wall of flame at my father, his bellow of rage echoing off the steep cliff and reverberating back tenfold. As I shove Mirren onto the horse, something like panic rises in my throat. I climb up behind her just as the familiar constriction yanks at my chest. My fire falters and I double over, clutching at my heart. My eyes pop and pain like I've never felt blooms beneath my ribs, billowing over my lungs and into my mouth; my father's rage made physical.

It's all I can do to stay on the horse as Ivo shoots another arrow, this one landing true and piercing my shoulder. I wrap myself around Mirren, becoming her shield in the open expanse of the canyon: the only thing I've left to offer. She clicks her tongue, urging Dahiitii into a sprint.

My flame is gone, and I barely feel as one, two, three arrows sprout from my back. Black edges my vision as the agony overcomes me. I only hold Mirren tighter as a wave bubbles up from the ground and rises behind us, a swirling wall of fury and power. It catches the remaining arrows as they sail toward us, halting the Praeceptor and his men in their tracks.

But walls have never stopped my father.

And above the roar of Mirren's wave and the rush of blood in my ears, one thought pounds in my head with the steady rhythm of a drum:

If the arrows don't kill me, my father will soon make me wish they had.

CHAPTER
TWENTY-ONE

Mirren

Shaw passes out behind me as we reach the end of the canyon, and it's all I can do to keep him upright on Dahiitii. When we reach the cover of the trees, I stop only long enough to tie him to the saddle and then keep going. Two arrows sprout from his back, another from his shoulder. Blood pours freely from the wounds and each canter of the horse must be excruciating, but I don't dare stop. The ground of the canyon was so dry, it had taken almost everything in me to raise the underground spring between us. I won't be able to do it again.

And the Praeceptor saw Shaw defend me.

A betrayal that will not be forgiven. However terrible Shaw is now, I won't give him up to his father to be tortured. Not when he risked everything to save me.

We run through the day, terrified and half-dead with exhaustion, until we finally reach the edge of the Nemoran. I know the creatures who reside here well and can only hope the threat of them will be enough to keep the militia at bay, at least for the night. And that Shaw's blood isn't scented by one of them before I can heal him.

I heave his prone body off Dahiitii, and the wind is knocked from me as we both tumble into an ungraceful heap. Rolling Shaw gingerly off me, I inhale deeply, attempting to catch my breath and slow my panic. I wonder where Avedis is now, wishing for the comfort of his presence while simultaneously hoping he's escaped somewhere far from here. The adrenaline of the day has faded and suddenly, I feel small and alone in the expanse of a cruel world.

It takes me over an hour to remove the arrows from Shaw's back and though I try not to cause more damage, the tips are ragged and barbed, embedded deep in the muscle. The wounds no longer bleed, the tissue appearing freshly burned as if his body somehow cauterized itself. He doesn't move as I work on them, the skin retearing with each ministration, and I pray he's far enough into unconsciousness not to feel the agony of each pull. By the time I'm done, blood coats us both, the metallic scent tinging the air.

I call my power to his skin, both to wash away the blood before a yamardu finds us and to heal his wounds. But the moment the water touches him, his entire body rears up as if seized by an invisible force. I scramble back in surprise, struggling to keep my *other* concentrated on his wounds. There's no way he'll survive the night if I don't heal him, let alone the risk of infection.

Crawling back to him, I try to hold him down as he thrashes violently. He screams, blood-curdling and horrible, as the water dips into the punctures. He claws the ground, bloodying his fingers as he tries to escape; then he begs me to stop, to take the water away.

Finally, he curls into himself, childlike and sobbing, relenting to my torture as if it's inevitable.

My fingers tremble and tears cloud my vision, falling into the final wound as I fight to close it. When I'm finished, my power recedes into slumber, exhaustion pulling heavily at both my limbs and my heart. I wrap Shaw's bare chest in the ragged cloak, and too terrified to light a fire, lie down next to him.

His skin is unnaturally hot, radiating from him in scorching waves and I worry infection has set in. My healing was shoddy and desperate. What if I was too exhausted to do it properly? What if he never wakes up?

I shiver against the night air, tucking the cloak more firmly around us. I should be grateful if he dies, prophecy be damned. Anrai would never have wanted to live the way he has, would never want to be responsible for the devastation he's caused. I realize now when Calloway spoke of killing him, it wasn't heartless—it was the greatest kindness he could think to grant his former best friend. Peace.

My throat aches where Shaw wrapped his hands around it, each swallow a reminder of his determination to end me. Every time I look in a mirror, I'll see the ugly wash of bruises, physical proof he truly wishes me dead.

But I didn't imagine what flickered in his eyes at the end, *lighting* like a new flame conflagrating in the middle of an ashen wasteland. And then, he'd wrapped himself around me, sacrificing himself once more to save my life.

I still don't know what it means, still don't have an answer for why I hadn't touched my *other* to save myself.

I should have drowned him.

I'm glad I didn't.

"Mirren," Shaw moans, his body twitching next to me. His eyes remain squeezed shut, but his fingers lift frantically, searching. I stare at them hesitantly, the way he cowered from my power like it was pure torture still fresh in my mind. "Mirren," he cries again, muscles contracting wildly, lost somewhere between sleep and pain. "Mirren, I miss you."

I grip his hand and he visibly relaxes, settling back down. "I'm here," I tell him softly.

"I miss you more when you're here," he sighs, before his breathing evens and he falls once more into sleep.

Hot tears well in my eyes for the thousandth time, because even with no soul, he speaks to my heartbreak. Being forced to watch his smile, his movements, his dead eyes and being allowed none of it has been more devastating than if he'd died. At least in death, I wouldn't be reminded of all I fleetingly possessed.

"We're going home, Anrai," I tell him, pretending for a moment the injured man next to me is the same one I met that day on the Boundary, cocky and ruthless and wonderful; pretending I didn't lose my home the day I lost him. "I'm taking you home."

CHAPTER
TWENTY-TWO

Shaw

When I force my eyes open, the sun burns my retinas.

I curse, shielding my face before slowly lowering my hand. Sun. I feel the *sun* on my face.

Which means I am no longer anywhere near Argentum.

The past comes back in sharp flashes, feeling at once intimate and acutely foreign. I had the ocean-wielder at my mercy and then, somehow, I'd decided to sacrifice everything I've worked for and keep her from my father. *Why?*

Our choices have doomed us both, and I don't even understand them. My father's hold over me remains and now, with no way to reverse it, all I can do is sit and wait for the moment he leverages it against me.

Pushing a pile of silky blankets off me, I attempt to stand but find myself hindered by the bite of iron. Glancing down, I realize both my hands and feet are bound in shackles. I squirm, searching for the pick I usually keep on me, when an amused voice freezes me in place.

"I wouldn't bother. You're the one who taught me how to thoroughly disarm a man."

I squint over the pile of covers as a lanky form unfurls from the corner of the room. I stiffen as the man comes to his full height before me, copper hair glinting in the buttery rays of sun. His presence echoes somewhere in the abyss as his russet eyes meet mine, sharply clever and grossly gentle. "Hello, brother."

His face swims in my vision, bringing with it a few empty memories. Tensing, I wait for the moment they sweep me away, but the man's presence doesn't *hurt* the way Mirren's does and despite their veracity, I remain rooted in the present. Twisting my lips into a cruel smile, I drawl, "Calloway. Still hiding in the shadows, clinging to those more powerful than yourself, I see."

His eyes narrow. "You forget yourself, Anni."

I yank roughly at my chains with a sneer. "I don't believe I do. I could melt these irons, and you along with them, without a second thought."

"You forget I have already seen the ugliest parts of your heart and never balked. You cannot scare me away because there is nothing about you I don't know. You've already tried and failed."

I frown, fidgeting uncomfortably under his gaze. Soft. It is too *soft*. "Perhaps you should learn a little self-respect and save yourself the humiliation. There is not one bit of me that cares in the least whether you live or die."

Calloway only smiles. "You gave your soul for me, brother. I think I can manage the sting of a little embarrassment." With that, his face sobers, and his eyes turn positively feral. "But I made you a vow that I would always keep Mirren safe, and I will not break it. Do you understand?"

I meet his unwavering gaze. His love for my former self aside, I've no question he will cut me down without hesitation if I so much as touch a hair on Mirren's head. My father has always said love is a weakness, but perhaps he hasn't witnessed the strength with which it reinforces loyalty until it is the tempered steel of Calloway's resolve. Even after my soul-death, he's willing to die to honor his vow to me.

Pathetic.

And useless. If I decide Mirren is worth more to me dead, a farm boy isn't going to stop me. There may still be time to kill her and bring her head to my father. To plead temporary madness and get back in his good graces.

Calloway's mouth twists in a mischief-edged grin. "Would you like to try?" he offers, reading my thoughts with irritating accuracy. "We could find out if your training is lacking."

Suddenly, I'm inside a memory of Calloway, with floppier hair and skinnier arms, grinning down at me in a gym on the first day he managed to best me at sparring. And me, taking his offered hand and popping up to clap him on the back. A worthy opponent, trained by my own hand. And I never do things in halves.

I grit my teeth. How aggravating.

Ignoring his offer, I relax against the headboard. There's no need to burn everything to the ground until I determine, why, exactly Mirren has brought me to my old home. Perhaps I will return to the Praeceptor with the ocean-wielder's head *and* the Chancellor of Nadjaa's war strategy. There would be no refusing me clemency then, even if I'll certainly have to spend time in the dungeons to make up for my previous failure.

"You've been unconscious for a week," Calloway continues, settling himself back into an armchair near the window. *My* armchair. Pushed up next to bookshelves that used to be mine as well. Looking around, I realize with something like dread that I'm in my old room.

Everything is as it is in my memories, except now, a smaller pair of boots rests next to one of my older pairs. A hairbrush lies on the vanity next to the sink and various shampoos line the shelf next to my tub. Even the bed I'm chained in, which should smell like nothing but abandonment, possesses a faint scent of night blooms.

It seems there is no end to what the ocean-wielder has taken from me, down to my very room.

"Mirren said she healed your puncture wounds, but that you—" Calloway stops, looking distinctly uncomfortable. I watch him with a hard gaze until he finally continues, "you didn't respond well to her power, so she couldn't heal all the infection. My best guess as someone completely untrained in magic *or* healing...I think your body has been keeping you unconscious while it worked on burning the poison away."

My power is made to destroy, not heal as Mirren's does, but it has granted me the ability to heal from wounds in my own way. In the depths of the Castellium, my father would watch as it cauterized lacerations and burn away various poisons. Including those used on the tips of militia-issued arrows.

I thought I'd dreamed the feel of Mirren's power inside me—the raw fear that I was once again drowning beneath the Praeceptor's ministrations. I was tumbling through the abyss once more, the raging sea determined to possess me. *Water is no place for a boy who burns.*

I am no place for a water-wielder's touch.

Why didn't I kill her? Why didn't I give her to my father?

"And you, Calloway?" I ask, spearing for the weaknesses

in him I know so well. "Where were you when I captured Mirren in Siralene? Still too cowardly to face your own demons? Too weak to cut down the witch responsible for the destruction of your family?"

The tips of his ears turn red, but he doesn't rise to my rancor. So I press harder, shoving my fingers into the unhealed wound. "How dare you speak to me of the vow you took when you've already forsaken it. You allowed Mirren to be stolen away by a bloodthirsty monster and dragged to the gates of Argentum. I was obviously a fool to believe you capable of protecting *anything*."

Anger flashes on Calloway's face and satisfaction threads through me at how deftly I crawled under his skin. The soul-ridden are so easy to manipulate with their raw hearts and pure intentions.

"Mirren has never needed anyone's permission to take risks she deems necessary. You would have been the first to agree, she is her own." He shoves himself to standing and I follow the light trail of his fingers over the hilt of his sword. "How far you have fallen, brother, to be so far from the Castellium and still be trying to claw your way back to grovel at your father's feet. Has losing your soul robbed you of courage as well? Even soulless, you must see there is nothing to be won at the Praeceptor's side."

Fire lines my skin, melting the metal of my bonds and singeing the wood floor around my feet as I strain toward Calloway. "There is still my vengeance! The girl has robbed me of what I deserve, and I will cut through whoever I need to *take it back!*" I snarl, half-deranged, as the last of the iron drips away from my skin.

I lunge at him, but he's ready, striking my jaw hard and fast. "You'll watch the whole world burn for vengeance!" He shouts, ducking as I shoot a ball of flame at his face.

It hits the bookshelf behind him, the blaze bursting through the wood and spreading through the pages of novels.

As I lift my hands to shoot another, something in the room shifts. As if the entire atmosphere has suddenly frozen.

It isn't just the air. My clothes, my skin, my hair, my very *blood*, turn to ice and I am mired where I stand, arm still reaching for Calloway's throat. Violent shivers wrack my body as the door opens quietly behind us and Mirren steps into the room.

She douses the flaming shelf perfunctorily, an unreadable emotion flickering over her face as she examines the half-destroyed books.

My body feels like it's made of frozen marble rather than muscle as I struggle to move. I gasp bitter air into my lungs, my teeth chattering so roughly, it jars my skull. Gods, is the ocean-wielder able to freeze my actual *blood*?

There is no flame left in my chest, nothing but ice and the abyss. And it is all because of the girl in front of me. "I will kill you for dooming me to the Praeceptor's wrath," I manage through a clenched jaw.

She ignores me completely, looking instead to Calloway. "We need a minute."

With a deferent nod, he relaxes and shoves his sword back into its scabbard. With one last taunting smile at me, he ducks out of the room without a backward glance.

Mirren's face is serene as she releases whatever hold she has. My blood runs hot through my veins once more and feeling returns to my extremities with painful furor.

"Your body contains a fair amount of water," she explains over her shoulder as she closes the door. I stare stupidly in face of her fearlessness. My mere presence sends the most seasoned of militia members scattering, and this petite woman makes to turn her back on me, as if I'm no more a threat than a field mouse.

I examine the vicious necklace of bruises that ring her throat.

And after I've almost killed her, no less. Has she no sense of self-preservation?

"And like all water, it answers to me."

Wonderful, I think bitterly. If the events of the tent were any indication, she doesn't need to touch her power to command my body. The way she touched me was its own delicious form of agony. Pain and pleasure blended so fully it was impossible to distinguish one from the other. And the worst part was, I hadn't wanted to.

In those moments, I'd lost sight of everything but her. I'd wanted to drown in the sort of pain she offered, because *gods,* for the first time in months, I felt *hot.* Not the tepid warmth that comes after I hurt someone, but a roaring fire, wild and uncontainable. If I didn't know better, I'd think *she's* the one who wields flame.

I watch silently as she moves about the room, opening drawers and collecting an armful of clothes. Her long hair hangs in soft waves down her back and instead of the ragged nightgown and cloak I've grown accustomed to seeing her in, she's wrapped in an airy pink dress that exposes her bare shoulders. My gaze follows the bruises along the curve of her throat, the morbid watercolor on otherwise unmarred skin summoning a wild storm within me. I want to peel that ivory skin from her bones: to feed on her pain and teach her all the ways to *hurt.* I want to run my lips across the subtle peaks of her exposed collarbone and drink in the light glowing from her.

Before I can do either, Mirren moves into the adjoining

bathing suite, the swing of her hips infuriatingly mesmerizing. Flame rises to my skin, and I struggle to tamp it down, as she turns to look at me over her shoulder, her mass of curls swaying. "You have two choices." It takes me a beat to realize she doesn't mean the two warring in my brain. "One, I can send you into hypothermia until you cooperate. Or two, you can listen to what I have to say."

Or I can punish her for all the ways she's doomed me. For the ways she's caused me to fail and the things she's stolen. Vengeance and escaping my father were the only things I was living for and now, I have nothing at all. Unless I finish what I started and bring her body to the Castellium.

She peeks her head out from the archway and I shift uncomfortably. I don't like the way she looks at me—like I belong to her.

I belong to no one. I am nothing but cold ash.

"First, you need to wash. After, you can make your choice."

Uncertain whether I'll listen or burn her until her last breath goes to the Darkness, I follow her into the bathroom.

∼

Mirren

He stares at me through the spirals of steam curling off the hot water as the large copper tub fills. The mud of the canyon mixed with his own blood coats him in a thick paste. It hangs heavy in the fabric of his clothes and smears across his face like warpaint. Until now, I've been afraid to touch him again, even while unconscious, terrified of causing him anymore pain. I still don't know whether it was the agony of my touch he feared or the water itself, but if he has any objection to bathing, he doesn't voice it.

Instead, he holds my gaze and drops the filthy cloak to his feet. He wears no shirt underneath, as it was left behind in the tent, and the bronze skin of his muscled chest gleams in contrast with the muck, seeming to draw and hold the morning sun's warmth. I bite my lip roughly and turn away when his hands go to his trousers. The water sloshes over the sides of the tub, slapping to the floor as he climbs in. I force myself to count to five slowly before turning around once more, praying he's completely covered when I do.

No such luck. He dwarfs the tub, his chest and knees towering above the water. My eyes are drawn to the gnarled scar above his heart, and then, to the multitude of newer ones scattered across his chest, legs and back. A sob barrels up my throat at what's been done to him, but I swallow it down under his silent scrutiny.

He makes no move to wash. Just watches me with those dead eyes. Averting my gaze, I draw a stool from near the sink and perch behind him. It seems easier to begin with his hair. To escape from under his barren stare.

I move slowly, remembering the last time I washed blood from him in that cave. He'd been embarrassed, then, to allow me to tend to him. Will he stop me now? Will the moment between us fracture, his murderous hands around my throat once again? I reach slowly for the water of the tub. Quick as lightning, he grabs my wrist, and my stomach leaps into my throat.

Closing my eyes, I force a shaky breath. But he makes no other move to hurt me. "I do not like water on my face," he says, his voice like the rough scrape of gravel. As if the confession costs him something.

I nod and to my relief, he opens his fingers, letting my wrist drop.

I pour water over his hair, careful to keep it from his

eyes. He is perfectly still as I squeeze shampoo into my hand and slowly begin to massage it into his scalp. A harsh breath escapes him at the contact, and I freeze, uncertain whether he wishes me to continue.

After a moment, he leans into my touch with an involuntary groan. My throat is thick as I imagine the things done to him in our time apart. What sort of horrors have made him fear both the water and my hands. Shaw has always worn the mark of his stories on his skin, but this —*this* is something else entirely. His entire back is covered with new scars: slashes, puckered stab wounds, stripes that look like he's been whipped. The newly healed wounds continue over his shoulders and down his chest and arms like the patchwork of a morbid quilt.

There's barely an inch of skin that hasn't been touched by pain since we were parted.

Tears blur my vision and I regret how selfishly I took from him in that tent, how greedily I hoarded his pleasure for my own. Soul or not, I should never have touched him with anything but care when he's been so mistreated. How had I been so caught up in my own sense of loss, I failed to see what's happened to him?

Tangling my fingers in his hair, I stroke his scalp much longer than necessary, the suds bubbling up and coating the thick onyx strands in froths of white. The citrus scent of the shampoo clings faintly to the air and the only sound is the quiet lapping of the water against the basin. I know Shaw is dangerous, that he isn't my Anrai, but something unfurls in me anyway, tender and aching. Because at least for the moment, he will know something gentle.

I rinse the suds out, careful to avoid his face. Shaw is so still, the tense muscles in his neck now so fully relaxed, I begin to wonder if he's fallen asleep. But when I move to the front of him, his eyes aren't closed. Pale and horrible, they follow my every movement. An empty wasteland that scrapes against the inside of my chest, but I force myself to work through it as I scrub the dirt away from his back and chest.

Moving perfunctorily, I dip the cloth into the bath and try not to think. Not of the echoes of horror etched in his skin. And certainly not of how good that skin feels under my fingertips, warm and alive. He doesn't speak as I move to his arms, nor as I wash each of his feet.

When his skin gleams and the water has turned a murky shade of brown, I hesitate, sodden cloth gripped in my fist.

Shaw's face is the only thing left to clean. He blinks up at me inscrutably as I raise the cloth in permission, pale eyes bright against the shadow of dirt. Without breaking my gaze, he circles my wrist with his long fingers once more, but this time, it isn't a warning.

Or maybe it is, but I've lost all sense of self-preservation as something *hot* sparks in his gaze. The same thing I imagined back in the tent and on the canyon floor, but perhaps not imagined at all, as here it is, burning like a signal fire. Never taking his eyes from mine, he tugs me toward him, gentle but insistent. Entranced by his sudden need, heart pounding against my chest, I allow myself to be pulled into the tub. Water sloshes over the sides and the thin material of my dress logs with water as I settle on his lap, his large palm planted squarely on the small of my back as we watch each other.

I should be wary. He doesn't have a soul. He's loyal to my enemy. He doesn't even need his power to end me right here.

But he's touching me without flinching. And his eyes—

they're *alive*. Not with the corrupt power his father has unleashed, but Anrai's own: the warmth of a hearth and the freedom of a wildfire. I drink it in, letting it settle at the base of my spine as I slowly clean his face. Emotion rises in my throat as he allows me to care for him; to begin to atone for tricking and using him; for abandoning him to the Darkness in the first place.

He watches me, even as I clear away the filth from around his eyes. The long black lashes bead into dark clumps and for a moment, Shaw appears almost childlike. After his face is clean, I drop the soiled cloth into the water. His hand holds me to him, loose but decisive in its presence.

We stay like this for what feels like ages and no time at all, our faces close enough to steal each other's breath: him watching me and me, staring back. The water has long grown cold, but the heat of his body is enough to keep me warm as he finally snakes his other arm around my waist, pulling me tighter against him. Shaw's gaze drops to my mouth and my heart leaps at the lightning that flashes there. Electricity against the night sky.

"The only time I feel anything is when I'm touching you." His voice is so unexpected that I jump. It's the first thing he's said to me that hasn't been laced with vitriol.

"What do you feel?"

"Warmth. Hunger. Comfort." He tears his gaze from my lips, meeting my eyes once more. "Pain."

I rear back, but his hands cage me in, keeping me pressed up against him. "Don't leave," he protests, the word strangled. All I've caused him is pain. I cannot be responsible for any more of it. But the desperation in his voice moves me to do as he asks despite my misgivings. The water splashes some more as I crawl closer, my dress swirling around us like an ethereal cloud. I straddle his waist, his bare skin hot against the inside of my thighs, the hard length of him pressing between us.

We shouldn't be this close. It's wrong for both of us. But like opposing magnets, we seem to only pull closer together in spite of everything that tries to keep us apart.

"I don't want to be empty anymore. I just want to feel *something*," he says, his fingers beginning to run over the curve of my spine. Shivers erupt in the wake of his touch, and it takes everything in me to remain still.

He hikes my legs around his waist, clenching me so tightly to him, I have to thread my arms around his neck to keep from toppling headfirst into the water. His heartbeat hums through the flimsy fabric of my dress as our chests press together, his breath a sweet whisper against my mouth.

Shaw doesn't close his eyes when he settles his lips against mine, drinking all of me in through his gaze. His mouth is hot and when his tongue strokes my bottom lip, a moan escapes me. It wasn't the manor I promised him in the Nemoran, it was *this*, us together, familiar and whole.

A strangled sob sounds from his throat and I breathe it in as he opens for me. Our tongues dance and his fingers dig into the small of my back, greedy and terrified. As if I'll slip through his grasp at any moment—as if none of this is real. His other hand strokes my throat, angling my chin upward just as his tongue sweeps possessively across my mouth. Insistent heat pools at my core as he reminds me how easily he's always been able to wring pleasure from me, how he's always known the facets of my body better than I do.

Tangling my fingers in his hair, I pull him closer, striving to taste every bit of him I can reach. His breathing hitches as my lips reach his jaw and I come away with the salty taste of tears in my mouth. Shaw slowly lifts his fingers to his cheek, brushing at the moisture. He stares at them in a detached sort of wonder. After a beat, he asks levelly, "is this your magic?"

I shake my head, eyes wide.

The tears glisten on his fingertips and he examines them for a long while. "The soulless have no tears," he finally says. Another rolls down his cheek. "You do something to me I cannot explain. It feels heavy and terrible—" He swallows roughly. "—but also...warm."

Max would tell me this is very clearly a trick and admonish my naivete, and she'd probably be right. But Shaw's voice isn't edged with the cold malice I've come to expect from the soulless assassin. He sounds...vulnerable.

And I am so tired of pretending I have no hope, when agonized hope is *all* I am. "Help me, Anrai," I whisper. His hands begin to move again, tracing the curve of my spine, stroking my scalp, tangling in my hair. Tears fall faster now, glistening on the sharp edges of his jaw, the blue of his eyes magnified beneath their sheen. "Help me bring back balance. *This* is how you get your revenge against Cullen. By using everything you have to keep his vision for Ferusa from coming to pass. Help me bring back the light."

His fingers tighten and he grits his teeth, blinking rapidly. "The soulless cannot be trusted. We only do what's best for ourselves—what will feed the emptiness the most."

I trail my fingers along his dark brow, studying the small flair of his pupils, the minute parting of his lips. He is the man who threatened to burn a city of children alive, who wrapped his hands around my throat with no remorse. But he is also the man who shielded me from the *legatus'* arrows, who risked his father's wrath to facilitate my escape; who's allowed me to touch him, even when it's painful. "You saved me, Anrai. That wasn't a selfish act."

His lips twist and he pushes me off him. I flail back, struggling to gain my footing against the slippery tub, as he climbs out of the bath. Water splashes everywhere as his feet pound against the floor. "Don't see that for something it isn't, Ocean-wielder," he barks, slinging a towel around his waist. I manage to scramble out of the tub after him, my dress clinging to my body and doing little to hide any of it. I swipe at the sodden tresses of hair sticking to my shoulders, trying my best to appear unruffled, even though my heart has yet to calm.

Shaw glares at the soggy floor and then at me, water sluicing down his carved chest in small rivers. After a beat, he says, "Even if it would benefit me to help, the Praeceptor controls my movements."

"What do you mean?"

Shaw eyes are cold once more, and with his mussed hair and swollen lips, he looks every bit the wicked heir. "My father holds a power over me and is able to *force* me to do whatever he asks. It is not just being soulless that has driven my actions over the past months. I don't know it's nature and had planned on staying close to determine how to overcome it. But you have stolen that from me. Now, he will never trust me enough to hand over his secret. Because of *you*, I'll be his slave forever."

My stomach in my throat, I move toward him, a path of water dripping behind me. "How far is his reach?" I ask in a low voice. Shaw instinctively takes a step back, before remembering himself and planting his feet.

I run my hands over the muscled expanse of his stomach, watching the water bead across his skin. "Does he control you now?"

Shaw's lip curls, but he allows my hand to trail up to his pectoral and over the knotted scar above his heart. "He needs to be near me to control me physically, but I can feel the echo of his command, even here." He twists a finger into a wet ringlet framing my face, watching it with rapt attention before returning his eyes to mine. A cruel smile carves his face. "This far away, I can move freely. It was only *my* will that drove me to kill you. Not his."

I look up at him through a thick curtain of lashes. He towers over me, eyes sparking like two embers. "And what does your free will say now?"

He brushes my hair back gently from my temples, his gaze scorching every bit of me it touches. "Promise not to trust me and I will help you. For as long as it serves my goals."

"What are your goals?"

Shaw pulls away abruptly, and his entire body seems to change as he steps back, somehow dimmed and sharpened at once. He eyes are ash once more as he regards me, a remorseless predator. "To gorge myself on revenge. To rip my father limb from limb, to peel his skin from his bones. And then be free...free to end the monotony of the Darkness." At the question on my face, he explains, "to be free to die."

CHAPTER
TWENTY-THREE

Mirren

The manor is quiet, soaked in languishing afternoon sun, and by the time I find everyone in the training gym, I feel like languishing myself. I haven't stopped since I left Similis, always rushing from one place to the next, always balanced on the precipice of destruction. I should feel relieved at Shaw's agreement to help with the prophecy, but instead, I'm more exhausted than ever. I'd been so full wrapped in his arms, only to plummet once more at his declaration. I'd hurried from the room with my heart in my throat and tears in my eyes, his last words a resounding rhythm in my head. *The freedom to die.*

I've already lost him; I should *want* to grant his body peace at last. But every molecule in me revolted at the idea, had wanted to fight against it with every bit of my waning strength. Even now, it seems I cannot follow the Keys—I cannot put Shaw's needs before my own.

Because I can't let him die. Since that day in Yen Girene, it's as if I've been existing in a dreamless wasteland: not truly awake, nor truly asleep. Never wholly myself, parts of me sifting away like sand on the wind. It is only in Shaw's arms that I awoke once again, alive and whole.

I push the door to the gym open and three sets of eyes turn toward me. Harlan holds a sword and his breaths come in winded puffs, his cheeks red with exertion. Though he appears positively beaten, his golden eyes are bright, and his smile is easy like he's never imagined anything as fun as drills.

Cal stands across from him holding his own sword and breathing as easily as if he were standing still.

"Mirren," Harlan grins, his warm voice drenching the room in amiable sunshine. Guilt immediately twists my stomach. Harlan is in Ferusa because of me. He's left behind everything he knows because he trusted his life partner to save Similis. And how do I repay his trust? By kissing the Heir of the Praeceptor, enemy of Harlan's home.

"Hi," I reply tightly, stepping into the room.

"Have you come to watch Harlan learn to be Ferusian?" Cal grins, ruffling Harlan's hair affectionately. "He's gotten quite good while you were playing prisoner."

Harlan blushes, smiling shyly. "More like, I've finally learned how not to trip over my own feet."

"Where's Shaw?" Max interrupts from her perch against the wall. "Cal said he's awake."

"He's resting in his room," I hedge. She narrows her eyes, her shrewd gaze not missing the guilty twitch of my mouth. I sigh in resignation. "He's unbound and isn't our prisoner any longer. He's agreed to help us complete the prophecy."

Max shakes her head, pushing herself to standing with an angry huff. "Mirren, this is naïve, even for you. He almost burned all Siralene's children. He *has* destroyed entire cities and shipped off the rest of them to Argentum.

Mothers and babies and fathers." Her eyes soften as she takes in the wobble of my lip. "You cannot trust him."

She's right. The way my heart shatters and rebuilds every moment I'm in Shaw's presence changes nothing. "We can't trust him. But we *can* trust he will do what's best for himself. He still has Anrai's sense of strategy, and this is the best way for him to get revenge on his father. He knows that."

Max glances at Cal. He sets his sword at his feet and crosses his arms, face scrunched in thought. "If he truly wants revenge against the Praeceptor, why has he been doing his bidding for months? Why not just take it when he was in Argentum?"

It feels wrong, to be discussing Shaw's secrets with his best friends, when *he* should be the one to tell them. But it isn't fair to keep the extent of the situation from them, not when they are as entrenched in this as I am. "Cullen controls him somehow. Back in—" my stomach flips "—in Yen Girene, he said 'you will swear your soul to me, forevermore.' I thought it was metaphorical at the time, but now... now I think he somehow took the last piece of Shaw's soul. I think he's using it to hold him. To control Shaw's power."

"I've never heard of being able to *steal* someone's soul," Max remarks doubtfully.

"Well, I'd also never heard of sea-speakers and wind-whisperers, but here we are," Cal replies wryly. He furrows his brow. "So, Shaw was doing the Praeceptor's bidding in order to gain his trust? To figure out how he controls him and how to break it. So he could kill him."

I nod.

Cal lets out a sharp sigh and turns to Max with a shrug. "It does sound appropriately soulless. Sacrifice villages worth of people just to break your own curse."

I press my mouth into a thin line, not telling them what Shaw intends to do once he's free. Or what I suspect he's suffered all these months at his father's hands. Though I mean nothing to him anymore, his revelations still felt intimate. I cannot give up his secrets when he's always been so delicate with mine.

Harlan sets his sword down and sweeps his arm across his sweaty brow. "If you believe Shaw will help us bring forth the prophecy, I trust you."

I smile weakly. "Thank you, Harlan."

"We're Bound, Mirren. Where you go, I go. Who you trust, I trust." He says it like it's the simplest thing in the world, his face handsome, his eyes perfectly open.

Nausea climbs my throat, along with the urge to run far away from his undying belief I'm better than I am. The only thing that keeps my feet planted to the ground is the reminder that Harlan deserves more than my fear. He deserves my honesty. "Can I talk to you for a minute? Outside?"

He tilts his head curiously, but nods. Cal watches us go, his face lowered in an indecipherable look. I wonder if he judges me for what I've done to Harlan—for what I've done to Anrai—all because I've never been adept enough to name my own emotions, let alone claim them. Outlawed because of their power, and I've been letting them run amok with no regard to the damage they reap. Maybe I am already just as soulless as Shaw.

~

We sit on the cliff nearest the manor. The cerulean waves of the Storven crash against the black rock, angry and powerful, and as I breathe the sea air, my *other* sighs in contentment. This is where we should always be, poised on the edge of the earth and the endless depths. No thoughts of whether to forsake the land for the waves, because here, I can I have both.

"I'm sorry we haven't had much of a chance to talk since Similis," I start out awkwardly. Even to me, my words sound stilted.

Harlan stretches his legs out in front of him and leans back on his elbows, turning his face toward the sun as if he can soak up every ray of warmth. How can I have dragged someone so light into such Darkness? Why did I not consider the cost or what I can give?

And mostly, what I can't.

"Saving the world has been more time consuming than I would have imagined," he says with a chuckle. And then, "I worried for you while you were gone."

He turns toward me with bright eyes, his movements easy even as the world crashes around us. It would be so easy to love this boy—like being Bound to the sun itself. Nothing would ever feel dark, only buttery and warm and light.

But the sea does not strive to reach the sun. Its waves ache for the moon, enigmatic and wild.

"Mirren, I know you worry about bringing me here," he says softly, angling his face closer to mine. For someone raised in Similis, he somehow reads my emotions like the pages of a book. "But I *want* to be here. With you."

Bile fills my mouth, and I stand up abruptly. "Oh gods, Harlan, I can't—" His eyes widen as he watches me pace, running a hand frenetically through my hair until half the curls stand up from my head in a frizzy mess. *Say it. Just say it.* "I'm so sorry, I just—my heart belongs to someone else."

The words feel like pieces of glass coming up, but once they're out, I feel instantly lighter.

Harlan takes them as he takes most things—calmly, and with no hint of judgement. His face is only vaguely concerned as he repeats, "Someone else."

I swallow down the lump in my throat. "When I was here before...when Shaw was...well, when he *was*. We were...I gave him my heart."

Harlan nods slowly, as if connecting my words to the soulless arsonist he witnessed in Havay and Siralene. "And now, his soul is gone."

"Yes," I answer miserably, turning toward the sea. "But it doesn't matter, because my heart is gone along with him. I cannot give it to you, no matter how wonderful you are. And I'm so sorry if you followed me into Ferusa because you thought we were truly life partners. And gods, I'm even *sorrier* you sacrificed yourself for me and I betrayed you with another. You're the entire reason Easton is alive, that *I'm* alive, and I don't deserve any of it." The words pour out of me along with hot, fat tears, but they are also edged in relief. Finally, Harlan knows the depths of my selfishness. There will be no more hiding behind a kind façade. No more cowering behind his imagined version of me.

But when I gather the courage to look at him, he doesn't look at all angry. His head is tilted, his lips curved in a sad smile. "I had no idea you felt guilty about that the entire time."

I shrug rather pathetically, unable to speak.

"Let me ease your burden, Mirren. I *didn't* sacrifice myself last spring for you. And I didn't follow you here because I want to be with you. When I told you friendship was a good place to start for life partners, I meant exactly that. I love you, but not in *that* way."

I stare at him in bewilderment, first at how easily the word *love* slips from his lips, and then, for what he implies. "Then, why—"

Harlan drops his eyes and flushes from his throat to the tips of his ears. After a moment, he says quietly, "It was all for *him*."

"Who—"

But as Harlan meets my gaze, shame and conviction mingling fiercely in the honeyed irises, I realize who he means—who he sacrificed everything for.

Easton.

My brother, Key-follower, is in love?

"We were together before he got sick, in secret, whenever we could find the time and space. But now—well, now he thinks the reason he was spared is to give him a second chance to follow the Keys. And he doesn't want to be with me anymore." Grief washes over Harlan, acute and familiar. Because don't I know exactly how it feels to have your heart torn from you?

"He has a second chance because you loved him. Not because of the godsdamned Keys," I mutter mutinously. Harlan's words to him the night we escaped are now astonishingly clear: *I wish I had seen how weakhearted you are.* Has my brother always been so weak? The outside of him has always appeared strong, like the stone façade of a building, but maybe there have been vines creeping through the cracks. Expanding silently until the entire structure is poised to fall.

Harlan shakes his head. "It doesn't matter anymore. I didn't come this time for Easton. I came because the Keys may have saved Similis from the curse, but they have wrought so much more damage. Things need to change. We should be allowed to *feel*. Love, no matter what form, can't be wrong. Look how far it drove you."

I stare at him.

Love. It sounds so innocent spoken in Harlan's honeyed voice, but nothing so consuming can ever be benevolent. It digs itself in your bones, embeds in the lining of your lungs until it is all you breathe, all you are. It nourishes and starves you all at once. And I'd been too cowardly to name it, to give myself over entirely and drown in its depths, unlike Harlan, who declares it in the daylight and gives it room to grow.

Maybe I deserved to lose it.

"There are others who agree, Mirren. Last year, they found me, and we've been planning a peaceful takeover. If there were enough who believed in change, we thought the Covinus would have to amend the laws." Harlan swallows audibly. "But someone turned and the Covinus...well, you saw what he did to them."

My eyes widen in shock. *The deserters.*

The entire time I felt suffocated, like I didn't fit and never would, there were people walking right beside me who felt the same way. And I never knew. In spite of the sorrow of all the lives lost, hope for my home begins to bloom anew. Because maybe, I am not as different as I always believed. "That—that's how you always know things. How you knew the truth about the Boundary." Harlan nods. "Are the dissenters how you survived being shot?"

Harlan stares at his hands and shakes his head, uncharacteristic darkness abruptly shrouding his features. "I was volunteering in the Covinus' building, filing old paperwork. I came across a file about your parents." My eyes flash to his in alarm. "There wasn't much information in it. It said your father was Outcast because of illegal emotions and that your mother was not."

I open my mouth, questions bubbling to the surface, but Harlan is already shaking his head. "I'm sorry, Mirren, it didn't say what happened to her. But there was something attached to the page. A coin. I knew Easton had nothing of his parents and even though it was rash, I loved him so much, I wanted to give him something. So, I put the coin in my pocket and gave it to him later that night."

The coin. The innocuous piece of metal that was never meant for me but has somehow made its way to my hands twice.

"I didn't know, but the Covinus had been searching for the coin and discovered my theft. The night you escaped was the perfect opportunity for him to bring me in. After they shot me, they dragged me in for questioning and I don't remember much, but I could barely handle it. To keep myself from spilling everything about the dissenters, I told the Covinus about Easton and me. It kept him from looking any further. And then—then they healed me. Because they needed a test subject for an experimental treatment."

I furrow my brow, my confusion palpable. "What do you mean? What kind of treatment?"

Harlan makes a noise in the back of his throat, something between a sob and a laugh. "For those they deem different. For those who don't *contribute* to their society in a way they accept. The fact that Easton and I loved each other was offense enough, but that we are two men? It's an unfathomable crime against the Community, not to reproduce." He presses his palms into his eyes, as if he can clear them of the horrors he still sees. "And it wasn't treatment, Mirren. It was torture."

Tears well in my eyes and instinctively, I pull his hand

into mine. "When you told me there were worse things the Covinus would do than banishment...Gods, Harlan, I had no idea."

He shrugs, but the movement is weighted by sorrow. "I didn't want you to know. I didn't want you to regret saving Easton. And it put me in a unique position. I convinced the Covinus I was a completely changed man and it gave me an inside tract to provide information to the dissenters." Harlan stares at our intertwined fingers. "And I wouldn't change anything that happened, because even if we aren't together, Easton is alive. And for that, I will always be thankful."

He raises his golden gaze to mine. "When I said I was honored to be your life partner, I meant it, Mirren. You are brave and good, and you refuse to just accept things that are unjust. Your side is where I choose. For life. Led by your kind heart, fighting for what's right."

A sob rips from my throat, and I throw my arms around Harlan with such force we both topple over. I've never done anything to deserve his goodness or his loyalty, but it is a candle in the dark cavern of my heart, nonetheless. "We'll find a way. To show our people the truth. Together."

Harlan nods, his throat working as he leans his forehead into mine.

At that moment, Calloway bursts through a manor door, looking distinctly disheveled. His cheeks are rosy and he's winded as if he's sprinted all the way here. Harlan looks at him in alarm, but before bothering to explain, Cal takes a beat to note our intimate position. His eyes narrow, as shrewdly observant as ever, but all he says is, "Come quick. It's Shaw."

By the time we reach the dining room, Shaw is a predator poised to strike. His teeth are bared, his body rigid with focused energy. A chair lies upended beside him, as if he sprung out of it in the middle of eating, and he grips a dagger in his fist with deadly accuracy. I wonder vaguely where he even found it, as Cal stripped him, and the room, of all weapons before he woke.

Max is to the right of Shaw, a sword in one hand, a raspberry scone in the other, looking uncertain whether to cut Shaw down or finish her lunch. Her sentiments of it being merciful to end Shaw drift back to me, and I hasten forward to step between them before she can follow through.

But when I follow Shaw's lethal gaze, the relief that washes over me in a cool wave erases everything else.

Avedis.

Not dead. Not strung up and tortured by the Dark Militia. Alive, whole, and handsome as ever.

I lunge toward him, and he catches me around the waist with a soft chuckle, pulling me up into a fierce hug. His eyes glitter when I pull back to whack him on the arm. "When you didn't show up at the manor, I thought they'd caught you! I was terrified you were hurt or dead...I wanted to come find you."

He sets me down, running a prim hand over his clothes to smooth them. "I did tell you not to worry, O Lady of the Sea. I am as uncatchable as the wind itself." He shoots me a charming smile. "There were things I needed to tend to before I could return." His dark eyes wander back to Shaw, an indication he will tell me no more in his presence. "I was on my way to inform you of my return just now, when I came across our wayward arsonist." Avedis nods to Shaw. "Tell me, *friend,* are you here to finish us all off?"

Shaw's eyes burn as they flash to me. "What *in the*

Darkness is the man who tried to *murder* you doing in this manor?" Every word snaps like a lick of flame and I don't miss the way he adjusts his grip on the knife.

Dread settles in my stomach as Avedis tilts his head, his fingers trailing over the hilt of his own sword. It seems traveling has not put him in an accommodating mood as his eyes flash to the ring of bruises around my throat. "I'm afraid *your* name is more recent on that list than mine, friend."

"Avedis," I warn. His glare softens and he relents with a succinct bow.

But Shaw doesn't release his dagger. I raise my hands, moving toward him slowly. He watches me as he would an approaching wolf, wary and heated, but he doesn't move. "Avedis is a friend. He's helping us with the prophecy," I tell him gently. "He helped me find *you*."

It's the wrong thing to say. His eyes glint savagely, and I suddenly remember the strength of Shaw's feelings were always as powerful as his cold soullessness. Driven by different things, but just as terrifying. It was foolhardy, to be assuaged by a few tears as if they are proof he is tame. Soul or not, Shaw has always been as untenable as a wildfire itself.

"So you *helped* her give herself up to a soulless monster? You *helped* her deliver herself to the Praeceptor to be tortured?"

Avedis is utterly unaffected. "This is beginning to feel like familiar territory. You, growling like a rabid animal about your paramour's weakness, and I...insisting there *is* no weakness."

Before I can blink, Shaw launches himself at the assassin. The two go crashing into Rhonwen's dining table, sending half-empty plates crashing to the floor. Avedis knocks the dagger from Shaw's hand, propelling it into a pitcher of ale. We all duck as the pitcher explodes, dousing the table and causing the candles to sputter wildly. Harlan wisely plasters himself to the nearest wall as the two careen past him, a tangle of fists and snarls.

"Hey!" I shout, my words lost in the din as soon as they leave my mouth. If either of them kills the other, we'll never complete the prophecy.

Max hops over them deftly, just as Shaw cracks Avedis in the jaw. She settles herself atop the table, curling her legs beneath her, and takes a bite of the scone with a small noise of satisfaction, content to simply watch the two men destroy each other.

I scowl at her, wading gingerly through the broken china and ale-sodden carpet. There is none of the restrained elegance Shaw usually fights with: only brutal scrapping, as if he can claw through Avedis with his bare hands and will relish every bit of skin under his nails. The assassin looks all too happy to return the favor, as he rolls deftly out from beneath Shaw, and punches him in the eye.

Cal dances uncertainly behind me, hands scraping for his bow. The sick sound of flesh-on-flesh rings through the room, but the two move too quickly for him to have any accuracy. He'd be just as likely to hit one of us as one of them.

Shaking my head in exasperation, I call the moisture of the overturned pitched and hurtle it toward their faces, just as Shaw gets his fingers around Avedis' throat.

The two men freeze, blinking up at me through sticky, sodden lashes.

"Get off him," I command Shaw. He stares at me hatefully, considering whether he can attack me without getting his blood frozen. He told me he didn't like water on his face, and in my urgency, I didn't consider that stopping him this way would feel like a betrayal. With a start, I realize in Shaw's eyes, I am just as terrible as the Praeceptor: using his weaknesses to control him.

Finally, Shaw releases Avedis' throat with a snarl. They both climb to their feet: Avedis looking like a scolded child and Shaw looking like he may burn down the dining room out of spite. I heave a weighted breath. "Shaw, Avedis is on our side now. He is the wind-wielder. If you wish to stop your father, you won't touch him again."

He doesn't nod, his dead eyes fixed on me. But he also doesn't argue.

"Avedis, stop taunting Shaw. He's—he's been through a lot."

The wind-whisperer merely tilts his head curiously. "My apologies, lady. I assumed it would be much harder to taunt a man who purportedly cares for nothing."

Shaw flinches. "I still have a want for vengeance," he grits out.

Avedis raises a brow and shrugs. "If you say so," he concedes, rubbing his throat lazily. We will bear matching marks of Shaw's malice, as there will most certainly be bruising and swelling, but there's no sign of a burn. Shaw didn't touch his power, even in the depths of rage. When we first encountered him in Havay, it seemed to burst from him, hungry with want of misery and pain. What does it mean that he now keeps it curled inside him?

Avedis smooths his fine clothes once more, before clearing his throat. "If you seek vengeance against the Praeceptor, you may be out of luck."

Shaw's gaze sharpens. "Why?" he demands hotly.

Avedis looks to me. "That is what I was attending to, lady. Once we stole the heir, I followed the movements of the Dark Militia. I wanted to be sure they were not mounting an immediate attack on Nadjaa in response to the slight."

Dread squeezes my stomach like an iron manacle. "Are they?"

"That's the thing. Even my winds cannot be sure. The militia has disappeared."

CHAPTER
TWENTY-FOUR

Shaw

The old witch is exactly as she is in my memories when I find her later that day. Hunched over her garden, gnarled hands deep in the dirt and silver hair hanging down her back in frazzled coils. She doesn't turn when I approach, and it isn't because her hearing has gone. "I'm too old to fear children and their fits of power," she says over her shoulder, answering my silent question of whether she's heard of my exploits.

After another moment of digging, a small sapling pulls free and she cradles it close to her face, cooing to it like it's a baby rather than a plant.

"I am no child," I reply obstinately.

Aggie ignores me completely, whispering to the sapling as she carries it away from the garden and nearer to the wood. Placing the sapling in the ground, she tucks it gently into the dirt before finally fitting me with a dubious look, hands on her hips. "*That* is exactly what a child would say, Anrai Shaw."

"Do not call me by that name," I rumble, eyes flashing.

The name is dead, buried in the Darkness along with my soul. I do not feel as Anrai felt; do not contain the weakness he did.

But when Mirren had uttered it, green eyes wide as a fawn, her body wet and warm and pressed against mine, I *had* felt a spark of him. Of the man whose memories I can trace the outlines of, the insides always stubbornly out of reach. The man who fought when he should have given up, who loved when he should have hated.

The flash of him had terrified me. The heaviness of it all, the consuming light that flared in my chest. I'd felt it in the depths of my abyss, my power sated for once. When I'd hurtled out of the tub, the feeling receded as quickly as it had come, and I was left cold and empty as ever.

Aggie pushes herself to standing, hands on knobby knees. Pieces of leaves and dirt cling to her wiry hair, but she doesn't seem to mind as she stares at me with milky eyes. "Names have power, Anrai Shaw. Consumed by the fire or not, that is yours and I will call you by it."

Her words snag something in my memories. "You knew?" I demand suddenly. My power surges to my fingertips. "You knew this would happen to me and you did nothing?"

The old woman doesn't even flinch as flames line my arms, conflagrating in the setting sun. "You have always had power. The old gods have yet to determine if yours will be the beginning or the end. Fire is both a source of light and one of devastation. It is up to you which you choose."

"That choice was taken from me, along with my soul."

Aggie makes a humming noise. "Was it?" she asks in a horrible sing-song voice. "As I recall, your soul was not taken, but rather, *given*. Therein lies the difference."

I grimace. I should have just tortured the information I

seek out of her, and spared myself the old hag's riddles, but Mirren wouldn't let me out of the manor until I'd promised not to kill Aggie. Good riddance. But as I have no wish to get my blood frozen, it hadn't been worth the effort of arguing. "Do you know where the Praeceptor's militia has gone?"

Aggie's eyebrows fly up her forehead, as if I've surprised her for the first time. "That is why you've come? To find your father?"

"Should there be another reason?"

She wipes soil covered hands along the front of her dress. "Is the state of your soul not more important than your vengeance?"

I set her with a dead glare, the hollow in my chest echoing like the wind outside a cavern as I draw my flames back toward my heart. "My soul is gone, there is nothing more to entertain. My vengeance remains. Breaking my father's control."

Aggie narrows her eyes and I work to keep myself from snarling.

I stretch my neck, trying to relax. Pain has begun to simmer in my blood, and I cannot feed it here if I wish to use these people to defeat my father. And after my stunt at camp, I've been left with few other choices than to accept their alliance. "Just because I have no soul doesn't mean I wish to have a master."

She tilts her chin up and I wonder why I feel inspected though the witch cannot see. "Very well, Anrai Shaw." Aggie stiffens abruptly and her melodic voice roughens. "Your father dabbles in things that have long slept and they begin to rear up in defiance. He controls them for now, but it will not always be so."

"How has he made an entire militia disappear?"

Aggie shudders violently. "They are not gone, only

hidden. Where the old magic sleeps, wound in the roots of trees and hearts of beasts. He claims power that is not his, to find what should not be found."

I push a loud sigh through my nostrils. "Is that it, then? I'm supposed to track down the Praeceptor on nonsense and whimsy?"

Aggie's demeanor shifts again, her body going pliant. "Is that not how you found your ocean-wielder?"

"She is *not* mine," I snap. "And your vision was manipulated by the Praeceptor so I would find her. *You,* and the ridiculous nonsense of your visions, caused all this. If I'd never met Mirren, my father would not control me now."

Aggie glares at me, and for an absurd moment, I have the urge to retreat from the old woman. "I hear fragments from the old gods, Anrai Shaw. The whispers of the lines of time cannot be manipulated, no matter the blood magic. It does not matter how it happened, you were *meant* to find Mirren and give her a piece of your soul in love."

My breath freezes in my chest. "What did you say?" I ask, my voice deathly quiet.

Aggie levels me with her cratered stare, though this time, it is lined with something close to pity. "You have been mired so long in the Darkness, boy, you think the light to be imagined. Your soul is not gone. It lives on in the one you gifted it to." At my dumbfounded look, Aggie sighs, "In Mirren."

~

Mirren

Gone. The entire Dark Militia is gone.

Even in a world so large, it should be impossible to hide an entire army. Especially someplace even the wind can't find. After brainstorming for hours, we'd all come up empty. Even Avedis hadn't been able to name a place in Ferusa large enough to hold the Praeceptor's forces, but small enough the wind couldn't enter.

Max had thrown her hands up in frustration and headed into Nadjaa to blow off some steam. Cal and Harlan had gone back to the training room and Avedis had retired to an upstairs guest room to catch up on sleep.

After hearing the news of his father, Shaw's eyes had gone positively feral. Smoke crawled around him, his power's own brand of Darkness, and for a moment, I feared what he'd do. But he'd only insisted on speaking with Aggie, and after repeatedly threatening to freeze his blood if he hurt her, I'd reluctantly agreed. Though, in all Ferusa, Aggie may be the only one who won't fear the Heir.

Alone for the first time since my return, I head into one of the manor's grand studies. It's come to be my favorite in my short time here, with its comfortably worn seating and mountains of books piled haphazardly around, as if they've begun to sprout from the floor itself. Books that have been read so many times, it must have seemed pointless to reshelve them, even to someone as ruthlessly tidy as Rhonwen.

When I arrive, the earth-wielder sits tucked into one of the deep armchairs. He smiles up at me, etching the lines in his face even deeper, his tongue pushed against the hole left by his missing teeth. A farmer from Ashlaa, Gislan is Darkness-weathered, but in his short time with us, he's proven to be an amiable ally.

"Hello, Gislan." I plop myself down on a chair across from him, pulling a large book into my lap.

Gislan nods over his tea. His smile, though friendly, is as tight as ever, like he's always prepared for the moment a smile will no longer be necessary. He'd been trapped with Akari Ilinka for well over a month, and though he showed no outward signs of abuse beyond severe neglect, his demeanor made it quite apparent he hadn't been allowed an inch of freedom while in her possession.

Someday, the witch-queen will be made to answer for her treatment of others. I'll be sure of it.

"Are you making yourself at home?" I ask.

"Yes, lady."

"Call me Mirren." It's bad enough Avedis calls me that.

"Mirren," the earth-wielder repeats rather shyly. "I am appreciative for everything you've done for me."

"Cal told me of your family. When this is all over, I hope you know I'll do anything in my power to help them. Maybe we can even bring them to Nadjaa."

Gislan shakes his head. "You have already given more than I could have asked for. You've not only saved me, you've gifted me the chance to make them proud." His gaze meets mine, his eyes the color of freshly turned earth. "You should know, I was a thief in Ashlaa."

I open my mouth to protest, as I'm the last person Gislan needs to justify himself to, but the earth-wielder continues. "There is never enough at home. We starve to death on the gates of the warlord's palace. And so, I kept my family fed. But I've never made them proud."

Closing my book gently, I lean forward earnestly. "You protected your family, Gislan. Surely you can see the honor in that."

Something like sadness flickers over his face as he looks at me. "Still so young, your compassion not yet ruined by the world," he says softly, and then, seeming to remember himself, he straightens in his chair and clears his throat. "Anyway, I thank you, Mirren. When the prophecy comes to pass and we give others the power I never had to rise up against those who would oppress them...then, I shall be proud."

He buries his face in his book, leaving only the pink tips of his ears visible. Fishing around for a change of subject, I say, "Your power must be extraordinarily strong. We felt your earth shake all the way in Similis."

At this, Gislan looks up once more, a line between his brows. "I didn't—"

But before he's able to finish his thought, the door to the study bursts open so brutally, it ricochets off the opposite wall. Gislan jumps, his gaze jerking fearfully to the hallway where Shaw looms, his hair brushing the top of the doorframe. At once, the air in the room heats. His eyes glow as he charges into the study, and he takes no notice of Gislan at all, except to growl a menacing, "Out."

Gislan needs no prompting. He's already halfway to the door, perhaps having heard rumors of Shaw's temper.

I stand up, steeling my spine as Shaw stalks toward me, his long strides eating up the space between us. Fire bursts to life at his fingertips, the flames eagerly licking up his arms and his chest. "What did Aggie say?" I ask, somehow managing to keep my voice even, despite the pound of my heart. Whatever it was, it obviously wasn't good.

He prowls forward, for once, showing no hesitation at all about touching me. I back up, matching his steps, but it isn't fear that threads through me. Something closer to anticipation blooms and my *other* rises in ardent fervor. I try to tamp it down, to remember why this is a bad idea, but one look at the hungry glint in Shaw's eyes and my power begins to flow through me in a heady wave. It sings to the call of his, rising to the surface of my skin as if it waits for him, and him alone.

Taking another step backward for no other reason than to take a breath, I bump into the wall. Shaw stops a hairsbreadth away, gazing down like he intends to devour me whole. Hatred, lust, and something wholly softer mingle on his face and I drink it all down, because it is all so much better than emptiness.

His hands come to my shoulders, before skimming up my throat to tilt my jaw upward. His flames graze over my skin, but they don't hurt or burn. They warm me from within, an extension of his touch, and I close my eyes with a small shiver. I've been so cold without him.

While my eyes are still closed, Shaw takes my lips beneath his, ravenous and demanding. The delicious weight of him presses me into the paneled wall so hard I can feel every ridge of his muscles, solid and inescapable. How odd that feeling powerless is so thrilling; how odd it somehow makes me feel strong.

His hand dives into my hair, the other running the length of my spine, restless, as if determined to explore every inch he's been denied in our time apart. He teases my breasts through my shirt, growling his approval into my mouth as my nipples peak in response. I push at his chest, only putting enough space between us to tear his shirt over his head before I throw myself at him once more. Shaw doesn't even tilt back on his heels as he catches me in the solid cradle of his arms, winding my legs around his waist and returning his needy mouth to mine. I breathe a sigh of relief. With the rest of the world, I've always held back in fear I am too much. I have tamped down my words, my power, *myself*, for so long: only gaining a respite in the few months we had together. Because I have always been able to throw everything I am at Shaw—to do my worst—and he never falters. The immovable mountain to my tempestuous ocean.

I claw my way across the bare skin of his chest, kissing and licking every part I can reach. The taste of him buzzes to my head and slides beneath my skin, until I am panting with want.

Taking my chin between his fingers, he swipes his tongue across mine. Flames roll over my skin, mingling with my waves until we've created our own storm. Barely breaking his lips from mine, Shaw yanks my shirt off, flinging it to the ground. He backs me up to the window, his tongue pulsing, his hands never ceasing. And I burn, burn, burn as he grinds his hips into mine until I'm writhing, a whimper rolling across my tongue, pinned between the heat of him and the cold of the windowpane against my bare skin.

He pulls back, breathing heavily as he gazes at me trapped beneath him. His dark hair is mussed, his pale eyes bright against the dark smudges of exhaustion beneath them. Even the small distance is too much, and I reach for him, but he holds me in place with a hand to my throat. It is the worst kind of agony, to be unable to chase the friction that will ease the ache between my legs, but I hold still beneath his firm grip. "It's true then," he whispers, his voice strangled. For a moment, the dichotomy between the two sides of Shaw is as visible as if painted in a crisp black line. Tormented. Reverent. And utterly inhuman.

"What's true?"

Shaw's eyes trail to my lips, and they linger there, voracious and burning, before lifting once more to mine. "You own a piece of my soul," he says, before abruptly tearing himself away from me. All at once, his power and mine recede, leaving the room empty.

I stare at him, folding my arms across my bare chest, the cold of his absence unbearably biting. "I—what?"

He gathers his shirt from the floor and pulls it over his head before turning to me. I flinch at what now lies in his eyes—the barren vacuum of nothingness. "It seems I gave you more than my father and my friends and my room and my *life* when I loved you," he says, his voice laced with razor-sharp anger. "I gave you a piece of my soul."

My throat feels thick, as if every terrible and wonderful thing I've both wished for and feared, is suddenly attempting to climb out of it. My body begins to tremble, a new sort of hope and dread mingling furiously. How many times have I imagined him whispering those words to me, the words I was never brave enough to say? And now—now he whips them at me, a dagger to the heart.

But a soul...if Shaw gave me his soul, could I somehow give it back? Could I save him from himself? "What...what does this mean?"

Shaw runs his gaze over me and for the first time, I feel ashamed to be naked in his presence. Because there is nothing but hatred there: no heart, no longing—only destruction. "It means nothing. Do not touch me with it again," he spits, his tone brutal. "I don't want it back."

CHAPTER
TWENTY-FIVE

Mirren

I find Asa by the same fire, the crowd of children around him now quadruple that of the one before. Word of his captivating temperament and enchanting tales must have reached Nadjaa, because now, it is not only Xamani who listen with rapt attention, little bodies soft and still.

Asa weaves the story with his hands, his voice winding through the air like a resonant song. Its melody draws me in, feeling for a moment like it lives inside me rather than in memory. My *other* curls up into a soft pool, content to sit and listen to the Kashan for the rest of the day.

But before I can settle in fully, I realize it isn't just children who've been drawn to Asa's stories. My father stands to the back, almost fully hidden behind one of the tents. He leans against his cane, his eyes oddly bright behind his glasses as he listens.

I stand frozen, wondering if there's still time to leave before he catches sight of me, when his head turns. Guilt threads through me, thick and unpleasant. There was a time my father's arms were infallible; the one thing in the world that would always catch me. Now, he just appears frail and exhausted, consumed by the act of living. Not so long ago, I would have blamed it on the Darkness, but I know better now. It isn't Ferusa or the curse that turns people into what they are. It's the choices they're forced to make. And living with them.

With a nervous breath, I draw up beside him. "I didn't realize you were back."

Denver nods, regripping his cane and adjusting his stance. His movements are jerky and pain-ridden and send another thread of guilt spiraling through me. "My trip to Siralene was cut short as Akari Ilinka would not allow any foreigners into her city, even under the guise of an alliance. Something has her spooked."

My father had left Nadjaa shortly after we did to negotiate an alliance between the two territories. The witch-queen holds no love for my father and his taste for peace, but I can't imagine my stealing Gislan from her helped matters.

I hum noncommittally, eyes still on Asa as he gestures wildly, earning delighted squeaks from the children. "Do you think telling a story like that is something that can be taught?"

Denver chuckles softly and it warms my chest. "The Xamani believe it is a gift, but one that can be nurtured to fruition, passed down from one Kashan to the next." He nods to Asa. "But I believe Asa was born with words pouring from every bit of him."

I smile lightly. Heavy silence settles between us, the past and the present suddenly feeling like an immovable wall. *You once told me stories of wild places and unlimited dreams. Do you remember?*

"Asa says he has not yet found the true story of the

Dead Prophecy, but it appears you've been busy in spite of this," Denver says amiably.

Cal had been purposefully vague on Gislan's origins when they turned up at the manor and by the time I'd arrive home with Shaw, Denver was gone. Though he rarely takes meals in the dining room anymore, preferring instead to eat at his desk in between meetings, by now, he's certainly noticed his former ward skulking around the manor.

This is the closest he's come to mentioning it, the Similian in him still preventing him from making me uncomfortable with accusations. But my father has been in the Darkness a long time, and I'd be remiss to think it hasn't shaped the few words he allows into cutting weapons.

"I am not Chancellor," I say levelly. "I care for more than just the wellbeing of Nadjaa."

Denver nods slowly, digesting my words. "And capturing Anrai? Was that a strategic decision or one made with your heart?"

I turn to him with a heated glare, my *other* simmering to the surface. "If you're about to tell me I've put Nadjaa's safety at risk by bringing him here, I will drown you where you stand. He saved your life."

Denver only tilts his head, lips turned down in disappointment as if I'm three years old and he's enduring an unreasonable tantrum. "The opposite, actually. It will be driving the Praeceptor to madness that I have his son in my possession. And I believe, a great strategic boon to our completion of the prophecy." My lips curl in fury at Denver's claim on Shaw, but he presses on, "My worry is for you, Mirri. If you brought the boy here because you think he can be saved, you are only setting yourself up for more sorrow."

I considering telling my father of Shaw's recent admission: that there's a piece of him living in me. I could tell him of my suspicion that Cullen also holds a piece and uses it to direct him like a warped puppet. But I don't say anything as the strength of my anger mingles with the strength of my power, and I'm forced to use all my concentration on keeping it from exploding out of me.

It's becoming harder to grasp, to keep myself poised on the edge of humanity, when falling appears so tempting: no heartbreak, no treachery, no love. Just power.

"He is soulless, Mirri. He will help you only so long as it serves his goal. And after, he is just as likely to kill you as he is himself. His anger will consume everything in its path, and if you don't let him go, you will be destroyed by it."

Shaw told me as much himself, but somehow, hearing it from Denver is worse. My cheeks flush, anger prickling, hot and sharp at the back of my throat. I grit my teeth and plant my feet, swallowing down my *other*; using the earth as a reminder to remain present. "I thought Easton inherited his weakness from our mother, but it's you whose spine bends to the whims of the world. Tell me, how do you so easily give up?"

Denver's nostrils flare, the only sign he'll give I've unsettled him. But it is enough. "Don't ever speak about your mother that way." His voice remains calm, but something unfamiliar edges it. Something primal.

But it's too late to rein myself in, to cage what's begun to thrash around inside me. The hurt I've felt since I was an abandoned child has grown into something far more monstrous. "Did you know she tried to keep from being Outcast by throwing herself at the Covinus? And it wasn't to stay with her children. It was to save her own skin. You were more perfect for each other than you knew, both selfish to the core."

Denver flinches like I've delivered a punch to his gut. "That is not true," he says quietly and though I hate myself a little, I can't catch the words as they pour from me.

"The Covinus told me before he tried to kill me. He murdered her for that weakness. How many people must be sacrificed for the weakhearted of this world? How many slaves made, how many children abandoned, how many innocents killed because of the choices of people like you? Like Mom and the Covinus?"

Denver studies me, and for the first time I can remember, I see the hard flash of anger in his eyes. "You can rage against the world, Mirri, but you will only fall further into the Darkness. And someday, you won't be able to find your way out." He turns away from me. "There is much you don't know. Do not speak ill of your mother in front of me again."

With a scoff of disgust, I whip around, determined to put as much distance as possible between the two of us. I'd come to the refugee camp intending to speak with Asa, but it will have to wait. Now, I can hardly think beyond the boiling wave of power threatening to crest over me.

Before I even make it past the next tent, I spot Sura hurtling toward me. Her silky hair has pulled free from its plait, her high cheekbones stained with a rosy shade of exertion. "Sura! Is everything okay?"

She shakes her head frantically, gasping to catch her breath as Denver hobbles to my side. "I was just in Nadjaa," she wheezes, grabbing her chest. "You both need to come right now!"

"She has a breathing condition," Denver explains gently, placing a hand on her back as she doubles over. I stare, momentarily transfixed by the tender gesture. My father has not touched me at all in the time we've been reunited, but apparently, he isn't opposed to compassion altogether. "Deep breaths, Sura. What's happened?"

Sura nods at Denver gratefully, her eyes wide and panicked. "The manor. The manor is on fire."

∼

Shaw

Strike, parry, move.

I repeat it to myself until sweat pours from my brow; until the movement is imprinted on my limbs and exhaustion saps every word except those three from my mind.

You are a weapon. You are made to destroy, never build.

Lacing my daggers with flame, I spin, shooting them into the heart of the nearest dummy. The outside training grounds are empty in the late morning light, and the chilly breeze coming in off the Storven Sea cools the heat of my skin as I gather up my knives and begin again.

Strike, parry, move.

My muscles ache in protest and my breaths saw out of my lungs painfully. I've been at this for hours. Since I fled the study and the raw hurt in Mirren's eyes—hurt I caused. Hurt she deserved.

But it wasn't the hurt that drove me away, it was what shone beneath it, tender as a new flame.

Hope.

The water is no place for a boy who burns.

My father is cruel, but even he has never been ruthless enough to give me hope. The ocean-wielder is vicious, to hold out light in the middle of the Darkness. For when it is inevitably stolen from my grasp, leaving me naked and desperate on my knees, the night will only be more suffocating than before.

My daggers sail into the heart of the target, one after another, with a *thwump, thwump, thwump*. Flames burst to life, and I watch with detached interest as they consume the dummy, just as they've consumed so many before.

Mirren can keep Anrai's soul and his love. I want nothing to do with them. I felt the rhythm of myself in the beat of her heart and found I could not bear it. For how could a fragment of a soul live beneath the weight of my sins? It is better to be empty than live with what I've done. Of what's been done to me.

Better to live with no regret. With nothing holding me back from doing exactly what I want to do when I want to do it. I am stronger without Anrai's weak soul. Strong enough to take everything from my father, the way Anrai never could. His humanity always held him back, his pathetic need to prove himself *good*. I harbor no such vulnerability. There is no sadness twined around my chest, no loneliness wrapped around my throat. If I can best the Praeceptor and defeat his control, I will be completely free.

Free to feed the emptiness however I'd like. And then, when I'm finished, the freedom to end it all.

Deaths like these are common for the soulless. Being unable to satiate the perpetual hunger, the endless cold is enough to drive even the most reasonable to madness. But I am not mad, simply pragmatic. And most of all, *bored*. There are only so many ways to fill the void, and with every passing day, it becomes harder and harder to satisfy.

The chasm grows hungrier, always searching for *more*, and eventually, I won't be able to keep up. The cold emptiness will overwhelm me, ceaseless and eternal, with nothing ever able to fill it.

Except Mirren. You were full when you touched her.

I push the thought away with a snarl. Mirren is the cause of all of this, the reason I'm enslaved to my father. Wielding those luscious red lips and silken skin as a warrior would a weapon, beckoning unsuspecting fools like Anrai with her soft words. I'll slit her throat before I let her touch me again.

Gripping another dagger in my hand and lining up my sight, I am about to throw when the air shifts around me. Something flares hot beneath my shirt. The coin. Mirren must have found it in my desk and brought it with us, because when I searched the manor, it had been nestled in a locked closet along with my militia-issued bandolier. There's no way Mirren knows of its magic. More than likely, it was her sentimentality that persuaded her to keep it. But I know its power, its searching hunger a mirror to my own, so I strung its weight around my neck.

Now, it pulses against my skin, alive and agitated. I still, listening for the cause of the disturbance, when my power suddenly flares to life. Not in devouring hunger, but as a flaring beacon, answering the familiar call of another.

Then I smell the smoke.

I palm my daggers and dash toward the manor. Sweat dampens my hair, my clothes, but I don't slow until the old house comes into view. It looks the same as ever, vines crawling up the sides, wild blooms painting the landscape in a riot of color. No fire, no destruction.

Maybe I'm going mad, after all.

I exhale sharply and make to turn back, just as an explosion rocks the world around me.

Flames shoot from ground level windows, their panes shattering on impact. I throw myself to the ground as hot glass rains from the sky. The shards slice my cheeks and the exposed skin of my arms, but I'm already up and running toward the front door. Rhonwen stumbles out, the housekeeper smudged in ash and looking dazed. I grab her by the shoulders, forcing her to look me in the eye. She rears back in panic at what she sees, but when I tell her to go get help, she nods in understanding.

Knives out, I step into the manor just as another explosion tears through the kitchen. Flames burst from the doors and into the entryway, a wave of boiling heat. Sheathing my knives, I inhale and attempt to focus on the call of fire. I've never tried to control flames that weren't of my own making, never had any reason to *stop* them. I've always bent to their whim, their wish for destruction a mirror to my own. But I'll never defeat Cullen if I let everyone in this mansion burn, so now, I close my eyes and reach for them.

Their rage charges through me, burning at the back of my throat. My power rises, entwining itself around them, and for a moment, I fear combining them is a grave mistake: that they'll combust, overpowering me in a maelstrom of destruction.

I will my breathing to slow, feeling the familiar edges of this body and commanding it as if it's mine and not Anrai's. I imagine the subtle flames of a campfire, the flicker of a candle against Mirren's skin, the warmth of a fireplace on a winter's night. I imagine the glow of a lantern against the dark and the smell of the hearth of a home.

My power softens, curling around my heart, and for a beat, I am warm. When I open my eyes, the flames around me have all calmed to embers. A relieved breath shoots from my chest, but it is short lived—the coin shudders and something shifts in the air once more. This time, it does not call to me. It's a vacuum, malevolent and endless, and I collapse to the ground as pure agony wracks my body.

Every bit of my power drains away, as if all the oxygen has been sucked from the room. Tremors raze through me, my bones so cold I fear they'll break beneath the least bit of pressure. My nerves scream and I can hardly think, but for one thing: I've felt this before. In the bowels of the Castellium and the dungeons of Yen Girene.

My throat spasms, my heart slowing until its beat is hardly more than a murmur. The flames crawl toward me, alive and hungry once again, and I know instinctively, if they reach me, I will burn as I've burned so many others. I look around wildly, the movement sluggish and awkward. My father cannot be here, in the heart of Nadjaa. He could not have gotten past the army that camps in the mountains, the Chancellor's guard that surrounds the city. And if he had, I would be under his control once more, the iron vice in my chest insurmountable. *I* would be the one destroying the manor.

But if it isn't the Praeceptor, who else has the strength to drain my power?

Another explosion rocks the east wing, the impact of it a searing wave that sweeps through the manor. I bury my head in my arms as my skin blisters, my chest already aching from the smoke.

You will die just as you've lived. Burning too brightly, until there is nothing left but ash.

Flame cracks above my head just as Cal bursts in from the dining room and stumbles into the foyer. His clothes are torn and covered in a layer of black soot, the copper of his hair obscured by gray ash. Blood streams from his forehead and a piece of shrapnel protrudes from his forearm. I feel the moment his eyes light on my decrepit form, the density of his love and the shape of his loyalty both a physical force as he runs toward me.

Wedging his hands under my armpits, he heaves me up with a pained groan. My muscles scream, as if they've been mired in the depths of a frozen lake. "I have to go get Gislan," he gulps, as the manor shudders once more. Flames shoot down the hallway from Denver's office and he shields us both against the bright light as I work my way gingerly to my feet.

Cal balances my weight against his own. "We can't lose Gislan," he manages, and I realize he speaks of the Dead Prophecy. If the earth-wielder dies, we won't be able to complete it. "But Max is upstairs." His eyes plead with mine and I understand what he asks of me. He'll risk himself to save my crusade against my father. But I must risk myself to save what matters to him: the venomous girl who's looked at me with nothing but pure loathing since I woke here.

There's no choice to make. Even without my power—without my flames, or my strength, or even a clear head—I'll never give up my vengeance. So I nod.

Cal inclines his head once, his eyes glistening with tears and something close to faith that curls my lip. I want to tell him this means nothing, I do not care for him or the angry woman, but before I can, he hugs me to him. "Be safe, brother," he whispers into my neck, before disappearing into the destruction.

Move, Shaw.

It's the voice inside me my father could never kill, the instinct that has kept me alive for so long given form. Even in the absence of flame, my shadows endure. *It is only pain.*

My jaw clacks with tremors, my teeth grinding together, but I move anyway, forcing one foot forward. Each breath feels like acid as I claw my way toward the stairs and then up them, scraping, crawling, and sometimes falling, one step at a time.

My fingernails crack and bleed as I scrabble upward, my breaths coming in short wheezes. Another explosion wracks the manor, and the impact throws me down two stairs. My knees crack against the marble, but I grit my teeth with a curse and pull myself back up. Using the iron spindles as leverage even as they scorch the palms of my hands, I climb higher.

When I finally reach the second story landing, I collapse on my back, coughing up black clouds of ash as the sounds of destruction echo around me. An absurd bubble of laughter climbs my throat, as I vaguely wonder whether I will burn to death trying to reach someone I care nothing for. Wouldn't it be fitting if I succumbed to flame, able to feel everything I've subjected so many others to.

Smoke scorches my lungs, so I rip off my shirt and tie it around my face. Flipping gingerly to my hands and knees, I slide toward Max's bedroom door on my belly, hoping she's there. If she's not, I have no way of finding her before we both die. And on the slight chance I manage to survive, Calloway will surely cut me down where I stand if Max isn't with me.

When I finally reach her door, it won't budge. Warped and swollen with the heat, I can hear Max on the other side of it, hacking at the old wood with a sword and cursing violently.

Using the iron doorknob to hold most of my weight, I pull myself to standing as my vision begins to blur with the sting of tears. I wipe my eyes impatiently, but it does no good, as thick, black smoke billows around me.

"Stand back!" I holler, before hurtling myself at the door. I have no strength, but thankfully, my pure mass still has some effect. Both the door and I topple over gracelessly into Max's room.

Flames race through the hallway just as I manage to stand up, and we both dive further into the room to avoid being burnt. And then Max is back on her feet, weapon drawn, even as I roll listlessly, struggling to determine which way is up. For half a heartbeat, I consider taking my chances with the fire rather than the heat of her fury. Even in the midst of absolute chaos, she manages to look haughty as she stares down her nose at me, hand on her sword.

"You can kill me later," I mutter weakly, finally managing to maneuver myself upright and stumbling toward the window. I don't even bother trying to force the ancient pane open, instead choosing to heft Max's armchair above my head with my remaining strength and hurtling it straight through the glass. "Let's go," I pant, motioning vaguely toward the now gaping window frame.

Her lip curls. "I'm not going anywhere with you, monster," she spits.

I take another singed breath, cocking my head in annoyance. "Would you prefer to burn to death?"

The floor rocks beneath us in demonstration, but Max doesn't relent. "We never should have let you in here. You did this! The least I can do is die knowing I've taken you with me and spared the world your horror." With that, she raises her sword and launches herself at me.

But I know her, trained with her. Have watched her habits for years. I shift my body, and using one last surge of energy, leverage her own momentum to send us both flying backward out the window. She screams, in fury and fear, and I wrap my body around hers as we plunge toward the ground. The impact is deafening and sharp, every bone in my body having certainly snapped.

Max wrestles herself off me, and as I stare up at her furious face, my breaths coming in whistled wheezes, I can't help but laugh. Wild, absurd laughter coughs out of me, each peel causing my chest to further feel like it's caving in. Blood seeps into my mouth, the iron tang coating my tongue as she draws her sword and presses it my throat.

My smile is positively demented as I glare up at her. "Do it," I rasp, spitting blood onto the ground next to me and laughing again. "Kill me."

As soon as the words leave my mouth, my power returns in a surge of flame. Each piece of me thaws, until only the cold chill of my soullessness remains. But I don't move against her. Instead, I lift my chin, pressing my throat further into her sword with an unhinged snarl. Her dark eyes flare with rage, and she presses her foot into my chest. "I will," she whispers, her voice laced with death. This is the Max from my memories, the one who's rage against the world is ceaseless. "I will gut you right here. Recompense for everything you've done with Anrai's body."

The air around us cools and the roar of the fire behind us suddenly falls silent. Eerie calm settles over the mountain top and I know why before I hear her voice. "Max!" Mirren shouts from a distance, panicked and winded. "Don't do it!"

Max doesn't waver as a cruel smile crawls over my face. She grits her teeth, staring down at me with hard determination. "For Anrai," she declares.

"Max! Stop! Look at him...he *is* Anrai!" Mirren pleads, her voice growing closer as she sprints toward us.

"HE IS NOT!" Max screams wildly. "My friend is gone! And this *monster* has destroyed everything Anrai loved!"

"Don't be weak," I taunt, baring my throat. "Kill me, Mahwell'ha."

Max grips her falchion, her eyes filled with fury as the name touches something inside her, just as I intend it to. Perhaps I've lost my mind after all, choking on my own blood, taunting her to send me to the Darkness. *End the boredom.*

Max's pupils flare and her sword twitches against my throat just as Mirren arrives at her side. "Max, I have a piece of Anrai's soul. And when I touch *him*," she explains breathlessly, jerking her head to me, "he feels it. Anrai's soul lives."

Max looks to Mirren and a small fissure appears in the armored wall she holds around herself; the one that guilds her eyes in anger and keeps the world from seeing the vulnerable girl who resides beneath. "That isn't possible," she breathes.

No. The ocean-wielder has already stolen so much from me, I won't allow her to take this. "I burned your manor, and I will destroy everything else you love." I laugh in Max's face. "Calloway, Denver, Mirren, Nadjaa. I will ravage it all because you're too pathetic to stop me."

But she doesn't rise to my taunt. Behind the wall of stone, buried as deep as she keeps her secrets, a new hope blooms in her eyes and gods, I want to howl in fury.

Mirren kneels next to me, her eyes burning as if sensing my madness, my wrath. "If you give up now, Cullen wins."

I scream in frustration, in rage at her truth, but when she weaves her fingers through mine, I scream for an entirely different reason. The weight of my own soul presses down on me, smothering the breath from me with its horror and its goodness and everything in between. It was never Mirren's power that caused me pain—it was my own self, my own shame and guilt and sadness that were unbearable.

And this time, I don't fight it. I let it settle over me until I think my bones will splinter and my chest will cave in. Because though it's agony, Mirren is right—if I give in to the emptiness, my father will never pay for what he's done.

When I open my eyes, Max stares down at me in abject horror. My first friend in the world, who saved me from becoming soulless so many years earlier. "Max," I whisper, and my voice breaks with emotion as I let Anrai's memories flood me, *my* memories. And not just the lines of them, but every bit of emotion that painted them in such vibrant splashes of life. "Max, I'm sorry I left you alone...that I haven't been there to shoulder the Darkness with you. The weight of caring for everyone so deeply."

The fissure in Max's wall becomes a gaping hole, and she lets out a loud sob, throwing her arms around my neck. Her weapon discarded on the grass beside us, I hold her to me as she cries. All the while, Mirren grips my hand, her own tears running silently down her cheeks. Finally, Max pulls back and inhales sharply, resurrecting her wall brick by brick.

And for a moment, she looks exactly as she did the first day I met her in the Castellium dining room. Defiant, beautiful, and sad. "I have missed you," she says simply, before turning to Mirren. "Thank you. F-for believing when I couldn't."

Mirren bows her head. "You believed enough for both of us all this time, Max. It was time I returned the favor."

Max nods, swiping at her eyes, before turning toward the smoldering manor.

Mirren stares at our intertwined fingers wistfully, her

tears falling freely now. "I'm sorry for touching you again," she says roughly, "but I couldn't let her kill you."

I want to tell her she should be sorry—that the weight of my soul is like the weight of the very sky, and I fear I will break beneath it. That when I ran from the study last night, it was not her touch I couldn't stand, but my own.

But I only stare at her. Even with the gaunt appearance of her once full face and the exhaustion marked beneath her eyes, she is the most radiant thing I've ever seen. And gods, *it hurts:* the strength of her beauty and her power and the things I've done to them.

She pulls her hand from mine, barely catching a sob in her throat. And this time, when the emptiness hollowness settles over me once more, I welcome it.

CHAPTER
TWENTY-SIX

Shaw

The little goodwill I garnered by agreeing to an alliance has been destroyed along with the manor. Though she didn't kill me, Max continues to shoot glowering looks in my direction all day. Mirren may have stayed her hand by convincing her my soul lives, but she still implicitly believes I orchestrated the attack.

Rhonwen has been inconsolable most of the day, hiccupping and muttering about the state of the manor floors. Though stern, the housekeeper has always treated me with maternal warmth. Even when I returned with no soul, she greeted me as if nothing had changed: by scolding me about the mud I'd tracked in and informing me there was bread in the kitchen, and I was to eat it immediately as she thought me entirely too skinny. Now, though, she too avoids my gaze.

The assassin had been out of Nadjaa at the time of the fire, having climbed one of the nearest peaks to attempt to get a better read on the Dark Militia. When he returns and sees the smoldering ruins of the house, it takes both Mirren and Cal to keep him from attacking me. A forcible gale rips across the hill as I grin maniacally, confirming his worst beliefs. He swears loudly, and with a shake of his head, stalks off into the trees to cool down.

And Denver.

He returned shortly after Mirren, his face unreadable as he gazed up at the smoking ruins. The man Anrai viewed as a father, a Chancellor worthy of admiration, now watches me with abject wariness as if I might channel the Praeceptor and set him alight at any moment. He hasn't spoken to me at all since my return, his demeanor so cold and detached, I wonder how I never suspected he was Similian. The manor was an extension of him, of his belief in community and family, and now, it's gone. But he does not mourn as the others do, or rage like the assassin. He simply watches, green eyes calculating behind his wire rimmed glasses.

They all believe I've done this.

I probably should have. Stolen the coin and burned them all while they slept.

And then spent the rest of your life running from the Praeceptor's control. I curse inwardly. Will there be any salvaging this? Or have I doomed myself to a life of looking over my shoulder, always waiting for the moment when my chest constricts, and my will is no longer my own?

So far, no one has attempted to restrain me. I sit propped against a tree, managing short, beleaguered breaths in between waves of pain, observing their anger, their heartbreak, their fear, with detached interest. The damage was miraculously contained mostly to the wings, the foyer and main level of the house still intact. All day, they go in pairs, carefully hauling out items they deem precious, grieving openly for what they've lost.

Sentimental nonsense. They should be launching an attack against my father. Or at the very least, investigating how the hell he got someone so far into Nadjaa. The moor is unapproachable by sea this time of year, the waves of the Storven crashing so hard against the cliffs, any boat would be reduced to splinters. The Nadjaan guard is posted all around the surrounding mountain ranges, all schooled in an elaborate messaging system if anyone so much as sets foot over the passes. Someone getting through all that—someone with the ability to not only replicate my power but *steal* it—is more than worrisome. It's a disaster.

My father wouldn't risk war with Nadjaa before he was ready. Their geography is too isolated for him to attack them outright and win. This wasn't meant as an assault on the Chancellor.

I hear his bellow of rage as I stole the ocean-wielder from under him, the pain he promised for the betrayal sharpening every line of him.

The attack on the manor was meant to destabilize *me*.

It's why he chose fire as his weapon, why whoever it was waited until both the assassin and Mirren were gone. So it would appear my loyalty lies with the Praeceptor.

Look at how easily you destroy, my father's voice seems to whisper. *You think to build an alliance to escape me, but you do not create. Only destroy.*

The assassin and earth-wielder set up a large tent in the nearby copse of trees. When they've finished, the assassin follows Mirren into it, the tent flap swinging closed behind them. I grimace as power surges to my fingertips and briefly consider setting the tent on fire before remembering myself. They already don't trust me. Burning Avedis alive would only serve to drive the point home.

"Is it true?"

Cal's voice comes from somewhere above me, and I keep my body still as I roll my eyes to him insolently. His copper hair gleams in the afternoon sun, wild and streaked with soot. Though blood still coats his exquisite clothes, the shrapnel has been removed and he's no longer injured, courtesy of Mirren.

"Is what true?"

He sits beside me without being invited, folding his long legs beneath him. "You feel your soul when you touch Mirren?"

"I don't see how it matters," I reply with an irritable sigh. The accompanying wave of pain leaves me more breathless than before. "It isn't as if I can cut her open to take it and shove it back into my own chest." Cal purses his lips in disapproval. I grin. "Though I could certainly try. Maybe I'll murder her and see if reverts to its rightful owner."

Calloway doesn't rise to my rancor, his eyes on the golden-haired man hauling another load of belongings out of the house. Cal just waits, his face an infuriating lesson in patience. He'll wait all day for my response to his true question, the truth lurking beneath my enmity.

"I suppose you'd just like me to hold hands with the ocean-wielder from now on? Turn myself into another of her tame little pets?" I snarl with a pointed look toward the tent.

"You've never been tame a day in your life, Anni, and I'm not fool enough to think Mirren's hand will change that."

I grit my teeth, hot annoyance climbing my throat. I don't like that Calloway purports to know me, like nothing that lurks in the deepest corners of my mind would surprise him, soul or not. I'm about to tell him so when Mirren finally emerges from the tent.

My breath catches as she straightens, the wild tangle of her curls haloed in the waning sun. The moment her eyes fall on me, my flames rise, reaching for her. Is it her power that calls to mine? Or is it the echo of my own soul, straining toward me?

If I could speak to it, I'd tell it to be grateful I gave it away. It's far better off in the depths of Mirren's goodness than in the hollowed abyss inside me.

The assassin ducks out of the tent behind her, his face flushed and his gaze something like reverent. I dig my nails into the flesh of my palm, but the sting of pain does nothing to ground me. At the moment, I'm numb to everything except the blatant desire to pluck Avedis' eyeballs from his head.

Mirren strides toward us, motioning for the others to gather. After a heated conversation with his daughter, Denver has already left for the council house to manage the political fallout of the morning's events. The earth-wielder skulks over, his eyes unreadable as he gazes up at the remnants of the manor. The golden-haired man places a gentle hand on his shoulder. "Come, Gislan. We're safe. That's what matters."

The earth-wielder nods, following the man toward Mirren, but I get the sense safety was not at all at the forefront of his thoughts. The two situate themselves next to Cal, the golden-haired one giving my former best friend a demure smile. When the man feels the weight of my gaze, he raises his eyes to mine with an open smile. "You must be Shaw. I've heard a lot about you."

Not fire-bearer or Heir. Just Shaw. I glare at him. "And who, exactly, are you?"

"Oh, I'm sorry. I'm Harlan, Mirren's life partner. It's nice to finally meet you."

He says it like it truly is, which only annoys me further, and flames surge to my fingertips as I digest his words. *Life partner.* "There's nothing nice about it," I bite back.

Harlan doesn't flinch as the bright tendrils lick up my arms, so he's either dense or entirely too brave. He tilts his head, watching them with curiosity. "Does that hurt you?"

I narrow my eyes, uncertain whether he mocks me, but am spared from responding as Mirren approaches. "Avedis has detected no one at the manor," she announces. "And there have been no reports of anyone in the mountains who shouldn't be there."

"So, someone who was already here had to light it," Max finishes for her, shaking her head with distaste. "I don't know why we're wasting Avedis' time," she drawls, her body limned with violence as her hard gaze falls on me. Whatever passed between us earlier has done little to temper her suspicion of me, which is no surprise. From Anrai's memories, I know Max does not waste time with forgiveness. "We know who it was. He may feel his soul when he touches you Mirren, but he's still a vile monster when he doesn't. *He* destroyed the manor, just as he's destroyed everything else."

I inhale sharply, grinding my teeth against the fresh wave of pain. "Perhaps I should do a more thorough job the next time and leave nothing standing of you or your precious *home.*"

Her eyes flare and her hand twitches toward her sword, but she masters herself. Pathetic. Another whose power has been leashed by the ocean-wielder.

Mirren ignores me completely, turning to the assassin instead. "Will you do another sweep of the passes?

Denver's guard is on alert, but perhaps you can find something they missed."

The assassin bows his head. "As you wish, lady."

Cal stands up and slings his bow over his shoulder. "I'll come."

Avedis nods, as if grateful for the help, and I turn away in disgust. *This* is who I've chosen to align myself with, who I thought would help me defeat my father? People who are too softhearted to gut a mercenary where he stands, too gullible to see through his proper words and helpful guise?

The mistake is mine, for ever thinking them powerful enough to stand against the Praeceptor.

Mirren looks to Max. "Will you take Gislan and Harlan to Evie's boarding house? She's offered up some rooms until we can repair the manor."

Max narrows her eyes. "And where will you be?"

Mirren straightens her shoulders, meeting Max's gaze. "I'm going to spend the night here and make sure whoever did this doesn't return."

I've told no one that whoever was here had the ability to sap my power, which means they'll also be able take Mirren's. Instead, I watch in silence as Max's face twists in rage. "With *him?*" She wipes furiously at the soot covering her face, in the end only serving to smear it further. "He should be locked up."

"Shaw did not burn the manor," the ocean-wielder says so decisively, my eyes snap to her in surprise. After the way I'd ravaged and then abandoned her in the library, I assumed she'd be the first calling for my blood.

"What proof do you have of that beyond your feelings for him?" Mirren's cheeks go pink, but Max presses on, unconvinced. "He's a danger not only to us, but to everyone in Nadjaa. It was foolish to trust him at his word.

He should be locked up until we need him for the prophecy."

Mirren sighs patiently. "He'll only burn his way out. Besides, he's too hurt to be moved anywhere."

I squirm as five stares fall on me, each seeking to determine the source of my injury. "He seems fine to me," Avedis remarks doubtfully.

"Why don't you come closer, and I'll show you just how fine I am," I growl, but when I reach for a dagger, I have to grit my teeth against the agony radiating from near my lungs. My breaths have grown shorter and more pained, each one requiring more energy than it sustains.

But I'd rather breathe acid than be healed by Mirren again. Even though I was mostly unconscious last time, the feeling of her power touching the rawest parts of me is not something I'm eager to repeat.

"He's broken a fair amount of his ribs and fractured part of his spine," Mirren explains succinctly, earning another of my sullen glares. "He'll stay here with me. Avedis, would you mind?"

"I don't need my spine to burn you alive, assassin," I bark, summoning flames to my fingertips.

"Sit in your consequences, Heir," he laughs, just as an errant gust of wind sweeps across the cliff side, blowing out my flame and hurtling me into the air. I twist for the ground, but another excruciating spasm has me biting my lip against the scream building in my chest. There's nothing I can do as I'm launched toward the tent.

"Avedis!" Mirren scolds from somewhere below me, and the wind gentles ever so slightly. It dumps me into the entrance of the tent, my face planted into a pile of furs like a dilapidated sandbag. I claw my way to sitting, bracing myself against the feeling of hot blades that slices up my legs with each fractional movement. Furious whispering sounds outside the tent for a few moments, before Mirren ducks inside, her face flushed, her cloak swinging around her legs.

"Do not touch me, witch," I growl at her. "I have no wish to be healed."

She raises an amused brow, something like laughter dancing across her lips. I wish furiously I didn't know the taste of them, both as Anrai and whatever I am now—didn't still crave it in some twisted way. "Suit yourself," she replies with a shrug. Turning her back to me, she shucks off her boots, placing them neatly near the entrance. Next, she strips off the cloak, folding it and setting it next to her boots.

I stare at her dubiously. "You aren't going to make me, then?" I ask, despising how much I sound like a sulking child.

"No," she snaps. Her sudden anger hangs in the silence of the tent as she weaves her hair into a tight plait. I've the absurd urge to tug out the leather strap and set her imprisoned curls free, but I focus instead on working breaths in and out. They've become sharper, less sustainable, and I wonder if one of my ribs has punctured a lung. As if I'd be so lucky.

"If you want to accept defeat and die a stubborn ass, I won't lift a finger to stop you Anrai Shaw."

I flinch as her mouth wraps around my name, wondering why it no longer feels as dead as it once did. "I never accept defeat."

Mirren laughs, humorless and ringing. "Please tell me, then, how exactly you're working to defeat Cullen. You refuse to defend yourself to your allies. You refuse to be healed. You will not even entertain the idea your father could be thwarted simply by gaining your own soul back. It seems to me you don't wish victory at all. You'd rather wait here to die and make me watch as some sort of infernal punishment."

I stare at her, momentarily dumbfounded.

I haven't thought of it, lost as I've been in my drive to free myself of him, but I *have* already bested Cullen, in a small way at least, by my soul surviving at all. He thinks he's destroyed every bit of the son who betrayed him, thinks he's ensured the viciousness remaining serves only him; but by loving Mirren, his plan was thwarted before it began. I thought being soulless has allowed me to think more clearly, unhindered by the shackles of emotion, but perhaps the emptiness of it all has clouded my rationale.

Because if I've bested my father in this, it stands to reason I'm capable of beating him in *all* of it. Freeing myself, completing the Dead Prophecy, and then destroying him entirely.

Adjusting myself primly, I say, "I'll allow you to heal me."

Mirren's eyes blaze, roiling like the waves of the Storven during a fall storm. "Oh, you'll *allow* me, will you?" Throwing her hands on her hips, she stalks toward me angrily, getting so close to my face, I can see the different shades of green swirling in her irises. "How about I don't? You're so keen to suffer, to inflict it on everyone else, then have at it!"

"Fine," I snarl back, pushing my face toward hers. "I'll die in this tent, and you'll be left without a fire-bearer for your precious prophecy."

"*I'll find another,*" Mirren hisses so furiously, I actually believe she will scour the entire earth to find another fire-wielder if it will spite me in this moment. Fighting the sudden urge to laugh, I purse my lips together. She waves wildly. "By all means, get on with it! I have things to do."

We stare at each other in furious silence. Insufferable woman: imperious as if she's been crowned queen by the old gods themselves. She will watch my last breath come in an agonizing wheeze and won't lift a hand to stop it. But somehow, her words still reverberate between us—*you don't wish victory at all.*

If there's one thing I am, one thing that remains in the barren wasteland of myself, it is that I do not surrender. As Anrai, or Shaw, or Heir, or Fire-bringer—through things that would kill most others—I persevere.

I inhale sharply, swallowing down both the urge to kiss her and murder her. "Will you heal me, Lemming?"

She only cocks a brow.

Gritting my teeth, I hiss, "Please."

Mirren straightens, throwing her braid over her shoulder with a small smile. I despise the victory on her lips at the same time I want to run my tongue across it. She kneels next to me, examining my chest so closely, I can feel the brush of her breath against my bare skin. Lifting her eyes to mine, something far softer glimmers behind her anger. "I'm sorry if this hurts you," she whispers, before pressing her hands to my skin.

I stiffen, biting back a cry, as the weight of my true self falls over me. My breathing quickens as my body prepares to be crushed by it all, but after a beat, I'm able to relax. Pain is my familiar, my home, but *this* pain is laced with home of a different sort. It is Mirren's heartbeat and Cal's smile. Max's cutting humor and Denver's patient faith. Through the fire and the bloodshed, the ache and the agony, it is *me*.

Mirren watches as I adjust, her face a mixture of brutal

longing and savage hope. Her tongue darts out and sweeps across her lips as she squeezes her eyes shut and pushes her power into me. For a moment, panic overtakes me, and I writhe beneath her hands, warring with the need to get away, to escape.

The water is no place for a boy who burns. I am back in the bowels of the Castellium, drowning over and over, unable to wake from my nightmare. My power gone, I am extinguished, left with nothing.

Swallowing down bile, I force my eyes open and focus on the dark sweep of Mirren's lashes against her pearlescent skin; the bob of her delicate throat; the fine line of concentration between her brows. Small pieces I've somehow forgotten until this moment, all settling beneath my skin along with her power. Mirren doesn't control the water—she *is* the water, as much a part of her as anything else.

And in spite of everything we've done to each other, I know deep down, she would never hurt me. My muscles loosen beneath her touch as the kernel of truth unfurls in my chest. I have not been safe in a long time, but with Mirren, I am. My power sighs, winding around hers as she mends my vertebrae. And as I settle, it's like the first time she allowed me to touch her, to claim her as mine. I am extinguished but not erased, content for once not to burn or destroy—but just to *be*.

When my last rib is mended and unhindered breaths barrel into my famished lungs, Mirren makes to move away, but I ensnare both her hands in mine and pull them to my chest. Her eyes flare in surprise and she stares at our intertwined fingers, mine appearing all the more scarred against her smooth skin. "You're right. I was giving up."

The words seem to echo in the small tent, heavy and

metallic, as I let go of her hand. The heaviness of my soul recedes and as cold washes over me once more, I shiver violently against the emptiness. When it passes, I push myself to standing. There is no more pain in my back or lungs, my legs strong beneath me once more. "Taking away my father's heir would be the ultimate revenge, even if we cannot bring the prophecy to pass. A warlord with no heir is one who leaves themselves ripe for a cous."

Before, when I'd left as a child, my father told everyone I'd been killed in service to him. It was easy to control the narrative with no one around to object. But this time, the entire Dark Militia witnessed me steal Mirren from him. If he doesn't bring me to heel, he will appear weak before the power-hungry beasts of his own creation. It will only be a matter of time before one of them comes to challenge him.

"And, perhaps, if I regain my soul—well, maybe it will break the hold he has on me."

Mirren leans back on her heels, eyes bright as she ponders my words. "I believe that's how he's controlling you. In those—" she rasps a trembling breath, steadying herself. "In the moments before you killed those soldiers, your father did something to trap the last piece of your soul. It did not go into the Darkness, Anrai."

I study her intently. "Mirren," I say slowly, her name low and dark on my lips. "Even when you touch me, I am not Anrai."

She stands up, brushing off her dress before facing me haughtily. "Your soul lives. Whether you wish to be or not, you're still alive. Changed, broken," she lifts her jaw defiantly, as if daring me to argue, "but Anrai lives."

I scoff in disgust. "You've never seen me for the monster I truly am, Lemming. Do so now and spare us both the humiliation of pretending I will ever be anything more."

A furious breath shoots through her nostrils. "Still Anrai and still an arrogant ass!" She folds her arms savagely over her chest, as if attempting to cage in her fury. "Do you think you're the only one who has suffered these past months? That you're the only one who knows the pain of living with pieces of their soul outside of themselves?"

"If you speak of Shivhai—"

"I do not!" she shouts so wildly the words die in my throat. "I speak of the piece *you* hold, the piece I gave before I could even name it. I have been living with a part of myself plunged into the pits of despair right alongside you. It has been with you the whole time."

I stare at her coldly. "I have nothing but the Darkness." How dare she speak to me of pain, when she knows nothing of the madness of void. When *she* is the reason for it all.

Mirren shakes her head, her eyes shining. And despite my hatred of her, I find I cannot look away from her wild desperation. "I am sorry for what happened that day. Sorry you thought you were only worth what you could sacrifice. But I am most sorry you gave everything without knowing how I truly felt. I was a coward." Her tears spill now and in spite of the pretty way they glisten on her cheeks, I feel nothing as I watch them.

Nothing, except for what now blooms in the emptiness: the thing that lives in the endless sea of my dreams, that's awakened in my darkest moments no matter how brutally I have starved and beaten it.

"You deserved someone brave." Her eyes meet mine, the color of the sea. I open my mouth to object, to stop whatever madness she will speak before it tears into what little restraint I have left. But she silences me with a fierce glare. "I love you, Anrai. I've never stopped. My soul has always been yours."

Anger threads through me and flames rise to my skin. They line my eyes and my fingers, straining for her, and I force myself to turn around and stalk out of the tent. Before I kill her and stave off the savage claws of hope. Before I take her, and taste that hope for myself.

I'm to the manor in no time, but she's only a few strides behind. I duck into the foyer, the place feeling eerily like death: ravaged and still. Mirren climbs up the stairs after me and ash rains down as she stomps inside, grabbing hold of my arm and spinning me around.

I shake her off, breathing heavily against the effect of her touch. "What is the matter with you?" I hiss furiously. "Have you no sense of self-preservation? I am a *monster*, Lemming. I have burned women alive, slit the throat of children and I *savored* it all. You think because I feel when you touch me, I am saved?" I glare at her, having somehow moved so close, our faces are only inches from each other. "I am not. As soon as I take my hands from you, I am evil incarnate once more. I will destroy your family and burn your innocents, all because *I want to.*"

"Then don't," Mirren says quietly.

"What?"

"Then *don't* take your hands from me," she says, taking my hands and pressing them to her chest. Her skin burns beneath my palms, and I don't know whether it's my power or her own heat. "We will find a way to restore your soul, but until then—" She runs a finger delicately along my jaw, watching as I tremor again beneath the weight of my soul. "Touch me, Anrai. Always. Do not make me live in pieces anymore. Even you cannot be that cruel."

Anger and flame still blaze through me, but their heat is now of a different sort. One that smolders. One that *wants*.

Drawn by some unknowable force, my hand tugs the

leather strap from her hair. Her curls spring free, and I run my fingers through them until the braid comes undone and they hang over her shoulders, wild and unkept. She does nothing to hide her hope now, her emerald eyes full and glistening as she gazes up at me. She goes completely still when I move my thumb over her jawline, as if she holds her breath. My flames flicker across her lips as I gently stroke her cheek and then down over the juncture of her throat, and for the first time, I understand.

My power has never hurt her, because it has always been able to recognize what I could not. She is a part of us, just as we are a part of her, incapable of hurting the other because we *are* the other. Mirren sighs, the noise satiated and wanting at once, as I finally pull her to me and come back to myself.

CHAPTER
TWENTY-SEVEN

Shaw

We crash together like waves of a great sea as I take her mouth beneath mine. She tastes of rain and smoke, and I yank at her shirt, determined to devour every inch of her, to drown in her depths. She needs no prompting, pulling away to tear it off impatiently, before throwing herself at me once more. I catch her, winding her supple thighs around my waist, thankful to be healed enough to match her strength.

Her curves fill my hands and I growl in approval, before sweeping my tongue along hers. She threads her arms around my neck, pressing closer, as if she seeks to meld us together by pure force of will. Her bare skin against mine is pure decadence, all softness and silk against my rough scars. I should be taking my time, savoring every breath she feeds me, but I've awoken from the depths of night, starving and mad with need. I cannot think, cannot slow—can do nothing but chase after what she offers, my compulsion an inescapable force.

I press her into the wall, causing more ash to rain down around us as she grinds her hips fervently against mine. A whimper of pleasure escapes her lips and settles beneath my skin like sparks of electricity. She reaches between us, her small hand working the button of my pants with such determination, I have to grit my teeth against the hard ache of my groin.

Taking a steadying breath, I pin her more tightly against the wall until there's no more room between us. "You won't be escaping so quickly this time," I whisper, running my tongue over the shell of her ear and delighting in her small shiver. "You asked for me to touch you," I remind her, peeling back slightly to run my gaze down her luscious body. Bare from the waist up, her perfect breasts heave with each breath. "So I'll give you exactly as you ask until you don't know whether to beg me to stop," I pinch one of the pebbled pink tips roughly between my fingers. "Or beg me never to."

Mirren's answering smile is so wicked, I shoot forward to taste its ardent heat. She moans and I nearly lose my mind as it reverberates against my mouth. Her body is luxuriant, trapped between the cold stone of the manor and the harshly etched planes of my chest. How did I ever mistake my yearning for her softness as hatred for it? There is strength in its lushness; in how well it yields to me.

I run my lips down her throat, her pulse thrumming like the wings of a hummingbird beneath her delicate skin. My flames rise, drawn to what sustains her, but I capture them inside my chest, adding to the maelstrom of chaos burning there.

Mirren drags her fingers through my hair as I take her breast in my mouth, palming the weight of the other. "Does touching me still hurt?" she asks breathlessly. Her eyes are heavily lidded and glazed as she watches me, curls tangled, sinful mouth parted.

I nip at the tip of her breast before soothing its hardening peak with a smooth roll of my tongue. "Pain and pleasure are not always indistinguishable."

I stroke her stomach indolently as I suckle her, watching as her skin pebbles beneath my fingers. Then lower, over the curve of her hip. Mirren doesn't take her eyes from me as I peel off her leggings and kneel before her. She is vulnerable and bare, entirely at my mercy, and yet, I am the one humbled. Emotion, foreign and demanding, climbs my throat as I run my hands up the bend of her knee, the expanse of her thigh. I am a wasteland, and she is an ocean. She shouldn't allow me to touch her.

Mirren lifts my chin, forcing me to look up at her. "More," she demands simply, as if she reads my every thought. "I choose, Anrai."

An echo of the first time I touched her, when time seemed stretched before us, hopeful and endless. I thought there would always be more of it: to touch her, to hold her, to learn her—but the Darkness is a brutal teacher. There is no time except now, and if you do not take what's given to you, it will be gone before you can.

I kiss the inside of her thigh gently, before settling my tongue against the core of her. She throws her head back against the marble with a sharp cry as I lick her in long, languishing strokes. She is wet and waiting and her taste empties every thought from my head, except for the primal need to drink her pleasure, to claim it as mine. How many times have I woken with her taste in my mouth, aching and desperate to devour her?

I flatten my tongue against the apex of her thighs, the swollen place where she needs me most, and she bucks against me in response. Suckling it between my lips, Mirren braces herself against the wall, settling her weight on my face as her legs turn to jelly beneath her.

She trembles above me, whispering my name like a hallowed prayer. *Anrai, Anrai, Anrai.*

It showers me like a spring rain, every droplet bringing with it a piece of who I was—who I am. I unleash myself on her until her moans echo off the cavernous ceiling and she writhes furiously on my tongue, chasing her gratification, demanding it as she should. I push a finger into her, followed by another, hissing a curse against her wet heat as the feeling of her slick warmth, pulsing and tight around them, threatens to undo me. I thought I knew hunger, knew ache, but everything before is a pale echo of what explodes in my chest now.

Mirren shudders, so close to tumbling over her peak. I scrape my teeth gently against her bundle of nerves, before sweeping my tongue around it in a soothing stroke. She cries out, her body gripping my fingers as the rest of her goes limp in my arms. And when I stand, it molds to mine, flushed and pliant and warm.

I kiss her once more and she opens eagerly, her tongue caressing mine until the edges of my mind go hazy, her sweet taste swirling between us. She palms me through my pants, and I bite out another curse as she deftly pops the button open. Somewhere distantly, I remember what this is to her—a first that can never be given back. But I have not been Anrai in so long, I'm incapable of making the selfless sacrifices he could.

There's no question I will take her, have her every way my mind has imagined, both with a soul and without; consume and claim her until she burns for me. My blood sizzles through my veins as she fists her small hand around the length of me.

My thoughts shatter into fragmented pieces and I freeze beneath her touch, attempting to gather them. I can at least make it to the tent outside. At least give her somewhere comfortable, somewhere that isn't ruined. Without a word, I sweep her into my arms, her wet core so close I could enter her with one small movement. She shakes her head stubbornly.

"No," Mirren protests. Her hands are restless, her fingernails running along my shoulder, her mouth suckling at my neck, but when she looks at me, her eyes are determined. "Not in the tent. Here. *Now.* In our ruins."

My power pulses in approval, but I shove it down. I should object, but I have no words. She deserves somewhere beautiful with someone else—someone like her life partner, who is always kind and has never felt the heat of someone else's blood on his hands.

Someone who doesn't destroy everything he touches, made of flame itself.

"I want you here, Anrai. All of you," Mirren whispers, her voice a warm breeze against my skin. I groan at her words, at the weight of my want for her. "Fire doesn't only destroy; it can also be a harbinger for new life. It begins with us."

Mirren's hands still and my body screams in protestation, but I set her down in spite of it because I understand her demand. She accepts me as I am, ruins and all, but I must as well; something I would have never thought possible, even before I lost my humanity. Because giving up my soul for the people I love was never going to be the hardest sacrifice—living with myself demands the steepest price.

A price that doesn't seem so insurmountable while imbued with the strength of Mirren's heart. Because what could be stronger than the fortitude it takes to remain soft in a world so very cruel? Power she gifted me before I even knew, that has kept me from breaking against the tide of darkness. For the first time in months, it is not just emptiness, or even my own soul I feel—for hers is beside it, soft and luminescent.

"I am not the same man I was, Lemming," I tell her roughly. I have no blanket, so I grab a half-burnt cloak that still miraculously hangs by the door. "Even if I was whole, my soul has been Darkness-touched."

Mirren spreads herself over the cloak, her bare skin flushed and waiting like a sensuous feast. I'm now so hard it hurts as she raises her arms above her head, her hair sprawled across the ground in a dark wave, her breasts heaving with each intake of breath, a small smile playing at the corner of her lips. My body *shakes* with the urgency to take her, both my power and my cock straining to make her ours, but I stay where I am. "I cannot be gentle." Both a warning and a promise.

She tilts her head, running her pink tongue over her lips as her voracious eyes trail the expanse of me. "You've never treated me like some breakable thing. Don't you dare start now."

Something in me releases, a knot untied, and I practically lunge at her. She doesn't falter, opening for me in a pillowed respite against the rigidity of the world. My equal in all ways, my only match in power and strength, she wraps her arms and legs around me in avid fervor. I tear off my pants, flinging them haphazardly across the foyer. I've never been so hard in my life, but the ache only intensifies as Mirren's wide eyes take in all of me. There is no apprehension in them, only a blazing desire.

I tangle one hand in her hair, using the other to guide myself into her. Our tongues dance, but our eyes remain open as I slowly push into her. She tenses, her muscles contracting tightly around me, and for a moment, I fear I might lose it. It's been so long since I've been touched with anything but cruelty, and Mirren is so warm and soft that unbidden tears spring to my eyes and I suddenly feel as though I'll combust. I bite my lip savagely enough to taste iron, the sting of pain grounding me until her body adjusts.

She relaxes beneath me, her own eyes shining as I move further inside her, inch by agonizing inch. I have been unmoored, adrift in the Darkness, and only now, seated fully within her, am I found. As I begin to move, words leave me entirely. It is beyond the modern trapping of language, only spoken in the ancient wash of the sea, the heart of flame.

Mirren closes her eyes, throwing her head back with a moan. I take her nipple in my mouth, suckling roughly as I begin to move faster inside her. "Give me *all* of you, Mirren," I whisper to her, an echo of the words I spoke in Siralene. I meant it then, as I mean it now. She may hold herself back from the world, from those too weak to worship her as they should, but she will not hold back from me.

I want all of her, every piece the world has deemed too much. Because for me, it will never be enough.

Power bursts from her, a sparkling wave that washes over my skin, and for once, I do not cower from it. I feed it with my own as I thrust into her faster, until we are the center of our own storm, our own force of nature.

Fire and water should be the death of one another, but we are not—we are the balance of the universe, the beginning and the end. Life and death in pure, unadulterated synchronicity.

My moans join Mirren's, echoing off the cavernous ceiling. Ash falls down around us as slick warmth builds between our bodies. I grip her hips roughly, angling her upward to drive even deeper, all thoughts of anything but *her* evaporated in the pleasure she gives. She digs her nails into my back, lifting her hips to meet my thrusts, urging me *faster. Closer. Harder. More.* Pressure builds inside me as she cries out and the warmth of her spasms around me. My flames dancing over her throat, my name lingering on her lips, she climaxes hard.

And it is my name, forgotten and then found once more, held in the safety and freedom of her voice that sends me spiraling over my own edge. For I could be no one, soulless and forsaken, but I will never be empty again. Because as pleasure washes through me, a flame hotter than any wildfire, I feel Mirren.

The soul she gifted me, shining like the reflection of a tropical sea, all sun and light and warmth.

Mirren gently strokes my spine as I settle back into myself, stunned and thoroughly satiated. For a moment, there is no pain, no ache, no Darkness. There is only the ash and us.

I push myself up onto my elbows, staring down at her in awe. Her cheeks are flushed, her lips swollen, thoroughly wrecked and thoroughly mine. "Mirren, before I gave up my soul, you claimed me as yours."

You are mine, Anrai Shaw. Do you hear me? Mine.

Her eyes soften, but they do not relent, and I understand it in the darkest parts of myself. She will claw her way through the Darkness, through the Praeceptor—through anything that tries to take what is hers. And it leaves me breathless, its ferocity more familiar to me than anything. It is the song of my heart, the thread of my power. "I claim you too, Lemming. We belong to each other."

CHAPTER
TWENTY-EIGHT

Mirren

"So," Anrai drawls hours later, when we're snuggled beneath a thick pile of blankets in the tent. After our excursion in the foyer, we bathed in the cliff pond, scrubbing the ash and sweat from our skin. It began innocently enough as we'd both been filthy, but after catching an eyeful of Anrai's muscled backside gleaming in the setting sun, it had not ended that way at all. "That puppy-faced blonde is your life partner, then?"

My body is sore in the best way, spent in pleasure, and the warmth of Anrai has sunk into my bones, lulling me into a comatose state where thoughts drift slowly. I run my fingers absently along the ridges of the binding mark on my forearm. Once an angry red, it has faded to a soft pink in the months since it was branded on my skin. "His name is Harlan. And it's not—it isn't like that."

"Harlan," he muses, twisting a curl around his finger and then letting it spring back toward the crown of my head. "Are you saying you're *not* forever intertwined with that simpering Similian?"

My cheeks heat. "We are, but it isn't...we aren't...it's more like—" I let out a furious huff of air as I realize Anrai is shaking with laughter.

"Relax, Lemming. I knew you were Bound when we first met," he admits with a grin. I haven't heard the sound of his happiness in so long, for a moment, I forget to be angry. And then his murmur is so wicked against my ear, my toes curl beneath the blankets. "I just didn't care."

I shove him away even as shivers rise to my skin. "You're incorrigible," I laugh. "And Harlan is not simpering. He is brave and good."

Anrai raises a brow. "If I hadn't just had you twice, and if he wasn't completely enamored with Cal, I might just be jealous."

Cal? Anrai has always been acutely perceptive. It would be no surprise he's observed something I've missed. Maybe Harlan really is finding a way to move past my brother's betrayal in the form of a well-dressed redhead. He deserves someone like Cal to love. Someone as kind as he is.

Anrai lightly traces the small mark, his fingers trailing over the three entwined keys. "Oddly brutal way to mark someone as married for a place that claims civility."

A laugh scrapes my throat. "There is no more civility in Similis than anywhere else in Ferusa," I mutter so bitterly, he leans back to study me. Night has long since fallen, the only light in the tent coming from two small lanterns, their shadows casting the planes of his face into sharp lines.

After a beat, he asks in a low voice, "What brought you across the Boundary again, Mirren? Where is Easton?"

A sob climbs my throat, and before I can consider it, I tell him everything. A rush of words, of heartbreak and triumph, so potent it may as well be a wave of power. Every terrible thought and every selfish action; all my loneliness and regret—he takes them all from me without faltering. Without trying to assuage it or think his way around it, Anrai just listens.

Give me all of you, Mirren.

When I finish, tears line his own eyes and a familiar shadow shrouds his handsome features. The kind limned with anger and death. Even if we manage to restore his soul, the Darkness will never fully leave him, for broken things cannot be made new again. They can be mended, become something different, but he will never be as he once was.

Perhaps I won't either.

"I left my brother behind. I left him, even when I knew he wasn't safe." It's freeing, to finally allow my guilt and sorrow out of the cramped cage I've kept them in. "The Covinus could murder him at any moment, and I left. Even though you gave your soul so he would live."

Anrai strokes my hair back from my face and sets his lips gently to my forehead. "Easton makes his own choices. You were right to leave. If you stayed to be killed, what would happen to the Similians then? It could be another hundred years before anyone comes close to the truth." His eyes darken. "I should go blow a hole through more than just the Covinus' fence," he says with an angry twist of his mouth.

At my look of horror of what that would mean for my brother, Anrai's face softens. "I'm sorry you had to go through all this alone. I thought—" he clears his throat, his voice suddenly thick. "I thought you'd be safe after my sacrifice, Mirren. Happy. That's why I did what I did."

I run a thumb over his cheek and then the sharp angle of his jaw. "I haven't been alone. I've had Cal and Max. Avedis and Harlan. You gifted me that. I was shattered when you were gone and I was never going to be happy, but their friendship was always a reminder of *why* you sacrificed what you did. You saved all of us, Anrai. I could never let that be in vain."

Anrai bows his head. "You saved me first."

I drop my eyes, the crack in my soul aching for the first time all day. The crack I'd willingly given myself to keep him from losing what was lost anyway. "It didn't matter. Not in the end."

He cups my chin softly, the calluses of his fingers scraping my skin as he forces me to look at him. "It mattered," he says, his pale eyes fervent. "No one has ever fought for me the way you have. No one has ever *seen* me and still thought I deserved it," he hesitates, shame flaring in his eyes. "I don't, but—it mattered."

Our legs twine together as he draws me closer, his skin burning against mine. There is nothing languid about the way he kisses me, as if, even now, he fights against the pull of time. Rolling me on top of him, he sweeps the thick curtain of hair from my shoulder. His irises flicker with heat and his hair has dried in a tousled mess, and somehow, he is mine. Beautiful. Broken. Through Darkness and flame, we fought our way back to each other.

Even if it's only temporary, if the world shakes around us, I will always have the memory of home in him. And that is enough to make me thank the dead gods every minute of every day for the rest of my life.

"What?" I ask with a shy smile, as Anrai gazes up at me.

"There is no beauty in Argentum. There is only gray," he explains. Smoke curls around him in snaking tendrils, the shadows of his Darkness made physical. "I find myself starved for your colors."

It's the first he's mentioned his father's city, the place

where his power was brought forth. I want to know everything that happened to him; to hear the name of every person who's hurt him and drag them beneath the fury of my waves. But it is still a raw wound, gaping and tender, and if I touch it now, I know I will only cause more pain. So instead, I press my lips to his, pouring everything I cannot say into the kiss.

His tongue sweeps across mine and his fingers roam in lazy circles over the small of my back and over the curve of my rear. "Have I ever told you how irresistible your skin is?" Anrai murmurs against my throat, running his lips so lightly over my pulse, I shiver beneath him.

"As I recall, you insulted my skin," I tell him pointedly, pressing my lips together to hide my smile. His hands graze lower, pressing into the sore muscles of my upper thighs. He watches with a satisfied smile as I arc into his touch with a groan.

"It was an observation, not an insult." He licks up the column of my neck, tastes the sensitive skin of my earlobe. "So smooth and untouched by the terrible things of the world."

I set him with a wry glare. "And right after, you allowed me to be eaten by the Ditya."

Anrai laughs, but his hands don't stop working. "I would never let a wolf taste you before I got the chance," he growls so wickedly, renewed heat shoots straight to my center. To illustrate his point, he ensnares me in his arms and nips at the swell of my breast.

I squeal, wiggling against him with no intention of escaping, when he suddenly freezes below me. His eyes grow wide as they land on mine. "The Ditya wolf. *Where the old magic sleeps, wound in the roots of trees and the heart of beasts.*" He sits up and shakes his head, scooping me with him so that I'm seated in his lap. "Mirren, I know where his militia is."

"Where?"

"There have always been stories of why creatures like the Ditya and the yamardu only exist in one part of Ferusa. The Xamani have always claimed it's because there's still magic there, that the trees absorbed it before the queen's curse could annihilate it all." Excitement and dread mingle on his face. "The Dark Militia is in the Nemoran Wood."

Foreboding, deep and cold as iron, falls heavy in my stomach as I remember what is housed in the heart of the wood. "The Praeceptor's army is going to attack Similis."

CHAPTER
TWENTY-NINE

Mirren

The Moon City is dark when we reach Evie's boarding house, the surrounding mountains holding silent vigil in the night. A few spare lanterns reflect in the black bay as we climb from the skiff onto the slick docks and head toward the quiet marketplace. The wedding arbor once arched over the purple doorway of the bakery and boarding house is gone, and I wonder if Evie is now a married woman. Anrai knocks with one hand, his other still enlaced with mine, as it has been since we left the manor. It's naïve to believe we won't ever be separated, but testing fate this early seemed unwise—the last thing we need is Anrai to have a crisis of conscious in the middle of the Nadjaan marketplace.

His own friends still don't trust him, and Denver, the man Anrai reveres, believes he's a lost cause. Only time will convince them otherwise. Time we don't have.

Anrai bangs again, rattling the old door on its hinges. Finally, a lantern flickers somewhere inside and the door whips open, revealing a stern looking woman holding a long-barreled gun. I flinch, still unaccustomed to staring down my own death after all this time, but Anrai just says, "Hello, Evie."

Evie doesn't lower her weapon. "You know better than to pound on someone's door in the dead of night, Shaw," she remarks, narrowing her eyes. "Especially now that word has spread of what you've done to the Chancellor's manor."

Anrai grimaces, shifting uncomfortably under Evie's gaze, and a wave of protectiveness rises in me. I push in front of him with an impatient sigh. "Is the Chancellor here?"

Evie's eyes and gun move to me. "And who are you to demand our Chancellor's whereabouts?"

I plant my feet. "His daughter."

Understanding flashes across the councilwoman's face, and as she lowers her weapon and leans it carefully against the doorjamb, I feel small relief. As far as I know, Denver has never told anyone in his new life of Easton and I's existence, leaving any regrets locked safely behind the Boundary along with us. But it appears he's told at least one person. Whether it's because he trusts Evie, or because he's confident in his control over her, will have to be determined.

Though, according to Anrai, the baker has always been levelheaded and fair. Not one to be swayed by the power of holding an elected position, but also not one to squander it.

"He's in the sitting room with the rest of them. Cal and that other charming young man returned about an hour ago. No one's slept a wink all night." Evie glances hesitantly back at Shaw, her face softening in concern. "What happened to you, Shaw? I've been so worried. Denver returned, but you never did. And there have been so many rumors running rampant...that you left to join the Praeceptor. That you possess dark fire and you've been destroying villages under his command. Tell me it isn't true."

Anrai swallows roughly as she looks at him hopefully. I feel his struggle as if it's my own. The guilt, the hurt, the anger.

"Shaw saved all of us in the spring and he saved us again last night," I tell the woman fiercely. "Now, are you going to make us stand outside all night?"

For a moment, I fear Evie will demand we leave, but instead, she raises her chin in approval and nods amiably, as if she's been waiting for someone to contradict the rumors. "Come in, come in. I've just started some pastries for the morning rush. I'll bring some to you in the sitting room." She takes in the gaunt set of Anrai's face with an appraising grunt. "You look in great need of them."

Anrai releases a breath from between his teeth, his relief at Evie's acceptance palpable, even as he mutters, "I'm going to develop a complex if one more person tells me I look like hell."

The bakery takes up most of the front of the building. An etched glass cabinet stretches along the side wall, already filled with so many freshly prepared delicacies, I distantly wonder when Evie has time to sleep. My mouth waters as I spot the chocolate scones Anrai bought for me my first morning in Nadjaa, tucked in between an array of other brightly colored treats. Curved iron chairs are speckled in front of the large glass windows, and draping flowers hang in wicker bowls from the ceiling, making the space feel both open and homey.

Evie leads us through the bakery and down a winding hallway, the smell of her goods that trails behind us so tempting, I wish I could fall face first into it. When we come to an elegantly appointed sitting room, it's clear no one has slept. Cal and Max are sprawled across a small settee, Max's stocking feet propped up on Cal's knees. Harlan is curled in a large armchair with a book spread across his lap. A fire roars in the hearth, and Avedis is spread out before it like a cat soaking up the heat, his hands behind his head and his eyes closed.

Upon seeing us, Cal immediately stirs. "Has something else happened?" His voice is slightly panicked, but Anrai's gaze is on the man seated behind a small desk in the corner. My father.

The corner of Denver's lips tighten as he takes in our interlocked hands, and though he says nothing, his words to me before the fire hang in the air as if nailed there. He stands, smoothing out his wrinkled pants and straightening the glasses that have gone slightly awry, as if the small motions serve to ground him. "Why have you come?"

Anrai stops breathing at the ice in my father's voice, as indifferent and wary as if he were addressing complete strangers. Or worse, enemy combatants. Anger flames inside me. "A warm greeting for the son and daughter who saved your life not so long ago," I spit.

Denver's face remains impassive. "Shaw is controlled by my enemy and Nadjaa was attacked today." He'd said as much to me before he left the ruins of the manor to check on the city's fortification. I knew better than to ask him to stay, to grieve for the home he'd built and that I'd known for only a short time but loved dearly.

"Anrai didn't attack the manor," I insist from behind gritted teeth.

Denver inclines his head, in neither agreement nor disagreement. "Be that as it may, I would be remiss to welcome the Heir of the Praeceptor with open arms. And you, daughter, seem to have chosen your side," he says with a pointed look. "I will address you as such."

A million acid-filled retorts throw themselves at my lips, but I focus instead on the small squeeze of Anrai's hand. A reminder, that in spite of my own feelings, I still need my father's help. "So be it," I tell him obstinately, yanking Anrai into the room and practically pushing him down onto a small couch. I plop beside him, sinking into the deep cushions and pushing a leveling sigh through my nostrils. "We have information on the location of the Dark Militia. Unless you'd rather us keep it to ourselves."

Denver's brow raises fractionally, the only sign of his slight surprise. For all his power and connections, he hasn't been able to find the Praeceptor, and I know it must irk him that we've found him first. My father has always thrived on not only finding the answer, but being the first to do so. "From whom?"

"Aggie," Anrai replies without meeting Denver's eyes. "I went to see her before...before the fire and she told me where they were. I've only just now figured it out."

"I don't suppose she gave you something useful," Max remarks dryly, bobbing her feet atop Cal's lap. "like, I dunno... coordinates?"

Cal laughs. "Or perhaps the old gods have drawn her a map?"

"I can only imagine any map drawn from the old witch's mind would resemble something like the pits of hell," Avedis quips without opening his eyes, apparently not asleep after all.

A smile tugs at the corner of Anrai's lips, and for a moment, I wish so badly to see it. To watch him laugh with his friends as if doesn't have the world tied around his throat like a yoke. "She said the militia is where the old magic sleeps, wound in the roots of trees and the heart of beasts."

Denver's eyes widen. "The Nemoran..." his gaze flicks to mine, something close to panic flaring there. But I must be mistaken; my father does not panic. He plots. "Cullen is invading Similis?"

Harlan sits up in alarm, his book fluttering to the ground in a forgotten heap of pages. "Now?"

"How has he hidden his entire militia so even the wind can't touch it?" Max asks doubtfully. "Have they climbed the trees or something? Hidden in a cave?"

Anrai stares down at our hands rather than meeting anyone's gaze. "He...he doesn't have power. Not like Mirren or me. But he *uses* something. I don't know what it is, or how he controls it, but he had a way of draining our power in Yen Girene. Before the fire, my power was drained again." Max's eyes snap to his, her expression unreadable as she realizes Anrai came for her, through flame, when he was able to be burned as easily as the rest of us.

Denver watches Anrai carefully. "Are you certain it was the same feeling?"

Anrai grunts. "I know the feeling well by now. My power was gone, just as it was in Yen Girene. And when—when I was in Argentum." He swallows audibly and shakes his head. "He must be using the same sort of thing to mask the militia. But the amount of power needed to do that... I don't know."

Calloway watches Anrai speak of his father, wearing his best friend's anguish as openly as if it were his own. Horror and shame cross his face in equal measure. "I didn't realize —I didn't understand how much you've been controlled, Anni."

Anrai still doesn't raise his eyes. "It doesn't matter," he mutters.

Calloway sits so far forward Max's feet fall to the floor. "I'm sorry, brother, for thinking the worst of you."

At this, Anrai finally meets his gaze, fierce determination burning there. "Do not apologize for honoring your vow to me. Ever."

Cal opens his mouth to protest, but Denver cuts him off, staring at Anrai in calculation. "My last intel indicated that the Boundary is still very much active. I don't see how Cullen would be able to bypass it."

Harlan shakes his head. "The Boundary is *not* intact. It's been faltering ever since..." he trails off, his gaze flickering to me. "Well, ever since Mirren returned. And the Covinus is in denial. He won't prepare anyone for an invasion, because it would mean admitting he's been wrong. He'll never do that."

Denver settles Harlan with an appraising look, before flicking his gaze back to Anrai. "Even at half its power, the Boundary cannot be infiltrated. I suspect the only reason *you* were able to penetrate it was that you already possessed the spirit of the fire, even though it lay dormant. And since you are the only of your kind, Cullen won't be able to break through."

"He could send his militia in one by one through the existing hole and wreak havoc that way," Max suggests. "He hasn't always taken over places with a large assault—"

"What if I'm not?" Anrai asks suddenly.

"What if you're not what?"

"What if I'm not the only fire-wielder?" His words are soft, but something about them lingers long after they've been spoken.

Denver's eyebrows climb up his forehead. "The Dead

Prophecy has not yet been achieved and won't until we bring together, water, fire, earth and air." I swallow guiltily, noticing how all my friends avoid meeting Denver's eyes as he goes on. My father remains blissfully unaware of Avedis or Gislan's proclivities for elemental magic. "It's doubtful Cullen could have created another fire-wielder without breaking the curse."

"I broke through the Boundary *before* my power matured," Anrai says. His eyes travel to the coin that now hangs from a chain between my breasts. He hasn't explained it's significance or how it managed to make it from Yen Girene to his tent in Argentum. He just silently removed it from his neck and fastened it around mine as we lay in the manor. And I'd accepted it without question, the cool bite of metal a reminder of Easton. "My father gave me that coin to find those with the potential for magic. I would send my power into it and press it to their chests and if they possessed the gift, it would burst into flame."

I snap my eyes to his, but he stares at the ground, thick tendrils of hair shielding his face from me.

"I sent thousands of them to Argentum."

"Where your father annihilated them," Denver finishes for him, his tone cutting.

Anrai hunches his shoulders, curling further into himself. "Eventually, I'm sure. But they...they were held in his dungeons first." Nausea rises in my throat as I imagine thousands of people subjected to the Praeceptor's brand of hospitality. And Anrai himself told me there were *children*. "What if he found one with the potential for fire?"

Silence blankets the room, as the repercussions settle over all of us.

Max crosses her arms, eyeing Denver with an

inscrutable look. "How did you know Shaw was a fire-wielder? Before the Praeceptor took him?"

My father frowns and does his best to avoid my gaze. He's silent so long, I'm certain he won't answer, but then, he says quietly, "Because of the stories."

"Xamani stories?" Cal asks.

"Not only the Xamani. Since I came to Ferusa, I've studied all histories in equal measure. You don't know what a gift it is to be able to learn all you want of history. It is not erased in Ferusa or twisted to fit one person's narrative. It is always there, waiting to be learned from." Now, my father's gaze lifts to mine and a lump of emotion forms in my throat. This is the man I remember from my childhood, who shared my desire to understand the world rather than accept it as it was told to us.

I've been so blinded by my hurt, I haven't considered how Denver must have felt, trapped behind the Boundary where knowledge is shunned. When he first crossed the Boundary, did he feel like I did? Terrified, but equally exhilarated at the expanse of the world around him?

It doesn't make his abandonment hurt any less, but it makes it more understandable.

"Each one is unique," Denver goes on, "but there are similar threads throughout all of them, specifically when it comes to fire-bearers." His eyes rove over Anrai. "They are different, you see."

Anrai shifts uncomfortably under his examination as Denver continues, "Most nature spirits summon their particular power. Mirri, you do not make water. You call it and shape it, but it already exists, in the earth and air. But Shaw—he *creates*. He makes flame where there was once nothing. And so, according to the stories, the fire spirits were not able to choose just anyone to bear them. They needed a particular kind of person, born with the capabilities and strength to withstand the act of creation."

Denver moves closer to the hearth, staring into the cheerfully flickering flame. "We'd spent so much time together, Shaw… And the more I learned, the more I began to notice these qualities in you." He doesn't look at him, and his voice sounds oddly distant, as if my father is lost in memory. "Heated. Able to move through pain like it was nothing. Since you were a child, you've always burned so hot in your rage."

Denver shakes his head, as if climbing out of the past. He turns back to us, his tone straightforward once more. "I wasn't certain until I found Asa in the north. One night, a dozen children at his knee, he told the story of a pale-eyed beast who spewed flame. None of the other accounts mentioned eye color, but I *knew* it to be true then. Eyes the shade of the hottest flame."

Max narrows her eyes. "Argentum borders Xamani land. It's entirely possible the Praeceptor has heard these same stories. That he can identify another potential fire-bearer."

Denver nods once. "Asa was held in his camps, tortured by his hand. It's entirely possible Cullen knew the stories even before I was taken."

Silence settles over the room. After a long moment, Denver straightens. "We cannot take the chance. If the Praeceptor invades Similis, the rest of Ferusa will be doomed. The Covinus hoards technology, and while he has been a benevolent leader," —my father ignores my loud scoff— "Cullen will not. He will be at too great an advantage to defeat with electricity on his side. He will come for Nadjaa. We must act before he does."

I breathe a sigh of relief. Until now, I hadn't known how

much doubt I harbored about Denver. In my mind, he was just as likely to take the warning as an opportunity to shore up his own territory's defenses as he was to help a country halfway across the continent who once took everything from him.

"I will call an emergency council meeting. Hopefully we can come to a vote by tomorrow night."

"Tomorrow night?" Harlan repeats in disbelief. "That's too long if the Praeceptor is already at the Boundary. We have to go now!"

Denver begins to gather the papers strewn about the desk, shuffling them into a neat pile. "That is the price freedom demands. Nadjaa will not go to war without its people's say so."

Desperation strangles my windpipe. The Dark World is expansive and if the slaughter at Yen Girene taught me anything, it's that sometimes, news travels slowly. Cullen could already having broken through the Boundary, my brother, and the rest of the Community, already subjected to his twisted depravities. "But—Easton is there!" His name is an arrow through the chest, pointed and painful. I left him in Similis, and now, he's going to face the Praeceptor's cruelty with no protection. Whatever happens to him will be my fault.

"I *know* who is there," my father snaps so harshly, I flinch. He grimaces, remembering himself, and his eyes shine behind his glasses as he sighs deeply. "In spite of what you may think of me, Mirri, I am not a dictator and cannot selfishly bend this city to my whims, no matter how I might wish to."

"But—you'll make sure they come, won't you? You won't leave Easton alone?"

"My vote means no more than any Nadjaan's, so I will try to make my words matter."

Evie chooses that moment to return, her arms laden with plates of sweet-smelling pastries. She sets the plate next to Anrai with a wink. "Eat. There's plenty more where those came from."

He smiles up at her gratefully before taking an obedient bite.

"Evie, I'm afraid the bakery will have to wait this morning," Denver tells her, gathering his things to his chest with one hand and leaning on his cane with the other. "We need to call an emergency council meeting."

Evie doesn't miss a beat, nodding determinedly. "Berik can run the store. I'll send out a messenger to the other members and meet you there." With that, she hurries from the room.

Denver makes his way toward the door slowly, the limp in his gait still evident, despite it having grown less inhibiting over the past few months. He hesitates before Anrai, who gazes up at him, not with the disdain and anger that embitter me, but with something like adoration. After everything my father's done, the ways he's failed him and the weaknesses he allowed to overcome them both, Anrai still sees Denver as the man who once saved him.

The man who first loved him.

For a moment, I hope Denver will tell Anrai what he means to him; my father has always had a way with words. Even in the depths of Similis, he could paint vibrant dreams that felt buoyant enough to carry us out of it. His words built Anrai up from the ruins Cullen created, what made him believe he was worth saving. If my father expresses his faith once more, perhaps it would be enough to make Anrai believe it now.

But all he says is, "It would be a wise strategy for us to inform the People's Council of your true identity. If they see we have the Praeceptor's son on our side, and a fire-bearer at that, they will be heartened in our potential strength against the Dark Militia. And hopefully see the wisdom in meeting them somewhere far from our shores."

I open my mouth vehemently to protest parading Anrai in front of the council—he is too vulnerable, too uncertain in his own humanity—but Anrai has already stood. "I'll do whatever you need."

My father nods curtly and when he shuffles from the room, Anrai follows, fragile hope gleaming in his eyes.

Shaw

"I'm glad to see you've healed," I say into the silence of the skiff as one of the city guards rows us toward the business district. "When we saw you in Yen Girene, I—I wasn't sure you would make it."

Denver doesn't look at me, his gaze on the spread of his city before him. It's quiet and sparkling, residents safe in their homes with no sense of the Darkness that grows on the edges of their borders. They rest their heads comfortably, knowing their voices are heard and their lives are their own, all thanks to the man sitting across from me.

When I first met him, I saw him as the polar opposite of my true father. He was kind when Cullen was not; he used words instead of weapons, logic rather than fear. He saw the plight of others as something to be rectified, not something to be exploited. Growing up in the Castellium, I never knew someone like Denver could exist. He was a fever dream outside my wildest imaginations, and I idolized him as such.

I still do, but now it is edged with the disappointment that comes with realizing the greatest people are still that —*people*. With all the weaknesses and limits that come along with it.

Because Denver is the man who saved me, but he is also the man who lied to me, who abandoned his daughter when she was small and again when she was grown. Who hasn't been able to look me in the eye since I returned, let alone ask me how I feel. I haven't had the time to make sense of the two sides of him together, to decide which matters more.

"Healed, but never the same," he replies quietly. His eyes finally settle on me, the color unnervingly similar to Mirren's. "I admit, I've been waiting for you to seek some sort of revenge for my betrayal."

I shrug with a casualness I don't feel. "I'm probably the only one who doesn't judge your choices under duress. I know what it's like to be in the dungeons of the Castellium. I know the price it carves from you."

Denver's eyes shine, and for an absurd moment, I expect him to cry. But he tamps down his emotions with the brutality only a Similian could achieve and smiles thinly. "I suppose revenge against me doesn't serve your greater purpose at the moment, anyhow."

"What is that supposed to mean?"

"Only that the soulless are driven by their own selfish desires. You are driven by a vendetta against your father. Is that not why you agreed to help? Why else would you care about stopping an invasion against a country that means nothing to you?"

So far away from Mirren, it's true the hollow has

ballooned inside me once more, painfully cold. But it is no longer entirely isolated, for now that I have felt the warmth of her soul, it seems I cannot *unfeel* it. It is odd—for such emptiness to live alongside something so whole, my body now the horizon where the void and light meet.

"It is," I admit slowly. *Or it was.* But when I offered to come to the council house, it wasn't revenge I'd been thinking about. "It's more complicated than that now. I have a soul when I touch Mirren."

Denver's mouth presses into a thin line. He's never once whipped me, and yet, I feel his disapproval now as deeply as one of Cullen's punishments. "You may have a semblance of a soul, Shaw, but do not fool yourself into thinking you are the same man you were. You will only be disappointed."

"You said yourself, none of us are the same as we were, Denver," I bite out irritably, as the skiff cuts silently through the sparkling water, the sound of the gentle lapping against the wooden sides heightening my anxiety with each moment. "But the soul Mirren holds is *mine*. It is who I was and who I *am* when I touch her."

Denver sets me with a piercing gaze. "It may be an echo, but it is *not* who you were. If it was—if you were the same boy I knew and cared for—you would never let yourself within ten feet of my daughter. There was nothing like the strength of your heart, or your will, and you would have never put her in danger for your own selfish desires. You would have done everything in your power to keep those you love *away* from something like... like you."

I stare at him, chastened, my power burning its way up my throat. I could cut him down where he sits and throw his body into the bay, treating him as carelessly as he's just treated me. I could shout all the ways he's used both me and his daughter for *his* selfish desires. But my hand won't go to my dagger and my mouth won't open.

"I do not doubt my daughter has pulled you from the depths of your own Darkness, Shaw. But it is dangerous to save a drowning man. She is just as likely to be pulled to her death right along with you."

The skiff clanks against the dock as the guard jumps out to tie us in place. The business district gleams, it's lanterns bright and cheerful against the dark sky. Gazing at the skyline once felt hopeful, but now, I just feel numb.

Denver maneuvers awkwardly out of the boat, his cane scraping the docks. Leaving me sitting alone, trying to staunch the wound of his words.

CHAPTER
THIRTY

Shaw

When we enter the expansive meeting room, the People's Council is already in an uproar. Furious mutters come from disheveled looking council members, most of whom look like they've been pulled directly from their beds and shoved into the stodgy mahogany chairs. A hush falls as Denver shuffles to take his seat at the head of the imposing table, one of the few things in the ancient building that has been here since its inception.

Probably because no one could figure out how to get the behemoth through the narrow doorway.

I take my place behind Denver, standing with my hands clasped rigidly in front of me. The position is familiar, having stood behind Denver in countless meetings, but I feel inexplicably uncomfortable in my own body, as if my skin has suddenly grown too tight for it. My flames strain in my chest. *This is not the Castellium,* I remind both my power and myself, *you are not a monster here.*

But by the way most of the council is eyeing me, they don't agree.

"Ah, *zaabi*," a deep voice says to my right, the Xamani word for 'cherished friend'. "It is so good to see you here."

I turn to find a man staring at me, his face crinkled in a kind smile. There is no way he means that look for me, so I glance around in confusion, but upon finding nothing but the wall behind me, turn back to him uncomfortably.

He is handsome, with high cheek bones and slightly upturned eyes that sparkle in amusement as he watches my confusion. His dark hair is tied in two thick braids and his clothes, finely dyed doeskin, denote he is highly respected in his tribe. My gaze trails to his bare arms where the bronze skin has been mutilated and recognition sparks in my memory.

"Hello, Kashan," I greet Asa. "I don't believe anyone here would believe I'm worthy of that term."

Asa doesn't smile, but his eyes twinkle all the same. "Ah, but they don't know you as I do, *zaabi*."

I want to point out that Asa doesn't know me either, as we've never actually met. He was long gone by the time I made my way out of the Praeceptor's camp last spring, and thank the gods for that, because otherwise, he'd most certainly be dead.

Council members have taken to their seats, the sounds of arguments and protestations now echoing across the table. The lanterns have all been lit, the brightest glow coming from the iron chandelier that hangs from the ceiling.

"It seems the Darkness has a sense of humor when it comes to the two of us," Asa says, his voice lilting and melodic. Tilting my head in confusion, he chuckles lightly, gesturing to the bustling room around us. "We are destined to meet only in the dens of vipers. Let us thank the old gods for the light of friendship in even the darkest pits of chaos."

Before I can respond, Asa has taken his seat to the side of the table. He's been invited only as a courtesy because of his role with the Xamani, and his opinion will hold no sway over matters.

"Just what is the meaning of this, Denver?" Jayan demands. His white-blonde hair pokes up in the back and his watery eyes are still heavy with sleep. When they find their way to me, I grin wickedly, pouring some of my flame into my gaze. A reminder that though he seems to have been forgiven for his actions against the city and Mirren in my absence, *I* do not forget.

Denver smooths his papers and heaves a leveling breath before beginning. "We have received information on the movements of the Praeceptor. He is believed to be in the Nemoran Wood preparing to invade Similis.

"I don't know why you woke us for this when you have Nadjaa's forces in a stranglehold under the guise of *peace*," Jayan retorts hotly, his mouth twisted.

"Good riddance to the pathetic lemmings. It's about time they felt some of the Darkness' scorn," another member says, an elderly man representing the Hithe district.

A few murmurs of agreement echo through the room, and I don't entirely blame them. It was how I once viewed Similis, safe in their electric homes with their warm heaters and full bellies. It never seemed fair that there were people allowed to live outside the punishments surviving requires.

If Denver objects to his home being spoken of so cruelly, it doesn't show. Instead, he nods as if he completely understands the men's viewpoint. Ever the politician. "Normally, I would agree. But I'm afraid the invasion of Similis has far more resounding repercussions for the rest of Ferusa than just a simple battle. If the Praeceptor gains access to the resources the country has, it will only be a matter of time before he turns them on Nadjaa. He has always hated what we stand for and will use anything he can to crush it. Dictators are threatened by acts of freedom."

Another wave of murmurs slides across the table, but Denver remains still, watching them all calmly. It has always been his strength, to remain calm and fair, in the face of others' more human emotions. To listen to things he may not agree with and give them the same amount of consideration as those he does.

"What of the Boundary? Surely, it can't be broken through," Sandeel Fermal, the councilmember representing the low farmlands, asks from near the end of the table.

I stiffen. Is this when Denver will shame me in front of his council? Is this when he will illustrate the horrible things I've done? Closing my eyes briefly, I settle myself. As upset with me as Denver is for being with Mirren, he is still who taught me how to be a man: and he has never been petty or vengeful.

"It has been compromised," Denver replies simply, confirming I was silly to worry in the first place.

Another councilmember, a dark-skinned woman with thick braids coiled atop her head, says, "We are protected by the mountains and the sea. Let the Praeceptor come. Even with Similian technology, he will find himself crushed against our rock."

"Would you really want war brought to our shores, Ajan?" Evie admonishes. "Near our children and our elderly? I agree with Denver. It is wiser to defeat the Praeceptor now, before he gains such power that we are forced to test the strength of our defenses at home."

Denver nods to the baker. "Thank you, Evie."

"Yes," Jayan agrees snidely, appearing to have fully woken now that he's realized war may be on the table. "We should defeat the Praeceptor's armies and take his territories for ourselves. Nadjaa has been stagnant too long in the shadows of these mountains. It is time for her to show her might to the rest of Ferusa."

"Are you truly advocating for war, Denver? It is a weighty decision to risk Nadjaan lives protecting a land that would never do the same for us," a wizened member says.

"I am *not* advocating for battle," Denver clarifies, and my breath freezes in my lungs. Despite what he told Mirren, he has no intention of leading an army to help the Similians. "But I *am* advocating for action. I propose another Blood Alliance to stay the Praeceptor's hand."

Ajan shakes her head doubtfully. "We barely got him to adhere to the last alliance, Denver, and that was only because he was sorely beaten. His militias were depleted, his wife kidnapped and hung by the witch-queen. It was only by agreeing to let him crawl back to his land that he ever agreed in the first place. Things are different now. The witch-queen only works for herself and the Praeceptor now has half of Ferusa's warlords in his control. Unless you're prepared to hand over the ocean-wielder, you have nothing else he would want."

I've spent years observing every detail of the man who saved me. The intelligent humor in his eyes, the skill in which he weaves his words. I was determined to emulate him, and so I memorized every facet of him—which is how I know what he'll say before he says it.

"I have his son."

A weighted silence falls over the room as every eye

turns to me. It feels like every bit of oxygen has been sucked from me and my flames falter, dying to nothing more than ash.

"Denver..." Evie says hesitantly, her eyes wide in horror. "Shaw is a son to you. Are you...are you seriously proposing we hand him over to that—that monster?"

Denver holds his head high as he surveys the council before him. His brainchild, the symbolism of ideas over bloodshed, come to life. He has never believed in using battle to solve issues. Denver's ideals have always been unshakeable; it was foolish to believe he'd give them up now, simply because his daughter asks it of him.

"The son I knew was lost when the Praeceptor took his soul. You have heard rumors of the man behind me and the destruction he has wrought at Cullen's hand. He has destroyed villages, decimated entire populations of Ferusa. As much as it pains me, my son is gone. And the man standing behind me is the only thing the Praeceptor wants —perhaps more than Similis."

I should burn Denver where he sits, rain flame down upon him until his council house is nothing but a pile of rubble. But instead, I remain rooted in place. The hollow inside me flares, until I taste it at the roof of my mouth, in the exhale of my breath. When I was a child, wretched and violent, Denver saw the good in me when I was convinced there was none. If he cannot see it now, it is because it doesn't exist.

I *am* my father's monster, his weapon. I am nothing but ash and destruction.

A brief moment of pleasure, the warmth of someone good, and somehow, I'd imagined myself as more. *Foolish.*

"The Praeceptor will use him against us if you give him back," Sandeel points out.

Denver folds his hands in front of him, the lack of scars jarring in comparison with the rest of him. "After his most recent betrayal, the Praeceptor will no longer trust him enough to use him as a weapon," he says matter-of-factly. "It is my belief he seeks vengeance against his son. Cullen risked war with Nadjaa to bring down his son...*that* is why he had Shaw attack my manor. Not to kill me, but to show us that Shaw will always be his. So, if we are to give him back, we should do it to our utmost advantage. Pride drives Cullen's need for power, for fear, and we are in a unique position to feed it. He will sign the treaty and Similis will remain safe. And so will Nadjaa for the remaining future."

"Denver, this is..." Evie shakes her head as she stares at the Chancellor, at a loss for words. "This is not how Nadjaa does things."

"This is how *Ferusa* does things," Jayan snaps back, his disappointment in the lack of war only sated by the opportunity to punish me. "As much as you and the Chancellor and the other idealists like to pretend Nadjaa is separate, we are just as much a part of the Dark World as anyone else. Eat or be eaten, Evie, you know that."

I hardly hear their words anymore, the sounds fading to a monotonous hum. Mirren's soul throbs in my chest, suffocated as it is by the Darkness swallowing it. I don't try to save it. Better she lose this one small piece than the entirety she'd lose tying herself to me.

Denver was right. I've always been drowning; I just didn't realize how far I'd sunk. Better to drown alone in the emptiness than take her with me. Better for Nadjaa to be spared from my monstrous appetites, for its Chancellor to ensure the people's safety by putting an end to me.

Empty. Nothing.

When the guards come for me, I don't raise a hand to stop them.

~

Mirren

"The council won't vote to help Similis," Max says morosely.

We've eaten an entire plate of pasties and gone to the front to raid the glass counter for more in the time since Anrai and Denver left. Calloway probably would have gone for thirds if Evie's husband Berik hadn't arrived, shooing him from the bakery with a threatening broom.

My stomach roils, uncomfortably full and unsettled at Anrai's absence. Images of Similis burning and Easton in the middle of the destruction have been pushing into my thoughts, until I have to squeeze my eyes shut in order to force them away.

"Why do you say that?" Harlan asks.

Max shrugs ruefully, stretching out on the floor, and clutching her own stomach. "As great as Nadjaa is, it's still the Dark World. We may help our neighbors here, but they aren't going to risk themselves for strangers. They're going to do what's best for their own city. The Darkness has no mercy and the desire to protect what little is yours has been imprinted over the millennia since the queen's curse. It can't be rooted out in just a generation."

Cal stretches out beside her, crossing his long legs at the ankles and closing his eyes. "What's best for Nadjaa is defeating Cullen. Denver will convince them of that."

Max twists her lips doubtfully, but doesn't reply and, for once, I appreciate her restraint. I can't bear to hear my own thoughts spoken aloud. They are too wild, too desperate.

He loves Shaw. He loves Easton. He will help us.

I repeat the words to myself once more, but even in my head, they sound flimsy. My father's love has never held the strength it should.

After a while, Max's eyelids flutter shut, her head leaned against Cal's shoulder. Harlan eventually succumbs to sleep as well, the book in his lap slipping to the floor once more with a soft flutter of pages. My eyes burn with exhaustion, but I'm too agitated to sleep, my blood like a river careening over rapids.

I jump up from the couch, the small movement grounding me slightly. Walking toward the hearth, I gaze at the flames as they spark and leap from the logs. They flicker and dance with the same sort of grace Anrai possess. Fierce and bright and beautiful.

"Who would have guessed the water-wielder would have such a thing for fire?" Avedis drawls from his place on the floor. His eyes are still closed as they've been most of the evening, but a mischievous smile graces his face.

"Isn't it wind that's supposed to feed fire?" I plop down next to his head and curl my legs beneath me.

"This wind is only interested in feeding itself," he chuckles, peeking an eye open. "You should sleep, lady." I shake my head, and Avedis nods in understanding. "There is no point in worrying about Similis until your father returns. There is nothing to be done tonight."

I press my teeth into my lip. "It isn't just Similis that worries me."

"Ah. Your assassin? Is he not in good hands?"

"That's still to be determined," I reply darkly. "It just feels wrong...with him so far away after—" I blush and attempt to reorder my words. "I mean, I worry how going back and forth between having a soul to not again will affect him."

"Do you think he'll get bored in the council meeting and set them all on fire? Anyone who's been subjected to one of those insipid processions would hardly blame him."

I shove his shoulder, but in spite of myself, I laugh. Avedis sits up, gazing thoughtfully at the fire. "You know I don't care for the man, but I will humbly admit, he has seemed to defy his soulless nature on occasion. I believe we can trust him to do so now."

"I do trust him." Implicitly. There is not a crevice of doubt anywhere that Anrai will betray us, soul or not. "I guess I just worry that he doesn't trust himself."

Avedis makes a humming noise. "Perhaps that is something that will come in time? Once we've found a way to return his soul permanently."

There's no irony or doubt in his words, and I smile broadly at my friend, somehow weirdly thankful it was him who was sent to kill me. "I'm glad you're here with us," I tell him sincerely. "I'm glad it was you the wind chose."

He smiles demurely. "To the Darkness' final calling, O Siren of the Deep." I roll my eyes as his wry grin fades and his face turns uncharacteristically somber. Staring at the fire, he says, "you asked me once if I have a soul."

"I did."

"You have not asked me since."

I smile softly. "I know you have a soul, Avedis."

He nods heavily, dropping his gaze, his throat working with emotion. "I was luckier than your Shaw. I escaped after only a few years and after that, I was able to choose my work sparingly to keep myself intact. And even then, it has only been to earn what I needed to keep my mother from starving to death. She is sick and her treatment—well, it costs a lot to manage."

"I had no idea. When this is all over, Avedis, I swear, I'll heal her."

Avedis shakes his head. "It is not a physical affliction to be healed, but rather, one of the mind. And that is not why I told you."

"Why, then?"

"So someone would know I never wanted any of this." He clears his throat. "I have no regrets for what I've done, but I want someone to know who I truly am. Or who I could have been, at least." At last, he looks to me. "Thank you for seeing it even when it was hidden beneath brutality."

"Brutality is often the price we pay for love," I tell him, stretching out next to the fire. Following my lead, Avedis lays down next to me and closes his eyes. "Similis isn't wrong in deeming it dangerous. They are only wrong to think the danger isn't worth it."

"Very wise, for a lemming," Avedis laughs.

My power finally settles in my veins, running through me like the soft trickle of a forest stream. Avedis is right, there is nothing to be done tonight. So, despite everything, I fall asleep.

As I linger on the edge of dreams, a sharp bang sounds at the front of the bakery. It's followed by successive pounding, desperate and loud. I shoot up, grabbing my bandolier and sprinting toward the front room, Avedis in step beside me. Cal and Max are close behind, the latter wielding her twin falchions and looking distinctly put out at having been woken.

Panic grips my throat as I determine the source of the racket. Sura, brown eyes wide with panic and cheeks flushed with exertion as if she's just sprinted all the way here.

When I whip open the front door, Sura practically tumbles into my arms. "Sura, what's wrong?"

Her breathes come in painful wheezes and I remember what Denver said about her breathing condition. She gasps and swallows, struggling to get her words out.

Finally, she manages, "It's Shaw. They've taken him."

CHAPTER
THIRTY-ONE

Mirren

"What happened?" Cal asks, hair still tousled with sleep.

They've taken Shaw. Over the thrum of my panic, of the blood rushing in my ears, the words reverberate in my head like the beat of a steel drum.

Sura wrings her hands nervously. "They...the Council—I think they've arrested him."

Max furrows her brow, as Avedis sinks to the floor to listen to the wind. "What do you mean they've arrested him? Where was Denver?"

But I'm already moving, buckling my bandolier, and shoving my feet haphazardly into my boots. Because it doesn't matter what happened. *They've taken Shaw.*

They've taken him from me.

Hot rage rushes through my veins. I allowed him to be taken from me once and it nearly broke us both. And now—now he's irrevocably mine, our souls entwined, and no prophecy or warlord will steal him from me. Certainly not some paltry council.

"I was waiting outside the council room for the Kashan when I heard shouting. The Kashan never raises his voice, but he sounded so angry. A few minutes later, they carried Shaw out in chains," Sura explains in a rush. "I think—I think the People's Council must have outvoted Denver."

I swallow down the anger clogging my throat and make toward the door.

"Where are you going?" Harlan asks in alarm.

When I turn back to him, there is no mistaking the determination on my face. "I'm going to get him."

He nods, something close to pity on his face. "Just pause a minute, Mirren. What if this is part of his and Denver's plan?"

I narrow my eyes. "You think Shaw wanted to be dragged to the dungeon?" I ask hotly.

To Harlan's credit, he doesn't flinch from my anger, apparently more accustomed to Ferusa than I've given him credit for. "Why else would he not be fighting back? He has no soul right now, Mirren, but he isn't burning anyone. That has to mean something, doesn't it?"

Calloway watches Harlan with an inscrutable look, before flicking his eyes to me. "I've seen Anni melt through irons like they were nothing," he admits. "If this is some sort of scheme, we could be ruining everything by bursting in there."

I force myself to level a breath, to consider my friends' words. But they don't settle. Instead, they remain unbalanced and wrong as I imagine Shaw—strong, undefeatable, Shaw—ensnared in iron. He has been chained by the Praeceptor for so long, he wouldn't willingly submit to shackles once more, no matter if it was Denver that asked it. Not unless something was seriously wrong. "They could have a different way of holding him. Like when we were in Yen

Girene." I steel my chin and meet Max's gaze. "I won't leave him there. He—he can't be in a dungeon."

She straightens, cursing loudly. "Give me five minutes to change," she barks, ducking through the doorway and heading upstairs.

Relief barrels through me as Cal throws his bow and quiver over his shoulder. He looks to Harlan. "We won't interfere with the council's plans for Similis," he says sincerely. "But if there's even the smallest chance Anni's been taken against his will, I hope you understand...we have to help him."

Something passes between the two and I'm reminded of Anrai's earlier observations. Cal's words seem to calm something in Harlan and after a moment, he nods. "What can I do?"

"Wake Gislan and bring him to Aggie's. We'll meet you there...after."

Harlan nods, touching his binding mark absently. "Be safe, Mirren."

By the time Max returns, Avedis has risen once more. "They have him in the dungeons. Seven guards posted outside his cell, ten more in the hallway above." He looks to me curiously. "As far as I can tell, it is only iron that holds him."

Why is Anrai not helping himself? Perhaps Harlan is right after all, and this *is* a plan between him and my father. Will I be ruining everything by storming into the council house?

My heart pounds in my chest, a frantic beat that won't be soothed until I see for myself that Anrai is safe. "Where's my father?"

Avedis closes his eyes once more. "He is—" His eyes fly open, his mouth twisted in violent disgust. "He is in his office dispatching a messenger." He hesitates, noting the surge of my *other*. It's seeped into my eyes, my rage mingling with that of the sea. After a moment, he sighs and says, "to Cullen."

The world is suddenly colored in shades of red, my father's face at the center of the maelstrom. He not only allowed the council to vote against Anrai, he's *using* it to his advantage. All thoughts of treading carefully empty from my head as water surges to my skin. I will tear that council house down brick by brick if I have to. "Max, I need you to stop that messenger."

Max grins devilishly. "Gladly," she replies, before disappearing into the night.

"Ready?" I ask, planting my feet against a tidal wave of anger and panic. It will unmoor me if I allow it, sweeping me away to depths I can't climb out of.

Cal nods. "Let's go get our boy."

I glance at Avedis in question. This isn't his fight. And for someone who wishes to remain invisible, storming the political seat of a powerful territory isn't wise. But he gives a quick bow and a small smile. "To the Darkness' final calling, my lady," he repeats with relish.

~

The Council House is eerily quiet when we dismount our horses. Built from the same material as the surrounding mountains, its bricks blend into the landscape almost seamlessly, as though the designer wished to camouflage its brutal purpose. Tall and robust, there is no mistaking the house was built to withstand siege.

And I'm about to break into it.

Avedis nods to a window five floors above us, a gauzy curtain blowing in the night breeze. "Shall we?"

Cal blanches. "And just how in the Darkness are we supposed to make that climb?"

Avedis doesn't answer, only sweeps his strong breeze beneath me, lifting me from my feet. It isn't nearly as terrifying as sailing off a cliff and after a short moment, I'm deposited gently inside the window.

Cal tumbles in after me, clutching his bow with white knuckles and muttering something under his breath that sounds suspiciously like a prayer. As his feet touch the floor, he shudders involuntarily, his face going slightly green. When Avedis steps lightly through the window, Calloway shoves him heartily. "Don't *ever* do that to me again."

"Do heights bother you, Calloway?"

Cal glares at him indignantly. "No! Sailing through the air with nothing to hold onto *bothers* me."

Avedis chuckles lightly as Cal straightens his trousers with an irritable flare. "There is only one entrance to the dungeon. It won't be easy to remain unseen."

His unspoken words linger. *Or to free Shaw without hurting anyone.*

I clear my throat, the fissure in my soul aching fiercely, remnants of the cost carved from me the last time I tried to save Anrai. "Don't fracture your souls for this," I tell them gravely, because I know they both will without question. For me, for Anrai. But it is my sacrifice to make, my soul that must pay to get back what's mine.

The door to the small office opens and Evie's hands fly to her heart in alarm when she notices the three of us, fully armed and conversing in the dark. "Gods help me!" she cries, stumbling back against the door until it shuts with a loud bang. Avedis has already pulled his sword and stands at the ready, his dark eyes wary on the baker.

I place a hand on his wrist, a sign to stand down, but when he begins to lower the weapon, Evie yelps, "Don't put it away, you foolish boy!"

Avedis cocks his head in curious astonishment, apparently not having been referred to as a 'boy' in a long while, but before he can comment, Evie rushes toward us. "Thank gods you've come. They've got him in the farthest cell. I'll take you down the back way, but after that...well, after that, it's up to you."

Finally noticing our confounded stares, Evie flutters her hands impatiently in front of my face. "Where is the girl who shouted at me in the doorway of my own establishment?" Evie mutters, shaking her head in exasperation. She plants her hands on her wide hips. "Do you plan to dally here in my office all night or are you going to use those weapons and free Shaw?"

"I—why are you helping us?"

Evie believed the worst about Anrai on Denver's word. As kind as Anrai tells me the woman is, I was under the impression she wouldn't go against my father, especially in political matters.

"Didn't the council vote for Shaw's arrest?" Cal asks, sounding slightly stunned. "I thought you were a true believer in the vote."

Evie makes a testy noise in the back of her throat. "I still am, Calloway. But if we don't let heart into our government, then we are no better than the Similians, are we? Now, string that bow and let's get on with it."

Without another word, she ushers us out the door and into the hallway. Here, the harsh stone is hung with brightly colored tapestries and in spite of the moldered age of the building, the hallway appears cheerful under the flickering lantern light. Evie leads us past doorway after doorway, before finally stopping in front of one of the largest hangings, an intricately woven work of the night sky above the Shadiil mountains. Evie pushes the tapestry aside, revealing a large stone stairway descending into the darkness.

"There you have it," she says perfunctorily. "This will lead you straight down to the dungeon entrances. It's heavily guarded, but I don't see how to avoid that unless you can somehow tunnel straight through the rock."

Calloway raises an eyebrow and I know what he's thinking. Gislan. Creating an opening in solid earth is exactly the sort of thing he specializes in. But he's already risking himself to help us with the prophecy; I can't involve him in this and put him in my father's sights. I nod to Evie. "Thank you for helping us, Evie. We won't tell anyone you did."

Evie's chin wobbles slightly, the first sign of vulnerability she's shown. "He is just a boy that no one has ever seen as one. But I always did." When she meets my gaze, her fierce determination mirrors my own. "I still do. And I won't let him be treated like trading chattel."

With a quick squeeze of my shoulder, Evie arranges the tapestry so it appears unobtrusive once more and the stairway goes dark.

Cal clears his throat. "Well, if there were ever a time for Anni's magic, I think now would be it."

I smile into the darkness, beginning to feel my way along the smooth stone wall and descend the narrow staircase. The air smells damp and abandoned, the stairs carpeted with a deep layer of dust. All is quiet but for our breathing as we slowly make our way down. If there is any life in the Council House at this time of night, the thick stone walls keep it solidly muffled. I may hold a piece of Anrai's soul, but I cannot feel him beyond the knowledge he lives.

Does he believe I'll come for him?

Does he even want me to?

Our progress through the dark is painstakingly slow, but finally, we reach the bottom, denoted by the feel of another thick tapestry. Cal moves the embroidered fabric slowly, peering into the hall outside before turning back to Avedis with a raised brow.

"Is this your handiwork?" he asks, brushing the tapestry aside so we're able to see what he means. "What exactly have you done to them?"

Indeed, three guards dressed in the crisp white uniform of the Nadjaan guard lie unconscious in a heap just outside the secret entrance.

Avedis shifts primly and shrugs. "They found themselves without air just long enough to need a nap."

"Now that's the kind of magic I can get behind," Cal grins with approval.

Gingerly stepping over the guards, we make our way through the empty hallway. It appears as if the entirety of the Council House is abandoned and yet, it brings me no sense of relief. Instead, dread, thick and viscous, wriggles its way down my throat.

As I move to turn down the next hall, Avedis throws an arm in front of me, hard muscle colliding so hard with my abdomen that I let out a grunt. He doesn't speak, but eyes Cal and I meaningfully as he draws his sword. We've reached the entrance to the dungeons.

Which means we've reached the Nadjaan guard.

Cal draws his bow, stringing an arrow, and nods once.

There is no need to call my *other*, for it has been simmering at the surface of my skin since Sura first said *Shaw's been taken*. All too eager to mete out justice, to take back what's ours, my power rises. It laps at my fingertips and crashes against my heart, settling my panic and then shaping it to be wielded as something dangerous.

When we round the corner, I understand why the rest of the building appeared uninhabited. There are not seven guarding the dungeon entrance—there are at least triple that, as if the People's Council pulled *every* guard on duty to keep someone from breaking in.

Or to keep Anrai from breaking out.

My eyes move past the first line of guards to the apparatus positioned behind them, pointing toward the dungeon entrance. Rusted and somehow outfitted to be used without the power of electricity, stands what is undoubtedly a water cannon. I've only seen them in the old films of the Dark World, where governments would use them against their own people to quell riots. I'd always thought of them as something long gone, same as most of the technology in those videos. But here one is, in the middle of what is supposed to be the most peaceful city in Ferusa.

Rage clouds my vision. Anrai's power is fearsome to be sure, but how could my father allow *this*? How can Denver not realize this—water—is how Shaw has been tortured? And these guards—who have sworn to protect Nadjaa in peace—are they complicit in torturing a prisoner who's done nothing to them? Is there no peace, no justice, anywhere on the continent?

The first guards move toward us with a shout. Cal tenses beside me, arrow nocked, but before they make it more than three steps, they both crumple into unconscious heaps. The rest of them swarm, their incapacitated brethren becoming a rock in the sudden river of bodies.

Cal's arrows soar, their sound a comforting *thwack, thwack, thwack* in my ears. Wind rushes through the room, as Avedis lunges toward the first group, the metal of his sword ringing as their blades meet his.

My heart flies frantically against my chest and my *other* bursts forth. It spears toward three of them, turning the water in their bodies to ice with barely a thought from me. They fall to the floor gasping and writhing, but I'm already moving to the next wave of men.

They don't balk from our power. Instead, they meet it with fury as if they've been preparing themselves to fight against it.

Two more fall under Avedis' spell, another knocked out cold by his fist. Cal's arrows fly past my head, his aim true, as they sprout from legs and shoulders. None of us has aimed to kill, but as the injured rise to rejoin the fight, I see the folly of our plan. The guards are an unending wave, ceaseless and untiring. Their faces blur together, their angry shouts blending into a cacophony of chaos I can hardly hear beyond my anger.

I'd just seen glimpses of the true Anrai—the man I first met with the fierce heart and tender soul—only to have him stolen from me once more. Locked back up in a cage, tortured and sacrificed once again for the good of someone else.

And still, he shows them mercy by not melting them all where they stand.

I find no such mercy in my heart. And this is taking entirely too long.

Reaching out, I feel for the ammunition in the water cannon. The soldiers have it loaded and ready, fed by an interior pipe and already pressurized by the pump. I feed my *other* my fury, my determination and in turn, the water in the cannon begins to move. Agitated. Angry.

And then, the cannon explodes in a torrent of water and debris.

Avedis throws a shield of air around the three of us, as the rest of the guards are swept away in a pressurized tidal wave. Some are hit by the debris, some still struggle against the current, but all are preoccupied enough for us to slip through the dungeon entrance.

And now, they will have no recourse from Anrai's power.

The three of us sprint down the stone stairs, weapons raised. Sconces flicker along the walls, their fuel almost depleted as morning approaches, casting the passage in odd moments of darkness. "Well," Cal says, wiping water from his eyes, "your way was quite a bit faster." Droplets cling to his lashes, giving him the impression of an oversize doll as he reaches for another arrow. "Though quite a bit *wetter* than I was planning for."

Seven guards rise to meet us as we round the final corner. Six of them crumple in unconscious heap. The seventh runs toward us with a shout, only to be hit over the head with the flat of Cal's longsword. It seems the guard foolishly put their faith in the strength of their numbers upstairs, along with the water cannon. In their fear of Anrai, they blinded themselves from their true opponent: me.

Cal grabs an unconscious guard's torch from the ground and raises it, lighting the dungeons more clearly. The place is an expansive exercise in metal and stone. The room is large, apparently built to house quite a number of prisoners, but the low stone ceiling makes it feel claustrophobic nonetheless. Rusted iron bars dissect the area into cells, which are empty of everything but a refuse bucket. There are no blankets, no straw. There is nothing soft here except for the torchlight.

Anrai is curled in the corner of the farthest cell, knees pulled up to his chest and head buried in his arms. His arms and legs are shackled, fastened to the wall behind him by a thick iron chain. The smell of mildew clings to my nose, the damp stink of the place a strong reminder of the depths of Yen Girene. Emotion clogs my throat as I run toward him. How can he stand this place, so empty and yet so suffocating? So similar to where he gave up his soul?

And though I've never been to Argentum, I can only imagine the dungeon he was kept in was similar. How has he kept his sanity, being reminded every moment of the torture he's suffered?

My *other* rushes toward him, its panic a mirror to my own; desperate to touch him, to reassure us he hasn't gone mad in this place. That he hasn't experienced anymore hurt.

Anrai lifts his head, watching detachedly as my power skates across his skin in sparkling droplets. It flickers and probes, searching for any source of injury. It calls to his flame, searching for the power it loves to dance with. But Anrai doesn't produce even an ember. And when he turns to me, I understand immediately he hasn't been physically injured; something much worse has been done to him.

Something to cause the deadened look in his eyes.

There is no spark of rage. No hope or relief.

The only thing reflected in the pale blue is absolute nothingness.

Cal rushes up behind me and shakes the bars, testing their strength. Iron, drilled deep into both the ceiling and the ground. "Melt these, Anni. The guards are all taken care of for now, but I'm sure some of them can swim, so we've gotta hurry."

A fresh wind rushes through the dungeon, clearing the air of the moldered stink, at least for the moment. "If we can get back to the stairwell we came from, I should be able to lower us down through the same window without anyone being the wiser," the assassin says, eyeing Anrai with something like sadness.

"Or I'll take my chances and jump," Cal mutters, rattling the bars once more for good measure.

Anrai's eyes lift to his friend, but there is no spark of recognition. "You shouldn't have come. None of you should have."

Cal furrows his brow, and his freckles disappear under a flush of anger as he comes to the same conclusion I have. Something has happened to Anrai. Something that's convinced him to give up his fight.

The freedom to die. His own words, echoed back to me. But surely, not now—not when I've just gotten him back.

"How did Denver let this happen?" Cal demands, kicking at the bars with renewed fervor. "Do any of the guards have a set of keys?"

"I believe they're only kept by council members," Avedis replies, running his fingers over the thick lock, before pulling a small pick from somewhere inside his tunic.

"Don't bother." Anrai shrugs and turns back toward the wall. "Denver is protecting what's his. I would have done the same."

Cal's head whips toward me in alarm, but the room has already gone unsteady beneath my feet as the implication of Anrai's words settle.

My father wasn't just making the best of the way the vote went, complicit in Anrai's arrest.

My father *arranged* the arrest.

He knows Anrai's scars, knows the depths to which he's been dragged beneath Cullen's feet. He's experienced the madness of Cullen's brutality firsthand, and still—*still*—my father put the welfare of his city before everything else.

There is no more thought of edges or limits, there is only the rush of an angry sea—the drag and the power and the magnificence. A storm to wash away an entire coastline, to demonstrate its rage at the boundaries nature attempts to inflict upon it.

When I close my eyes, I am no longer Mirren. I am endless, powerful, the beginning and the end.

As every pipe in the council house explodes.

Avedis throws himself at Cal, raising his shield just in time as they tumble to the ground. The boom is deafening, the sound of time itself raining down upon us. And the entire fortress, as old as the Averitbas Mountains, trembles.

I hope every council member feels it in their bones, in the depths of their selfish hearts, as I send the force of the flood at the bars that hold my soulmate.

Broken and patched together, we belong to each other. Let this be a message to my father, to the Praeceptor, to *anyone* who would try to take him from me again.

I open my eyes as the bars are blown apart, the iron hinges now rusty and mangled. Water and debris shower down from the ceiling as I walk toward Anrai. Shouts echo from the floors above us, the ground shuddering as wall after wall tumbles down. Avedis shoves his air shield at the ceiling, and I know we're on borrowed time.

But as I finally cradle Anrai's face between my hands,

his stubble scratching against the pads of my fingers, I see none of the ruin around us—I only see his anguish.

How he drowns so deeply in it, there is nothing left of him on the surface.

My father, his idol and his mentor, has told him there is nothing redeemable left in him. And the small bit of faith in himself, the goodness that was so hard won, has been completely shattered by it.

Anrai shakes his head, the irons clamped around his hands clanking as he desperately tries to pull my hands from his face. "You shouldn't have come," he implores, gripping my wrists. "I will only bring you ruin. Just leave." His voice cracks, and he speaks so softly, I can barely hear him above the chaos as he repeats, "Please. Just leave."

Struggling to keep hold of him, I lift his chin even as he paws at my hands. *Look at me.* "Are you his...or are you mine? Will you let his words be your truth? Or the words of the woman who holds your soul? And whose you hold in return?"

Anrai squeezes his eyes shut. And then, his entire body shudders like the walls of the Council House, as he breaks down into sobs. The sound is so ragged, it is as each one has been dragged from the depths of his chest; all the horror and the shame, the cruelty and the shattered hope of the past few months, mingled with the Darkness that's plagued him his entire life. It all pours out of him in wave of sorrow so powerful, it embeds itself in my bones.

"You do not ruin me," I tell him fiercely, brushing his hands aside so I can press my forehead against his. Our tears mingle together, hot and sticky. "I have been so terrified to fall into the depths of my power, Anrai. So scared of losing myself. But I just did it for you without a thought." I stroke his jaw and then wipe his cheek clean of tears. When I force him to look at me this time, hope sparks in my chest.

Because though his face is tortured, it is no longer empty. "And I'm still here," I tell him with a wet laugh, peppering soft kisses over his tear-stained jaw. "You do not bring me ruin. You *ground* me. You lift me up. You are an adventure, and you are the way home. I'm more myself *because* I hold a piece of you."

For a moment, I think he'll send me away. But after an agonized pause, he pulls me to his lips. His hands tremble as they tangle in my hair, angling me closer. Our kiss tastes of ash and ocean, of open air and tortuous dungeons, of blood and time—every bit of our story, imprinted on our embrace.

"So sorry to interrupt," Avedis interjects, not sounding at all apologetic as he struggles with the collapsing ceiling, "but we're in a bit of a hurry here."

With a weak laugh, I step back. Anrai takes a steadying breath as he stands. Then he flares to life, all beauty and heat and light, and his shackles melt into a pool of molten metal at his feet. Following me from the cell, he steps over the mangled bars with a low whistle. "Remind me never to make you mad," he laughs. It's weak, but it's a *laugh* and the warmth of it balloons in my chest.

"If you wanted a firsthand account of how unpleasant it is to be on the receiving end of the lady's wrath, I could have happily provided one without all the theatrics," Avedis remarks with a shudder.

I roll my eyes.

Cal, who is bleeding freely from a gash on his forehead, rushes Anrai. Anrai tilts on his heels under the ferocity of the hug and more tears spill down his cheeks as he wraps his arms around his friend. When they pull apart, a thousand unspoken things pass between them.

"What about Denver?" Cal asks gravely.

The question is clear, and it isn't for me. My father and I have our own tangled history to settle eventually. As enraged as I am, today isn't the day. Not with Similis on the verge of invasion and my brother so close to Cullen's grasp.

Anrai straightens his shoulders and tilts his chin in the haughty way that reminds me so much of the man I first fell in love him. "We leave him be," he says sternly, pulling a dagger from my bandolier and twirling it deftly through his fingers. "Today, we go save Similis."

CHAPTER
THIRTY-TWO

Mirren

The sky is a creamy pink by the time we reach Aggie's property at the edge of the valley, the early morning air edged with a crisp chill. Getting out of the Council House was far easier than getting in; we'd picked our way through the rubble, skirted around pipes still furiously spewing water, and easily avoided the guard, most of whom had been distracted with rescuing council members from where hallways and rooms had collapsed entirely.

I tensed every time we rounded another corner, half expecting my father to come charging down the passageway and drag me off to the dungeons. A shameful part of me *wanted* to see him: to study his face as he took in the damage I'd wrought. *Look around, father. This* is what my heart looks like, your abandonment, your betrayals, made physical.

He'd left me alone so many years ago, and in the shadow of his abandonment, ugly, dark things have grown around my heart. My anger hadn't been solely about Anrai, not really—it was that it was unbearable to watch my father repeat his mistakes with another. In Anrai, he'd had the chance to be the father he never was to Easton and me, and he'd sacrificed that chance in service of his vision.

Nadjaa is the only thing that means anything to Denver and in my moment of rage, a terrible part of me had wanted to take it from him. Steal it as he's stolen so much from us.

And in doing so, I've put myself firmly on the opposing side of the Chancellor. There will be no help for Similis. I told my father he was no better than Cullen, but in truth, neither am I. In my moment of anger, I couldn't think outside my pain, couldn't breathe beyond punishing those who would take what's mine.

Cradled between Anrai's arms as he holds Dahiitii's reins, I wiggle closer against the heat of his chest. I am sorry for what I've done, but not nearly sorry enough.

Because I would do it again.

Without thought, without question, I would ravage the entire world if it kept Anrai from being hurt.

He pulls Dahiitii to a halt, nodding to Avedis, who rides astride a large black mare. "Have you covered our tracks?"

Avedis nods once. "I've whispered misdirection in the ears of those who search for us, and the breeze tugs them down false paths. It should buy us a few hours to determine our next move."

"Thank you," Anrai says sincerely, earning a flattered look of surprise from the assassin. I don't know that Anrai will ever fully forgive him for trying to kill me last spring, but his assistance in storming the Council House has somewhat tempered his anger, at least momentarily.

Though we are still a good distance from Aggie's cabin, Anrai swings himself off our horse before offering me a hand down. To Cal and Avedis, he says, "We'll meet you at Aggie's shortly."

They exchange an amused look but keep their comments to themselves as they clear the thick copse of trees and gallop toward Aggie's cabin. As the sound of hooves fade away, I allow Anrai to help me down, my confusion palpable. "Is everything okay—"

The words die in my throat as he lunges at me, tangling his fingers in my hair and slanting his mouth against mine. I stumble backward with a laugh, gripping his shoulders to keep myself upright as his tongue sweeps past my lips, hot and desperate—as if he seeks to possess me with only a kiss. I groan when his fingers dive beneath the waistband of my leggings, and he smiles wickedly against my mouth at how ready he finds me, how desperately I need this.

Without breaking our kiss, he peels my leggings off, exposing my wet, aching center to the cool air of the forest. He curls his fingers into me with a reverent curse, his other hand climbing up my shirt to pinch the tips of my breasts.

We stumble backward, tongues dancing as my back hits the wide trunk of a tree, the bark catching at my cloak. Anrai pulls it off, and the cloak flutters to the ground beside us as his fingers keep moving in a steady rhythm. Electricity sparks beneath my skin and sizzles up my spine. I pull him toward me, tugging his shirt over his head. Running my fingers over the ridges of muscle, I reach between us with my other to stroke the hard ridge of him already straining against his pants.

Anrai catches my hand with a snarl. "No playing," he bites out, his voice a wild murmur against my throat as he draws me against his chest. Sinking to the ground, he pulls me with him until I'm straddling his waist. "I just need—"

I interrupt him with a kiss, yanking his pants aside in a desperation I hardly recognize. There is no explanation needed for what is imprinted on my own heart—the demand for reassurance that no matter how the earth shakes, *we* do not. We are the bones and the foundation on which life sits, not to be blown about by the whims of the world.

Pulling back, our eyes lock. The glacial blue of his burn, the color of the hottest flame, as I slide myself onto him, inch by steel inch. He bites out something halfway between a curse and a prayer as my body welcomes his, warm and stretched and full. The first time, the pleasure came with a bite of pain, but now, only ecstasy washes over me in scorching waves.

My inner walls clench around him, the heat between us almost unbearably decadent.

Then, I begin to move.

Slowly at first, the delicious agony of it enough to make my legs shake as I lower myself onto him once more. When he first touched me all those months ago, Anrai had trembled with the exertion of his restraint, but now, he is unbound. Wild. His long fingers splay across my bottom, his touch a brand on my skin as I leisurely rise, and he greedily guides me back down.

"You are so fucking exquisite," he rasps, running his teeth up the side of my throat, before licking at the sensitive spot behind my ear. He licks at the swell of my breast, before pulling the tip into his mouth and suckling roughly. "So soft and delicious, I could spend the rest of my life devouring you and it would never be enough."

His hair sticks up where I've run my fingers through it, and his eyes, half-lidded and ravenous, are positively feral as his flames erupt over his arms and trail over his chest. I roll my hips on top of him, and a thrill runs through me as the flames flicker brighter, lighting his bronze skin until he glows like the warmth of a hearth.

His mouth pulls into a devilish half grin, and the tendrils jump from his skin to mine. They dance their way over my stomach and my whole body heats, until I feel as though I'll come undone. Unmoored, unbound, held to earth only by *him*. When the flames reach my breasts, I dip my head back with a sharp cry, pushing them needily to him, the warmth as luscious as if it was his mouth.

"Look at me," Anrai orders, his voice threading up my spine as if my body lives for his command. So I look—and he is so beautiful, all mussed black hair and sinfully sharp angles. His lips are swollen and his eyes flicker, half mad, as he thrusts into me over and over again, until my legs feel like jelly beneath me. His flames circle the tips of my breasts, and his fingers slowly work the bundle of nerves at the apex of my legs. Pupils blown wide, he whispers, "tell me."

I know what he demands. Know the empty ache that's opened up inside him after being torn from me once more. Because the same ache is mine: only relieved by him inside me, close enough to meld our souls.

"I claim you," I breathe, scraping my nails down his chest and clenching my inner walls. His answering groan is a rumble against the curve of my chest. "You are *mine*. No one will take you from me." I take his hair in my hands, before running my teeth down his throat. His pulse thrums frenetically beneath my mouth, as if it fights its way out from beneath his skin. "Not your father or mine. Similis or Ferusa." I slam my hips down, a moan working out of my throat. "Not even the Darkness itself."

His hands dig into my hips as he thrusts deeper. Faster. *Mine. Mine. Mine.* The word echoes in the heated air between us, weaving its way over our sweat-slick skin until it's imprinted on the darkest corners of our hearts. There will be no dragging this out: no games, no teasing—only chasing after the primal need to claim more of each other.

"Mine," I growl. "Now make me yours."

Flames burst anew from Anrai's hands as if my touch ignites them. They skitter over my skin, joining the tendrils flickering over my breasts, to circle around my throat. Fire and hope and lust burn between us, and I cry out as he slams into me, a merciless rhythm that both sates my ardent compulsion and ignites it anew.

"I stole you for mine the first moment I saw you," he murmurs and adrenaline shoots straight through the center of me as the flames around my throat squeeze tighter, pinning me in place until the only thing I can move is my hips. I roll them wildly, thrashing on top of him even as he slows the pace of his strokes.

I whimper as he only gives me enough to edge my need. Anrai smiles arrogantly, knowing the depth of my hunger.

"Show me what I've stolen," he tells me, the words so guttural, they skitter over my skin as if they, too, are flames. "Show me what's mine."

There is no thought to obeying, only wanton submission as I spread my legs wide, offering him everything. Because he owns every inch of my pleasure.

My body, my soul, my power—they are his and they always have been.

His ravenous eyes spark as he watches his rigid length disappear into my wet folds. And then, fire still squeezing my throat, he winds a new flame down my stomach. Lower.

My skin is electric beneath it, shivers rising in its wake as it curls over my hips. And when it circles my throbbing core, I scream. At the moment the heat mingles with my own, Anrai slams up into me and I am entirely lost. I thrash on top of him, the pleasure almost unbearable.

His hands everywhere, his fire at my throat and breasts and core, I become the wild, uncontainable thing I've always been to him. I ride him, chasing my gratification as my power bursts from me, circling around the forest in maelstrom, encircling us in sparkling isolation. Anrai is relentless, whispering lascivious decadence against my ear as he thrusts into me.

The flames at my throat squeeze harder once more, and my entire body clenches, a wave of pleasure hotter than any fire cresting over me. Anrai grips me to him, pressing me to the hard muscles of his chest, and as I shake in his arms, he finds his own climax with a roar.

His flames curl back into him and lays his head on my chest, arms and legs still tangled, sweaty tendrils of raven hair falling against his forehead. When his breathing slows and his heartbeat has evened, he opens his eyes and looks up at me. "I'm sorry," he mutters somewhat sheepishly. "Similis is being attacked and the Nadjaan guard is out for our blood, and I couldn't even control myself long enough to have you inside a proper building. Again. I just needed—"

The words tumble out of him in a tangled mess until I press my finger to his lips with a smile. "I know what you needed...because I needed it too."

The strength of my need should frighten me, its power greater than any emotion Similis purports to ban. Even now, when he is still buried inside me and his taste lingers in my mouth, I *want*. And there will never be enough to sate the ravening hunger, never enough time to find the limits of it.

Anrai's eyes shine as he brushes the tangle of my hair over my shoulder and then kisses my bare skin. "You blew up the Council House for me."

"It was more like a flood," I hedge, blushing.

Anrai runs his lips along my cheekbone, as if he can taste the flush under my skin. "I love you," he murmurs against my jaw, before pulling back to look at me. His eyes are earnest, the flame in them now flickering like the embers of a campfire. "I love you, Mirren."

The words light in my chest, sink beneath my skin. *Love.* Terrifying, wonderful. Agonizing and rare.

"I'm sorry I first admitted it in anger. I—" Anrai curses and runs a hand through his hair. "You deserved to hear it differently. Softly. I know it scares you, and that it's against the Keys, but I don't know how long I'll be able to feel my soul or how long I'll even survive, and I need you to know... You called to me in the Darkness when I was unmade. You cooled me when all I could do was burn. Even in the depths of soullessness, when I was nothing but an abyss, I have loved you."

I never knew a heart could break and somehow, feel better than when it was whole. Because as Anrai gazes at me, eyes shining, mine does. It shatters and comes back together as something different; something new. *The Darkness will change you.*

"I don't need you to say anything. I just... no matter what happens to me, I just—I needed you to know that."

I smile broadly. "I love you, too." There is no more agonizing over whether to name it, no more fear of the cost it demands. Because spoken or not, it has always demanded all of me and now I know—I will freely give it. Freely now I fall, into the depths of him, the beauty of us, because it is all worth the sacrifice, whatever it may be.

Shaw taught me that, once. And now, with Anrai, I feel its truths in the depths of our entwined souls.

I run my fingers over the cupid's bow of his lip, up over

his razor-edged cheek bones. Over the small scar dissecting his brow. His long lashes flutter against the palm of my hand as he gazes up at me with the hearth of a home in his eyes. And then I tilt my head as a thought occurs to me. "How *would* you have said it?"

He lets out a breathy laugh. "Well, I definitely would have liked to have a soul when I did." I laugh as he trails his fingers lightly along the ridges of my spine, his gaze oddly intent. "I would have told you in a soft moment. When you were happy and safe." Anrai's fingers widen their path, running up the sides of my stomach and then over the curve of my breasts until goosebumps rise in his wake. "Not when we were arguing or running…or when we were trying to kill each other." He pinches me lightly. "*Or* someone else."

I laugh. "So, you would have *never* told me, then?"

He nips at my shoulder playfully. "We do have an auspicious lack of quiet moments, don't we? Well then, maybe I should have just told you every time I thought it."

I furrow my brow doubtfully. "Like when?"

Anrai presses a kiss to my shoulder and then the edge of my jaw, his fingers never stopping. "The cliff pond," he growls in my ear. "*Both* times." A kiss on my chin and another on the line of my throat causes me to shiver. "Watching you dance at the lunar celebration. When you offered to feed Luwei and Sura. When you were in my bed with a knife," he cocks his brow so wickedly, another laugh escapes me. "In my father's camp when you were willing to give up everything to save Asa."

"And what about after? When I stabbed you?"

"*Especially* when you stabbed me," he laughs, the resonance of his voice rolling over me.

I snort. "You did *not* love me then."

He pulls back, gazing at me intently. "I did," he insists, "it was the first time I saw you as you are. Not as a lemming, not as what the world expected you to be, but *you*. Brave and determined and soft and powerful." Anrai tilts his head. "And a tad murderous, which I find wildly appealing, of course."

I shove him, guffawing loudly, feeling lighter than I ever remember. And as Anrai laughs alongside me, I think it's the most beautiful sound I've ever heard.

After he's helped me dress and we've smoothed our hair into looking somewhat presentable, we walk hand in hand toward Aggie's house. Max is already halfway across the lawn when we emerge from the trees, her stride determined, and her swords still strapped in an 'X' on her back. Without a word, she drags us both into a hug so fierce, it knocks the wind from me.

When she takes a step back, her gaze finds Anrai. "Even when I thought you destroyed the manor, I would never, *never*, let you go back to the Praeceptor."

Anrai nods, the movement weighted. Though we aren't touching now, his words are still somehow warm. "I know, Maxi."

Righteous fury burns in her eyes and her lower lip trembles as she struggles to keep her emotions from spilling over. "What he did Shaw—"

Anrai swallows before threading his fingers through mine once more. "Is done," he finishes sternly. "He was doing what he thought was best for Nadjaa."

"What's best for Nadjaa is a leader with a brain *and* a heart," Calloway mutters from the porch, his face uncharacteristically savage. A large gash at his hairline has begun to clot, staining his hair an even deeper red than usual and his normally immaculate clothes are caked in mud.

I blanch, rushing over to examine the injury. "I'm so sorry, I should have healed this right away. Is this...was it because of me?"

"I *did* tell him to beware of brick walls. It isn't your fault the hair product has clogged his ears," Aggie cackles snidely from her doorway.

Cal looks to the sky with measured patience. "You failed to mention the walls would be *exploding*."

"I'm just an old woman, Calloway. You can't expect me to know everything," she shrugs, to Max's great amusement. Aggie is dressed much the same as the first night I met her, in rich fabrics of aubergine and woven gold, and I realize with a start, tonight must be the lunar celebration.

And I've just blown the Nadjaan Council House to high hell. Something like shame winds its way around my throat as I push my power gently into Cal's wound. I feel Anrai's eyes on me, his steady gaze a firm reminder not to make myself smaller. He loves all of me, the depths and the dark of my power, and his face is clear: *don't degrade me by making yourself less than what I love.*

Cal shudders as I remove my hands. "Gods, that feels weird." He runs his palm gingerly over his newly healed skin. "And itchier than I expected."

Still rubbing his forehead, he sniffs sharply before narrowing his eyes at me. "You smell like a campfire."

Blushing furiously, I clear my throat loudly and ask Max, "Did you stop the messenger?"

She shoots me a roguish grin. "He never even knew what hit him."

"What *did* hit him?" Harlan asks worriedly, poking his head out from Aggie's door. He grips a chipped mug of tea and is now clad in an outrageously patterned sweater. At my incredulous look, he mutters, "Gislan and I were near the Council House when it exploded, and I got wet. He stayed at the edge of the forest to keep watch and I came here to dry off. This was the only change of clothes Aggie had."

"The messenger is fine," Max replies with an impatient wave. "I stowed him in the hull of a merchant ship headed for the southern isles. By the time they find him, his message won't matter anymore." She laughs at Harlan's look of horror. "What? The man should thank me. I saved him from an entire *building* being brought down on his head."

I blush furiously. "The damage was pretty terrible, wasn't it?"

"Damage is an understatement," Avedis says with a wry grin, from where he lazes in the grass. "Though as far as I know, no one was killed. Your mercy is still something to be admired, Lady of the Deep."

Something uncoils inside me at the knowledge I haven't killed anyone, specifically, my father. He deserves so many things for what he's done, but still—we share the same blood. He is at the core of who I am, the weaver of so many of the dreams that kept my childhood in Similis bearable. Do I truly wish him dead?

Anrai moves beside me, squeezing my hand. If anyone understands the entanglement of feelings Denver evokes, it's him.

"Do you think Denver will still help Similis?" Harlan asks.

Cal sighs doubtfully. "Well, considering we just blew up his Council House and stole his prisoner, I'm going to guess he isn't feeling particularly magnanimous."

Something heavy settles on Harlan's shoulders, the same as the weight pressing against my own chest—fear for Easton. And it is not just the threat of the Praeceptor. The Covinus has already proven he's willing to hurt his own citizens to keep hold of his power. What will he do now that he's threatened with losing it?

"But he understood," Harlan insists, unwilling to accept that unless it means war for Nadjaa, my father will be no help. Even if it means sacrificing another of his children. "He understands the gravity of what will happen if the Praeceptor invades. Not just for Similis, but for all of Ferusa."

"We can't afford to wait to find out," Anrai interrupts. "My father will burn Similis to the ground while the People's Council still sits in their house debating. If we're going to stand any chance of stopping him, we have to bring magic back. Now. And hope it's enough."

Worry lines Harlan's face. "What if we're too late by then? Won't the combined power of the four wielders be enough to defeat him? His militia is only mortal and you... you're all so powerful."

Anrai gives Harlan an assessing look, before inhaling sharply and shaking his head. "Maybe if it were a typical militia, but it isn't. My father takes babies from their mothers and raises them as weapons until they can no longer remember what it was to have a soul. We will find no mercy there, no humanity. My father does not follow the rules of civility. He doesn't fight fair—he fights *well*. And there's a huge difference. We can't risk getting to the Boundary and having him steal our power. We'll be defenseless and no help to the Similians at all."

He exchanges glances with Max, the only one who has witnessed the inner workings of the Praeceptor's forces. Her jaw hardens and for a moment, she looks terrifying as she recalls her time in Argentum. "And that's if we were only facing the Dark Militia. My father has spent the past year infiltrating other territories. Over half of the warlords are now loyal to him." Anrai curses and shakes his head. "Even if Nadjaa were to come, there's no guarantee we'd win. We have to defeat him a different way. By interrupting his plans and bringing balance back to Ferusa. At least that way, the people he's trying to annihilate will have a chance to fight back."

Harlan looses a shuddering breath. "I hate this. I hate that we're so far away."

I reach toward him, but Cal is there first. He places a hand on Harlan's shoulder and squeezes gently, his eyes shining.

"We don't even know what the rest of the Dead Prophecy says," Max points out, examining her nails like the conversation has grown dull. "We have no supplies and no idea where we're going. And by this point, the entirety of the city guard, if not the entire Nadjaan militia, will be after us for destroying the Council House."

"I'm sorry," I say earnestly. Because of me there will be no militia. No reinforcements. Only our small group trying to evade half the continent. I've become the worst of the Dark World, everything the Covinus warned us about: too overcome by emotion to make rational choices.

Max waves me off. "You should have brought the entire thing down on all their heads," she snipes venomously.

Avedis grins, his eyes lighting in approval. "A woman after my own heart," he purrs. "The wind speaks misdirection and Gislan is keeping watch at the edge of the property. He'll send a signal if anyone grows close, so we should at least have a few hours to plan."

I'm about to thank him when Asa appears at the edge of the property.

"Asa!" I cry in relief. Sura said the Kashan had argued against Shaw's imprisonment, but she hadn't known what happened after. A terrified part of me wondered whether Asa had been banished for his disagreement. Once, I would have thought dissension was only punishable in Similis, but I'm no longer so sure. Because dissension is not individual or selfish like the Covinus preaches—it's risking your own safety to stand up for the mistreatment of others. And my father, for all his words of the importance of balance, sacrificed someone broken for his own cause. Just like the Praeceptor, just like the Covinus. It isn't farfetched to assume punishment for disagreeing ideas is next, even in a place as progressive as Nadjaa.

Peace is only sustainable as long as the people work for it.

My relief is palpable as I hug the Kashan. "Are you alright?"

His dark hair is slightly disheveled, his shiny braids having come loose in some places and tangled in others, but he looks decidedly unharmed as he nods. "I am well enough and have managed to gather you a few supplies. Luwei is waiting with them along with Gislan."

With a crinkled smile, Asa grips both Anrai's hands in his. Anrai tenses, as if bewildered anyone would touch him so willingly. "I am sorry, *zaabi*, that I could do nothing to stop the injustice against you. But I am glad to know you are so well protected," he says with a wink at me. Another hot blush washes over my cheeks.

Anrai relaxes, grinning. "She is a fearsome thing, to be sure. And there is nothing to apologize for. You risked your tribe's refugee status to bring me help. I won't forget it, Kashan."

Asa waves irreverently. "I only risked a temporary sky, a

sun that is not ours. You risk something far greater to defy the selfish tides of the land. Your father—" Asa swallows, before raising his chin. The Kashan has felt the Praeceptor's rage, the permanent brand it leaves on a person. "Well, he will fight until there is not a droplet of blood left in his body to destroy whoever tries to take his power. And you, *zaabi* —" Asa's eyes shine. "You and your soul-bonded risk his wrath to save this land. There are warlords and entire armies that do not possess your same bravery."

Anrai gazes at the Kashan for a beat. "I don't know where to start, Asa," he admits softly. "His forces are hidden somewhere in the Nemoran and it's only a matter of time before he attacks. I don't even know if we can make it there in time, let alone figure out how to free magic."

Asa presses his mouth into a small smile. "I wished to tell you before the council meeting, but I did not want the Chancellor to overhear. Now, I realize my silence was guided by the old gods."

I furrow my brow, my confusion mirroring Anrai's. "What do you mean?"

"I've found the story to guide us. The Praeceptor may have his militia, but we, dear friends, possess words. The most powerful of weapons."

CHAPTER
THIRTY-THREE

Shaw

Aggie's cabin is humid and cramped. Max's elbow sticks into my ribs, and Calloway's knee knocks against mine as eight of us squeeze ourselves around the rough-hewn table. The heedless manner in which they touch me, with no fear of the pain or destruction it could cause, brings a familiar wave of humility to my chest. Mirren settles herself on my lap with a happy wiggle, and though it only makes the cabin feel hotter, I wrap my arms around her waist, pulling her into me to savor her softness.

"Did you discover the full prophecy?" she asks Asa.

The Kashan shakes his head. "*That* story remains stubbornly hidden in the depths of time. But I have discovered another I believe will help guide us."

Asa takes a deep breath, and after a long moment of rapt silence, begins to speak.

Long ago, when the First Queen's curse was still new and the Darkness had not yet settled, the old gods still lived. These gods were older than our world, having come from another. A place of thick nights and oily evils, they migrated here seeking light to dance in. When they found this land, they knew it was not perfect, but they celebrated the perfection of the balance we possessed. Light and dark. Water and Fire. Earth and Air. It was through their worship of balance, and the spirits worship in return, that the old gods' power grew.

For an eon, there was bountiful peace, but the souls of the people became restless and brought the curse down upon themselves. It was a curse of Darkness, of the soul and the land, but it was also a curse of compulsion. For any that tasted the Darkness were unable to resist tasting it again, until they were entirely consumed.

And the old gods could do nothing but watch as the land was torn apart by the same Darkness they'd sought to escape. Brother turned against brother, mother against child, and the Darkness multiplied. The earth rotted and rivers dried, and balance was no more.

Man began to hunt the spirits of the earth. Some blamed them for forsaking the land and wanted them punished. Others sought to use their power as a weapon. One by one, the spirits were annihilated. Some were driven into hiding, while others were killed, the Darkness feeding on the echoes of their sacrifices until it was impenetrable. It settled over the land and in the souls of its people until no one could remember what the light looked like.

The old gods grew sickly. With no one left to worship them, they withered into little more than dust. But they loved this world they had found, and with the last of their power, wished to protect us from ourselves. We had already tipped so far into the Darkness, the gods could not right it, but they could keep it from being swallowed completely until someone else had the power to swing the pendulum.

So, with the last bit of their power, the gods went to a cave in the depths of the oldest forest. Forests are rooted in time itself, their own sources of ancient magic. Here, the gods bound the last of the nature spirits together.

Earth would never against exist without air. Without fire or water. One could only exist if the others did, an eternal gift to our earth to keep what little balance we had. If one fell, so did the others. If one thrived, the others would, too. In binding them to each other, their power increased tenfold. Instead of controlling a forest stream, the water spirit could now wield oceans. It was not enough to save us from ourselves, or even to save the gods, but it kept the rot from expanding. From tipping into the edge of Darkness and being swallowed whole.

And then, with the gods' dying breaths, they uttered the final story. A plea and an edict to the remaining spirits to sleep until they found hearts full enough to hold the strength of them. And once they did, the curse of Darkness could be lifted by the light.

And so, our race has lived, balanced on the precipice of destruction, but never able to fully fall.

Asa's word drift into silence and for a long beat, no one moves.

We all stare at the Kashan, his words still woven around us as if they live apart from him, their own source of magic. They transported me from the small kitchen and into a memory I've never lived, memories of beings both foreign and powerful. Unknowable. And yet, through Asa's words, I felt as if I *was* them.

"Are you—" Mirren hesitates, her voice wavering. "Are you saying that if one of us dies…"

It's Avedis who finishes her thought. "The rest perish as well. In service of balance."

Asa collapses heavily into a chair, his strength sapped by being the conduit of the old gods' stories. "Words often hold meaning outside the literal. But I do believe if one of you loses your power, the rest will as well. There always has to be four."

Gods.

If I'd actually carried through with my plan to free myself from my father's hold and then die, I could have inadvertently sentenced Mirren to death. And what if she hadn't stopped me from plunging my dagger into Avedis last spring? Would both of us have dropped dead at his side? And before that, when I was a slave child for my father, constantly straddling the line between life and death? Had I held three others lives in my hands without ever knowing?

Judging by the look on the assassin's face, his thoughts run similar to mine.

Cal stares at the muddy cup of tea in front of him, face scrunched in consternation. "How does that story help? It takes place after the curse and doesn't tell us what we need to do to complete the prophecy. If anything, it just makes it seem more impossible. *It was a curse of compulsion.* What does that even mean?"

Of course Cal, who has never taken a life, wouldn't understand the same line of the story that ensnared me. He has always believed so much in my goodness, in *everyone's* goodness, that he wouldn't understand the allure of the Darkness. How the first fracture in your soul creates an opening for the shadows to breed. How you begin to welcome each crack, each painful fissure, because it's the only way to feel anything at all. Until there is nothing but Darkness and its rapacious hunger for more.

"The commenia tree," Aggie pipes up from behind Cal, her voice rising and falling in a lilting song. I startle, having been so mesmerized by Asa's words, I forgot the old woman is here. She steps from her kitchen, cratered eyes glimmering as they fall on Mirren and me.

"Here we go," Cal mutters dubiously and I'm struck with the urge to laugh.

"The commenia tree holds the answer," Aggie says again.

"Well, alright," Cal concedes with a shrug. "Let's go ask a tree. But I draw the line at getting naked to do it."

Avedis raises a brow. "Do you normally get naked to talk to trees?" He asks mildly.

"Well, if you have to be naked to thank the moon, one would assume—"

Mirren squeaks in sudden understanding, her body tightening in my arms. "The gods' power!" she yelps, her excitement tugging at my heart. Even before she knew the questions, Mirren has always found joy in the discovery. Curiosity, a search for knowledge, has always been a driving force in her. She was denied it for so long in Similis, now, her pleasure in it is contagious. It makes me want to build her a cabin on the coast and fill it with books and spend the rest of my life watching her try to read them all.

My breath hitches and my power freezes in my chest. I have no right to any sort of imaginings of the future.

As far as I know, I could very well be marching myself right back into my father's possession by going to Similis. And even if I somehow miraculously escape his clutches, the future doesn't belong to the soulless.

"The gods' power and the nature spirits were like the commenia tree," Mirren explains in an excited rush. "The gods had power because the nature spirits worshipped them. And the nature spirits had power because of the gods worship of their natural balance. *That's* why they slept.

When the gods crumbled to dust, there was no one left to imbue them with power."

She stands up suddenly, her gaze appearing far away from this cabin as she paces before the door, her nose scrunched in thought. "It wasn't just the gods and the spirits who made it work," she says slowly. When her eyes flash to mine, the irises churn like the waves of an emerald sea. "They needed us for balance. They needed our good *and* our bad. It's why our power feeds on our emotions. Without it, there's no balance. It's a circle that's been broken and we need to repair it."

Her face shines with a conviction so great, I find myself nodding in agreement. It sounds impossible—fantastical, even—but Mirren is the one thing I've always been able to believe in. Even in the depths of Darkness, she has always been real. "Balance is a delicate thing," I say, though she knows better than most. It only takes the smallest of breezes to tilt your entire world from its axis and send it spiraling out of control.

"And the old gods are dead," Max reminds us brutally.

The Similian's eyes widen, giving him the appearance of an overgrown teddy bear as a thought occurs to him. "But they gave the last of their power in that cave!"

Mirren nods and claps her hands together excitedly, and for an obnoxious moment, I understand why the Covinus matched the two of them. Hot jealousy grips my throat. Not that Harlan possesses her—after the wood, she's mine more surely then ever—but for some alternate universe where he could have given her the life she deserves. Light and airy and somewhere far away from the Darkness.

"What if their power is still in that cave? What if that's what we need to bring back magic? The story says the spirits still lived after the curse, so it wasn't the curse that killed them. With the death of the gods and the anger of humans, the nature spirits had no one left to worship them. *That's* what caused them to die out. We don't need the Dead Prophecy to bring magic back. We just need us!"

Max twists her mouth in doubt, her leg bouncing next to mine. "This doesn't make sense. If the Dead Prophecy doesn't bring back magic, what was the point of it? People have killed each other for centuries to keep it from being unearthed. Why, if not to keep magic dead?"

"Because if there is no light, the Darkness is all-powerful," I answer, my voice sounding far away. In the dungeons of the Castellium, or in the depths of your own mind—when there is only dark, it is so easy to forget how to get back the light. "Magic isn't going to fix the world. It won't break the curse and it isn't going to magically turn Ferusa into a good place. But it will light a candle. It will remind people that it wasn't always so black. That things can be better." I drop my gaze to the table, examining the scratches etched by time and love. "Sometimes, a reminder of hope is more powerful than any militia."

My words hang in the air like mist as Mirren threads her fingers through mine. So small, and yet her touch is proof. She is my hope, my candle in the endless of tunnel or turmoil I was trapped in. Her undying faith, Calloway's compassion, Max's loyalty. All lanterns on a path, leading me from the depths of my own despair.

Asa watches me, his face inscrutable. Then he heaves a deep breath, setting his hands to his knees. "It is my belief that the curse was the First Queen's punishment for man's selfishness. It destroys everything electric, keeping us in perpetual darkness, but it is also a moral curse. It is an addiction, feeding itself in depravity. And once it touches someone, it steals their chance for redemption. By breaking the curse, I believe we will be opening up Ferusa to the light. And bringing back magic is the first step."

Suddenly, the ground trembles beneath us. The trinkets lining every surface of the cabin rattle and clink, and the lanterns swing violently from the rafters. My feet feel like they are planted on the hull of a rocking ship rather than on solid ground, and I swallow forcefully as my stomach leaps into my throat.

"Gislan!" Harlan yelps, as if suddenly remembering the earth-wielder. "Perhaps he can help us find the cave."

Asa clears his throat, rising to his full height, thin body poised and strong. "I'm sure the earth-wielder will have much to say on what we have learned, and as that is his signal, perhaps you should go fill him in now, rather than later. We packed as many supplies as we could, but I'm afraid it isn't much."

"Thank you, Asa. You've done more than we can ever thank you for," Mirren says warmly. Chairs scrape as everyone climbs to their feet, the cramped cabin feeling three times smaller as everyone begins to move. Avedis is already checking his weapons. Cal swings his bow and quiver over his shoulder, oblivious to Max's cries of protest as the string catches in her hair.

She swats at him viciously, before stomping outside, having never removed her armaments in the first place.

Asa bows to Mirren. "You freed me when you did not have to. There is no repayment needed." Then his clever eyes flick to me. "May I speak with you alone a moment, *zaabi?*"

I nod as the rest of the group steps onto the porch, lively bickering echoing behind them. Mirren squeezes my hand before slipping out the door, my body feeling as if it's been plunged into an icy lake in the absence of her touch. Only Aggie remains, quietly sipping her tea, her blind eyes shrewd on Asa. I swallow down my revulsion, having had the unpleasant experience of Aggie's tea on several occasions.

"Forgive me for the timing, but the Darkness is swift, and I don't know when we will get another chance to speak," the Kashan says hurriedly.

I smile at Asa, but the gesture is lacking. No longer touching Mirren, cool calculation has settled where just moments before, hope dwelled. And if Asa has asked for an audience while I'm soulless, his request must be something ruthless. "Speak then, Kashan."

"I only wanted to ask...did you know your mother?"

I stare at him in startled surprise. I'd expected a demand for brutal revenge on my father, Asa's torturer for months on end. And yet, when I meet the Kashan's eyes, there is no vengeance or anger. Only sincerity edged with something like sadness. I narrow my eyes. "I've never had a mother."

Both a truth and a lie. Everyone *has* a mother, but in my entire life, I haven't spent more than a few moments considering the woman who birthed me, and even then, only in the worst depths of loneliness as a child. All I'd ever known was she was not my father's wife and that she was dead; another faceless victim of the Praeceptor's twisted predilections. Energy was a finite resource, and I couldn't afford to waste mine wondering about a woman who was the same as so many others. She wasn't coming to save me, and that had been all that mattered.

The Kashan doesn't falter beneath my cruel gaze. "Am I safe to assume it was not your father's wife who was killed prior to the Blood Alliance?"

I watch him indolently and he takes this as confirmation. "I only ask, because you weave words like a Kashan. Life clings to them, Shaw. Faintly, but there."

I don't move, now baffled twice in the space of a minute. "What are you saying?"

"I believe you are Xamani." Asa looks at me the way Denver used to, both welcoming and proud, as if there's nothing to earn. I want to physically shrug it off, to cut it down before it can settle in the abyss. Because Darkness knows, looks like that never come without a cost.

Forcing myself still, I bite out, "What does it matter?"

Asa tilts his head, his fingers clasped loosely before him. "It matters because you have always been alone, and perhaps, that is the way you need to live to survive what comes next. But after, when your world has settled, there is a place for you."

"I'm sure the Xamani would welcome a half-breed, soulless monster as their Kashan with no objections," I scoff acerbically.

Asa only watches me steadily. "Half or whole, soulless or not, you are Xamani and that means you are always part of our tribe. In Darkness and in light. I tell you now, only so you will remember to think of the possibilities the future holds."

I feel stripped, as if the Kashan has peeled my skin down to my rawest thoughts. "The future doesn't belong to me."

Asa reaches to take my hand, but when I flinch violently, he drops his palms to smooth his trousers instead. "The future belongs to no one," he says firmly. "It is a story that unravels moment by moment. Do not discount yours."

At that moment, Aggie chokes on her tea. We both jump

in alarm, whipping around to face the old woman, but her white eyes already stare past us as her rattling cough echoes in the small room. I know what's to come with an acute sense of dread as her frail body stiffens. The same thing that brought me to Mirren; that lost my soul to my father. A harbinger of the best and worst parts of my life.

"Light and dark, dark and light. There is not one without the other," she rasps. Her usual teasing sonance is gone. Now, her voice is weighted and full, like more than just her speaks from her mouth.

Asa makes to go to her, face pale in alarm, but I hold him back as she continues. "But balance will be betrayed. A heart thought to be light is only filled with Darkness and it will bring death."

Aggie blinks wildly and settles back into herself. Asa says nothing, staring at the old woman in mixture of wonder and abject horror, as he finally sees her for what she truly is. Not mad, not a fraud. A conduit of whatever remains of the old gods, perhaps a piece of whatever is locked away in a cave somewhere in the depths of the Nemoran.

And they've just told her I will get my friends all killed.

CHAPTER
THIRTY-FOUR

Mirren

We leave Nadjaa under the full moon, a night meant for celebration, but I only feel an acute sense of foreboding. Why am I always leaving this place too soon? Will life only ever allow me enough of a taste of something to know exactly what I'm being denied? Because in spite of all the ways Denver has betrayed me for this place, something of my heart lives here. In the vibrancy of its people and the quiet shade of a cliff pond, Nadjaa brought me to life last spring, and it will always beckon to me as the place of my rebirth.

Thanks to Gislan's warning, we missed the arrival of my father's guard. The affable earth-wielder took the information about being bonded to the rest of us much better than I had, with only a quiet nod of acceptance.

I stare at him sidelong as we begin our journey north. "It...it doesn't bother you? Your fate being tied to us?"

Two assassins and an ocean-wielder who's almost gotten herself killed numerous times in the past few months are not exactly the safest group to have one's life tied to. If I were Gislan, I'd be pleading with the old gods to release me, earth power be damned. But he only tilts his mouth into a knowing frown. "Are our fates not all tied together under the Darkness, anyway? We are all dragged along by warlords or killed by someone needier than we and it is all only because of the circumstances of our birthplace. I am no more damned than any other Ferusian by being tied to you. We all do what we must to survive, do we not?"

The earth-wielder glances back at the trail in front of us and his jaw tightens as he slides a large boulder from our path. If I thought the Shadiil mountain pass was treacherous, it's nothing compared to the one we now traverse. The main routes all guarded by Nadjaan forces, we've been reduced to a small path that seems better suited for goats than a party of people and horses. It hugs the side of a steep cliff, barely wide enough for one horse, with no room for a misstep.

The boulder falls down the ravine, the shattering shale echoing in the silence. Gislan turns to me, his crinkled eyes suddenly grave. "To be honest, lady, the magic is meaningless to me. I do not care if it returns to the land or not. But it is a tool to save my family from the Darkness they've been forced to live in, and I will use it however necessary to ensure their safety." Something flickers in his gaze and the corners of his lips turn down. "I hope you understand... all I do is for them."

Miraculously, we make it over the pass without anyone tumbling over the side by the end of the night. We travel through the next day and by the time we reach the edge of the Breelyn plain, my feet ache and I feel as though I could sleep for days. After a mostly silent dinner from Asa's stores, Avedis offers to take first watch.

To my surprise, Anrai gives no argument. Having never traveled with two headstrong assassins, I assumed there'd be a power struggle over who makes decisions, but Anrai's shoulders sag as if he's too tired to even consider it. Worry gnaws at my stomach. How long has it been since he's actually slept?

He crawls into our bedroll without bothering to remove his boots. I peel off my own, before gingerly placing my bandolier—still Anrai's old one—within reach, before crawling under the blanket. He hasn't commented on my possession of it, choosing instead to continue using the black one he had in Siralene.

I wonder what it means, that he still uses his father's weapons. That he hasn't claimed anything of his old life.

He circles his arms around me, pulling my bottom snuggly into the cradle of his hips, his large hand splayed lazily over the curve of my stomach. Burying his nose in my hair, he curls his body around mine. He's been unusually reserved since joining us outside Aggie's cabin. Perhaps only a result of exhaustion, he hardly spoke on the journey here, leading us over the pass with barely more than a word.

"What did Asa say to you?" I whisper into the dark. There's no point in keeping the question to myself. No point in pretending worry for him isn't threading through me like a poisonous vine.

Anrai stiffens behind me, but his reply is unbothered. "He thinks I have a gift for storytelling."

"You do," I agree. Our first journey to Nadjaa, I wiled away the hours under the spell of his words. Anrai has never spoken like Asa, but his voice has always possessed its own magic.

After a long beat, he says, "he thinks I might be Xamani. Or that my mother was."

I jerk my head toward him in surprise. His features are cloaked in the darkness, the curve of his lip and slash of his jaw only visible in the soft light cast by the moon. "Truly? Anrai, that's—that's amazing."

"Is it?" He sounds surprised.

"Haven't you ever wondered about your mother?"

"No." There is no hesitation in his answer.

But it can't be true. I used to spend so many nights wondering where my parents were; if they were like me, if they loved me. Even now, I wonder about my mother. Was she truly who the Covinus says? Or was she the person Denver thinks she was, someone who understood what it was to love with all of themselves?

Anrai has been subject to such horrors throughout his life, how is it that he's never considered there was a person somewhere who would love him better? How has he never even dreamed of it?

"There was nothing to wonder about," he says, answering my unspoken question. "If she was Xamani, she came to the Praeceptor as a slave. Another nameless victim in an endless line of them."

"But—what if you have family among the Xamani? After all this is over, Anrai, you could...you could have a home."

He makes a noise in the back of his throat. He's never allowed himself to claim the word, never thought himself worthy of it, even before he lost his soul. "*You* are my only home," he whispers into my hair, his words barely more than a soft breeze.

And because his eyes are my hearth, his mind my doorway, his heart my foundation, I allow him to draw me close.

He makes love to me slowly, worshipping my body as if it isn't just his home, but his alter. Until I forget the nagging worry, the looming dread—until I forget everything but him.

～

In the morning, we ride northward, Avedis' gift allowing us to keep to the Old Road. Anyone we happen across suddenly hears the wind pulling them in a different direction, and unhindered, we make good time across the plain. There is no sign of the Dark Militia, their eerie presences felt only by their absence. Only a few weeks earlier, when I'd ridden across the plain with Anrai unconscious in front of me, the road had been crawling with them.

That the Praeceptor has called them all away to wherever he hides doesn't bode well for Similis.

Days pass atop Dahiitii. Nadjaa's sharp peaks level out into rolling plains of amber grasses. As we grow closer to the Nemoran wood, the ground begins to gradually climb once more until we're surrounded by undulating hills of verdant green.

There is no talk of how long the journey takes or what we'll find when we make it to the Boundary. Avedis still hasn't been able to detect the militia's whereabouts, and when I ask him to check on Similis, he informs me the Boundary has always kept the territory from his sights.

I glance at him in surprise. "But—didn't you keep tabs on me when I was in Similis?"

The assassin smiles sheepishly, chastened. "I only knew of your movements once you stepped outside."

Though disappointing, it makes sense Avedis' power doesn't work inside the Boundary, when mine also falters.

It brings me small hope that my brother is still somehow protected by the ancient wall, hole ridden as it is. As long as Avedis cannot see Similis, I take heart the Boundary still stands.

At the very least, Cullen's attention to breaking through should grant us enough space to search for the cave of the old gods. Gislan is confident that once we're close enough, he'll be able to delve beneath the surface with his power, but there could be a countless number of them to search in the hills surrounding the north side of Similis.

Anrai rides atop his own horse, a more expedient option than sharing Dahiitii, but one that surprised me, nonetheless. I assumed he'd want the reassurance of his soul as we journey toward his father, but he appears to have no interest in it at all. He hardly looks at me during the day, only touching me under the cover of darkness. And even then, I feel the war waged in the tremble of his hands: his need fighting against whatever keeps him from me in the sunlight.

Maybe it's that he needs to be soulless to face what's to come: to meet his father on even footing. Or maybe it's that Anrai refuses to become accustomed to the feel of something he fears he'll lose. I don't press, hoping he'll confide his fears, but his silence only grows heavier.

My anxiety grows, as day after day, he surveys the landscape with a set jaw and dead eyes. I thought he'd been adjusting to having a soul once again—laughing with me in the forest, smiling with Max and Cal at Aggie's cabin—but it seems the small joys he allowed himself were temporary. He responds only when spoken to directly, offering no further words. His power remains hidden in the depths of himself, tendrils of smoke wreathing his head, as though he, himself, is a dying fire.

I miss the days we spent nestled together atop Dahiitii, his words a balm against my ear as he regaled me with stories of the all the things I've never seen. Miss the days when he would laugh with me, fight with me—when he felt everything so brightly, his vibrancy was addicting.

We make camp for the night when we reach the edge of the Nemoran. I feel the forest's pull as if the trees twist invisible vines around me, snaking through me. The air is heavy here, but not with mist—with something untenable. Ancient.

It calls to me. *Ours. Ours. Ours.*

How have I never noticed the forest's presence before? Alive and *reaching*.

"Enjoy your last evening without wondering if you'll wake up to a yamardu drinking your blood," Calloway tells Harlan with a clap on the back, his eyes glinting with mischief.

Harlan swallows audibly and I notice he's pulled the rifle from his pack once more. He's been lucky enough to have never witnessed the twisted creatures that live beneath the canopy of this forest, and for all our sakes, I hope he never has to.

When the fire is low, and our bellies are full with rabbit stew and freshly picked berries, Anrai stands before us. Harlan gapes up at him, surprise flickering across his face. Max narrows her eyes warily, planting her feet more firmly into the ground as if readying herself for an ambush. I can't blame them—this is the first Anrai has spoken to any of them since we left Nadjaa, beyond the occasional barked order.

His face is impassive, his jaw set like marble, as he surveys our motley crew. His lips twist in disappointment, as if he's imagined us against his father and found us severely lacking. "We need to talk about what happens tomorrow."

Avedis takes a delicate sip of his stew. "I believe what happens is, we search for a cave of long dead gods, while trying to avoid being strung up and gutted by the madman you call a father." He dabs the corner of his lip primly, before raising his eyes to Anrai. "Unless I'm missing a step?"

Anrai's gaze flickers coldly over the assassin. "And if my father takes control of me? What then?"

Avedis shrugs, leaning back lazily against a fallen log. "You'll be with Mirren," he replies, as if that settles it. And it should. With me, Anrai has a soul, and he would never hurt any of us.

"You should chain me up."

My blood freezes, dread curling low in my stomach. "You don't need to be chained," I tell him slowly, gazing up as his barren eyes refuse to meet mine.

Cal nods in fervent agreement, the crusted bread he'd been chewing on abandoned halfway to his mouth. "As much as I've missed your inconvenient desire to be a martyr, Anni, this is overboard, even for you. You haven't tried to kill any of us since you've arrived—"

Avedis clears his throat loudly.

"Well, any of us but Avedis," Cal amends with a roll of his eyes, "who clearly deserved it."

The assassin shrugs in concession.

Anrai's eyes flash, his anger suddenly a living thing, wild and untenable. The air in the small clearing grows hot, but still, his power remains strangled inside him. "Just because I haven't doesn't mean I won't." He spits out a curse in the language he so often murmurs, which I now realize with a spark of surprise, is Xamani. Running his fingers roughly through his hair, he shakes his head angrily. I stand to go to him, to bring him some peace, but he throws a hand out in front of him. "Don't," he grits out harshly without looking at me.

My own anger churns in my stomach, hot and insistent. To keep Anrai, I will fight the Praeceptor and my father and even the Darkness itself—but how do I fight *him*? I cannot wipe away the traumas that warp his mind and blind him from what's true. Cannot fight against what he won't let me see.

"You've had multiple chances since I kidnapped you to hurt us, Anrai. And instead of making the selfish choices you say the soulless make, you've always put our wellbeing first. You saved me from your father. You saved Max from the fire, even when you had no power. You let Denver imprison you instead of burning everyone in Nadjaa." Everyone has gone silent, their wide eyes volleying between the two of us. "We trust you."

My body tremors, anger sparking like a livewire through me. "By the Covinus, when will you start trusting yourself?"

"That is exactly the kind of weakness that will get us all killed," he spits furiously, finally looking at me. His eyes rove hungrily from the top of my head over my lips and down my chest, as he takes note of every facet of my being. Every bruise from the world, the crack in my soul, every chink in my armor—he knows them all. "Will you forgive yourself if your soft heart gets your precious brother burned alive?"

Now, sparks explode from his hands and flames lick up his arms. He stalks toward me, lithe and enflamed. "Because I will burn him, Mirren. And you will only have your own foolish heart to blame."

Acid climbs my throat as I stare at the man I love. My *other* rises in agitation, and for a moment, I forget that I know Anrai—forget that he only lashes out to protect. Fury roars in my ears, and I feel breathless with heartbreak as realization slices through me, sharper than any blade.

It doesn't matter how hard I try. I could tear apart the world, give every drop of strength and blood I possess, and I will never be able to fix Anrai. My faith is not enough. My love is not enough.

He is the only one who can climb out of his darkness.

And he won't.

"Don't you *ever* use Easton against me," I hiss at him, turning away before my tears fall.

∽

Shaw

It will bring death.

The words have resounded to a harrowing beat the entire journey here. They are behind my eyes when I close them, in my ears with the rush of wind. And no matter how I've tried, they remain unmalleable.

I will betray them, no matter that I have no interest in doing so. We are bonded by the elements and their deaths will cause my own. Why would I choose that?

I wouldn't. Even soulless, it makes no tactical sense. Which can only mean I'll betray them because I won't be able to help it. Even touching Mirren, my father must still be able to control me. And he'll use me to rain down destruction on everyone, until there is no more magic, no more prophecy. Until he overtakes Similis and then Ferusa.

I will watch the world burn at my hands, controlled until the very end.

You are a weapon. Only made to destroy.

My father has always known what I could never accept about myself. I've accepted it now.

I thought about telling Mirren of Aggie's prophecy that first night on the Breelyn Plain, of warning her of my betrayal, but when she spoke so earnestly of her hope of a future, I knew I couldn't. If I did, she would keep me far away from my father. She loves me enough to let Similis fall, and her brother with it, in order to thwart my fate.

I know, because when her soul touches mine, I would do the same for her.

But when I am empty again, I remember I can't let her. My father cannot win, cannot be allowed to dictate the balance of the world and the lives of those in it. I cannot live in fear of him finding me once again, never knowing if my wants are my own, or some outline of his. I have to be here to find that cave.

So, I'd tried to goad her into restraining me instead, which had gone over about as well as a brick to the head. Her eyes filled with righteous anger and anguish so deep, for a moment, I thought she'd drown me where I stood.

"Staring down the barrel of your weaknesses?" a sly voice asks from behind me.

Irritation rises that I didn't hear the assassin coming. He's probably the only person in the world silent enough to sneak up on me, a fact I find infuriating.

He motions to the stream beside me. Small enough to be unnamed, its cool waters trickle cheerfully over the smooth pebbles of the creek bed. I've been staring at it for over an hour, feeling simultaneously repulsed and drawn to it. My downfall and my savior. Love and hate.

"Have they sent you to talk me off the ledge?"

"Would you rather I push you off it?" Avedis asks

conversationally, sitting against a boulder a few feet away. "If you haven't noticed, I'm rather self-serving. As your death causes mine, I'd prefer you alive."

"That's the nicest thing you've ever said to me."

Avedis bows his head with an indulgent smile. "With the way you've been provoking the lady, it appears as if you have a death wish for us all."

I glare at him, but don't argue. He's right. I know Mirren. And with that, comes the knowledge of the darkest parts of her, the keys to unleashing the wild creature crawling beneath her skin. I've never used them against her before, and if I had a soul, perhaps I would feel ashamed for doing so now.

But I only feel justified. If I could have just provoked her enough to restrain me, she might be able to save me from ruining my own vengeance.

I toss a rock into the water, and the small splash echoes in the empty space of my chest. A tranquil enough sound, but my body freezes with it anyway, rebelling against what always came next. I could run to the edges of Ferusa, and it will never be far enough. I will always be imprisoned in the dungeons of the Castellium, unless I put an end to my father.

Glancing at Avedis, my mouth curls distastefully. The assassin says he is free, and yet, he isn't, never fully. Not while the witch-queen breathes. "Why does Akari Ilinka still live? It would have been simple to suck the air from her lungs."

Avedis watches the stream thoughtfully. He's mostly unarmed, having left his swords behind with the others, but old habits have me noting the two daggers still hidden inside his boots. "She has already stolen pieces of my soul. I won't give her another," he answers simply.

And then he smiles, though the gesture contains no warmth. Only the same madness that coats my mouth every time I hear the Praeceptor's name. "And you offend my creative sensibilities. Death is not extravagant enough for the queen. When I have my revenge, it will be far more thorough and impossibly entertaining."

Something like a grin tugs at my lips, but I press it away as I examine the thick scar that runs the length of his face. Avedis is handsome by anyone's standards, a small gift in the Dark World, but an important one when you're a starving child. The witch-queen chose to mar his beauty for a reason, to take what little he'd been given in this world. "When I was in the Castellium, my father—" I suck in a leveling breath and try again. Try not to feel the bite of that metal table, the burning of the water. "The Praeceptor... well, you know what happens in the dungeons of warlords."

Avedis watches me calmly, but there is something feral in the glint of his dark eyes. In the set of his jaw.

"He used water." It's the first time I've admitted the intimate horror of it. Mirren has guessed, but I've never confirmed it. I've been hanging onto humanity by the small thread she's given me, and I feared the weight of acknowledging what's happened would be enough to shred it to pieces. "He would drown me, over and over again, for hours and then days. Until I was only a wraith, clinging to the edge of life. In those times, my power would recede because it had nothing to feed from. I was no longer human. I was— I was an empty shell."

Avedis raises his chin, and I know, in that moment, he understands why I've told him. Understands in a way none of the others can, a soul-deep pact melded only in the forges of blood and death. Because only another monster can know the importance of handing over the one weapon that will break you before you destroy everything around you.

And I will die before I ever allow my father to control me again.

Avedis opens his mouth to speak his own truth, but I shake my head. "Don't. Don't forget what I am."

Avedis tilts his head, his mouth turned down. "Perhaps it is you, friend, who must forget."

Chapter
Thirty-Five

Shaw

When we enter the shade of the trees, the Nemoran feels restless around us. Its dark womb has always been edged with danger, but the reality of my life as a child always made it all the more appealing, for there was nothing in the forest more horrible than my father.

But now, knowing the Praeceptor is housed somewhere in the expanse of wood, the forest is more foreboding than ever. It is not the Ditya, or the yamardu, or any number of other malformed creatures who reside here that causes dread to slither along my spine.

Gislan presses his power into the earth, and we watch as the enormous roots begin to wriggle and crawl, as if suddenly alive. They rise like snakes before settling once more and I am reminded of the cracks in the dungeons. After all this is over, perhaps Gislan will accompany me to Argentum and bring the whole city crashing down upon itself. As an Ashlaan, so close to the Castellium, he's surely felt my father's poisonous shadow as acutely as any.

The earth-wielder's power rumbles, the pressure

building in my chest as the minutes tick on. Finally, he tells us there are no caves on this side of the forest. So, we walk.

The foliage grows so thick only slivers of sunshine peek through the canopy, buttery slices of light that serve to make the darkness more disorienting. Mirren places her hand in mine, my calluses scraping against her soft palm. I remember the feel of her the first time we were here, tangled up outside the Boundary.

All velvet curves and delicate skin. My first thought then had been, *breakable.*

I know better now. The world cannot break Mirren. Only I can.

And I will. I can only hope once my father takes control of me, Avedis uses what I've given him, and they have enough time to bring back magic. The Praeceptor wanted to create a weakness by giving me a fear of water, to keep me from ever aligning with Mirren, but instead, he created a failsafe. A way to stop the soulless monster from burning the world.

A howl echoes in the distance and Mirren shudders beside me. An amused smile pulls at my mouth, but when she shoots me a hot glare, I quickly press my lips together. Apparently, she doesn't recall her first meeting with the Ditya as fondly as I do.

Avedis closes his eyes from time to time, allowing Harlan to lead him blindly through the trees as he listens to the wind. After one such instance, he growls in frustration. "There should be *nowhere* the wind cannot touch."

"Do you think they're underground?" Harlan asks, dropping Avedis' hand and hoisting the Similian rifle more tightly under his arm. "Maybe they've found the caves?"

Gislan's weather-worn skin crinkles in a doubtful frown. "I don't know of a cave that could fit an entire militia, but I suppose it's possible. Or perhaps the Praeceptor has cloaked them with some sort of magic."

I stare at the coin hanging from Mirren's neck. It's what allowed me to channel my power into others to find their ability for the same, but my father never said where he'd gotten it. Does Cullen somehow possess another trinket powerful enough to hide an entire army?

If so, the Similians will be completely ambushed, overwhelmed by an invisible enemy.

We make camp next to an old ruin, the most defensible place we're likely to find. Constructed of large stone and rusted steel, whatever it used to be has been lost to the influence of the wood. Vines and roots crawl over it and a large spruce sprouts through the foundation.

I haven't actually slept in days, in fear of waking up in my father's control once more, so I take first watch and Cal offers to sit with me. Rather than risking giving away our location with a fire, everyone piles their bedrolls close together and huddles beneath them. It's much cooler this far north, the air already tinged with a winter bite. A part of me aches to go to Mirren, to keep her warm in my arms, but instead, I burrow deeper into the emptiness of my chest.

Remind myself of what I am, even if there are no certainties in it.

I am a monster, but monsters don't love. I am a weapon, but weapons don't feel.

Cal leans against the tree beside me, laying his longsword carefully over his thighs and yanking his cloak up to his throat. I haven't spoken to him at all on the way here, and though he hasn't pressed, I feel the weight of the way he watches me. His worry claws at my ribs, his hurt brushes against my spine. But there is no point in pretending I am saved when I'll only betray him in the end.

He loves me too much to believe it, and even if I could somehow convince him, I can't ask him to cut me down before it happens.

I've already asked him to leave me once. It would break him to do it again.

"Have you fucked him?" I ask, nodding toward the mop of golden hair poking out from under a pile of blankets. "Is that why he looks at you like a puppy that's been kicked?"

Cal looks over at me mildly, not even having the decency to blush. "You're a real bastard without a soul, you know that?"

I shrug, staring out into the night. "I was a bastard with one, if you recall." Instead of replying, he offers me a piece of jerky. I shake my head; my stomach has been in upheaval since we left Aggie's. I've barely been able to keep down more than a few morsels at a time, constantly poised on the edge of nausea and dread. "Does being perceptive make one a bastard?"

Cal rolls his eyes to me, a laugh playing on his mouth. I watch it detachedly, memories of his laugh swimming before me. His laugh used to ease something in me, but now, it is only an empty reminder of my foolishness. Had I really thought I could be who I was?

With no soul, no heart, hands covered in ash and blood?

"No," Cal sighs, "but your lack of tact does. I hear all sorts of things coming from your bedroll, you know. But I have the good sense to keep it to myself."

If I had a soul, I might blush. But instead, I grunt irritably and push down the possessive wave of flame that rises in me. Cal is only making a point, but I don't even like the whisper of implication on his lips. What happens when I touch Mirren is *mine*. And it hasn't seemed to matter that I should keep my distance from her. My hunger for her skin, her touch, her taste—the Darkness may be my compulsion, but so is Mirren.

Only her anger has kept me away the past few nights—and the fear that even that isn't enough to make her distrust me.

"And to answer your question, I won't touch Harlan. That's probably why he looks so hurt."

I look to Cal in surprise. "I've never known you to turn down a handsome man in your bed."

"He's Similian," he answers shortly, as if this explains everything. And in a way, it does. "And in love with someone else."

My eyebrows lift as I catch the slight edge of bitterness in his voice. Have I been so caught up in my own turmoil, I somehow managed to miss something so obvious? One glance at Harlan had told me he liked Cal a lot—is he truly in love with someone else?

Someone like his green-eyed life partner?

Flame flares inside my chest, but I tamp it down as Cal shakes his head. "Don't, Anni. It's been a long night. Forget I said anything."

He suddenly looks so miserable, I know I should say something, but I have no idea what. I used to know the man beside me better than myself—I would know whether a crude joke would be cutting or would lighten the mood, would know exactly how much warmth was needed to assuage his hurt.

But I am not Anrai, not Anni—not a man who has a right to any of it. So I stare into the shadows of the trees, and don't say anything at all.

∼

We walk all through the next day and the day after that.

Restless agitation settles on my shoulders. It squirms in my stomach, crawls in the recesses of my mind. With each step, I grow closer to my father. Closer to the moment of my betrayal—to my last breath of freedom. Will my being in the cave with the other three be enough to free the gods, before Avedis is forced to take me down?

The creatures of the forest keep their distance, and it's this, more than anything that unsettles me the most. Something slithers between the trees that keeps even the most fearsome beasts at bay.

At the end of the third day, Gislan halts abruptly. He's taken off his shoes, preferring to keep nothing between him and the earth, and now, he wiggles his bare toes into the loam. My stomach surges as the ground rumbles beneath us. I don't think I'll ever get used to the old Ashlaan's power. The ground is not something that should *move*.

"There's a cave system beneath us," he says breathlessly, eyes suddenly shining in triumph. "It feels almost...*alive*. Sprawling. As if it grows."

A year ago, I would have scoffed at the imprecise nonsense of his sentiment, but now, I only nod in understanding. We all have our own ways of putting our power into words—to try and shape something unknowable into something familiar.

He points to a thick grove of trees, their gnarled trunks the size of the skiffs on the Bay of Reflection. "The entrance is there."

Dread wiggles in my belly. I avoid Max's gaze as she drops her pack and adjusts her weapons. Cal does the same, gripping his bow in one hand, an arrow in the other.

Max and I choose to be here, Anni.

Would he choose to be with me now, if I told him the

truth? If he knew the extent of my depravation, the shadows of my selfishness? If I tell him now, will he honor his vow to me and drag Mirren far away from here?

Her grip tightens on my hand, and she takes a leveling breath. "Well then, that's where we go."

Everything inside me screams as we move toward the grove. Gislan pushes aside vines thicker than my arm, revealing a gaping hole leading underground. It isn't ragged like the breach in the Boundary, but uniform and smooth as if constructed by man and not nature.

Mirren steps forward, and gods, I've always loved her bravery—from the very first night, when I was a stranger and she picked up that gun to help fight—but suddenly, it terrifies me. I want to yank her away from the entrance and steal her far away from this twisted wood. Far away from the Praeceptor who would hurt her and the vengeful gods who would use her.

Away from me, who, in spite of my love for her—greater than any truth I've ever known, even in the depths of my soulless existence—will betray her in that cave.

You are a weapon. Fire or storm, blood or darkness, you do what needs to be done.

My father cannot be defeated unless we wake the old gods' power. And though his reach is endless, I can take heart that he isn't here now. If he were, it would already be over, my power in his thrall once more.

I still have time to do what needs to be done.

Soul or not, a ruthless heart has always beat inside me. Honed by cruelty and loss and horror, it determinedly beats on, driving me past every shadow of a moral line. Taking a deep breath, I allow it to do so now as Mirren and I step underground.

CHAPTER
THIRTY-SIX

Mirren

Anrai's hand is tight around mine as we descend between the roots of the trees. The walls of the tunnel are wide enough for four of us to fit comfortably side by side, the ceiling tall and spacious. Made of thick cement with neat corners and straight edges, it is nothing like the roughly carved tunnels of Yen Girene, though the earthen smell and the way the damp air clings to my skin sends a shiver down my spine, nonetheless. The tunnel reminds me more of the hallways of the Covinus building than anything I've encountered in Ferusa. Flames flicker to life in Anrai's palm, before hopping to each of our lanterns and sparking to life. They shine softly, but their glimmer does little to pierce the sterile darkness, the dancing shadows appearing distorted along the walls.

Avedis shudders, his face having gone so pale, the scar dissecting his left eye looks starkly red in contrast. "There's no wind here," he explains, sounding ill. "The breezes here are stale. Older than the trees themselves. And they—they've gone wrong, being trapped for so long."

Anrai appears to agree, his body unnaturally stiff next to me, his eyes restless as we venture down the tunnel. Maybe because fire can't survive without oxygen to feed on, or maybe it's remnants of our fight. Neither of us has broached the topic again, let alone apologized, and he's remained as stonily distant as ever in our few days beneath the Nemoran canopy. Now, in the desolation of the tunnel, his agitation is palpable, written in the indents his fingers leave on my hand.

The tunnel is eerily silent, like it exists under a thick blanket, and after a while, I find myself missing the sounds of the Nemoran. Even the screech of the yarmardu is a reminder something else exists aside from ourselves, but here, there is only isolation and the muted echo of our footsteps.

Of the group, only Gislan appears entirely at ease, moving through the tunnel as if he were born under the earth. On the surface, he's always walked with an awkward gait, never entirely comfortable with his own body, but here, his strides are surefooted and confident as he leads us into the darkness. Even his face appears younger somehow, as if vitality pours from the damp earth into his skin.

His comfort eases the tightness in my chest somewhat; at least we won't be crushed to death by a cave in with Gislan here.

Harlan and Cal follow Gislan, both of their gazes steadfastly avoiding the other. Harlan's sleek rifle normally looks out of place against the rustic Ferusian climate, but its unadulterated curves now appear at home in austere light. Calloway eyes the gun with distaste, as if barely able to stand the sight of it in Harlan's soft hands. And indeed, a part of me hated Harlan coming along, just as I'd hated him crossing the Boundary into the harsh wild.

He glances back at me with a steadying smile. And in spite of my reservations, I return it sincerely. Because Harlan hadn't been dragged into this tunnel or across the Boundary. He made a choice that love, even one that had broken him, is worth fighting for.

We walk for hours, Anrai at my side. My feet grow sore atop the hard stone floor, but no doubt remains about whether we're heading in the right direction. A heaviness lingers here, and the further we walk, the more it seems to expand. Ancient and raw like my *other,* but altogether different. It weighs on my lungs and buzzes against my ears, its familiar cloying scent clinging to my nostrils.

What else could it be, but the old gods' powers? Excitement threads through me. After all this time, could a piece of their power, their sacrifice, still be buried beneath the roots of trees I've lived beside for so long?

Sweat beads on Avedis' brow, his freshly shaved head shining in the lantern light. He readjusts his grip on his sword, the movement uncharacteristically insecure, but when he meets my gaze, he only nods. He feels it, too. And doesn't like it at all.

Anrai's sharp exhale tells me he senses the same thing. His palm has grown damp in mine. "We're going west," he mutters, but when I look to him in question, he doesn't elaborate. Only folds further into himself, somewhere far away I can never follow.

The darkness is so isolating, we could be moving upside down and I wouldn't be able to tell. Our torchlight and Anrai's flame fight against it, but our vision is still limited to the few feet in front of us. By the time the passageway begins to climb upward, I feel as though I'm swimming through viscous fluid. It pulls at my feet and tugs at my hair, determined to possess and repel me at once.

After what feels like hours, the shaft widens to a small antechamber. The room is barely larger than the tunnel before it, constructed of the same sharp concrete, but these walls have been covered in murals. Perhaps vibrant at one time, but now, the depictions have all faded, the paint peeling off entirely in some places. Gislan stops in the middle of the chamber, hands on his knees, his breathing as labored as mine.

Max, who doesn't appear at all winded, runs her fingers over one such painting, ink so faded the subject is hardly decipherable. "It says something," she muses. Her voice is steady, as if she's passed through the air without a fight. "But that's no language I've ever seen."

She's right. The few marks that remain legible are completely foreign. With a sigh, my eyes climb upward. When they reach the ceiling, my heart surges. "Anrai, your stories!"

He swallows roughly, like he's attempting to keep down his dinner, and his voice sounds strangled when he says, "I don't think now's the time, Lemming."

I shake my head exasperatedly. "When we first met, you told me stories on the journey. Of the ancient world, before the curse. Where did you learn them?"

A line appears between his brows. "I don't know," he replies uncertainly. "I've always had a mind for stories. If I hear it once, I'm able to retell it like I heard it yesterday. For all I know, I heard it when I was nine and locked in a Baakan prison."

I point to the chamber ceiling, his eyes following my hand to where a sun is painted into the corner. Faded, but still beautifully intricate in the spiraling details. And beside it, something that looks like a bird gilded in metal. "You told me about flying machines! In the time of the old gods."

He studies the ceiling, but he doesn't share my excitement at the discovery. He only tightens his jaw.

"They're on the other side of this door," I insist. "Can't you feel them?"

Avedis swipes at his forehead, appearing by all accounts, extremely nauseous. "If this is what the old gods feel like, perhaps we should leave them dead."

Cal looks to us curiously. "I don't feel any different than usual."

Harlan, who's been examining the murals with an excited gleam in his eye, nods in agreement. "Other than slightly claustrophobic, I don't feel anything either."

The assassin doesn't look convinced. "You know I'll follow you to the end of time, lady. But something here feels...*rotted*."

Anrai looks inclined to agree. He's said nothing more of being chained, but I know the idea hasn't left him so easily. Though his hesitance in venturing underground, and perhaps through the door ahead, have nothing to do with the old gods. It's himself he doesn't trust.

"I agree, something feels corrupt here," Gislan says, eyeing the metal door. "Though what choice do we have but to press on? Whatever they are, however they feel... we cannot defeat the Praeceptor without first bringing back magic."

Avedis twists his lips doubtfully but offers no argument. And Gislan is right. If we don't go through the door, Similis will fall. Bringing magic back to life may not break the curse, but it will right some of the balance that's been lost and give the oppressed at least a fighting chance.

But dread tugs at me all the same. There is something familiar about what lives in this room that I can't put my finger on. A memory just out of reach.

Max turns away from the murals and looks to Shaw. "Do you feel the same as the others? If you feel something is wrong, we should turn around and leave now." It's the first she's spoken to him since we left Nadjaa, but at the soft glint in her eye, I realize it is more offering than words—she asks him to come back to himself: to trust his instincts once more, just as she has always trusted them.

Something ticks in Anrai's jaw. "The last time you followed me into a tunnel, it didn't end well for any of us," he snaps.

Max glares at him, but she doesn't back down, doesn't look away. Instead, she smacks his arm with the flat of her sword. Anrai's eyes flare, and for a moment, I fear he might attack her as he did in Siralene. But instead, he yells, "What was that for?!"

Her lips peel back from her teeth, and she practically growls her reply. "Apparently losing your soul has jarred your brain. I thought I'd do you a favor and hit the memories back into their proper places."

Anrai glowers at her. "My memories are perfectly *fine*."

Max smacks him again and he reaches for a dagger with a warning snarl. Only my hand in his keeps him from using it. But Max isn't finished. "The last time I followed you into a tunnel, you saved all of us. And while I'll be the first to admit that it was stupid as hell to sacrifice yourself, nothing about what happened was because of your instincts. Your instincts got us out of there and are the reason Denver is alive. So, if you'd be so kind as to pull your head out of your ass and help us bring back magic, it would be appreciated."

I almost laugh as Anrai stares at Max in a mixture of shock and fury, but instead, I steel my spine. The gift of another's soul is as much a burden as it is a boon. Anrai's soul has given me peace in the turbulence of my mind and the strength to keep going. And now, it is my turn, to hold it up when he cannot. To imbue it with fortitude he can't see.

"Avedis, do you sense anyone else here?"

The assassin shudders, closing his eyes. After a moment, he shakes his head. "It is just us, my lady. As far as I can tell, it is not an ambush that awaits on the other side of the door. At least, one human in nature."

"Then we do what needs to be done," I say determinedly, reaching for my *other*. "We've come this far together."

Avedis nods, raising his sword. Anrai already holds a dagger ready. Max, Cal, and Harlan set down their lanterns, arming both hands. Only Gislan holds no weapon, but when you hold the power of earth in your palms, there's no need.

The ground rumbles, undulating beneath us, above us. Chunks of cement shake free and small waterfalls of debris shower down from the ceiling. Anrai's grip on me tightens, and he flashes me a consternated look.

The deep groan of the earth's shudder vibrates in my chest. As solid as the concrete appeared around the metal door, it now moves as if made of liquid, before finally giving way and shattering completely. Max grips Harlan's arm, for his protection or her own, I have no idea. Only Gislan remains still, his arms raised, his weathered faced entirely peaceful as the world crashes around him.

When the rock around it has all crumbled away, the metal door crashes in on itself in a spectacular cloud of dust. For a moment, none of us move, staring in front of us. There is only darkness beyond the gaping hole. But I have ventured into the darkness before.

Gislan raises a lantern and gives me a reassuring nod.

"I'll make sure the ceiling is secure. Let's go change the world, shall we, lady?"

For those who've been abused by the more powerful—the downtrodden, the forgotten, the weak—Gislan steps into the dark.

Cal follows with his bow raised, his copper hair disappearing into the shadows. Harlan and Max step in behind him, weapons raised.

Turning to Anrai, I ask with a cheeky grin, "Light up the dark?"

He doesn't return it, his face the stone mask of the assassin. He only sheathes his dagger and ignites a small flame in the palm of his hand once again. Its light flickers, warming the sterile feel of the concrete room and bathing his eyes in a subtle orange glow. I let out a satisfied sigh, his flame reviving in the cold of the tunnel. Hundreds of feet underground, about to disturb an ancient power, but somehow, when I meet his pale gaze, I only feel strengthened. Whatever we face, whatever the world throws at us, we do it together.

I tug on Anrai's hand. He gives me a resigned look and grits his teeth, no doubt against the thousand objections in his head.

Trust yourself, Anrai. Trust yourself as I trust you.

"I shall see you on the other side, lady." Avedis steps through the doorway.

A terrible noise sounds from his throat—strangled, like all the air has been stolen from his lungs. His body seizes and as he tries to turn back around, his eyes bulge and he collapses to the ground.

"Avedis!" I cry out.

"Mirren don't—" Anrai roars as I let go of his hand and lunge toward the fallen assassin.

It takes less than a moment for me to understand, because as soon as I cross the threshold, I recognize the feeling of the antechamber. Why it was so familiar, so repugnant, so all consuming.

It feels like the Boundary.

Like Similis, suffocating and dead.

I fall to my knees with a crack as my power drains from me. The cave tilts around me, the walls swimming in my vision. Without hesitating, Anrai rushes through the opening to my side and I have no voice to protest. He claws at his chest as his own power is stolen away. Darkness edges my vision and I struggle to remain conscious as agony rips through me, searing my nerves, my heart, my head, until there is only pain.

Somehow, Anrai's hand finds mine and it is only the feel of his skin that grounds me to the present. He gathers me to him as the familiar agony scrapes my throat, feeling like thousands of shards of sand with every swallow. He holds me as my bones cry out, stabbing into my skin. "We fight," he whispers into my hair. His voice sounds tight and weak, like its trapped beneath a frozen pond. "With or without power, you and me, we never give up. We can make it out of this cave and save Similis, even if we have to crawl on bloody knees. Do you understand?"

I swallow down my nausea, blinking furiously as the dark room comes back into view. Harlan and Cal haul Avedis up by the arms, dragging his significant weight slowly back toward the antechamber. I need to get myself back over the Boundary, but everything *hurts*. It hurts like it did when I was alone and Anrai was gone, and suddenly, I can't remember it ever not hurting. The pain won't ever stop, I'll always be alone—

"Fight, Lemming!" Anrai barks from beside me, and my

body obeys. In spite of the agony, I move, pulling myself inch by agonizing inch toward the door. He yanks at my shirt, dragging me along as we slink slowly back toward the dim light of our lanterns. In Yen Girene, when he had his power stolen before he'd ever claimed it, Anrai fought. Even then, he moved through the pain, ever vigilant. And it's this, more than anything, that spurs me on.

We fight. We always fight.

I claw my way toward the door, my fingers stretching toward the light.

Almost. A few more inches.

I inhale sharply, my throat on fire as I gather the last of my energy for the final push.

Then, the opening to the antechamber caves in and all the light is snuffed out.

Max's furious yell echoes as more debris tumbles down around us. I hear the scuffle of feet as Harlan and Cal struggle with Avedis' unconscious form.

"Gislan!" Cal yells from somewhere near my head, his voice panicked and winded. "Use your power! Help us!"

But the earth-wielder will have no power here. It will have been sucked from his bones, just as ours has.

When Gislan responds, it takes a moment to place what unsettles me about his voice. "I could, Calloway," he says. He does not sound pained, or even panicked—he sounds... victorious. "But I'm afraid the Praeceptor won't allow it."

CHAPTER
THIRTY-SEVEN

Shaw

The Boundary. We're *inside* the Boundary.

And now there is only cold. Cold like the bowels of the Castellium, empty and biting.

We're under Similis. And Gislan, that two-faced piece of shit, led us straight here.

Straight to my father, to the depths of my nightmare.

But—there isn't only emptiness and pain. There is the feel of Mirren's hand in mine, soft against my calloused palm. There is the sound of Max's outrage, of Harlan and Cal helping Avedis. I may not have my power and my father may very well be on his way right now, but this is not the Castellium.

Determination and anger bloom in place of my fire, filling my chest and urging me to my feet.

I am not the traitor.

Mirren was right all this time, able to see my soul more clearly than I ever could. How much have I lost because I assumed the worst in myself? How much have I given up in service of self-destruction?

If I hadn't believed in my Darkness so fervently, I would have trusted my instincts. Instincts that have always kept me alive, for better or worse. I would have pulled Mirren from that tunnel the moment something felt wrong. And when we continued further and further west, I would have acknowledged the sinking feeling in my gut about where we were going, instead of allowing my friends to walk blindly to their deaths.

My father has never even needed a piece of my soul to control me. He planted the seed of self-hatred years ago—nurtured it until its vines entangled in every part of who I am.

No longer.

The earth trembles once more, no doubt, Gislan's way of alerting the Praeceptor of our presence. How long has he been in my father's thrall?

Ivo. That night he disappeared in Siralene, when I was too caught up in madness to question his absence. He never wanted to capture the earth-wielder. He wanted to find him and force him into the Praeceptor's service. I *know* my father; know he always has a contingency plan. And yet, I was so convinced *I* was his plan, I hadn't even questioned he might have someone else in his command.

The old Ashlaan moves thousand-pound boulders as easily as Avedis commands the air, a sight both impressive and terrifying. Rocks tumble, creating a small opening and light spills from the antechamber where Gislan still stands. I half expect the earth-wielder to have grown fangs or claws—something outward to demonstrate his inner treachery—but he looks the same as ever. Middle aged, unassuming. Sad.

He glares at us through the small space between the

boulders. "If any of you try anything, I will bring the entire city of Similis down on top of your heads."

"Gislan, what have you done?" Cal asks, shouldering Avedis' weight. The assassin wheezes, strung up between Max and Cal. His head lolls as he struggles to come to. Of all the horrors in his life, he's never experienced the raw agony of having his power stripped from him.

Shame washes over Gislan and I wish I didn't see it. I want to hate him for what he's done to us.

Another victim of the Praeceptor, another turned by the Darkness' compulsion.

"It was never the witch-queen threatening your family," Mirren says in slow realization. Betrayed and about to be handed over to certain death, and still, empathy pours from her. She's never had the sense to protect herself from the monsters of the world, but I no longer find it weak or terrifying—if there were more of what makes up Mirren's heart, perhaps there would be no more warlords to fear. No Darkness to fight.

Gislan straightens, his face resigned. "This is the Dark World. I do what I must to protect my family. Everything I do is for them."

My own words echo back to me. *This is Ferusa, Lemming, and I will do whatever I have to do to keep the ones I love safe.* I've always made the hard choices, done whatever I needed to for survival. But have I ever actually had a choice? Has Gislan?

For the first time, I understand Asa's story and the nature of the First Queen's curse. It was never about magic. It was a punishment—for those who allow the Darkness in, to never be able to rid themselves of it. For once it's taken root, there is no digging it out. It grows like a tangled vine until it is all that you are. There are no second chances under the curse, no room for growth.

And we've all been doomed from the start, whether born to warlords or loving parents, because whose soul remains entirely pure? We are only human, mistakes a part of our nature.

"This is insane. You're going to get yourself killed," Max snarls. If she has any empathy for the man, she's buried it deep beneath her anger. "You're all bound together. What do you think is going to happen to you once *he* gets ahold of them?"

Gislan's face tightens. "Those are only stories," he replies. "Stories do not fill my daughter's belly. They do not keep my son from the workhouse." For the first time, fear flickers in his eyes, remembering whatever my father has threatened. "Stories do not keep horrors from my doorstep."

His gaze turns cold. "And the Praeceptor has no plans to kill them."

Icy dread settles in my stomach as Mirren tucks herself into my side. Of course, he won't kill us. He'll whip Ferusa into a frenzy of hate against the nature spirits, all the while using them to reinforce his own power. He's committed genocide against an entire population to make sure the only power left belongs to him.

The thought of Mirren in the Castellium brings a fresh wave of nausea up my throat. When my father controls me once more, will he use me against Mirren? Will he force her to drown me, over and over again, until she goes mad with misery?

An echo of the abyss roars inside me. Even before my power matured, the abyss has always been there—fueled by my rage and shame. I feed it now, letting it climb from my chest to my fingertips. It isn't fire, but it moves like flame. Flames made of pure shadow.

When Gislan speaks again, I watch him through new eyes. The calculating gaze of Shaw the assassin, the ruthless power of the Fire-Bringer—and the heart of Anrai, the man who loves. I have been trying to live as one or the other, certain if I allowed them to coexist, I'd combust and destroy everything around me.

But I cannot live in pieces any longer.

I have always been all three. Long before I lost my soul, long before I set anything aflame; in the depths of the abyss, they've all been there.

"The Praeceptor will be here soon. And then, I will be able to return to Ashlaa in peace. My family will finally be safe from the Argentians."

Calloway shakes his head sadly. "You are one of the four wielders, Gislan. You must know he will never allow you to be free again."

Gislan's eyes shine and his chin wobbles, but he doesn't relent.

I dip into the abyss, allowing the shadow fire to swirl inside me. I no longer feel the icy cold of my lack of power. Since I was child, I've always burned; terrified of hurting those around me, I turned it inward, letting it consume me instead.

But Mirren is right. Fire isn't only destruction.

It brings light and warmth. It has melted the chains of slaves and saved the lives of my friends.

It burned through the Boundary and freed the woman I love.

The Boundary.
It burned through the Boundary.

When I had nothing but desperation—I was able to get through the Boundary. How?

"Are you just going to stand by the door until your master gets here? The ride from Argentum could take weeks," Max snipes doubtfully.

Gislan tilts his head, his eyes oddly bright. "The warlord isn't in Argentum." His laugh cuts through the muffled silence of the room.

I force myself to think beyond where my father is, or that I may only have moments left with control of my soul. Instead, I close my eyes and *feed* the abyss inside me. It accepts the depth of my self-hatred; the raw bite of my anger; the warm curl of my love. It devours them greedily, having been so starved since I gave up my soul. I feed it until it swirls in my chest like its own brand of wildfire, untenable and frenzied.

Harlan's voice sounds far away when he breathes one word with dread, "Similis."

Mirren eyes go wide in horror, but instead of reaching out to comfort her, I feed my worry to the abyss as well.

Avedis wheezes, the scar slashed across his face appearing almost crimson in the lantern light. "Why...I couldn't...find the militia..." he gasps, his eyes meeting mine.

It isn't just the Praeceptor who hides inside Similis. The entire Dark Militia has taken over.

The very Boundary built to protect the Similians is now a cage to hold them all prisoner.

Mirren's eyes shine with unshed tears. Her face is lined with guilt, her worry palpable, and I want to smooth it away. To take her in my arms and tell her none of this is her fault, but I force myself still. To concentrate on feeding the abyss. "We need to get him into this cave," I whisper from the side of my mouth, barely more than a breath. "Even if it's only a finger."

The opening Gislan created is only large enough to see the man's face, but it's enough to steal his power as he's stolen ours. Mirren's eyes widen, before she moves fractionally to relay the message to Harlan.

Calloway meets my eyes, a thousand unspoken thoughts passing between us. But the one I hold onto, that steadies the nerves causing my hands to shake, is that he trusts me. Through everything, he is still my brother and will follow wherever I ask him to go.

Harlan nods toward Calloway. "Here, let me," he says softly. Something flickers in Cal's jaw, but he allows Harlan to take Avedis from him without comment. I watch Gislan, hoping the earth-wielder doesn't see the offer for what it is —moving into place—but he isn't looking at us at all.

His gaze is on the tunnel we came from, and I steel my jaw as my father's voice echoes behind him.

Once, I would have allowed that voice to unravel me— to fill me with self-hatred and shame and fear. But now, I raise my chin. And in spite of the tremble of her body and the agony ripping through her, Mirren rises next to me. Pride flares in my chest. Made of different things, the same ruthless heart beats in both of us.

"Well done, Gislan." My father's voice slides like ice down my spine. It contains all my pain, all my fear, all my loneliness. Cold dungeons and scorching brands. Steel daggers and leather whips. And drowning. Always drowning.

But I do not relent.

I never understood why the fire chose me, never thought about it beyond the destruction it caused. But it never fed on pain—it was drawn to the shadows of my abyss, the part of me that has always burned. Made of agony and love in equal parts, every horrible and beautiful thing in between. I pour all of it into the abyss: the despair, the violence, it is mine to claim.

Because in spite of it, I rise.

From the depths of Darkness, from the depths of flames, I choose to rise to the sun.

I take a deep breath, ignoring the icy agony that cuts through my lungs, and throw the entirety of my abyss at the Boundary.

For a moment, the world appears to teeter on its axis. Time slows as I drain every bit of me and push it into the unnatural perversion of the Boundary. It rises up, greedily accepting everything I pour into it. Whatever it is made of —death or something entirely worse—it *consumes*.

The first time I broke through, I was filled only with desperation. But now—now I am filled with everything.

And somehow, the Boundary knows. It knows I seek to destroy it with everything I push into it, and it begins to fight back. To squirm and writhe: to try and give back everything it has taken from me. But I hold on. Nausea climbs my throat as the clammy desiccation begins to overcome me, but I push further. More shadows, more of my own brand of flame. Breath empties from my chest, and I am drowning once again. No air, no light. Only ever Darkness.

Hold on. A few moments longer, just hold on.

Pressure explodes behind my eyes and blood begins to trickle from my nose, the coppery tang staining my lips and coating my mouth.

And then, something shifts. A pinprick of light in the swirling black.

The ground shakes like the entire continent is rearranging, like the clash of mountains older than the sun, seas more ancient than the moon. Gislan's eyes go wide in horror as he realizes the earth now moves according to someone else's direction. Boulders crash to the floor, falling away from the antechamber until there is no more cave in.

My father's eyes narrow on me and I feel the familiar pull of his control in my chest. But he's too late. I've broken through once more. With one last gasp, I push more shadowfire into the small puncture. Bile fills my mouth and I collapse, my head colliding with the smooth concrete floor. Black edges my vision and I wonder vaguely if this is how it feels—the Darkness' final calling.

It doesn't seem so bad.

Distracted by his panic, Gislan doesn't see Cal coming. He lunges at the earth-wielder, wrestling him from the antechamber. The Ashlaan claws at Calloway, desperation widening his yellowed eyes. Harlan jumps into the scuffle, and the three tumble backward in a tangle of limbs.

And then, just as my eyes close, the world around us goes to hell.

CHAPTER
THIRTY-EIGHT

Shaw

When I come to, the world jolts like it's come untethered from the universe. Giant slabs of concrete tumble from the ceiling and shatter around us with violent crashes. Shale and granite fall, the sound so loud, it reverberates in my chest. Punishing screams of an angry earth, its vengeance echoing across the continent for what I've done to it.

What have I done?

Mirren falls to the ground beside me, and with more instinct than thought, I throw my body over hers, shielding her head between the cradle of my arms. Panic flares for the rest of our friends as the cave and antechamber collapse around us. Jagged pieces of rock tear through my shirt, ripping through the skin of my back. But I hardly feel it as I cradle Mirren. I only feel her. "I love you," I breathe against her throat. Her pulse pounds against my lips, stubborn, even in the face of death.

Have I doomed us all?

The earth tremors so violently, I swear I hear it shriek. If these are my last moments, I'm glad to spend them with Mirren in my arms, sound in the knowledge that if we die, at least we have taken the Praeceptor with us and spared the rest of Ferusa of his scourge.

Gods, is this all I get? It should be enough, but it isn't. And maybe I'm not as soulless as I thought, because as the world crashes around me, all I can think is how much more I *want*. More of being inside her; more whispers of how I love her; more of everything.

I no longer feel the pull of the Boundary, only an echo of the abyss. It is empty now, not even an ember left to flicker in the Darkness. Not even the whisper of a shadow. I clutch Mirren to me, tensing as I wait to be crushed beneath thousands of pounds of rock.

But it never comes.

Suddenly, something far more potent than shadowfire floods me.

I gasp as power fills my bones. Fire races from the middle of my chest to the tips of my limbs, melting the ice and imbuing them with strength. As I come back to life, the angry sounds of crashing stone still echo around us, but nothing hits us, as if we're shielded.

Peeking my eyes open, I stare up at a thousand-pound boulder poised directly above our heads, held in place by an invisible string.

Avedis.

Thank the gods for that arrogant assassin.

I scramble up, tugging Mirren with me. She appears dazed, her breaths coming in full gasps as if she's just emerged from the depths of the ocean. The boulder falls, the crash like an explosion. My ears ring and dust fills my lungs as we stare at the destruction of the place we lay only seconds before.

Debris is scattered everywhere, and huge towers of newly moved earth shoot from ground to ceiling, blocking us from where, moments ago, the rest of our friends stood. With one final roar of rage, the world around us stills. And then, there is only silence.

Only our labored breathing sounds in the eerie stillness of the cave. Fire flickers to life in my palm, but it does little to pierce the absolute quiet. If we've awoken the old gods, they've escaped somewhere far from here.

Leaving us buried beneath granite and concrete. And unfortunately, both are mostly fireproof.

I managed to break through the Boundary and restore our power, but at what cost? Have I doomed us all to dying in this cave, after everything we've been through?

"Cal! Max!" I shout desperately into the silence. My own voice rings back to me, trapped beneath the roots of the Nemoran just like us. I will my panic down. If Avedis saved Mirren and I, he must be somewhere close; Max and Harlan were with him. He'll have been able to save them, too.

But Cal. *Oh gods.* He'd been with Gislan, so close to where the Boundary collapsed.

"CAL!" I roar, digging into the wall of crushed rock, suddenly determined to dig him out with my bare hands. "Calloway, where are you!?"

"Would it be wrong to let you wonder a little longer? Really, Anni, your concern is touching," Cal rasps, limping out from the darkness. A new gash on his brow bleeds openly and he keeps his left arm tucked gingerly to his abdomen as Mirren hurtles toward him, enveloping him in a hug. He meets my gaze with a cock of his head. "How is it you're worried about me when you don't have a soul?"

I have no idea and I don't take the time to ponder it.

Something akin to a whimper leaves my throat, a sound I've never made in my life, as I fling myself at my best friend. Relief is a cool breeze that soothes the panicked fire burning at the back of my throat. Calloway hugs me back with his good arm. "I was separated from everyone else during the collapse, but I think they're okay." Pulling back, he looks at us gravely. "Gislan is dead. The Boundary stood long enough that he didn't have his power to save him from the cave in."

Mirren gasps and silver lines her eyes, but I feel none of her regret. "Good," I snarl, the hollow in my chest expanding. The earth-wielder almost cost me everything—I hope he rots under the roots of the Nemoran for eternity.

As if sensing my sudden savagery, Cal looks around with a shudder. "I hope you have an idea to get us the hell out of here. Darkness knows, I've never liked enclosed spaces."

"Enclosed spaces and heights," Mirren says with a weak chuckle, earning an injured look from Cal. "I'll add it to the list."

More stones clatter from a far corner of the cave. I coax the flames in my palm up my arm, shining light into the darkness. Huge slabs of concrete have fallen from the ceiling and electric lights lie shattered all around. Even wrecked, the vestiges that remain look entirely foreign. Mirren picks up one such lamp and examines it with a twist of her lips.

"Why were the old gods somewhere like this?" she says slowly, turning the dead light in her palm. "This room looks like something in Similis. But...they were older than Similis, weren't they?"

Before I can answer, someone appears in the far corner of the cave. I yank a dagger from my bandolier and push

Mirren behind me. She pushes me back with an indignant huff, and in spite of my wariness, I'm struck with the urge to laugh. Stubborn woman.

A boy stumbles from the darkness, eyes round with shock. Dark smears of blood cover his Similian jumpsuit, the sticky substance matted in his light hair. Mirren goes taut next to me, a silent cry poised on her parted lips. Before I can stop her, she leaps at the boy, throwing her arms around his neck. Relief and terror in equal measure flicker across his face and he raises his arms as though he means to hug her back, but then thinks better of it, leaving them suspended in the air like an odd sort of marionette. Mirren appears to need no encouragement and, as she runs her hands reverently over his face as if he's something from a dream, I realize who he is.

Easton. She never thought she'd see him again.

"What are you doing here?" she scolds, suddenly remembering we're in a cave of the gods buried in piles of rubble. "You could have been killed!"

"I was trying to find *you*, Mirri. I followed the Praeceptor to the tunnel and when everything collapsed, I found my way through an offshoot," he explains, motioning to the direction from which he's come. Easton shifts uncomfortably as he watches tears pour down his sister's face and a wash of anger crashes against me. So strong, I have to grip Cal's shoulder to keep from swaying on my feet. He may be her brother, but I will never forget how he broke her heart. How she gave up everything for him, and he was too weak to give up his home for her. How he was too selfish to realize Mirren *is* home.

"I don't care how you got here, I'm just s-so happy to see you!" Mirren says with a watery laugh. "When we found out the Praeceptor invaded Similis, I—I thought the worst happened. I thought you were dead, Easton...or—or worse."

Easton purses his lips, his jaw tightening. "There's so much I need to tell you—" He stops abruptly, appearing to take notice of Cal and I for the first time. His eyes travel from the dagger in my hand, to the blood coating my clothes, before finally resting on the flames lining my arms. His mouth twists in disapproval and it's all I can do to keep myself from snarling at him.

Mirren steps back to me, threading her fingers through mine and gazing at me with a smile. She nestles into my side, her presence serving to cool my anger slightly as my soul settles over me. "Easton, this is Shaw. He's the man who helped me save you last spring."

Easton says nothing. Though he's as tall as me, he gives the impression of softness, like one strong breeze would blow him over. However, he doesn't flinch from my gaze. His eyes flick between Mirren and I, whatever he sees there thinning his mouth. But he only says, "The Praeceptor didn't invade Similis."

My eyebrows flick up, but Cal, who's been examining Easton with an alarming amount of hostility, speaks first. "What do you mean?"

"He means the Praeceptor had no need to invade," a cool voice says from the shadows where Easton first appeared. A man steps forward, his white-blonde hair shining in the light of my flame. "When he was welcomed as an ally."

Mirren goes deathly still and dread wriggles in my stomach. The man's eyes flicker from black to an odd shade of gray, but it isn't their color that forms a sheet of ice in my lungs as I realize who he is—it's the deadness in them, their barren emptiness a mirror of my own whenever I'm away from Mirren.

The Covinus is soulless.

When he sets his gaze on Mirren, I'm struck with the urge to jump in front of her, to shield her from the horrible depths of those eyes. I've always been comfortable in the Darkness, have always lived with it inside me, but this man —he *is* Darkness. Fathomless and horrible. "Do you have any idea what you've done?" he asks and though his face hardly moves, anger vibrates beneath his calm words.

Mirren's power crashes against our bond, felt in the piece of my soul she holds, but she remains silent, eyes churning as they take in the man who stole her father from her, who murdered her mother and forced her to leave her brother. The man whose actions have left her entirely alone.

"I'm afraid it was me who blew a few holes in your little fence," I drawl in an attempt to draw those malevolent eyes away from Mirren. The Covinus bristles at my arrogance, so I paste a broad grin on my face and weave my fire around my chest and down my legs. Let him see how arrogant I can actually be.

He regards me emotionlessly. "You did not put a *hole* in my Boundary. You brought down the *entire* thing."

I stare at him, words lost on my tongue.

Cal claps me on the back. "Is this how you two keep your relationship spicy? She wrecks a council house and you one up her by blowing up a thousand-year-old wall? Should I get you a city to destroy as a wedding present? A continent to ruin?"

I glare at him, and for once in his life, Cal takes the hint and falls silent.

"It has always been the foolishly prideful that thought

they could thwart me," the Covinus remarks, walking slowly toward us. He has no power and judging by his physique, would pose no challenge in a fight. But still, I feel like I'm being herded. My flames blaze hotter, and the Covinus just watches them, expressionless. As if there is nothing in this world that surprises him.

"Queen Iara thought to stop me with her silly curse. But it was never electricity or magic that earned me my riches. It was my ruthless brilliance and my ability to always adapt. Iara conspired with the nature spirits to curse me, so I waged war. And the humans, who the nature spirits loved so much, were *so* easy to turn. But war is messy and dark. And when everyone is dead, power dries up." His eyes move to Easton. "You are only as powerful if there is someone to rule over."

The Covinus clasps his hands in front of him with a resigned sigh. "And then the old gods, with their pathetic attempt to outwit me one last time, instead, gave me exactly what I needed to thrive once more in the world Iara had created. They gave up all of their remaining power in that cave."

My flames flicker as something like horror curls in my stomach.

"I siphoned it for myself. Transformed it into something malleable, something I could use to control the tide of the continent."

"*You*...you're the reason the land was cursed?" Mirren asks, aghast.

The Covinus shrugs noncommittally, as if the curse that has destroyed thousands of lives, stolen the food from the belly of children, is hardly exciting.

"And...the Boundary? You've been stealing the old gods power to keep Similis unaffected by it."

For a moment, I don't know whether to be impressed or horrified, as my mind attempts to wrap around the fact that the man standing before us is thousands of years old. He has seen warlords rise and fall, the ruin and rebirth of civilization, all the while safe in his own cocoon of power. The Covinus has watched children starve, and brothers war, all lost in the depths of the Darkness he is responsible for.

My flames flare, racing through my chest and over my fingertips. Sizzling anew in the depths of my abyss until I can feel nothing but heat: my power and Mirren's hand.

Easton dances uncertainly on his toes, staring at the man he's trusted as his leader with outright terror. And I realize how much bravery it took for him to break the rules and come find Mirren; to admit every certainty in his life was wrong. He may have given into his fear before, but when faced with the same choice, this time, he made the right one. Admitting weakness can be its own sort of strength.

"The Boundary has kept order for a millennium and now you've destroyed it. Similis will be invaded by monsters, your neighbors torn apart by war and poverty. And for what, Ms. Ellis? To selfishly save yourself?" His eyes flick to me momentarily. "The soulless monster you love? Have you been so twisted by the curse you would put your own life above the wellbeing of thousands of your Community members?"

Mirren swallows audibly. "Don't speak to me of selfishness," she hisses. "Your pride cursed an entire continent of people, and instead of living with your own consequences, you stole even more from them. The old gods meant their power to save *everyone*, not just those you deemed fit." She raises her chin, as the water from inside the earth begins to move toward her as if drawn by a magnet. "The people of

Similis will thrive without the cage you built around them. They'll be free."

The Covinus tilts his head. "Don't you see, Ms. Ellis? The Boundary did not keep them contained. *I* did. By taking away their ability to love, I took away their reason to fight. They have no connection to anything but *me*. They will *never* be free because the true Boundary is in their mind." His face is still the picture of calm. Is it that he's learned to control his emotions so well in his thousands of years on earth? Or is it that the passage of time has stolen the meaning from them, only pale echoes of what they were once meant to be?

The man raises his chin as if he's already won something, and the back of my neck tingles with anticipation. Reflexes beaten into me as a child, now as innate as breathing, that have kept me alive against countless enemies. Alive, even when I didn't wish to be.

Something is coming.

"You have not freed the Similians. The consequences of your arrogance will take years to clean up, for how will their Covinus protect them when their wall is gone? Their electricity and livelihoods? Your recklessness cannot go unpunished. You know better than anyone, Mirren. There are consequences for breaking the rules."

When my father steps from the shadows, his mouth twisted in a terrifying sneer, there is no surprise. Only a suffocating sense of inevitability. I hadn't really thought he was crushed by the cave in, had I? Something as benign as nature would never be the downfall of the heart of horrors. The Praeceptor would never give into the subtle ways of the world, would never allow anything but victory against it.

I know this, and yet, I am no longer afraid.

Because when I feel the familiar pull of his control, the tight squeeze of my lungs, I am able to breathe through it.

My father holds me no longer. Because even a man who directs the tides of nations, who holds the ear of a thousand-year-old dictator, cannot overcome Mirren and I's bond.

My flames flare, fed by love and agony and heartbreak —and they are entirely my own.

A grin crawls across my face as I stare at the man who has taken so much from me, the worst not being my childhood, or even my soul—but my own sense of worth.

I am the Heir of the Praeceptor, but I am not my father.

I am not selfish. I am not hateful.

And that's why, when his eyes land on Easton and he raises his dagger, my decision is easy.

For love, for a better world, for the sake of every pinprick of light in the wash of darkness—I let go of Mirren's hand and my soul, and take the blade meant for Easton.

CHAPTER
THIRTY-NINE

Mirren

A silent scream sticks in my throat as Cullen's dagger lodges in Anrai's back. With wide eyes, he stumbles forward, long fingers gripping Easton's jumpsuit to keep himself upright. My brother buckles beneath Anrai's weight, his face a blend of shock and horror as he struggles to keep them both on their feet.

And then, Anrai straightens.

Slowly, but smoothly—like the dagger isn't there at all.

And that's when my scream finally sounds.

Because in my gratitude for Easton's life, in my terror for Anrai's—I forgot.

Our hands are no longer entwined.

And he's slipped through my fingers like fine sand. It's why the Covinus spilled his darkest secrets, why he was in no hurry to escape from us when we held all the power. He only needed to wait.

The Praeceptor's control restored, the Heir returned.

Anguish rises, but I refuse to let my tears fall. Instead, I feed them to my *other*, coaxing it to the surface of my skin. The dark room glitters as the water rises to my call, swirling and vengeful. Waves of an angry sea crash against my heart, but I no longer worry whose rage it is that echoes: it is ours together—our heartbreak, our terror, our love—that wash over me like armor.

Anrai reaches over his shoulder mechanically and pulls out the knife, a small twitch of his jaw the only sign he feels anything at all. Blood pours from the wound as his body works to cauterize itself, but he doesn't seem to notice as he narrows his eyes on Easton. My brother, who in his panic and shock, remains rooted in place directly in front of Anrai.

Cal lunges forward, pushing my brother behind him. He raises his chin and plants his feet, his sword steady as he raises it to his best friend. "I'm afraid I can't let you do that, Anni," he says calmly.

Flames burst forth from Anrai's palms and he snarls, inhuman rage carving the planes of his face. Inhuman as that night in Havay, as the one in Siralene. Has he truly gone so quickly, when just a moment ago, his heart was full enough to sacrifice himself for my brother?

Calloway only laughs. "Afraid to spar without your power, brother? I thought better of you."

Anrai rolls his neck and his body twitches as he reaches for two of his daggers. His flames sputter and then burst forth once more, and with a start, I realize he fights for control of himself.

He's still in there.

Pride flares in my chest. How many times have I wished for him to understand his worth, to know he deserves every bit of the fight? And now, forced to relive his worst nightmares, he hasn't lost hope. My vigilant assassin, who will shred himself apart to save others, has finally realized he is worth the same.

We fight. You and me, we don't give up. Even if we have to crawl.

I call to the underground streams winding their way through the ancient roots of this forest. My *other* twists around my fingertips and curls around my throat.

Fight, Anrai. Just a little longer.

With a scream of rage, I thrust all of it toward Cullen.

Anrai roars, clutching at his skull with one hand even as his other raises like the arm of a puppet to shoot a wall of flame toward me. I'm forced to drop the wave as I roll to the side, squeezing my eyes shut as I'm buffeted by a boiling rush of heat. The wave crashes to the ground, splashing up the sides of the walls in a torrent and drenching all of us.

"Enough of this," the Covinus says softly to Cullen as I struggle to climb to my feet. "Your pride is the reason my Boundary has fallen. I have given you endless power and you have wasted it on petty revenges. Do not make the same mistake again. Destroy them and take the coin."

The coin?

The Covinus' hard gaze falls to my throat, where the coin that started everything still hangs beneath the layers of my shirt. The coin Anrai used to determine who possessed the potential for power. Could the coin have something to do with the prophecy?

Cullen furrows his brow, his face a terrifying combination of fury and concentration. Anrai doubles over, his teeth gritted in pain. His body wrenches violently, contorting unnaturally until his muscles bulge.

Fight Anrai. Fight long enough for me to break your father's control.

He lets out a roar, feral and wild. His breathing comes in

violent rasps as his body twitches and for a moment, I think he's done it.

But at once, the convulsions cease. Anrai straightens, the movement fluid and unhindered.

"Cal!" I scream, as Anrai cocks his head at his best friend. I scramble up, throwing the weight of my *other* at Anrai, but I'm not quick enough. He raises a wall of flame, his expression unchanging and blank, as he hurtles it at Calloway.

Cal flies backward, slamming into the crumbling wall with a sickening thud. The acrid smell of burning skin tinges the air as his head lolls. Panic grips me, hot and bright, as Anrai emotionlessly surveys the damage his flames have wrought. Nothing human flickers there. Only vague satisfaction.

"Get him out of here, Easton!" I shout.

My words unfreeze something in my brother. He races toward Cal's prone body and desperately pats out his singed skin, before hauling him up by the armpits. There's nowhere to go, the only remaining exit blocked by both the Covinus and the Praeceptor. But he drags Cal anyway, heading for the cover of a fallen slab of concrete.

"The coin, Cullen," the Covinus snarls. "It is the only remaining piece. *Get it.*"

The coin seems to shudder against my chest in response as I call another wave to me. Water threads through my veins, cool and endless, as I advance toward them. Cullen hardly spares me a look, as focused as he is on controlling his heir. But the Covinus meets my eyes.

And they are as black as I first thought they were.

Nothing flickers there. No sadness for his Boundary, no fear for his people. Nothing but fathomless dark.

My *other* crashes against my lungs in fury as I gaze at

the man responsible for murdering the other nature spirits. The man who took everything from both of us, leaving us orphaned and alone. The water undulates, rising so high, I can only see the Covinus' gaze through its shimmer.

There will be no freedom while either of them lives.

My words or my *other's*, it no longer matters. The fissure in my soul aches, as I grit my teeth against the strain of the wave.

Anrai snarls in rage at the small step I make toward his father. Before I can blink, he twists his hands and more flames burst to life, an explosion of heat and light. They rise around him, a boiling whirlwind of destruction so strong, the roar of it shatters against my eardrums.

Realization settles like a heavy stone in my stomach. The Praeceptor will make Anrai kill me before I ever get close to him.

And if he somehow survives his father, Anrai will not survive my death on his hands. The only remaining lifeline to his humanity will go into the Darkness with me.

You could fall.

The edge of the cliff I've feared for so long is now a siren's song. If I leap into it, I have a chance of killing the Praeceptor. I could end his reign of terror and avenge so many horrors—but at what cost?

Will I be forced to drown my soul-bonded? To terrorize and torture him, to bring his worst fears to life?

He would understand. He knows the sacrifices the Darkness demands.

I could be as ruthless as Anrai. I could end this.

But my *other* chose me, not because I carry a heart for vengeance. It chose me in a mountain cave when my heart carried mercy and healed an assassin with a loyal soul.

The Praeceptor's atrocities will never be forgiven, but if I meet them with my own, I am only layering darkness upon darkness. What if I choose light instead?

Love, instead of hatred. Bravery, instead of my fear.

Healing, rather the tearing more of the world apart.

There has been enough destruction.

I have spent the past few months ruined and heartbroken. Terrified that if I admitted I loved, the world would have even more to take from me.

But on the occasion I have been brave enough to name it, to rise up and claim it as my own, I have not been torn apart. I have been made stronger. Different, reshaped—but fortified.

My *other* shimmers in my chest, light and strong and free. *Be brave now.*

Anrai thrusts his hands upward and his flames explode. I squeeze my eyes shut against the chaos of light, the boom of ruination in my ears. Controlled by Cullen, he will never allow me near enough to touch him.

So, I touch his power instead.

My waves reach for his flames. They wrap around each tendril, until every part of me, of my *other,* is tangled around every part of him. His eyes widen as he realizes what's happening, but it's too late to unravel himself. I feel the hollow anger, the biting hopelessness, and let it join the melee swirling around us. Cullen fades away as Anrai and I are wrapped in a hurricane of power, the center of our own storm, just as we've always been.

My arms begin to shake with exertion and sweat beads on my forehead. The only sound is our labored breathing and the cyclone of power around us, a mirror of when we met in Siralene. I'd been so afraid, then, of what existed over the edge. I stubbornly hung on, bound by fear of the unknown.

I'm not afraid now.

This time, I jump freely into the dark sea of power that awaits.

And I pull Anrai with me.

CHAPTER
FORTY

Mirren

Anrai's power thrashes as I bind it to mine and pull it into the depths.

It shrieks and flares, but it's grown weak being starved for so long, and is no match for us.

Together, we free fall.

Hours or days pass. Anrai struggles, his anguished screams careening off my heart and burrowing into my soul. But I refuse to let him go.

Because there is light at the end of our fall.

Somewhere, at the bottom most depths of myself, lays the source of my *other*. Its dazzling glow sings me home, to a place where healing exists.

Anrai's flames are drowned by heavy moisture, and they begin to fade as we plummet closer to the blaze of light. When we reach the bottom, it is not with a violent jolt, but instead, a gradual slowing until we lay gently on a swath of cloud.

Around us, the world shines, soft and billowing like silk in the wind. The sound of water gently lapping at a sandy shore surrounds us, but somewhere further, beyond our sight, echoes something wholly more powerful. A storm behind the curtain of blue sky.

I am powerful here, renewed and full, no longer expending all my energy on fighting the draw of my *other*, terrified of where it might lead. I know now, it leads only to myself. A balance written in the beginning of time. The depths I so feared are of my own creation, dug by heartbreak and love in equal measure. And they are mine to explore, to wield.

Anrai is still as I gather him to me. Only in our minds do we touch, in the depths of our power, but it feels as real as any caress of skin. And though it is my *other* and not my hand that begins to press into his heart, I know the pain he feels is as real as the cut of any blade.

He jolts and writhes. Cries and screams.

But I don't relent.

Healing is never comfortable.

Sometimes, it is agony. To reopen old wounds and sew them neatly back together. To grow new skin over them. To forget the echo of pain they caused, the ache of betrayal lining them.

And a soul is an awfully big thing to heal.

My eyelids flutter and my heart races, but I press on.

The light around us flickers and dims, as I feed it into Anrai.

The storm beyond our sight grows, its fury reverberating in my chest, its roar resounding against my skull.

It will take every blazing ray of light to heal what has been so broken. There will be nothing left to aid our climb back to ourselves, nothing to keep the storm at bay. But still, I pour more.

As he once gave everything for me, I will do the same for

him. I won't lose anymore of myself to fear, won't waste one more minute worrying about what could be taken from me.

Instead, I will give. Everything that shines in the depths of my *other*—friendship, freedom, exhilaration. And love. Everything Anrai's broken soul gifted me with.

He deserves everything he's given; everything and more.

So I hang on to him, feeding him all of it, until there is nothing left in me but the dim flicker of a single candle. The power beyond shrieks and crashes.

I could stop now and hope it's enough. That a little healing is better than none at all.

But now I understand. Giving yourself was never something to fear. It is a blessing, to have those in your life worth giving yourself to.

"I love you," I whisper to Anrai, to the depths, to the world.

And then I push the last bit of my *other* into his soul.

~

Shaw

It burns, burns, burns.

My lungs, my heart, my eyes—everything *burns*.

The flames rise as I scream, until they are all I can see, conflagrating into a whirlwind of torment.

The flames swell, and I gasp in terror as they overtake the hollow inside me. They rise and they rise, until I can no longer contain them, and then burst forth, consuming everything in their path.

Everything is agony.

But—I am warm.

I am *full*.

And the flames, my power, no longer ache with hunger. Satiated, they do not feed on my internal wounds, nor do they spear out in search of more.

Because now, I am enough.

Climb, Anrai.

Climb.

There is no pain here, no thirst, no ache. For the first time I can remember, there is only peace.

After a lifetime of unrest, I could finally, *finally*, know the serenity of the Darkness. There would be no more fire, no more yearning hunger. In the depths of wherever we are, I know, I don't have to climb. I can choose for this to be over and be welcomed into the arms of the shadows.

My flames curl around my lungs and settle over my heart.

Ruthless heart, they beat. *Ruthless heart, loyal heart.*

You persist.

Born in the Darkness, baptized in pain, I persevere. Broken, but never shattered, pain does not defeat me—it drives me.

I have worn my steadfast heart as an instrument of self-flagellation, but instead of shredding it apart piece by piece in service of others, what if I allowed it to beat for itself? What I stopped tearing it apart out of shame and gave it room to grow?

I have scraped and crawled and suffered, but I have never done it for myself.

And so, I climb.

Living is pain, but it is so much more than that. It is the gasp of Mirren's breath against my lips, the curl of Calloway's smile, the tenacity of Max's fight.

I climb for all of it, for every bit of the agony and ecstasy of life.

But the reason I don't slip—the reason I push past the shredding pain in my limbs and the burning in my lungs—is because this time, I climb for me.

CHAPTER
FORTY-ONE

Shaw

I rise.

My skin is no longer too tight, my bones no longer too sharp for my body.

My heart pumps, and my lungs fill, and I command all of it. My body is *mine*.

There is no more emptiness, no more ache. My soul is entirely whole.

Mirren, that miraculous, stubborn, impossibly brave woman, somehow managed to heal my soul. And not just the piece I gave to her, but *all* of it. Every fissure has been mended, the Darkness rooted in me since I was a child, dug out. And gods, without it, I am so light.

When I open my eyes, the destroyed room of the old gods comes barreling into view. Mirren lies a few feet from me, eyes closed, dark hair sprawled in a wild curtain around her head. My heart jumps into my throat as I race to her side. *Oh gods, oh gods.* Her arms fall limply to her sides as I gather her to me, her skin deathly cold. Holding my breath, I press my fingers to her throat, desperate for the feel of her pulse. It always beats so determinedly, relentless even in the face of death, but now, there is only silence.

Rage and grief billows in my chest, clogging my throat. *Don't leave me. Don't go where I can't follow.*

A cutting laugh echoes across the ruins.

My father lounges against the wall, watching my desperation with something close to amusement. Flames climb my throat, mingling with fury. "What. Have. You. Done."

Because whatever this is, whatever is wrong with Mirren, is my father's doing. He has always been threatened by the beautiful things in life, has always torn down anything that shined.

Cullen runs his tongue along his teeth and pushes himself to standing with an arrogant tilt of his head. "I think you mean, what have *you* done, dear son," he says with vicious relish. "After burning your best friend alive, the girl gave herself up to *heal* you." He laughs mirthlessly, the sound ringing against my ears.

It isn't true, can't be true. Cal isn't dead, cut down by my power. Mirren isn't gone, can't have given herself up for *me.*

No, *no...*

Flames shoot from my chest, lining my skin in an outward conflagration of the despair building inside me. My father doesn't even flinch, just watches me with that flat gaze that tells me he finds me lacking.

As if reading my thoughts, he smirks. "I have never needed your soul to control you, boy. You are only ever what I made you and you are unmade just as easily. *I* carved you. You are *my* weapon, my monster, and you will never be anything else." He saunters closer to my flames, his stride relaxed as if they pose no threat. As if I'm exactly what he says—his to control. "You are only made to destroy, never to build." The same words he's repeated since I was a child echo in the vulnerable place forged by my loneliness and shame.

Cullen's eyes trail from Mirren to Calloway—to the pieces of my heart I've destroyed. "And it looks like you've done exactly the job I forged you for."

Mirren's skin is like ice against my burning palm. Her eyes are closed, sooty lashes fanned across the delicate skin of her cheek. The vital essence that normally pours from her is gone, as if the woman I hold is only an echo of the one I love. And *gods,* the entire earth feels darker because of it.

It is not gone. It was given. Therein lies the difference.

My love, my sacrifice, everything I thought I needed to give in order to be worthy; Mirren found a way to give it all back.

"Well done, my son," the Praeceptor says, my flame reflected in his pale eyes as he bends down in front of me. "You've destroyed the prophecy more thoroughly than I could have imagined. The ocean-wielder is dead."

Dead. Why am I not with her as the story promised?

"Now bring me the coin and take your place, Heir. It is only *I* who will cherish the ruination you bring. Only I who understands you and will not try to change it."

Once, I would have believed him.

Believed that everything I touch turns to ash. I would have torn myself apart, buckled under the weight of blame. I would have thrown myself to the whims of the Darkness, certain I deserved them.

For burning Calloway, the same way his family was burned.

For stealing the life from the woman I love.

But no longer.

I am not my father's weapon.

I am Anrai Shaw. Brutal assassin, loyal friend. I have done heinous things, but I have also fought for good. And I have chosen to let the good matter more.

Calloway and Mirren saw me for who I truly am. And it's time I honor them by truly seeing myself: every horrible, wonderful, raw piece.

I raise my flame and let an arrogant smile crawl across my face as I stare down my father.

The man who made me. The man who destroyed me.

The man who no longer has any power over me.

"You may have made me, Father, but you have never known me. And you do not learn from your mistakes. You have always underestimated the power of hope. It is unbreakable, unmalleable. It cannot be cut down, no matter how hard you rail against it." My flames burst forth, leaping from my fingers, and crawling across the floor toward Cullen in a slow path of promised agony.

"Hope," my father spits in disgust, watching the flicker of flame. He stiffens, but he doesn't cede a step. "Hope is the food of the weak. Imagined and useless, they are always left starving."

My flames crawl, just as I have crawled before him. "Hope of something better is what keeps us alive. Hope is what can turn even the most vicious of monsters against their creators."

Fire explodes before him, a conflagration of my grief.

Rather than responding, the Praeceptor does the one thing I don't expect.

He turns and runs.

CHAPTER
FORTY-TWO

Shaw

I would laugh if my throat wasn't clogged with grief. If rage wasn't barreling through me, entwining with my flames until it's acidic and destructive. All my life, I have feared nothing but him. Not the horrors of the Nemoran or the torture of the cruelest warlords—not even death itself.

Only him.

And the whole time, he's been a coward.

I tear after him, the sight of Mirren, vulnerable and alone on the cave floor, imprinted behind my eyes. The emptiness where her heartbeat should be, the lifeless pallor of her skin: it rises up, threatening to smother my chest until my flame is gone. I've just managed to claw my way back to humanity and the reality of her truly being gone will surely send me spiraling into the Darkness once more.

So, I don't think. Don't breathe. I do what I'm good at—I turn into a weapon.

And I hunt.

Cullen disappears into the darkness, aided by his training and the simple fact he knows where he's going. He melts into the dark like a wraith, his footsteps silent as he disappears into the small passageway. Hidden behind piles of rubble, somehow the small escape shaft survived the Boundary collapse. It's how Easton and the Covinus found us and as I hurtle after my father, I have a vague idea where the tunnel leads.

I run anyway, fueled by anger and exertion and fire. When I come to a fork, I turn right, hoping the left leads back to where we first entered the chamber of the gods. The gods who we risked everything to free, who may have never even been there in the first place. It must have been the Boundary we felt the entire time, the viscous perversion of it permeating the walls of the chamber.

Cal and Mirren sacrificed themselves and magic is still chained. Despair thickens my throat and I push myself further, not feeling the burn of exertion in my muscles, only the burn of vengeance. My father will pay for everything he's taken from me. For everything he's taken from the world.

I don't relent until the tunnel begins to climb. Scrabbling up the sloped concrete, I slip on the marbled stones that coat the floor until my fingers find the ceiling. Heavy wood, roughly hewn, with thick iron hinges at one side. I know what I'll find on the other side, because I know my father. He is never at a disadvantage, always armed with a plan behind a plan.

It's why he never fails.

Always adjust. The moment you grow stagnant is the moment you're dead.

I pause for a fraction of a beat, to run my fingers along my bandolier. The one that still smells like Mirren, still *feels* like her. The carved ridges of the daggers ground me, sending a fresh breath barreling into my lungs. Through Darkness and fire, I'm alive.

Because of Cal. Because of Mirren. Because of *me*.

I burst through the door, my daggers flying before my feet fully touch the ground. Around me, all I see is red. The red of my father's militia, the red swirl of bricks.

And then—the crimson of their blood.

Most of Similis has gone dark, but the two closest Boundary lights flicker in and out with a sharp clicking sound, dousing the square in disorienting bursts of light and then falling dark, as the militia falls beneath my blades. I hardly see them, all my focus on the Praeceptor. He stands calmly behind two lines of his men, commanding them with an iron voice. He watches detachedly as they succumb in service of his goals, not people, but instruments.

Nothing flickers on his face, though I don't miss the exerted pump of his chest. Satisfaction threads through me; the first sign of his humanity.

I will show him how human he truly is.

My abyss flares, no longer a gaping hole where rage breeds and Darkness feeds. Now, it is full—of fire, of life, of love and I allow it to climb through me. It threads through my chest, sizzling down to my fingertips. It climbs up my throat and powers down my legs.

An impenetrable wall of flame rises around me, painting the night and the red square in licks of flame and shadow. Ash rains down and soldiers scream, backing away in terror. They've witnessed my fire's hunger, its need to destroy, and they fear meeting the same end.

But Mirren not only mended my soul, she somehow healed the rift that kept my power from being fully mine. It no longer spears from me, uncontrollable and apart. Now, I *am* the flame. It is only my will, *our* will, be done.

But the Praeceptor commands nothing less than absolute loyalty, the fear of his retribution more harrowing than the threat of burning to death. I have stood where the militia stand, my own wellbeing superseded by my need to please him.

They throw themselves into my flame, swords raised. Some of them burn, their uniforms igniting in a red-hot burst. Others press on, ignoring the sizzle of their skin, the scorch of their clothes. I could stop them with hardly a thought—melt the muscle from their bones and relish their screams of agony. A part of me still craves it; the same part that will always long for the Darkness. But my soul is whole for the first time since I was seven, when, terrified and sick, I took my first life.

I broke my soul for the first time on the Praeceptor's command. He ensured I fractured it only for him.

Now, I will ensure the same.

I pull my sword, meeting blade for blade. I duck and weave, the familiar dance of violence imprinted in the memory of muscle, the lining of my skin. The song of metal rings out, the sound of flesh hitting brick, and still, I move. The Boundary lights flicker in a strobe effect as soldier after soldier falls to my blade, succumbs to my hand.

Others are overcome by flame, their hair burned to the scalp, their skin and clothes singed as they fight their way toward me.

There are so many of them, an endless wave of my father's fury, but I never falter. My limbs don't tire, my lungs don't ache. The burn of my power roils and rises, sustaining my every move, imbuing each act with the strength of a wildfire. Not one movement is wasted, each jab of my fist, each slice of my sword, landing with precise efficiency.

Rifles sound, but the bullets are melted in the air before they reach me. The Boundary lights whine and flare, before finally falling dark for good.

I raise my flames higher, buffeting an entire line of soldiers back. The small trees catch fire, lighting up the red square in the absence of the lights. The flames race from treetop to treetop, before bursting at the foot of the largest building. And still—my father doesn't move.

He will let his entire militia fall before me without flinching, his arrogance too great to ever admit defeat.

It is only when the last of his men finally crumple, when the only sound in the square is the moan of the injured and the pounding of my heart, does my father reach for his sword. Rage rushes against my ears as the blade gleams black in the firelight, the color so deep, it hides the stain of blood it has drawn from so many. My blood, both as a child and a man, has adorned it so many times.

Cullen raises it with a resigned sigh.

I stare into his eyes, my own reflection mirrored back to me in the pale blue. My clothes are torn, dusted white with ash and debris. My hair is matted with sweat and my eyes burn with madness and grief. Blood coats my face and hands, none of it my own.

I look exactly like the monster he created, with one distinct difference.

I am too wild—with heartbreak and anger and love—to ever be controlled. Unrestrained and relentless as flame itself.

I never stood a chance of being what my father wanted, because he is not fire. He is death incarnate.

Nothing flickers on his face now, not even as he stares down his greatest mistake. The loss of his empire, his heir. His son.

Would I have become what he wanted if Max hadn't saved me? If Denver had never loved me, if Cal had never made me laugh?

If Mirren hadn't given herself to heal my soul, would I have finally become what my father is?

Empty.

Emotions have no place on the battlefield.

And yet, as my father lunges for me, I cannot push them away. There is no killing calm, no silence of the abyss. They rise up and ensnare me, wending my way through my lungs and my heart. Tears cloud my vision as I bring my blade against his, my arm vibrating with the power of the blow.

He has devastated so many. He has taken my soul and my life. And it was never enough.

And now, he has taken Cal and Mirren. My laughter, my heart. My soul.

I let out a roar of anguish and fury. Spinning, I bring my blade toward his side, but he is a step ahead of me.

He's been a step ahead of me since birth.

Cullen brings his second sword up from behind his back and knocks mine from my hand. His chest rises and falls in rapid succession, but his blade is steady as he brings it to my throat. "I have given you the power of the world, and *still*, you flounder it on emotions. Pathetic," he spits, his face twisting in disgust. "You spent so long in your conscience, wrapped in your shame, you never even recognized the flame inside you. You are too weak, too soft, to ever be the heir of mine. And now you will die just like your precious *love*," he draws so close to me, I can feel the heat of his breath on my cheek. "Because I am strong enough to root out every weakness. Even you, *son*."

I steel my spine, bracing myself for death, but my father's blade moves no further. His eyes flick around the dark square, as if looking for something. Or someone. *Why is he hesitating? Why hasn't he killed me?*

Cullen has never understood emotions, and in that, he has always underestimated their power. He does not love, so he cannot fathom how it drives a person. But now, with the edge of his sword poised at his son's throat—his heir, who has betrayed and humiliated him—he hesitates. Has he underestimated his own emotion?

"And yet, here you stand, unable to kill me?" I ask in a low voice.

At this, his gaze settles back on mine. Something flashes there, venomous and dark. "You think I spare you because I *love* you?" His laugh rings across the crimson square, embeds itself in my heart. "I spare you only to spare *myself.*"

My eyes widen in sudden understanding.

Praeceptor, scourge of the Dark World. Terror of my dreams and annihilator of thousands of innocent people—still has a soul.

How?

I have seen him cut off a man's fingers and shove them down his throat; slice open a person's stomach and burn them from the inside out. I've watched him order the slaughter of entire villages, burn his way through cities, string up women and children.

But—I have never seen him kill someone. Not himself.

He's always ordered someone else to do it, namely me. He's fed thousands of his militia's souls to the Darkness without flinching, but the whole time, selfishly held onto his. And isn't it always those in power who never get their hands dirty in the name of their own wars? There is always someone lower to be sacrificed, always someone more expendable in their climb to power.

But the Darkness can only be eluded for so long. Eventually, it will come to claim its right, the power forged in its name. Even the worst dictator will fall to those they oppress. To those they deem beneath them, too small to ever challenge anything.

I look my father in the eyes and let a smile creep across my face. I've always thought he was too advanced to allow his emotions to rule his decisions, but fear is just as powerful as any other. In his fear of the Darkness he tried to control, in his need to keep his soul, he's made a brutal mistake.

He hesitated.

My abyss flares to my skin, invisible to the eye as it heats the air around me to boiling. It reaches for my father's blade until the black metal turns red hot. My father cries out in pain as the blade brands his palm, his sword clanging to the ground. I lunge for it, just as he brings up the other blade with a roar of fury.

At the first ring of our swords, something in me shatters. And at the second, it is remade into something new.

He is faster than me, even with the fire raging through my veins, but I meet his every move with one of my own. My father was always a patient fighter, always telling me more fights were lost by impatience than by ineptitude. He measures his movements now, waiting for the moment my emotions overrule me and cause me to make a mistake.

My fire rages, my blood boils.

Mirren's face, pale and wan and beautiful, flashes in my mind.

But I am my father's son. And I force my body to calm, to meet each movement with precision and restraint.

Sweat springs to Cullen's brow and he grits his teeth as I break through his guard, slicing through the sleeve of his left arm. Not enough to break the skin, but enough to break through his calm. To free his anger. He whirls and I duck. I kick and he evades.

His breathing becomes heavier, and he snarls as I bear down on him. Our blades ring once more, and I laugh, the sound ringing over the ash of the square. The militia members who survived have crawled off somewhere to nurse their wounds and now, it is only my father and me. The Praeceptor is no longer the monster of my dreams—he is only a man. A man who tires, who sweats, who falters.

Same as any other.

He bares his teeth as I laugh again, the power of his blow vibrating up my arm as his anger begins to drive him. Anger that someone he's deemed weak is matching him. Anger that someone *he* trained, he *made,* dares to fight against him.

His movements become more powerful, but messier. Edged with something like desperation. Lined with fury.

Human. He is human.

The last piece of my soul, the miniscule fissure that still exists after Mirren's sacrifice, heals over.

He lunges toward me, and at the last moment, I step around him and swing my blade in a wide arc.

When it meets his flesh, he bleeds, just like any other.

"How does it feel?" I growl at him. The abyss roars its approval at the scent of his fear, at the taste of his blood. "To know that in spite of everything you've done, your legacy won't be remembered. After I watch you die, I will go to Argentum and burn your city until there is nothing left but wasteland. Until nothing will even grow on the cursed ground."

My father leaps toward me once more, with no thought other than to tear me apart, opening up his guard. I slice through his side with no hesitation. He snarls in agony, his eyes flashing. I drink it in fervidly, as he grips his side and stumbles sideways, his weapon shaking. Then I swat his sword from his hand with another laugh.

"Go into the Darkness knowing you have no empire, no heir, and no son. You will only be remembered for your weakness at the end, cut down by your own blood." I slice him at the knees and he falls with a groan. "Your legacy will be torn apart in the depths of the curse, tortured by the screams of the thousands you've destroyed."

My father's blood is not made of ichor as he kneels before me. It is the same crimson as mine, the same as my mother's and Asa's and Denver's. The same as every one of his victims. It seeps into the bricks, disappearing into the scarlet square as if it were never there.

The Praeceptor is human and now, he will die like one. I have hated him, and I have loved him, and this time, when I pierce his heart with my blade, I imbue it with the fire that forged me.

CHAPTER
FORTY-THREE

Shaw

Anrai.

Anrai, come home.

But I have no home now.

I tasted it briefly, in her—her voice, her smile. But it's gone. And I hate her for it, for healing me and forcing me to live without her, in the same breath I love her for it.

"Anrai!"

I awake with a violent shudder, drawing my dagger out of pure muscle memory. Breath barrels sharply into my lungs and I blink into the bright light blearily as I remember where I am.

Similis.

Nausea climbs my throat and my flames flicker and then die once more as I burrow back into myself. I despise the burn of the Boundary lights, the way they illuminate every dingy corner and every small crack. I miss the soft glow of Ferusa, the cover of darkness. I should have done a more thorough job of destroying the blasted monstrosities.

Someone beside me breathes a deep sigh of relief, and

when she speaks, my heart tumbles over itself. "It's nice not to *always* be the one fainting."

I peek an eye open and am greeted with the vision of Mirren, sleep-edged and dream touched. She isn't here, the void where her heartbeat should be still a physical thing in my chest. My grief has conjured up hallucinations, bringing to life what I wish was true. Because dream-Mirren is radiant, even under the glare of the lights. She is not empty, as she was on the floor of the gods chamber, absent of whatever made her *her*.

"I didn't faint," I tell my hallucination obstinately. After I burned my father so thoroughly his remains were left to blow away with the light fall breeze, I'd barely been able to crawl into this alley. With the Praeceptor finally gone and Mirren avenged, my fire receded, and my soul seized me.

There hadn't been time to feel it when I first woke healed, but once the adrenaline faded, every horrible thing I'd done while soulless crashed down on me. It was heavier than the sky and it cracked my ribs, severed my tendons, stole my breath while I tried to hold it up. The blood, the burning, the *children*. Every feeling I didn't feel while soulless now come to rest inside me, tenfold.

It had been all I could do to force rattled breaths into my lungs, to try not to choke on my own bile. Eventually, exhaustion overtook me, and I curled up behind a dumpster to wait out the pain.

As if pain is something that ever recedes. I know better than anyone. It is only ever something you become accustomed to, and that's if you're lucky.

"Well, it certainly looks like you did. Unless you enjoy napping behind trash bins." She wrinkles her cute nose. "And smelling of burnt sewage."

I grumble at dream-Mirren and with a concerted effort,

push myself to sitting. The building scrapes against my back and my tongue feels too thick for my mouth. Vomit rises once more, and I wince as I swallow it back down my sand-coated throat. "You're awfully rude for something I've conjured. You'd think I would make up a version of you that never argued, did exactly as you were told, and consistently pointed out how handsome I am."

I squeeze my eyes shut against the infernal light and bark out a curse. My pupils feel like they're on fire.

"You would conjure me exactly as I am, because someone needs to keep your ego in check for the good of the world," dream-Mirren responds haughtily, her voice resonating in my chest. "But Anrai, you haven't imagined anything. I'm here."

And then, she touches her hand to mine.

It's an explosion of the best sort, all warmth and light and power, as her fingers brush my palm. My eyes snap open, and gods, when she meets my gaze, it is the most beautiful thing I've ever seen. And I cannot have imagined her, could I? Even an imagination as vivid as mine could never get the churning emerald waves of her eyes just right, nor the way she seems to glow in the dingy alleyway, her face a mixture of love and relief. "You're... alive?" my voice cracks, desperate and ridiculous, but I don't even care as she nods fervently, her radiant smile breaking out into the open. "H-how?"

But I find I don't even care. Tears pour down my face, trailing through blood and grime and ash, as I pull her to me and bury my face in her hair. And when I feel her heartbeat, strong and beating in rhythm with my own, full sobs rack my body. "I thought I'd lost you. I thought you'd given everything for me."

She runs her fingers reverently over my face, her own

eyes shining with unshed tears. She traces my jawline until she comes back up to my lips, before kissing me fiercely. The taste of her mingles with the taste of tears and smoke, and a fresh wave of nausea roils over me. I don't deserve to be here, to hold her once more. Not after everything I've done. But I won't ever let her go.

"Gods, Mirren, how could you do that to me?!" I shout at her, before sobs overcome me once more. My shoulders shake and my body trembles, as I whisper, "how could you do that *for* me?"

Her eyes shine as she tilts her head. "Because I had faith in you, Anrai, as I always have. I knew, even if I gave up everything to heal you, a part of me *is* you. As long as you lived, I would, too. You just had to choose it."

I only cry harder, wrapping her in my arms. She's so warm and alive and so am I and I never thought I'd be so lucky. To be whole enough to love her without the edged knife of Darkness. I have done so many terrible things; so many heavy things.

Pulling back, I stare at her, taking in the set of her lush mouth, the flush of her skin, the rolls of her curves. "Cal?" The words lodge in my mouth, the truth of them enough to break me once more. "Is he—did I..."

"He's alive," Mirren assures me quickly. I sense her hesitation more than hear it, but I have no energy for anything other than relief I haven't added Calloway's name to the long list of people I've destroyed. "Where's the Covinus? The militia?"

"We can talk about everything when you're stronger," she tells me and though I hear the edge in her voice, I don't have it in me to argue. Sitting up is hard enough beneath the weight of everything. "For now, we're safe. You need to rest. I'll take you to my quarterage."

My limbs feel like they're made of cement, and the idea of lifting them, of having to move at all, threatens to sweep me into another haze of exhaustion. My stomach clenches, and though its empty and aching, I have to turn my head to vomit once more. My throat burns as I swipe at my mouth with back of my hand, before looking back to Mirren. *I am a mess. She is a goddess.* "I don't know if I can," I tell her honestly, without saying the rest.

I don't know if I can make it to the quarterage. I don't know if I can live with what I've done.

I don't know if I can stay whole for you.

But Mirren only smiles. "Then let us help you."

She looks past me, and when I follow her gaze, I see Avedis and Max lingering hesitantly at the opening of the alley. Max's face is scraped, and she holds a bandaged hand to her abdomen; Avedis' normally black hair is dusted in white debris from the collapse, his clothes torn. But they both look decidedly alive.

I narrow my eyes on the assassin and he lifts his hands innocently. "I swear to be gentler than the last time I moved you," he promises.

"What about the time before that?" Max asks genially. "I hear his trip down the cliffside wasn't exactly a treat."

Avedis tips his head in grudging agreement. "I may have allowed his head to hit a few rocks, but it was purely on principle, I assure you." He grins, before meeting my gaze. Awaiting my permission.

With one last look at Mirren, I dip my head. Perhaps I'll be able to manage the weight of it all, if I have my friends to help me shoulder it.

CHAPTER
FORTY-FOUR

Shaw

I spend my days in a dark square room learning to bear the weight of my soul. The gray curtains remain drawn, as sweat soaks my clothes and the mattress beneath me. My stomach is sore and my throat raw as I vomit up everything I eat, rarely able to keep down even water. My head pounds and my skin burns, and I writhe and jolt every time I close my eyes to sleep. But through it all, Mirren stays by my side. She strokes my hair through the tremors and soothes my itchy skin with salves. She feeds me ice chips slowly and changes my soiled sheets. She presses cold cloths to my forehead and sings softly into the darkness until I finally pass out from exhaustion.

I drift in and out of consciousness, lost somewhere between dark and light, until I am finally strong enough to stand beneath the heaviness. At first, I only manage a few minutes at a time. My bare feet touch the cold floor of the quarterage and when my legs begin to give out, I grit my teeth against the pain, and force myself to withstand it. In my moments of lucidity, I wonder if everyone's soul is as heavy as mine or if it was only made so by the life I've lived.

Surely everyone has different burdens to bear, but they've grown conditioned to lifting them every day. The time I spent soulless has weakened me, carrying on without lifting anything at all. When I was five, I could hardly pick up the wooden sword we used for sparring. The *legatus* who trained me showed no mercy, thwacking me with his own sword time and again. Welts bloomed on my arms and legs until I was finally strong enough to raise it against him.

I remind myself of this story time and again in that room.

You will be strong again, if only you persevere. Ruthless heart, you do not give in.

And so, I stand beneath the pain until my legs give out. And then, I try again.

A week later, when I've managed to stand for an entire hour, the door to my room opens. I expect Mirren and her hourly attempt to coax more of that disgusting broth down my throat, but instead, Cal appears in the threshold.

He looks the same as he has since we were fourteen—neat and handsome, his hair done within an inch of perfection. Except he's no longer perfectly handsome, is he?

My gaze immediately goes to the leather patch tied over his left eye, the one I took from him. It's the first I've seen of it, though Mirren gave me a full account of his injuries in order to prepare me. But nothing could prepare me for the way the skin glistens around the patch, new and stretched and colored an angry red. The burn stretches up over where his eyebrow used to be, spreading a few inches into his hairline.

Vomit climbs my throat so suddenly, my knees give out and I crash to the ground. Cal's eyes widen in alarm, and he reaches to help me, but I shake my head. Retching, I crawl onto the bed and curl into myself, unable to bear witness to anymore of my destruction.

And Cal, gods, *Cal*.

Cal, who has never hurt anyone.

Mirren is not the first pure thing I took for myself. Cal, with his brimming joy and infectious light, was the first thing I coveted. If I could never shine, the temptation of experiencing it tangentially had been too great in him. And being the person he is, Cal has only ever loved me, never asking anything for himself in return.

And look where it's gotten him.

"Come now, Anni," he says, closing the door gently behind him. His steps fall closer. "It isn't that bad."

I double over, clutching my stomach and burying my face in the scratchy Similian sheets.

Look at him. Look what you've done to your brother.

But I can't. Because if I do, I'll unravel all of Mirren's work. I already allowed the Darkness to pierce my new soul when I murdered my father, and if I acknowledge what I've done to Cal, whatever holds the new pieces together will shatter. I'll be nothing but ash once more.

So, I say nothing and keep my eyes squeezed shut.

Leave me. You should have left me long ago.

But Cal does nothing of the sort.

Instead, the bed dips beneath his weight as he crawls across it. He settles next to me, snaking his arms around my shoulders and pulling me to his chest. He tangles his legs with mine and for a few moments, we just lay silently like this. His presence has never sparked in my chest the way Mirren's does, but his weight is a steady, solid force that opens up something inside me anyway.

I bury my head in his chest, and the scent of him, of

sandalwood and spice—of home—fills my nose as I sob. Cal holds me while I shake. There are no tears, for I have none left in me, just silent wrenches as my body expels every horrible thing I've done. I've held my darkness so close for so long, terrified of poisoning those around me. But now, it's like I've opened the vent of a chimney. Oxygen feeds the flame until they crest out of me in a burning wave.

Cal doesn't even flinch. He meets my darkness head on, absorbing every bit of it into his light. I dig my fingers into his back, clinging to him like he'll disappear beneath me. But he doesn't disappear. He just holds me tighter.

Later, when sobs only come sporadically and my body is exhausted and spent, he presses his lips to the top of my head. "I'm so glad you're home, Anni."

I swallow roughly, keeping my face buried in his shirt. It feels safer in the dark. "I don't deserve you," I tell him. "I don't deserve any of you. I'm so sorry, Cal."

He forces me to look at him, his remaining eye shining with resolve. "We deserve each other," he tells me fiercely. "You have given everything for us, Anni. It was our turn to give something back."

"But Cal, your eye—"

"I have another," he says impatiently. "And besides, you've given me great qualifications to go after a hidden dream of mine."

I furrow my brow doubtfully. "And what's that?"

"I *have* always wanted to be a pirate on the Storven Sea. I don't see how they could reject me now."

I let out a surprised laugh.

"And you've made things much more even." At my consternated look, he clarifies, "It really wasn't fair to the rest of you for me to be so perfectly handsome. It's better to have at least *one* flaw. Makes me more relatable."

"How magnanimous of you to give the rest of us a fighting chance," Mirren laughs from the doorway. "Cal, Harlan would like to speak with you."

Cal gives me a wink and slides off the bed with the grace of a cat. With a quick peck on Mirren's cheek, he disappears down the hallway with a flourished spin.

Mirren's gaze roves over me curiously, her lips tilted up at one corner. I can't imagine what she sees, beyond the wasted echo of who I once was, but after a moment, she closes the door behind her with a quiet *snick* and turns back to me.

I've been so sick, my hunger for her has lay dormant, but as her eyes light on me and her full hips sway with her saunter toward me, it flares now like the spark of a wildfire.

"You look like you're feeling better," she remarks with a wry smile. I pull her into the bed and roll her beneath me. Even in my diminished state, she is still so much smaller than I am. She tangles her arms and legs around me, settling my hips into the plush cradle of her body. My muscles have wasted with malnourishment, my bones weak and brittle, and though I am in no shape to take her, a powerful part of me suddenly demands it.

Instead, I say, "I killed my father."

Mirren's eyes slide to mine, full of unwavering resolve. I broke my vow along with the shiny new soul she gifted me in order to end my father. Though Mirren understands the darkness that edges life, that doesn't mean she wishes to be around it. "Does that scare you?"

"No," she replies with no hesitation.

"I shoved a dagger into his heart. And then I burned every nerve ending in his body until all he could feel was agony. And then I melted his skin and burned his bones to such ash, they were taken by the wind." I run my fingers lightly down her throat to the soft skin between her breasts, and then say in a low voice, "And it was not because I had no soul."

It's important she know this—know how far I'd sunk into the depths of depravity, mad with grief. My brutality against my father was not because there was already Darkness growing inside me. I had a pure soul when I took his life and chose to sully it. It was a betrayal to Mirren and everything she gave me, so now, I must give it back. An offering and a question.

I brace myself for her scorn, her disgust. But she just nods. "Good," she says simply. Her eyes answer any question that still lingers.

I see all of you. Every dark and jagged piece. And I do not shy from it.

I have never given much thought to destiny—have always fought my way through life one step at a time because that's what was expected of me. But now, I understand the draw of the universe. Whether it was the remnants of the dead gods or the Darkness itself, I am grateful to whatever it is that brought me to Mirren. Someone who doesn't bend to the shadows but doesn't try to change them either. She just makes them beautiful with her light. Once, in a dungeon, I vowed to never be on my knees again.

But for Mirren, I will willingly kneel day after day to give thanks.

I crush my lips to hers, tracing the seam of them with my tongue until she opens for me with a small exhale of pleasure. Consuming it, I angle further to sweep her mouth and taste every bit of her I've been denied. I thought regaining my soul would erase the tinge of desperation I feel every time I touch her, the aching fear I will never get enough, never be satiated, but as I take handfuls of her curves and drink in her taste, the desperation remains.

But it no longer feels hopeless. It feels beautiful—like we could live forever and there will always be more to live for.

"Now that you're feeling up to it, there are things we need to talk about with everyone," Mirren whispers breathlessly against my lips.

I move down her throat, kissing and suckling her sweet skin. "Later," I groan against her, before sucking the peak of her breast into my mouth. She writhes beneath me, and I stop only to catch her moans with my tongue. My fingers find her soaking core, and when I curl them into her, I know all thoughts of talking leave her completely.

Because along with my soul, Mirren has given me the gift of time. Moments to heal, to rest. To love.

There will always be another crisis looming, another dive into the Darkness, but for a small moment in a nondescript quarterage, there is only us. My soul and hers, intertwined.

CHAPTER
FORTY-FIVE

Mirren

When we emerge from the bedroom, Anrai looks around the quarterage curiously. He moves slowly, his gait uneven and sore, so I duck beneath his arm, and he allows me to take some of his weight. Together, we shuffle awkwardly down the hall toward the living room.

He takes in the blank walls, the impersonal air, the electric lights that no longer shine, all without comment. I know how the quarterage appears to him as an outsider, because now, I see it the same way. There is no sense of belonging here, no welcome feeling of home. Only sterile unfamiliarity, as if the quarterage could belong to anyone.

And I suppose, now it will. In the wake of the Boundary collapse, the Similians have split into two factions. Those who still believe the Covinus' lies about the Ferusians have holed themselves up in what remains of the Covinus building in order to protect themselves, Farrah and Jakoby among them. The remaining Community members are reticent but hopeful and have stayed in their sectors to help their neighbors rebuild and heal. To me, these are the ones who truly embody the Keys.

Anrai squeezes my shoulder as if I've cast my thoughts into the air. He knows the loneliness I've felt in this place, the complicated feelings being here evokes. "No matter where you are, you are always home now, Lemming. With us."

And indeed, it's true. Laughter rings out as we hobble toward the living room and my chest warms. The quarterage may feel impersonal, but it has not been unbearable with my friends residing beneath its roof. In spite of everything, they have made it feel like a place belonging, their presence seemingly enough to make anywhere feel warm.

Harlan jumps up from the table when he sees us, ducking under Anrai's other arm and shouldering a significant amount of his weight. Together, we maneuver carefully toward the couch.

Anrai lowers himself gingerly into the cushions, looking up gratefully at Harlan. "Thanks, Life Partner."

Harlan grins sheepishly, his cheeks and ears turning pink. "If I'm hers, I suppose I'm yours as well. Glad you're feeling better, Shaw."

"Then what does that make me?" Cal asks genially, clapping an arm around Harlan's shoulder. Harlan turns, if possible, even pinker.

He's spared answering by Max, who sidles between them. "Desperate," she teases. Cal laughs, swiping her into a playful headlock.

As I sit next to Anrai, my eyes go to my brother. Easton stands apart, watching the exchange with an unreadable expression. We've tried talking a little in the week we've been here, but the words are always strained. He didn't follow Farrah and Jakoby to the Covinus building, but he hasn't warmed to the Ferusians either. Even after everything that happened beneath the red square, he watches them warily, as if they may turn on him at any moment.

Easton knows he was wrong about the Covinus, but undoing a lifetime of conditioning will take more than a week. And even so, my brother, who has always so selflessly embodied the true meaning of the Keys, won't ever be comfortable giving them up completely.

And I won't push him to. In spite of what the Covinus used them for, the Keys are not all wrong. In theory, in a world where humans aren't selfish or power hungry, they could have been something wonderful. And maybe they still can be, for someone like my brother.

Cal and Max pile onto the threadbare sofa until we're all squeezed together on the sunken cushions, but Anrai doesn't seem to mind as he watches his friends with shining eyes. His face is gaunt, the dark smudges beneath his eyes only serving to make the glacial blue look even more otherworldly. Strain lines his diminished muscles and I know the short walk from my room has exhausted him. His soul has been repaired, but healing isn't stagnant. It requires work every day, strength to make the choice to live —strength I know he possesses.

He smiles at me, his hand laced with mine. Not because it has to be, but because he loves me.

The world may still be unstable, but right now, that feels like enough.

A breeze blows through the quarterage as Avedis steps through the front door. He's allowed his hair to grow longer than I've ever seen it in our time here and now, the thick black tendrils are in a constant state of movement, as if the winds delight in playing with them. He looks windswept and handsome as he takes note of Anrai. Dark eyes meet light, assassin to assassin, and something like understanding passes between them. "I am glad you've found your way out of the dungeon," Avedis says.

And though I don't understand his meaning, Anrai does. He swallows audibly and nods once, familiar determination hardening his gaze. "Your time will come," he replies. And then, with a wry smile, adds, *"friend."*

Avedis laughs, a light breeze swirling through the room. It's edged with the smell of the approaching winter, of first snows and decaying leaves. "It will have to wait, I'm afraid."

Anrai nods, steeling his jaw. "Tell me."

"The Covinus has absconded from Similis."

"I figured we weren't here on his good graces," Anrai mutters.

I've wanted to tell him everything since the moment I found him in the alley, wanted to know his thoughts, his ideas. Hear his words of comfort. Fear kept me from it. He could barely stand beneath the weight of his own actions; I couldn't bear to add more worry. As if reading my thoughts, he squeezes my hand and whispers, "I won't break, Mirren. I won't leave you again."

I nod, accepting it for what it is. A promise and a prayer. "He's taken the Boundary Men and what remained of the Dark Militia."

"That isn't all," Easton says from the corner. He crosses his arms over his chest, as if he can somehow keep everything in him from spilling out. "He's taken Community members."

I glance at my brother. He's spent his days since the Praeceptor's death in the Community, volunteering alongside Harlan to help with rebuilding quarterages, cleaning up debris and distributing food. When the Boundary crumbled and the ground shook, entire blocks collapsed in on themselves. There were deaths, the number of which we haven't even been able to guess yet.

"How do you know for sure?"

He bites his lip and shrugs, determinedly avoiding Harlan's gaze. "I know my Community," he says sadly. "People are missing."

Cal furrows his brow. "Someone who's been in power for a millennium wouldn't just give it up. The Dark Militia and the Boundary men make sense, but why random citizens who don't even know how to use a weapon?"

Max purses her lips. "Slaves? Hostages? Evil men will always have need of innocents."

I push a leveling breath through my nostrils. "My coin is also gone."

At this, Anrai whips his head toward me. "What?"

"When I...well, when I woke up in the gods' chamber, it was gone." It had felt as though no time at all had passed. One second, Anrai and I were at the bottom of my *other* and the next, I was blinking into the darkness, alone in the ruins. I scrambled to my feet, disoriented and panicked. Anrai and Cullen were nowhere to be seen and the memory of the last time they'd disappeared thumped against my chest in time with my heartbeat.

By the time I'd found Cal and Easton, anxiety had fully lodged in my throat. Time rushed past me, a blur of moments and colors, fueled by adrenaline. It had been late by the time I realized my coin was missing.

Anrai looks thoughtful, watching the slow strokes of his thumb across the back of my hand. He opens his mouth to speak, but his words are lost, as the quarterage begins to shake. The earth rumbles beneath us, the floorboards looking more like rolling waves than solid ground. *Gislan.*

Anrai is on his feet in an instant, yanking a nearby dagger from the kitchen table before sprinting out the door. Despite his labored gait, he's still faster than any of us, with only Avedis able to keep pace. Plaster falls from the ceiling and the quarterage groans as the walls billow and recede. Cal grabs Harlan and Max, ushering them outside. I throw my hands over my head, reaching for my *other*, and dart out after them.

Avedis and Max found Gislan's body, crushed beyond repair beneath piles of rubble in the gods chamber, and confirmed the death by checking his pulse. But aren't I proof death isn't as permanent as it seems? And as the rest of us still remained alive and powerful, we'd begun to hope Asa's story had simply been wrong, and that Gislan hadn't somehow survived to join the Covinus.

People scream around us, Community members already traumatized by their leader and their new exposure to the world at large. I've never felt like one of them, but I feel for them now. For their terror and heartbreak. For the crumbling of the world around them. I know the feeling of the world shifting beneath your feet, something that should have been steadfast, failing before your eyes.

Anrai and Avedis stop short in front of me, their eyes on something crouched in the distance. I sprint to their side, a tidal wave ready to be unleashed at my fingertips.

But when I follow their gaze, my power recedes.

We stare in silence for two long beats, before Anrai whispers, "we've done it, Lemming." He exhales a wondering breath and mutters a curse. "We actually did it."

I don't need to ask what he means.

Because it is not Gislan at the middle of the earthquake.

It's a child.

EPILOGUE

Covinus

It has been years since I laid eyes on the mountains and the sea; a millennia since I've seen anything other than the rotted trees of the Nemoran. That wood, borne of my own mistakes. Physical proof of my power—and my own prison.

I have endured the weight of Iara's punishment, but I have also suffered under a different curse: that of memory.

Hundreds of years have done nothing to dull their sharp edges, nothing to blunt their heat or blur their colors. The order of things has been lost to time, but the images are always with me—Iara's gold spun hair and mischievous laugh. The shine of the moon over the black bay. The feeling of absolute freedom as we reveled in each other.

I have grown stagnant in my punishment. Power, riches, control—I'd had them all and I did the worst thing possible with them: I accepted them as enough.

Before Iara, before the curse, nothing had ever been enough. How is it that I remember the glow of her skin, but could forget that?

Never again. My Boundary has been destroyed and

though I felt its destruction in the depths of my soullessness, I have adapted. Its ruination has set me free from my prison of grandeur. Awoken me from the depths of my comfort and roused my insatiable need for *more.*

I should thank the ocean-wielder before I strip her of everything she holds dear. Thank her for granting me my sense of self lost in the depths of time.

I will start with my home. The place I met Iara. The place she banished me from.

And I won't stop until I have the entire continent beneath me.

PRONUNCIATION GUIDE

Mirren: *meer-inn*

Anrai/Anni: *on-rye/onn-ee*

Calloway: *cal-oh-way*

Avedis: *uh-vee-dis*

Gislan: *giz-lon*

Luwei: *loo-way*

Sura: *soo-ruh*

Asa: *ay-suh*

Evie: *ee-vee*

Akari Ilinka: *uh-carr-ee ill-inn-kuh*

PRONUNCIATION GUIDE

Covinus: *coh-vin-us*

Praeceptor: *pray-sept-or*

Legatus: *lay-got-us*

Xamani- *zah-mon-ee*

Similis/Similian: *sim-ill-iss/sim-ill-ee-an*

Nadjaa: *nod-juh*

Argentum: *are-gen-tum*

Castellium: *cass-tell-ee-um*

Siralene: *seer-uh-leen*

Dauphine: *doe-feen*

Ashlaa: *ahsh-luh*

Yen Girene: *yen geer-een*

Nemoran: *nem-orr-enn*

Yamardu: *yah-marr-doo*

Dahiitii: *dah-heet-ee*

Zaabi (Xamani word for friend): *zah-bee*

Acknowledgments

The concept for Flame of Shadow has lived in my head since before the first draft of Tide of Darkness was even complete. And while it is obviously fantastical in nature, I wanted the bones of the story rooted in reality—the reality of battling mental illness. It is not something to be fixed by magic or love, but something that requires the fortitude to wake up every day and choose to fight, even when some of those days feel impossibly heavy. I wrote this book after watching my sister bravely take on her own darkness and survive to tell the tale. To Kirstin—your courage inspires me every day. I love you and hope I did you justice.

Thank you to Shan for your encouragement, but also, for always knowing exactly when I need my ass kicked into gear. To Lindsay, thanks for always letting me borrow (steal) your books and for the countless driveway drinks and discussions on all things writing. To Christin, your love of the story has kept me motivated on more occasions than I can count.

To my fabulous beta readers—Janeen, Rebecca, Laura, and Michelle, thank you so much for your time and feedback. The story wouldn't be what it is without you all. Thank you to Sarah Hansen of Okay Creations for another gorgeous cover. You seriously blow me away every time. Thanks to Emerald Frost Media for your expertise in all things marketing and design.

Huge thanks to my editor Tiarra Blandin, for your

expertise and for continuing to put up with what can only be called creative comma usage.

To all my family and friends—your encouragement has meant the world to me. You showed up in the biggest way for Tide of Darkness, and your support and enthusiasm honestly left me speechless. It won't ever be forgotten and I love you all so much. Thank you for always believing in me.

To Jas, my biggest supporter—you are the reason any of this is possible. I know I write about grand gestures of love, but yours has always been evident in the quieter spaces that come with sharing a life together. I am so grateful for your kind and selfless heart. (Your face isn't too bad, either)

To my children, with their wild hearts and wilder dreams, I do this for you.

Lastly, and most importantly, I want to thank every reader who's taken a chance on this series. Your reviews, your messages, your likes and follows have been beyond everything I've ever imagined. From the bottom of my heart, I thank you for giving me the chance to be an author, to share these characters and stories with you. It's truly an honor.

About the Author

Amarah Calderini grew up in the Rocky Mountains, and spent her time imagining magic living in the shadows of the peaks. She writes fantasy imbued with equal parts magic, angst, and steam, featuring strong yet flawed heroines and the fierce-hearted men who love them. When not writing, she can be found soaking up the sun and singing along to the same dramatic songs she's listened to since high school. She currently lives in Colorado Springs, Colorado with her husband, two children, and their geriatric German Shepherd.

Check out my website for my newsletter and up-to-date info about what's next.

www.amarahcalderini.com

- facebook.com/authoramarahcalderini
- twitter.com/amarahcalderini
- instagram.com/amarahcalderiniauthor
- amazon.com/author/amarahcalderini
- goodreads.com/amarahcalderini
- tiktok.com/amarahcalderiniauthor